"This fantasy story is truly brilliant."

— GAY BOOK REVIEWS

"A book that provokes thought as it entertains."

— BINGE ON BOOKS

"Engaging characters, interesting and compelling world, and outstanding story telling. I wholeheartedly recommend this book to any fantasy lovers out there."

— JOYFULLY JAY

"We're completely hooked into the story, wanting to know more..."

— OPTIMUMM

"I can't wait for the final installment!"

— RAINBOW BOOK REVIEWS

"...a fun, exciting finish to Nichols's trilogy."

— PUBLISHERS WEEKLY

"I would highly recommend them if you like epic fantasy/erotic romance with graphic violence."

— SCATTERED THOUGHTS AND ROGUE WORDS

"...both met and exceeded my expectations."

— DIVINE MAGAZINE

BLOOD FOR THE SPILLING

STUDIES IN DEMONOLOGY

TJ NICHOLS

BLOOD FOR THE SPILLING

Sheets of ice are spreading across the human world, ushering in an ice age as the magic drained from Demonside turns that world into a desert. Angus and reluctant warlock Terrance have defected from Vinland to the Mayan Empire—a land of dark and potent magic. But the Mayans aren't offering sanctuary for free.

Nor is the world willing to stand back as Vinland attacks, and the backlash will affect all magic users.

Mage Saka has no tribe. He is now just another refugee fleeing the dying Demonside. He knows the conflict brewing now will be worse than the first demon war. Countries are banding together—not just against Vinland, but against all magic. Where will the powerful Mayan Empire stand?

Angus might have the power to fight Vinland and the Warlock College, but the cost will be terrible. Saka is torn between helping Angus and stopping him. And Terrance would do anything for Angus, but he's terrified of the man Angus is becoming, even as Saka is warming to the idea of a relationship between the three of them.

No matter what choice they make, victory will be bittersweet, and when the ash settles and the snow melts, nothing will be the same.

Angus Donohue never wanted to be a warlock despite the magic in his blood, but his father, a powerful and well-connected member of the Warlock College, insisted. On his first demon summoning Angus is taken to Demonside by his demon, Saka, where he learns the truth about the way the warlocks damaged two worlds with their use of magic. After joining the underground to help over throw the Warlock College Angus discovers they are just as bad.

The underground use his human boyfriend, Terrance, to keep Angus in line. Angus's training with Saka is limited by the amount of time he can spend in Demonside, which is regulated by the underground. They don't approve of his use of sex magic and Angus soon realizes that Vinland is no longer safe for him or his friends, but escaping and defecting to another country is just as dangerous.

When Saka's tribe declares war on the warlocks and they insist all humans be killed Saka chooses to protect Angus by leaving. He heads toward the distant tribe he has made contact with via the telestones. With no other options Angus and a few friends decide to flee to Demonside. They are horrified to arrive in the desert, miles from any tribe, but all they can do is press on until they reach the distant tribe. A tribe aligned with the Mayan Empire.

CHAPTER ONE

THE CITY of Uxmal was spread before Angus like a feast he could see but not taste. He was too high above the roads and trees to do much more than glimpse the ant-like inhabitants. That didn't stop him from leaning over the balcony of the high-rise to peer as far in either direction as he could. Uxmal seemed to grow out of the jungle. He was used to neat parks scattered among gray buildings, but Uxmal seemed to be the reverse, with buildings scattered among the greenery.

The structure was smooth, and the distance between balconies was too great for him to climb down. Climbing up was also out of the question, so escape from his *accommodation* seemed impossible. Magic tingled across his skin, but he wasn't sure how to use it to escape, and even if he could get out, he didn't know where he was going and he'd eventually have to find a way back in. But he was tired of being trapped indoors when there was a whole city to explore. He leaned farther out until his balance was more precarious than was safe, but nothing he'd done recently was remotely safe.

It had been dangerous to defect from Vinland, even without the trek across the desert of Demonside. He winced and tried not to let the pain of Norah's and Dustin's deaths tear open the still-fresh scab.

His fault.

He'd led them.

The other Vinnish defectors, including Terrance, had been separated when they arrived on the human side of the void, so he didn't know if everyone else was still alive. Were they all isolated? Were they even in Uxmal?

He drew in a breath of heavy wet air. The humidity clung to his skin, and the heat was a blanket he couldn't throw off. He slapped at an opportunistic mosquito, and blood smeared his forearm next to the scar where a beetle larva had been cut out some months before. He tried to work out how long it had been exactly, but the time he'd spent walking across the desert in Demonside and then the days spent here recovering and being questioned had blurred.

The color had gradually returned to Angus's eyes. By the time they reached the demon tribe that worked with the Mayans, his eyes were barely blue. Terrance's had been pale gold. And the other trainee warlocks who'd thrown their lives into his hands, had they recovered fully? Had Terrance? He didn't even know if Saka was alive. He rocked back away from the edge of the railing in case falling became a temptation.

The people who came to see him ignored his questions. Everyone seemed to think he was a spy for Vinland, and he hadn't been able to summon Saka, because the room was full of magical dampeners.

He moved to the far left of the small balcony and leaned out to catch a glimpse of the grand, glassy temple. From a distance it appeared to be made of smoke, but he knew it wasn't. The priest, the Mayan equivalent of a warlock, Cadmael Och, had answered that question in detail. If Angus were found guilty of being a spy, he'd be killed there. It appeared the Warlock College in Vinland hadn't lied about the Mayan Empire's love of human sacrifice.

The Warlock College also hadn't mentioned that the Mayans were using magic at a level Angus had never dreamed of—and he was seeing only the barest glimpses. When Cadmael sifted through Angus's thoughts, there were no side effects, but there was also nothing he could hide. The carefully constructed bubbles around his relationship with Saka had been stripped away.

At least the damage the college had done had been healed. While Cadmael might be the priest in charge of questioning defectors, he didn't seem to want them to suffer, which gave Angus a small amount of hope. He wasn't in chains, and the apartment wasn't a filthy cell, even if he couldn't leave because the fall would kill him.

He glanced down at the ground and willed the dizziness away, but his heartbeat increased. He wasn't going to jump, but he wanted to get out and see more of the city. Where was Uxmal on a map? How far south was he? Or was he near the border of Vinland?

Where were Saka and Terrance and the others?

He spun away from the railing and stared at the glass door. All that waited for him on the other side were the empty rooms of his apartment. He was done with resting and sleeping and tired of answering the same questions—questions they had probably already stolen the answers for when Cadmael sorted through his mind like it was a library for browsing.

He closed his eyes. For just five minutes, it would be nice to feel safe. As though he didn't have his neck in a noose and weren't waiting for the chair to be kicked out from beneath his feet. For several breaths he didn't move. If he went in, the magical dampeners would press against his skin. The humidity and the heat were more bearable.

He pressed his nails into his palms and squeezed a little harder. It would be so easy to draw blood... and do what?

He couldn't magic up wings.

He couldn't do anything but wait while the world froze over and Vinland and the Warlock College locked up all magic until demons and Demonside died. Even if there were no demons, magic would need rebalancing. He still didn't understand why the Warlock College was so against rebalancing. The free flow of magic was better for everyone. Wasn't it?

The door to his apartment opened. They never knocked when they came to talk to him. What would it be today? He'd been hauled before Cadmael in the middle of the night, hooded and questioned. He'd been brought food and questioned over a meal. While a demon with the face and antlers of a deer looked on, he'd been treated by a doctor and questioned by a woman he could only assume was a priestess. They were always asking the same questions, and he always gave the same answers—the only answers he had.

When they didn't want him to know what was going on, they spoke in a language he couldn't grasp. Yet they all seemed to speak Vinnish when they needed to.

Priest Cadmael stood in the doorway as though unwilling to step onto the balcony. His lilac pinstripe suit and yellow tie were almost subdued... for him. Angus still wasn't used to the color. Everyone wore color. The walls were painted and patterned like the Mayan city was a demon village. Nothing was left white or sterile. "It is time for a testing."

Angus uncurled his fingers and wished he hadn't been so keen to leave his room.

He could refuse, but they'd drag him off to whatever it was they wanted him to do anyway. At first he'd refused to talk. The old habit of keeping college secrets was hard to break, especially when the Mayan Empire was considered an enemy.

Both countries used demon magic. They were more alike than different. The Mayans took rebalancing very seriously, and Cadmael had been disgusted by the college. Angus didn't need to speak his language to understand that. His expression and tone said all that was needed.

Today he'd come to Angus instead of having Angus delivered. Was that a new approach to get him to say something?

He had nothing more to say. "What kind of testing?"

"You are a priest among your people, no?" Cadmael smiled, but it was the kind of smile that promised to trip Angus if he weren't very careful.

He had no idea if he was passing or failing—a refugee to be granted sanctuary or a spy to be put to death. At least his death would go toward stopping the ice sheets that were smothering the world. Maybe it would even bring rain to the drying Demonside. Cadmael wouldn't let his blood be spilled without it being used, but it was grim comfort.

"Warlock," Angus insisted. He wasn't sure of the difference between a priest and a warlock, and he didn't want to make false claims. Cadmael had never taken the hint and referred to Angus as a priest, which kind of implied more training and responsibility than Angus had ever wanted when it came to demons and magic.

"Your abilities with your demon and anchor will be assessed."

His heart lurched. "I get to see Saka?"

Saka was alive. His heart gave a wobbly flip, and he had to fight to keep the smile from his face. For five minutes with Saka, he'd do anything Cadmael asked, even for just two.

Cadmael nodded. "He is your demon." The smile was sly.

That was the trap. Humans weren't better than their demons. "And I am his warlock."

The slight inclination of Cadmael's head was the only response he got. Should he just start using the word priest? He didn't feel like a priest. He didn't know enough to be able to claim that rank. Priests were well-regarded in much the same way that warlocks were well-regarded, or so it seemed. Everyone deferred to Cadmael, but maybe that was because he was head of the Intelligence Temple.

Outside Angus's room, two green-uniformed soldiers waited. Both wore knives. Arrowhead patches marked their ranks.

Angus slipped on his sandals and followed Cadmael. He expected the cloth hood to be put over his head, but no one approached him. He was getting to see Saka and the city?

Fuck. That could only mean one thing. He was about to be cut open like an overripe fruit and bled out in the temple.

He swallowed and glanced at the soldiers and then at Cadmael. His heart beat fast, as though readying to flee. But if he ran, where exactly could he go?

He couldn't go home. The Warlock College would torture and kill him.

He couldn't hide in Demonside, because it would gradually drain him, and hiding in Uxmal was impossible. His red hair and fair skin would make him stand out. He lacked money, papers, and everything he'd need to live as a citizen.

So he was in limbo with no country and no home. He existed because Priest Cadmael allowed him to until his usefulness ran out… which was today.

He wasn't dead yet. There was still time to do something, but his brain refused to give him anything remotely close to an idea. At least he'd get to see Saka again.

In the foyer of the building, the woman on the desk didn't even look up. Two more soldiers stood by the door. Maybe this place was some kind of prison. On the street the heat and sticky air assaulted him. It was hard to believe that Vinland was icing over and Demonside was drying when even the air here needed wringing out.

No cars traveled the road. Instead, some other vehicle, like a bus that ran on a track, transported people to where they needed to be. But they weren't getting on. They were apparently walking and in the direction of the smoky-glass temple.

Soldiers walked the footpath in pairs, but no one seemed bothered by their armed presence except him. He wasn't used to having so many military people around.

Demons, some scaled, some feathered, and some with antlers—kinds Angus had never seen before—strolled along the footpath, and no one looked at them either. He tried not to stare.

But everyone stared at him as though they knew exactly what he was.

Defector.

He was the enemy.

He lowered his gaze to the path and kept up with Cadmael as the soldiers walked behind. To escort or protect him? Or both?

Across the entrance to the temple, something was written in gold glyphs. He didn't get a chance to memorize them or ask what they said before they entered. The cool of the temple was a relief, and the eyes of the Mayans no longer watched as though expecting him to do something awful.

The inside of the temple was gray stone, and the walls were decorated with vivid scenes that probably had meaning. But to Angus they were just scenes of people and demons and death.

He fully expected to be taken to the top to meet his fate. Instead Cadmael opened a door and ushered him into a room that was empty except for a hooded man sitting on a chair. The hood didn't matter. Angus knew who it was. He had to stop himself from running over and pulling off the hood. This was the first time he'd been allowed to see any of the warlocks who'd fled Vinland.

It had to be a trick or a trap. His feet remained rooted to the floor, and he was unsure what he should do. He glanced at Cadmael, seeking a clue but got none. The door closed, and the soldiers remained on the other side. Cadmael paced the room, his footsteps soft as a snake slithering over stone until he stopped close to the man.

Cadmael tapped the man's blue-shirted shoulder. "This man betrayed you to the college. He reported on you to the underground, brought you into their treachery. His loyalty changes depending on the breeze. Yet he is your anchor." He shook his head, and a crease formed between his eyebrows as though he couldn't understand. "That is all that is keeping him alive."

That word again. Anchor. What did that mean? What did Cadmael think was going on? Or know. No doubt the priest had rummaged thoroughly through everyone's thoughts.

Cadmael pulled off the hood and let it drop to the floor.

Angus took a step forward and then stopped himself, but his heart lurched.

Terrance blinked in the bright lights, but didn't get up, even though he wasn't tied down. His eyes were brown again and his hair longer, shaggier. Angus bit back the smile. He didn't know if he should stay where he was or rush to embrace him. Would that be frowned upon?

Was Terrance glad to see him?

Cadmael's gaze moved slowly between them, assessing and finding something lacking.

Terrance gave Angus a fragile smile and then a nod as though to say he was all right. Angus took another step forward. He had no words but so many questions.

"You trust him, despite his repeated betrayals," Cadmael said.

"I knew." He'd known from the start that Terrance was watching him for both the college and the underground.

"You betrayed your own people—the Warlock College and the underground. Your loyalty wavers depending on your mood."

Angus faced the priest. "Wouldn't you have done the same? The college was destroying the world. The underground became infected with warlocks who were tired of the college but still wanted power. I've been trying to save Demonside. Saka trusts me." Didn't he?

"Trust is a very flimsy thing. You have engendered none with me. Fleeing your country and surrendering all of its secrets. How do I know you won't do the same again?" Cadmael's hand was still on Terrance's shoulder.

"They wanted to kill me. What choice did I have?"

"How can I trust people who change loyalties so swiftly?"

"My loyalty has never changed. It has always been about the magic and not killing two worlds." What had Cadmael seen in his head? What had he seen in Terrance's?

"You gained followers."

"They wanted to flee. We did it together." Angus glanced at Terrance. What was going on? It wasn't like the other times Cadmael had questioned him.

"This one," he said, tapping Terrance's shoulder, "isn't like you."

"What do you mean?" Angus said. Terrance didn't need to be like him. Did he?

Cadmael went on as though Angus hadn't spoken. "He likes magic but fears the deeper connection. He wants to fight but doesn't know who to fight for, so he fights for all sides."

"I had no choice," Terrance said. His voice was no longer cracked and dry from the trek.

"There are always choices." Cadmael stepped away.

"The college would've killed us all. We did what we had to do to survive."

Cadmael shrugged. "Death is a choice."

But not a good one.

"It's better to fight." Terrance stood. He was as tall as Cadmael.

Some of the muscle he'd gained playing rugby had been stripped away over the weeks in the desert, but no one would ever call him scrawny.

"Only if you know what you're doing. Fighting everything and everyone is a fool's game." Cadmael smiled. "You may still get your wish. Our ball game always requires new players."

Something flickered over Terrance's face but was quickly masked.

What ball game?

Cadmael flicked a switch, and a circle lit up on the floor. "Your excuses bore me. Summon your demon."

CHAPTER TWO

Saka made his way along the dirt track to the wooden structure where everyone came to get treatment from the healers. There were enough trees in that part of Demonside to cut them down and make permanent buildings. He'd stopped running his fingers over the purple-tinged wood a few days after he arrived, but he still marveled at it.

No one lived in tents either.

This tribe didn't move around, not as a whole, anyway. People came and went to see other tribes, but this was where they lived. There were even buildings for visitors—demon and human. He had a room, and in the corner was his folded tent and the sled he'd dragged across the desert in the hope of getting his warlock to safety.

He hadn't heard anything from Angus since he and the other humans had been taken across the void by the Mayan priest. For all he knew, Angus was dead. It was a thought he didn't like to linger on but one that haunted him at night when he tried to sleep.

Had he done the right thing, or had he acted selfishly in leaving his tribe?

While his home had been drying, this place was lush in comparison. There was no need to draw up water from underground rivers. The river flowed along the surface.

The dirt track widened, and the town center came into view among the trees. It was still an arresting sight, unfamiliar and strange. He didn't belong among these demons with their fur and antlers and long muzzles or their scales and wings and feathers. There were so many kinds he'd never seen before that it had been hard not to stare at first. Even now, some of them stared at him as though they'd never seen a horned demon in their lives. Maybe they hadn't. His kind of demon didn't exist here, and his dark, reddish skin set him further apart.

In the healers' building, there was already a line of people waiting to be seen. The humans came there willingly, and most of them didn't come to die. They came to look at the demon town or to get treatment. Mage Iktan had put him to work there. Saka wasn't sure if it was so he could be closely supervised or if they actually realized he had a talent for healing.

He had been the main healer in his tribe. How were they managing now, or were they not coping with the dry at all? Guilt stabbed like a splinter he couldn't get to. He had to believe he'd done the right thing. Killing all humans was wrong, even though his tribe didn't see it. They wanted blood to stop the drying. They wanted war.

This tribe didn't, but while he was still afforded the title of mage, he had no standing.

He sat down at his place, and the first human approached with a friend. As was often the case, it was the friend who was making the blood sacrifice as payment for the magic that would be used in the healing.

For all his training and years practicing, he didn't know how the transaction worked. It was emotion that gave the blood power, yet there was no fear or lust involved. He'd watched on the first day and had questioned what happened to the blood. He wanted to know how the humans came and left so freely and had maddeningly been given no answers.

Iktan gave him professional courtesy and a grudging respect, but no trust. If Saka had lacked the ability to heal, he'd probably be planting and harvesting crops.

That might be preferable.

Saka listened to the human talk as he used magic to find the true source of the illness—words didn't always match the body.

"Healing can be painful." How many times did he say that each day? But they seemed to already know. Maybe a human on the other side of the void had warned them. All his questions about the human side of the void remained unanswered. Did they think him a spy? Who was he going to tell?

Angus?

Maybe they thought Angus was a spy.

This man's bellyache was caused by a festering in his gut. It was something that should be cut out and not something Saka could treat on his own.

He glanced at the human couple. "This requires a cutting."

The woman offered her arm.

Saka shook his head. While he could understand the words they spoke because of the magic-imbued jade now piercing his ear, he couldn't speak it. It was much easier to talk to demons using tele-stones when language fell away and thoughts were understood. Here he stumbled like a child learning his first words.

He got up and spoke to the demon in charge.

Noe understood Saka's demonstration of cutting open the belly but didn't deign to speak to him. Saka was there under sufferance. Until he heard from Angus, he had to do something, so Saka gritted his teeth and did what was asked of him. If he was busy, his thoughts had less time to rattle in his head, his worries less time to chew on his guts, and his panic less time to smother each breath.

Noe and the man with the belly had a rapid conversation that Saka was just able to follow. He was going to be moved to one of the back rooms where some very specialized demons would make the cut and heal him. He'd then be sent home to be watched by priests.

"Is there a problem?"

Saka snapped his head up at the sound of Iktan's voice. While the tone was soft, the words were full of bite.

"This patient is beyond his ability," Noe said as if Saka were a new mage.

"That's not true." Saka could treat the man if he had an assistant. "You have a different system." It had just been Usi and he in his tribe until Wek and Tapo joined them, but they rarely treated humans. Humans from Vinland would never come to a demon for help, but he'd saved Angus, much to the disgust of several mages who wanted to spill warlock blood.

The two furred demons glanced at him, and Saka wasn't sure if they understood a word he'd said. He needed to learn their language, but to do so, he would have to remove the piercing and actually hear the language.

"Your... warlock...." Iktan stumbled over the word as though it were one he wasn't familiar with. But it was the one that made Saka's heart tighten with anticipation. Angus was alive. "Will be summoning you soon. We will wait at the doorway." Iktan turned and walked away without waiting for Saka's agreement.

Saka shot a look at Noe and then followed Iktan. Angus was alive and about to summon him. Hope and other things a mage shouldn't dabble in flitted through him like the luminous insects that filled the night. The wait was over, and now they could do something to stop the college. But what had taken the Mayans so long?

They left the building, passed through a doorway, and then walked away from the town. What exactly was this doorway? Every other question had been met with a brush-off, so Saka didn't bother to ask.

They walked in silence until they reached an area that had been paved with several large stones. There was no door, just two pillars engraved with glyphs. Two ferocious-looking armed demons with long fangs and spotted skin guarded the area. Why did they need to be here when a warlock could summon their demon from anywhere?

Iktan stared ahead.

"What is this?" Saka pointed to the stones.

Iktan ignored him. It would be easy to assume that Iktan didn't understand, but Saka knew he did. Iktan was Priest Cadmael's demon, and the two of them were powerful. Because of their influence, Saka was tolerated in the tribe. But he wasn't an apprentice, and he should be given answers and allowed to learn.

He pressed his teeth together and forced his frustration out on a breath. Angus was going to summon him. It would be best if he were calm and prepared for anything, but he was sure it wouldn't be what he wanted.

On the trek he'd grown used to sleeping with Angus at his side. He missed him in a way he hadn't thought possible. A familiar tug bloomed in his blood. Once he'd been annoyed at having to answer a human's summons, but now he welcomed it. He needed to see Angus like he needed to breathe.

A tear in the void appeared between the pillars. It shimmered black as it widened, and Saka took a step forward, not willing to wait a moment longer.

Iktan put a hand on his arm to stop him.

The void was open, and the summoning was for him. He could feel it calling to him. Angus was on the other side. One of the soldiers peered into the void. Was he expecting an army to pour through?

It was only when the soldier stepped back that Iktan released Saka.

"Why did he check?"

"All openings get checked. All openings happen here at the doorway."

"But if I get summoned, and I'm in town, what then?"

Iktan gave what passed for a smile. He drew back his lips to reveal large square teeth. "You won't receive a random summoning."

What about the other mages? Did they sprint from town to the doorway? A twenty-minute walk was still a ten-minute run. Putting the doorway so far away made no sense. That they could control where the void opened was both amazing and concerning. And he had no idea how it worked. Would he be stepping through to Angus or was it a trap?

"Go, or your warlock will fail a simple test."

Saka didn't think a mage would lie to him, and Angus was waiting, so he stepped onto the warm stones. The closer he got to the tear in the void, the cooler the stones became. As he stepped through, the familiar chill sunk into him, and then he was in a white room with three humans.

His heart lurched at the sight of Angus, but his human looked well —fully recovered from the trek and well looked-after. Saka wanted to embrace him, but that had been frowned on in his tribe and he wasn't sure of the rules in the Mayan Empire. Rushing to Angus's side could make things worse. He curled his fingers with his need to touch Angus, but he didn't step closer.

He glanced at Terrance, who looked better than he had the last time Saka had seen him. He was glad that Terrance had survived, for Angus's sake. With training and some courage, Terrance would make a fine warlock… priest. He could be more than a wizard if he chose to push himself.

If he had five minutes alone with Angus….

Saka swallowed down the hunger to touch his human. He missed him, craved him. He didn't want to think that was a weakness to be healed. Miniti and Usi thought it was, and he'd proven them right by fleeing from the area of Demonside that linked with the Vinnish and abandoning his tribe to protect Angus instead of killing him.

The demons of Iktan's tribe didn't demand the death of humans, because the human country they connected with through the void didn't threaten and demand that. The Mayans worked with their demons. The relationship between Mayan and demon was something he'd only heard about from his mentor when she talked about a time before the first demon war. He hadn't thought it still possible.

Were they now in the second?

Had the Mayans ever had a demon war, or had they always had peace between the two worlds? If he could get answers and speak his mind, he'd be able to piece together a greater picture of Demonside.

There were many tribes with different customs, but they could unite to save Demonside.

"Mage Saka." Priest Cadmael looked unimpressed. It was perhaps his only expression. That was the way he'd looked every time Saka had seen him.

Saka inclined his head. He wasn't there for the priest. He was there because Angus had summoned him, albeit at Cadmael's request. Saka smiled at Angus but didn't step closer. None of them had moved. The humans seemed to be waiting for permission to do something. And Cadmael watched them all.

Saka didn't need permission from a human warlock or priest—they were the same as far as he could tell. He closed the distance to stand before Angus, close enough to touch if he reached out his hands. "Your eyes are blue again."

"Yes." Angus brushed Saka's hand for just a moment. Saka wanted to grab hold. "And you?"

"You may leave now," Cadmael said to Saka.

"I just stepped through. I want to be able to talk with Angus."

"I'm sure you do, and you can after the other one has called you back."

Saka flicked a glance between Terrance and Angus, but they looked just as perplexed.

"You are the anchor in this?" Cadmael pointed to Terrance.

"What is an anchor?" Angus asked. He seemed aware that the situation was sliding away from them.

Saka grasped Angus's fingers. He could take Angus with him if he had to.

Cadmael narrowed his eyes, but he didn't step closer. "Someone has to be on this side to bring you back."

Angus shook his head. "We all came through because we had to leave Vinland. I told you that. We all told you that."

"But usually you have an anchor."

Angus paled and looked at Terrance.

The conversations Saka had overheard in the village started to make sense. "They do not share a demon."

"But you both share Angus." It wasn't a compliment. There was more than a hint of disdain. Cadmael knew a little too much about who was involved with whom.

No one said anything, and the silence swelled until it vibrated in the air with each breath.

Cadmael took a few steps, his sandals a whisper on the floor. "If Terrance is not your anchor, then he has no use. You can find a better one, one whose loyalties are not so easily for sale."

"No." Angus put his arm out to stop Cadmael from getting any closer to Terrance. A crackle of magic shimmered through the air and between their linked fingers.

Saka didn't know how powerful Cadmael was, but he doubted any of them would get out of the room alive if Cadmael decided they were all too much trouble. And if, by some small chance, they got to Demonside, there was nowhere else to go. Saka wasn't ready to consider another trek across the desert. Then there were the other refugees, the humans who had followed Angus from Vinland. Saka brushed his free hand over his ear and removed the jade. Angus needed it more than he did. He'd claim it fell out and get a new one if questioned, or he'd just work harder to learn the language.

"You haven't even explained what an anchor is." Angus's fingers tightened on his.

"I just did," Cadmael said without any emotion.

But he hadn't explained well enough. Saka shouldn't have to take on the role of teacher. "A human who shares your demon, and can open the void so you can come and go at will," Saka said. There was probably more to it, but that was all he'd gleaned. He placed his other hand over Angus's and gave him the jade. He might not get a chance to explain what it was, but Angus would work it out... hopefully. "It's not that yet. But it could be."

"I am not in the position of granting visas on a maybe. Terrance, of all of you, is the one who arouses suspicion."

"I was in the underground. I was the one who talked everyone into fleeing. Why am I not a danger?" Angus said.

Cadmael walked up to Angus until he was almost standing on his toes. Saka took a step closer, but Cadmael ignored him except to calmly lift their linked hands. "You acted out of a love for magic and the need for it to be used correctly. You have a mage as your counterpart, someone who understands magic. He"—Cadmael inclined his head at Terrance—"had an animal that was killed and acted to save his own skin with no regard for others."

"That's not true." They were the first words Saka had heard Terrance say. While he hadn't liked Terrance at first, he had grown to respect him on the trek.

"Really? Then let me offer you a test to prove that your skin isn't all you value," Cadmael said.

Terrance considered for a moment. "What is your test?"

"Pitz," Cadmael said like it was nothing.

Saka had heard that word in relation to a large offering of blood and human sacrifice. Pitz was important and bloody. "What is pitz?"

"A game. A ball game." Cadmael smiled, and Saka decided that he much preferred his indifference. "You like ball games, Terrance."

"That depends on the game."

"This one is simple. The loser gives their life for magic to be balanced. So either you can play, or Angus can play. How precious is your life when weighed against the human you claim is so important to you?"

"We were in the process of making Terrance the anchor and cementing the relationship." By "in the process," Saka meant they had talked about the three of them raising some magic when they were safe and not thirsty and half dead in the desert.

Cadmael shot him a glare that cut through his web-thin truth.

Angus pulled his hand free, turned to Terrance, and gripped Terrance's shoulders. "You don't have to do this. We didn't come all this way to die." He glanced at Cadmael. "We came to get help to bring down the Warlock College and fix the way magic is used. I thought you'd help us."

"Help has a cost."

"If you do nothing, Demonside will dry, even your lush little part. The demons talk about the lack of rains and the shrinking of the jungle. And the ice that covers your world will continue its march. If you do not act, your way of life will unravel," Saka said. Didn't the Mayans want to stop the ice?

"I do not need to be told by a demon who abandoned his tribe to save a human. You had the chance to rebalance, and you didn't take it."

"I have rebalanced many times, as has Angus. One death is a drop when the warlocks are hoarding and storing." Killing Angus and staying with his tribe would've accomplished nothing. The warlocks controlled when the void was opened. That meant that demons were victims of chance. A warlock would grab as many demons as he could and then flee. All demons could do was arm themselves and wait to kill as many humans as they could. Both sides would pile up the bodies until someone was ready to make a treaty. Saka didn't think the Vinnish warlocks wanted a treaty. They wanted all the magic.

"A drop in an empty bucket is better than nothing," Cadmael said, dismissing Saka's argument.

"Give me a day with Angus, and I can fill your bucket. You do not need to send his human lover to his death."

"Your method is crude and for the untrained. Anyone can fuck." Cadmael's face twisted into a sneer.

"I have been trained in blood, soul, and sex rebalancing. You seem to thrive on taking souls. That is considered crude and simplistic where I am from. Why would you kill the offering when you can reuse it many times?"

"You will watch pitz and see why. Terrance, will you do me the honor and play, or will you sacrifice Angus and save yourself."

Terrance shook his head. "If I refuse, Angus dies playing in my place, and you still don't trust me because I've proven I act only for myself. Maybe I have... maybe meeting Angus made me think there was something worth fighting for, but you don't care. You just want one of us to be sacrificed. Either way I'm a dead man."

"You don't have to do it. We'll get a boat and try somewhere else. Someone will help stop the college," Angus pleaded with Terrance.

Cadmael laughed. "The world is at war. The Sindu are targeting all magic users. New Holland is under attack, and even the Institute for Magical Studies is asking for all demon magic to be ceased. You will get no asylum anywhere. Flee to Demonside. I won't stop you, but consider how far you can get. What country will those demons be aligned with? Not all demons are accepting of humans. You may find yourself stoned… at best."

The world was at war. What had changed while they walked? Saka was blind without other mages to talk with. He lived in a village but wasn't a part of it. He was there only because Cadmael and Iktan allowed it. If they changed their minds, he'd be forced out, and then what? What would happen to Angus if Terrance played this game and lost?

Terrance stood and hugged Angus. "It's a ball game. I always wanted a crowd cheering my name. I think these games must draw them in. They're a big deal, aren't they, Cadmael?"

Cadmael was expecting Terrance to die and clear the way. Saka bit back the horror that Cadmael expected him to be bound to another human, to be shared like a toy between children. "If you send Terrance to the game, then Angus needs to find an anchor."

Cadmael glanced at him. "He and you will be assigned one. He does not need to like or bed the anchor. And neither do you."

"You will have someone watch me you mean," Angus said, his face set.

"For your own good." Cadmael's smile was slippery.

Angus pressed his lips together. "Terrance should be given the opportunity to train. It should be a fair match, not against one of your star players."

"This is wrong. Death is not a game. Human sacrifices should be given respect and thanks, not treated as a spectacle," Saka said. What kind of people took life so casually? Angus had warned Saka that the Mayans had a reputation, but he hadn't expected this.

"Life and death are all part of the same game. You will attend and watch. Until then." Cadmael put his hand on Saka's chest, and the void swallowed him whole.

CHAPTER THREE

ANGUS SPUN AWAY from Terrance and reached for Saka, but he was already gone. "Why did you do that? He's my demon. I wanted to see him." Needed to see him. It had been too long, and Saka had been so close. Angus's skin was warm from holding his hand. He wished he hadn't held back and tried to be respectable.

"And he was no longer required. My questions have been answered." Cadmael turned toward the door.

"And what about mine? When do I get to explore the city? Summon my demon and—"

"And what? You cannot practice magic here without an anchor. Your relationship with him has already taken unnatural turns because you have lacked proper guidance."

Angus flinched at the judgment. He'd heard the same thing too many times in Vinland. *Skitun.* Demon fucker.

It wasn't the word they used here, but no doubt they had one.

"Why is it unnatural? Why not use any means to raise power?" Angus took a step toward Cadmael. Terrance put a hand on his arm to hold him back, but Angus shook it off. He stalked closer, not sure what he was going to do, only that he had to do something. He wanted to use magic and live his life. Would he be forever judged?

"It's a cheap way of working."

"And death is better? One life can't do much."

"That's where you are wrong." Cadmael glanced at Terrance. "One life can do so very much if used correctly. You will get your visa and be able to move freely about the city. But you are banned from using demon magic until such time as an anchor can be established."

"And if I don't want the anchor of your choosing?" He wanted Terrance as the anchor... if that was what Terrance wanted.

"Then you will not see Saka again. We have ways of ensuring...." He thought for the word. "Rogues do not operate."

Once again he was a dangerous rogue.

"Enjoy the rest of the day with Terrance. He will be collected come dawn for training." Judging by the way it was said, Angus wasn't sure there'd be any training.

That Terrance was going to play the game made his blood cold. Cadmael meant for Terrance to die.

"Let's make the most of what's left of the day," Terrance said softly. "It would be nice to be out."

Angus closed his eyes and curled his fingers into fists. It wasn't supposed to be like this. They were supposed to be safe, supposed to get help and bring down the college. But he couldn't strike out at Cadmael unless he wanted swift punishment. They were all dependent on the goodwill of the Empire. He uncurled his fingers and opened his eyes. Cadmael was watching him. Waiting for him to screw up?

He forced a smile. It would be nice to be out, even if half a day was all they got. His heart squeezed hard at the thought of losing Terrance; it had been too close in the desert. This would be so much worse. His safety would be paid for in Terrance's blood.

No. Terrance would survive. Angus nodded in agreement. "Yes, let's see some of the city."

And talk. And plan.

Cadmael opened the door. "The guards will follow you to make sure you remain safe. We are at war with Vinland, and you might be mistaken for the enemy."

Angus slipped whatever it was Saka had passed to him into his pocket. He took Terrance's hand and followed the soldiers onto the street, where the air blanketed him and almost smothered him in wet heat.

The scent of food from a street market drifted down the road.

"Where have you been staying?" Terrance squinted up at the sky as a flock of bright yellow parrots spiraled over the city.

Angus pointed. "That white-and-turquoise building. You?"

"I don't know. There was no view."

"What do you mean?" He turned to face Terrance.

"I mean this was planned from the moment he first sifted through our thoughts. From the time they offered sanctuary, one of us had to die."

Angus shook his head. "No."

The soldiers were standing too close, so Angus bit his tongue on his next words. He didn't know if the guards spoke Vinnish, and Angus didn't want to say too much in case they were playing dumb and reporting back.

Terrance drew in a breath. "We need to find out what pitz is." He turned to a soldier. "Hey, pitz?"

That was the last thing Angus wanted to do. "Do we have to?"

"I want a chance to see the game. It might be a ritual, but I'm guessing it's played in the streets. If they have champion players, they have to learn somewhere, and kids want to be like their idols."

The thought of the ritual game turned Angus's stomach, but Terrance squeezed his hand. "It's just a game."

Angus couldn't say anything to that. They both knew the stakes. If either of them had a chance at winning, it would be Terrance. Sports were his thing.

The soldiers looked at each other and spoke a few rapid sentences that meant nothing to Angus. It appeared they weren't in agreement. The first one shrugged and started to walk. They followed with the other soldier at the rear.

Angus tried not to feel the prickles of the stares from the people on the street. His palm sweated against Terrance's. They were the enemy, the cause of the cooling and the approaching ice age. There must be other refugees, people who took the risk to cross the southern border from Vinland. Or were they fleeing west instead, through the no-man's-land and into the Nations territory? Maybe that's what *they* should've done.

But it would've been his luck to arrive in an area that didn't tolerate demons at all, even though magic use linked the Nations. If the trek through the desert had been bad, trying to get out of Vinland in Humanside would've been nearly impossible. He didn't even know where the underground—the wizards and warlocks who were trying to stand against the college—had been housing them most of the time. The underground had deliberately kept them in the dark... to keep them safe.

They passed the food, and Angus's stomach rumbled. It looked like flat bread things filled with meat and vegetables and beans. But he had no money and no way of earning it.

Cadmael had only said he couldn't use demon magic, which meant he could still use his wizard skills. There seemed to be others in the market. Glyphs advertised their skills and rates—or at least he assumed they did—and there was definitely magic in the air.

"Can we get something to eat?" Angus pointed at the food stall. Eating would provide a temporary distraction from his thoughts. "Are you hungry?"

Terrance shrugged. "Not really, but who knows how many more last meals I'll get. Maybe I used up my luck in the desert." He grinned, but his smile had an edge.

"Don't be like that."

"Like what? Truthful? I thought I was going to die in Vinland, first at the hands of the college and then the underground. I survived. Then again in the desert, and I'm still here. Who knows. Maybe I'll survive this too. Kicking a ball isn't that hard."

Under protest, the soldier bought two wraps and handed them over. Angus almost expected him to spit on them. Then Angus and Terrance followed the guards into a park and to a long, thin court with wide ends. Four teens were playing a game that looked impossible.

"Oh shit," Terrance said with his mouth full of food. There was no kicking a ball or even catching.

"Pitz," the soldier said with pride.

Angus stared in horror. It wasn't like any game he'd ever seen before. The ball bounced between elbows and knees and never touched the ground or the hands of the players. How did one even learn how to do that? How was Terrance going to learn? He glanced at the man who'd only moments before been almost cocky about his chances.

Terrance was staring, tracking the game, the food forgotten in his hand.

One of the boys sent the ball through a ring on the side, and everyone cheered.

"He scored a try. It's the same… ish." The note of concern was clear in Terrance's words.

The losing team knelt in the middle, and the winners pretended to cut off their heads. The losers died silently without any flourishes, and then got up and started a new game.

"It's not the same at all." No one died at the end of a rugby match. Those kids were acting out ritual deaths.

"There's a ball and a scoring area and rules, so it *is* like every game." Terrance sat down on the stone bench around the top. The steep walls of the court angled to give a view of the players, and he ate in silence as he studied the game in a way that only a sportsman with his life in the balance could. Angus didn't dare interrupt. He left his food half eaten as his stomach betrayed his anxiety.

How long before Cadmael would force Terrance to play?

Did they only have tonight? He wanted to summon Saka and run away again—there had to be somewhere safe in a world that was falling apart. The kids laughed and cheered each other on and then mock-decapitated the losers again. All in good fun.

Birds chattered, and people talked. Life went on despite the war. How had he ended up here? He was a nobody with few skills beyond screwing a demon and leading people into danger. Angus rested his elbows on his knees and cradled his head. He should've stood up to his father and never gone to warlock school, but then he'd be ignorant about the truth and he'd have never realized what an oppressive regime the college had created. If he'd followed college rules and not opened his eyes to the truth, he'd still be there learning how to abuse magic and kill demons.

Maybe if he hadn't dated Jim and been introduced to the underground…. But he was erasing half his life, and even then he wasn't sure if he wouldn't have ended up in the same situation. Magic was in his blood, and he couldn't stay away from it.

Terrance got up.

The teens beckoned him over, no doubt hoping to make the foreigner look like a fool. If Terrance suspected that was their aim, he didn't let on. He smiled as they showed him how to strike the ball with his elbows, and they laughed as he made a mess of it.

He was going to die. He'd lose the game and be sacrificed.

Angus's eyes grew hot, and his throat thickened until the air was choking him.

Terrance continued to practice until the teens tired of teaching him and arranged into two-man teams.

It wasn't *the* match, but it was still awful to watch. Terrance and his teammate lost. They knelt at the end and bowed like they were ready to have their heads cut off, which the other two teens did with a little too much glee, reaffirming their hero status.

But no one died. It was just a game. There was a round of farewells, and Terrance jogged back to Angus's side. His shirt clung to his skin, and his dark hair was glued to his forehead.

He used his sleeve to wipe his face and gave Angus a grim smile. "Let's hope I get better."

CHAPTER FOUR

Terrance was fucked. Pitz wasn't like any game he'd ever played before, and he'd never played for his actual life. But there was no way he was going to back down to the jerk priest and put Angus's life on the line. He would play as best he could. It was still a better chance than the underground had given him and more than he'd thought he'd get in the desert. If not for Saka, he might not have made it. Angus's talents lay with magic and not balls. Terrance couldn't live with the idea of throwing him onto the court. And he'd done plenty of shitty things to survive over the years.

The ride up to Angus's apartment was silent. The soldiers took up too much space in the small elevator and left no room for conversation. He bit back a sigh and leaned against the wall, his elbows and knees smarting and bruised from the game.

It was the feeling of the ground beneath his knees and the mock execution after his loss that had done the most damage. His heart gave an extra squeeze of panic. But he couldn't let it take hold. He had to focus and learn everything he could.

It was just a game, and he understood games. Given enough time he could play and win. He was sure of it. But he doubted he'd be given the time he needed.

In fleeing with Angus, he'd swapped one dangerous life for another.

If he'd stayed in Vinland, the college or the underground would've found a reason take his life sooner rather than later. His back still bore the faint marks from a whipping, even though Angus had healed them. They'd used him to keep Angus in line, and it made his stomach turn. That hadn't changed. His role hadn't changed. It wasn't fucking fair.

They were still not safe. He was beginning to think they never would be. This was it. And if this was all they were going to get, playing a game in front of thousands was a reasonable way to die. He didn't care about the magical rebalancing the way Angus did, but he cared that the world was icing over and the people in power didn't seem to give a damn.

Magic had always been a means to an end for him. It wasn't his life, but it was Angus's.

Angus's eyes lit up and he got excited when he talked about magic —and not just because he was screwing Saka. Terrance glanced over at the warlock who'd stolen his heart. Angus's skin was fair and freckled, his hair a tangle of red that should probably be trimmed, but Terrance liked it messy. Angus stared straight ahead. His lips were pressed into a thin line, but his fingers worked, picking and tearing at the edge of his nail. Terrance wanted to reach out and pull him close, but he didn't. The soldiers were watching.

He didn't deserve Angus and never had, but Cadmael was right. He was selfish, and he wouldn't give Angus up without a fight.

If he somehow won the game, he would work out what the anchor thing was and do it just to spite Cadmael. It wasn't the best reason, but his reasons had never been good. Magic had never been good to his family.

It certainly hadn't been good to him.

The elevator doors opened, and the soldiers stepped out and escorted them down the hallway to Angus's apartment. Would they come in or stand guard outside? How closely would they shadow them? Into the bathroom? Into bed?

Angus opened the door with a fingerprint, and Terrance followed him. He glanced over his shoulder, but the soldiers remained on the other side of the door when Angus closed it.

"Are you always so popular?" He tried to make his words light, but Angus didn't smile.

"I can't do anything right. This was supposed to be better." Angus tucked a lock of hair behind his ear. The sun had bleached some of the red strands golden, and it hadn't been cut in months. But it was no longer stiff with sand and sweat, and Terrance wanted to run his fingers through it. It might be the only chance he got.

He'd been living with that thought for too long. In Vinland he thought every training session was his last, or that every visit might be the last time he would get to see Angus. Escaping to Demonside had seemed like a damn good idea, the only one any of them had for getting out. "The weather is better."

Vinland was caught in permanent winter. At least it was warm in the Mayan Empire.

"Could you be serious?"

Terrance inhaled and then exhaled slowly. "Why? What will it change?"

Angus scowled at him. "We need a plan. Maybe I can get you to Demonside and you can hide out there."

"Until it sucks the life out of me? Nope. I'm done with hiding and pretending and running." He needed to make a stand, and this was it. He'd play the best game of his life and hope that he was good enough.

"You'll be killed."

"Thanks for the vote of confidence." But he totally agreed. He'd need months of training to compete.

"Do you actually think you have a chance?"

Terrance was silent for a moment. He expected to die. The game was hard and he wasn't used to it. Would he get one training session or several? Would he get to watch some games and analyze them? How skilled would his opponent be?

Even if all of those factors aligned in his favor, which was unlikely, the odds were still marginal. He wasn't dumb enough to give false hope to himself or to Angus.

He shrugged. "Maybe." Long odds but sometimes the underdog won. That was why he liked sports. Nothing was a given, and no game was ever the same. Angus only watched it with him because he liked to look at the legs on the men running. They had that in common too.

And magic.

And they'd both worked for the underground for a time.

If he were smarter, he'd have let Angus go and tried to keep his head down, but the college had jailed his parents for being wizards, and as far as he was concerned, anyone who wanted to bring them down was a good person.

Angus genuinely was a good person. Terrance would never to be able to live up to that goodness. Someday soon Angus would realize that Terrance was exactly how Cadmael had described him. But he'd be dead before that happened… which wasn't terrifying at all.

His last words would be something like "Look, I finally did something right, and it worked."

"We need to make a plan and get you safe."

Terrance put his hands on Angus's shoulders and kissed him. His lips were warm and stiff, but then he relaxed his mouth and sank into the moment. That was what he'd been missing while he hung out in his windowless room or cell or wherever they were keeping him. Angus slid his arms around his waist, and Terrance pulled him close.

"I want to enjoy the rest of today and maybe tomorrow morning." He didn't want to dwell. There'd be time for that later. Today he would live.

Angus looked up at him. "You don't hate me?"

"No." Angus was the kind of person everyone should be. The world wouldn't be so fucked if more people cared, and Angus had made him care. He wanted to do the right thing because he should and not because of what he could get out of it. "You didn't drag me into this. I happily followed."

Angus tightened his embrace for a moment. "Have you seen the others?"

"No, but maybe they have swanky apartments too."

Why had he been put away? Was he really that untrustworthy? From the moment Cadmael rifled through his thoughts, he'd known that nothing good was coming for him. No, it hadn't been good from the moment they'd been brought across the void. They'd been so relieved to get out of the desert, to know death was behind them. But then they'd all been separated. He thought the Mayans were going to take back their offer of refuge and cut them down to use their blood.

"We needed to get out of Vinland or we were all dead. And we're out. We have a chance. That's so much more than we had before." He kissed the top of Angus's head. "I need a shower. What are the chances you'll share it with me?"

Terrance smiled, but the edges became strained, and when Angus didn't immediately respond, the smile started to fracture.

Did Angus not want him anymore? He should've seen that coming.

Fuck, he should've stayed in the desert and given up. But then he'd have never gotten to see the things he had.

The Mayan Empire was amazing, even the little bit he'd seen.

"Pretty good," Angus said eventually. "I don't want to waste this chance."

"I'll ask for another." If he trained really hard, maybe they'd reward him as they had in Vinland. He was so obviously for sale that people could see the price written on his forehead.

If he survived, he was going to change that, even though he didn't have a clue how.

He led Angus through the apartment. It wasn't big, but it was bright and airy and had a balcony that overlooked the city. The bedroom door was open, and through that was the bathroom.

It was a bright combination of green and orange, and the tiles formed patterns that edged the walls and the mirror. Everything was artwork here—functional yet beautified. He could get used to that. His childhood in his grandparents' home had been functional and barely getting by.

But he liked pretty things.

Terrance glanced at Angus. The moment he'd seen him in the

common room he'd wanted him. It was unfortunate that the college wanted Angus watched. It had made what could've been simple and fun into something complicated.

He dragged off his shirt, which was still sticky with sweat. Angus watched, and his gaze drifted over the old scars. For a heartbeat Terrance thought Angus was going to say something about what had to be the worst night of his life—the night when Angus had stepped in, stopped the whipping, and proven how valuable Terrance was alive. If he hadn't, the underground would have killed him.

He reached into the shower but couldn't see any taps like there'd been in Vinland or dials like his room had. A rose dangled from the ceiling. Angus reached past him and gave it a twist, and the water jetted out.

Terrance caught him before he could pull away and crashed his lips onto Angus's. "I'd have worked it out."

"Uh-huh."

Terrance stepped into the shower and dragged a fully clothed Angus with him. The water was warm enough, though not as hot as he liked.

"You've got no other pants to put on, and these are getting wet," Angus said against his lips.

"I don't care. I'll wear nothing on the balcony and scandalize the neighbors." He worked open the buttons on Angus's shirt, still half expecting him to change his mind and leap away.

"Please don't. They might send the soldiers in to arrest you."

That was a very good point. He didn't know enough about the society to know the rules about… well, anything. "Does your shower have a timer?"

"Yes. All the taps do. It's like they don't have that much water."

"Less rain. Vinland is freezing, and they're drying." He shucked out of his wet shorts and left them on the floor of the shower. "I'd better make this wash quick." He squeezed out some soap and lathered up.

Angus removed his clothes and shoved them to the side. Then he helped. He glided his hands over Terrance's soap-slicked skin as the shower beeped at them.

"That's the one-minute warning."

He wanted more than a minute, but he stepped under the water fully to rinse and pulled Angus close. He kissed Angus under the water and tasted his lips and his skin as he made his way down Angus's throat. Each touch firmed his desire about what he wanted to spend the rest of the day doing, and Angus pressed his hips closer.

The shower beeped five times and shut off.

They remained pressed together, Angus hardening against Terrance's leg. It was better to steal happiness now than to wait for the perfect time. He hadn't had Angus to himself since Vinland, which seemed like another lifetime.

He reached up to get the water going again, but nothing happened.

"There's a ten-minute delay to stop people from doing that." Angus smiled. "It was the first thing I tried. Of course I had shampoo all over my head at the time." He found Terrance's dick with his fingers and closed around it. "Do you want to stay here?"

A shiver raced through Terrance's body. He'd be happy if Angus just kept going. "Why not?"

It wasn't cold. They were both naked, and he didn't want to give Angus the chance to freak out about what was coming. He should be the one freaking out, but his impending death was really so overdone that he couldn't be bothered. If someone told him he was going to live and he had to get his act together, that would be much more terrifying.

Angus stroked and then ran his thumb over the head. "Are you hoping to wait out the ten minutes and get another shower?"

"Maybe. Maybe we'll need another one." He took Angus in hand. He'd always liked the way Angus's dick curved as though begging to be touched... or licked.

Terrance dropped to his knees, and his pants cushioned the impact. Angus gasped before Terrance's lips had even brushed the head.

"Been a while?"

Angus nodded, and Terrance bit back a smile at knowing he was getting in before Saka. They were sharing Angus, and at one point there had been a serious implication that the three of them could get together.

As pretty as Saka was—in a metallic, red-skinned demon way—Terrance wasn't sure if that was what he wanted. It didn't matter either. Thoughts of pitz tried to invade, but he swallowed them down, along with the length of Angus's dick.

Angus pressed his nails into his shoulder and threaded his fingers into his hair. Terrance pressed his tongue to the underside of Angus's hot, hard flesh so the tip rubbed against the roof of his mouth, and then he almost released him. He teased and tasted with his tongue and flicked around the crown. He was barely even trying, but it didn't matter. Angus's eyes were half closed, and he rocked his hips in rhythm.

Terrance cupped Angus's balls and slid one finger farther back and traced the seam to his ass. That was all it took for Angus to groan his release. Terrance swallowed the lot and then got to his feet, his dick aching to be touched. Lust was hot and heady in his body and his skin was too tight.

Angus cupped him almost gently. "What do you want?"

It wasn't his last meal before death, and he wasn't going to treat it as such. "Whatever you want to do."

Angus pumped some conditioner into his hand then coated Terrance's dick with it. Every stroke was torture.

"Now I'm definitely waiting for the water."

"And I know how to waste those last few minutes." Angus turned and put his hands on the tiles.

"It's not a waste." He kissed between Angus's shoulder blades while he teased Angus's tight hole with his fingers. Angus pushed back as though he were done with waiting, and Terrance obliged and pushed in.

He gripped Angus's hips and deepened each thrust while still trying to draw out the moment. He didn't want it to be over.

Angus rocked back to meet each thrust and shuddered. The tightening of his ass was enough to push Terrance over the edge. He gasped and let the tremor subside and then rested his head on Angus's back.

After several heartbeats he reached up. The water came on, but neither of them pulled away. He should. He couldn't waste this second shower.

But he needed to say something in case he did end up on some sacrificial altar. "I might be falling for you."

It was supposed to sound like he didn't really care, but it sounded half-broken. He couldn't say the real words. He never had. And he never would if he died.

If he couldn't say them to Angus, then what was the point? He'd never be able to say them to anyone.

Angus glanced over his shoulder, murder in his gaze. "Don't."

"You're right. I shouldn't lie." He pulled out and turned Angus to face him. "I do love you."

Water drummed on the tiles, and Angus looked like he wanted to kill him.

"You don't get to say that and then go and die."

"That's exactly why I need to say it. You don't need to say it back." He wished Angus would, though, even if he didn't really mean it.

Angus bit his lip and shook his head. "I don't want to love you. I don't want to fall, because it's going to hurt. I don't want to have to watch you play."

"But that's all going to happen anyway." Terrance stole another kiss and then started to wash off. He tried to convince himself that it was fine. Angus had said he didn't want to fall, which meant that he was falling, and that was good.

Angus picked up his clothing, and something fell out and rolled across the floor toward the drain. Terrance put his foot over the hole as Angus reached for the thing.

"What is it?"

"Whatever Saka gave me. I'd forgotten about it." Angus turned it over in his hand.

"It was in his ear."

Angus held it for a moment. "I think it has magic."

He offered it to Terrance, but Terrance didn't have the kind of magical ability that Angus had. He had never wanted to be a warlock. All he wanted was to play rugby. The college had bought him with a scholarship. In hindsight, they probably wanted to supervise the child of some dangerous wizards, and he'd fallen for it.

He handed it back. "Maybe. What do you think it does?"

"I don't know. But if Saka had it in his ear…."

"You're going to stick a random magical piece of jade in your ear? And you think *I* take risks."

Angus lifted his gaze from the piece of jade. "No, *you're* going to stick it through my ear."

Terrance looked at the jade and then at Angus's ear. "This is a bad idea."

"I have plenty of them. Loving you tops the list." He gave a tentative smile.

Terrance took the jade spike. "Are you sure?"

"No, but Saka gave it to me for a reason."

"Then you're going to want to hide it under your hair or Cadmael will rip it out."

The shower beeped, giving them one minute to finish.

"Before the water runs out." Angus brushed aside his hair.

"You're mad. And this is going to hurt." He ran his finger over Angus's ear to work out the best place to stick it. It was all gristle up where it would be hidden. "It's going to hurt a lot." And he was going to have to push really hard.

"I'm ready." He put his hands on Terrance's shoulders and closed his eyes.

"On three." Terrance lined up the spike. He held the ear with his fingers and had his thumbs on the flat end of the spike. He pushed without even counting. He'd cut up a roast chicken once—all wrong according to his grandfather—but cutting through the chicken gristle and bone was kind of what this felt like. Blood welled and spilled over his fingers, but the jade was in.

Angus hissed and cursed, and his nails cut into Terrance's skin. Terrance pulled him close. The pain was nothing compared to what was coming. He should have kept his mouth shut about loving Angus.

He didn't want to die and leave him. But even if he miraculously won, he didn't see it ending well. He cupped Angus's chin. "Do you forgive me?"

"There's nothing to forgive." Angus gingerly touched his ear.

Blood dripped on the shower floor and spiraled down the drain, and the water cut off.

CHAPTER FIVE

"I WAS INTRODUCED to three would-be priests today," Wek said as she picked her way along the trail.

Trees arced overhead and dappled the light. Vines and other plants reached to block the trail. It wouldn't take long for it to be swallowed up. The plants around Lifeblood Mountain had never been this lush in Saka's lifetime.

Out on the trails, they could walk and be alone. He had started to miss walking. There was no time to be lost in his thoughts and think about magic when he lived in a village surrounded by people and helped the healers all day.

Alone they could talk freely, and no one was staring at the strange-looking demons. Saka wasn't used to the attention or the suspicion, and he didn't like it. He'd thought other tribes would be more welcoming and would want to find a solution to what was happening. But because their part of Demonside was less affected by the drying—possibly because their warlocks and priests made sure to rebalance—they weren't that interested. It was a human problem for humans to fix.

"Why were you introduced to the priests-in-training?" Saka stopped and let something orange scuttle across the trail and out of sight. After his meeting with Cadmael and his only time with Angus, he had a bad feeling about why Wek was being touted to the priests.

"Mages are supposed to have priests, and I don't have one." She lifted her gaze as something flitted through the canopy, and she reached for her bow before she let her hand fall away. They didn't need to hunt for food. It was provided. "Unlike warlocks, priests will only bond with mages."

"What choice do they have? When the void is opened that first time...." Unless.... Just because it was that way where he was from didn't mean it was that way here. "They choose somehow?" Mages could turn away the pull from across the void as a warlock sought a demon. Too many of the mages in his tribe had. They viewed the bond to a human as a bad thing. But choosing was different than turning away. He hadn't chosen Angus, or at least not consciously, nor had Angus chosen him. Although, to the college-trained warlocks, the first demon a warlock-in-training summoned was an indication of sort of warlock they were becoming.

Wek nodded. "The priests-in-training meet some mages first, and then a connection is established so that when they open the void for the first time they get that mage."

"So the mage helps teach the priest, and the priest can't abuse a helpless animal." The warlocks in Vinland probably would've found a way to ruin a mage. Some people hungered after power and cared little about the bodies that fell around them.

"It also makes the priests more powerful. It's why they have kept you and Angus apart. They are worried about what he can do."

"He's barely started training." While Angus understood magic and was learning control, he still had a long way to go.

"He's Vinnish, and there is an amount of fear regarding them."

Saka kept walking. He didn't want to dwell on that. Angus had looked well when he'd seen him, though it hadn't been for long enough and they hadn't been able to talk without supervision. Terrance was much revived, though his health would be wasted. He didn't want to dwell on what Terrance's death would do to Angus either.

"What of this anchor the priests require?" He hadn't been able to find out any more, but if the priests were happy to talk to Wek, then she could get the answers he needed.

"Ah." She smiled. "That's rather clever and solves the problem Angus always had while in Demonside."

"He couldn't get home." No one could open the void from this side.

"The anchor shares the demon but never crosses the void and will open it at an agreed-on time."

"And the mages agree to have two priests?" It was enough trouble to have one human.

"That seems to be the way it is." She shrugged. "They were happy to explain because they want me involved."

"You would get two priests."

"I don't want any." Her words were as soft as the whisper of the leaves.

The trail ended at a hole in the ground that was at least three body lengths wide. They sat at the edge. Far below them, water glittered, and large things moved in it. They were far enough below that they weren't in any danger sitting where they were.

They had found the place by accident and came there to talk.

"You've never had one," Saka said. What had started out as a duty to his people, to get a warlock, had become so much more. It hurt to not be able to see Angus, to hold him and hear him breathing as he slept. He'd never wanted such simple things so badly.

"I was close to my trainee, and now… now she's dead," Wek said. Norah had been left for scavengers in the red sands. Magic and life had drained out of her until there was nothing more for Demonside to take except her skin. It had made the other humans more careful. "What about you? When will Angus be back?"

"I do not know." He wanted Angus the way he thirsted for water. If love wasn't a weakness for mages, it was at least a distraction.

It was also something the priest Cadmael disapproved of. Was that true for all Mayans? Was it something that shouldn't happen? It didn't feel wrong, and the magic raised….

He sighed and told her about Terrance and his fate. Then for a time, they were silent as they contemplated what should be done and what had to be done.

He'd made the right decision to leave Lifeblood. He had to believe that, but with every passing day he was no longer sure. "What will you do about the priests?"

"I don't think I can refuse."

"They respect demons." They didn't kill them for power the way the Vinnish warlocks did.

"Yes." She swung her legs over the water hole, reminding Saka that she was young—barely out of her traineeship. "But I don't want to be bound. I'm thinking of leaving."

Saka turned his head. "To go back?"

She couldn't make that trek on her own and survive. It had been hard enough as a group—a mock tribe with two demon mages and a few terrified humans.

"I don't think that's possible."

"No." It probably wasn't. "Miniti would've told everyone." They would be outcasts and untrusted by all.

If he went back with Wek, would that help anyone?

Was he helping anyone here?

He wasn't rebalancing the world and healing Demonside. He was muddling around with a tribe who didn't quite trust him and trying to learn the Mayan language. Even his reason for leaving had been taken from him. Angus might as well be on the other side of the world and not just the other side of the void.

"Do you regret following me?"

Wek was silent for a few breaths. It was better to take the time to put together the right words than rush and be wrong, but the silence still clawed at his skin. He understood the guilt that Angus felt over Norah and Dustin's deaths, despite not having caused their deaths directly.

"Regret isn't the right word. I think you did the right thing to save the humans… but I think it could've been done better."

"It was a plan put together in haste." He couldn't deny that, but he wouldn't change it either. Angus would be dead if he'd stayed. The order to kill all humans on sight was wrong. Usi would've taken far too much delight in spilling Angus's blood on the sand. Saka would never have recovered from that wound.

Angus had already given too much blood to Demonside. Terrance's death would only wound him further, and Saka wouldn't be there to hold him together. His heart twisted. Once he'd have been glad that Terrance would no longer be stealing some of Angus's affection. Maybe his heart was hurting because he'd started to care for Terrance too. He'd been brave on the trek, always willing to help. He could've been a good anchor, and Saka wouldn't mind being shared by Terrance and Angus—though he probably shouldn't think about that when he should be sleeping.

"Do you think we could try the telestone?"

"To contact Tapo? Or to see if another tribe answers?"

"Both." She glanced down at the water and the dark bodies gliding through the sun-sparkled surface. "I want to explore. There's so much more to Arlyxia than I ever thought. I thought Lifeblood Mountain was the center of our world, but it's not. There could be other tribes that have a solution."

BEING SUMMONED to the doorway was enough to make Saka quicken his pace. It had only been days since he'd last seen Angus, so maybe the priests were going to loosen their hold and things could go back to the way they had been.

He hesitated just before he stepped onto the stones.

Was today the day Terrance was to play pitz? He didn't want to be there for that, but at the same time, he needed to be there for Angus. Delaying wouldn't help.

The void opened, and after inspection by the guards, Saka went through, into the same white room, or at least a similar one. Terrance wasn't there, but Angus was. His arms were crossed, and he was scowling. Cadmael and several other men in bright suits stood nearby talking.

Saka could only understand a few words of their rapid speech—it appeared no one was happy—but he was learning the language much faster now that he wasn't relying on magic.

Angus glanced at him and walked over. He embraced Saka, eliciting a hiss of disapproval and another round of chatter. "They're talking about us and how I need to be brought into line. One of those priests is to be the anchor."

Saka kept his arms around Angus. He smelled of fragrant soap, and his clothes were crisp and bright, but not a suit like the others, just pants and a shirt that was pulled over the head with a few buttons at the neck.

"Are you well?"

"Yes. Terrance hasn't played yet. Or if he has, they haven't told me."

"They will tell you." And if they were introducing possible new anchors, it couldn't be far away. "Do we have to choose one of them?"

"Apparently. I have only just arrived, and I was told to summon you, so they haven't told me anything yet."

Saka brushed a lock of Angus's hair back and felt the warm jade in his ear. Angus grimaced at the soft touch, and Saka let the hair fall back in place.

"Angus, Mage Saka," Cadmael said. "If you could join us."

They pulled apart. Saka's fingers brushed Angus's, and for a moment he thought about keeping hold, but he had already stirred up enough trouble.

"These priest candidates are looking to be an anchor—"

"Can you explain what that is, exactly?" Angus said with a smile. "You all seem to know, and I feel it's only fair that I know in detail what I'm signing up for."

"An anchor shares a demon. They are the second, lesser priest, always there to help and open the void so you don't become trapped. It's a very important role."

Saka glanced at the three candidates. None of them looked like they were happy with the idea of being second to Angus.

Angus tilted his head. "It sounds like one that could be misused. If I were to die, say by being accidentally left in Demonside, they would get Saka and then bring in another priest of their choosing to be their anchor. Wouldn't it be better for everyone to be on equal footing?"

"There is no such thing. You are only the main priest because you have the existing connection," Cadmael said through gritted teeth. He didn't like that Angus had a bond at all.

"We didn't come here to study the way the Mayan Empire uses magic. We came for safety and to fight the college, to liberate the trapped magic," Saka said.

"We *are* fighting. But you must follow our laws. You said yourself Terrance was going to be your anchor."

"And where is he?" There was a little too much desperation in Angus's words.

"Practicing the way you asked. You will get to watch the game. Now you must pick an anchor." Cadmael swept his hand out to indicate the three other men.

Saka walked along the line as though he were selecting just the right sacrifice. The man at the end stepped back. Maybe horned demons scared him. "Not him."

Cadmael sighed. "You haven't spoken to any of them yet."

Saka didn't need to speak to any of them to know he didn't want them. He didn't want to work magic with someone who only tolerated him. And he certainly wouldn't bind himself to a warlock by another name. As Angus had said, they could kill Angus and then bring in another priest. He stepped back. "Angus, what is it that you'd like to know about these hopefuls?"

Angus didn't move. He kept his gaze on Cadmael. "Why did you select them?"

"They were the next to be assigned. We grade our priests. Some will be firsts and others seconds. They were not selected just for you."

Saka didn't believe that, and from the snort Angus gave, he didn't either.

Angus walked past the first two and stopped at the last one. "Why did you flinch away from Saka?"

"I've never seen a demon like him before."

Angus's eyes narrowed. "Now tell the truth."

The priest swallowed and glanced at Cadmael, who nodded. "I didn't want him to lie with me."

Cadmael winced.

Saka pressed his lips together. "I do not want you."

"That business will all stop. Angus will learn the proper way to harness magic to use and how to rebalance."

"I have a most effective way already," Angus said.

"You have a small-time way. You cannot fight a war on your back." Cadmael bit out the words.

That was true. If the Mayans had a better way, it would be good to learn it, but Saka had no intention of no longer kissing Angus.

Angus nodded. "I agree with Saka. Not him."

The priest in question left the room.

"And if I have sex with my demon for fun?"

One of the men quickly hid his grimace. The other one looked at Saka as though considering the possibility. "If it's for fun and doesn't interrupt magical workings—"

"Priests and mages do not have that kind of relationship," Cadmael said. "You may leave the room but see me after," he said to the priest.

"Stay," Saka said. That man wouldn't follow the rules. While Saka didn't want an anchor, Angus needed friends.

Cadmael looked torn, as though his world were crumbling and he didn't know who to save.

Angus stared at Cadmael. "What does it matter what I do in my spare time?"

"It's not right."

"Because?" Saka asked.

There was no answer from Cadmael.

"Because you don't like it," Angus answered for Cadmael. "There are many magic users in the world. Surely some study sex magic?"

"There are some...," ventured the priest-in-training who had been told to leave and then to stay.

"No one in the magical community takes them seriously. It's small magic." Cadmael smiled. "You can do better."

"I never wanted to be a warlock or a priest or a whatever. I never wanted any of this. I will wait to choose an anchor. Terrance might win. Then he can be my anchor." Angus looked at Saka, hope bright like the sun in his blue eyes.

Saka wanted to open the void and vanish. Angus was holding on to a fragile chance, but Saka didn't want a stranger to intrude, and he didn't want to be entangled with the Mayans. "I agree we will wait."

Did he wait?

Wek's idea to explore more of Demonside had swelled in his mind, but that would mean leaving Angus—Angus who still didn't want what he'd been given. For all of his training at Saka's side, magic wasn't his life. It was something to do. For Saka it was everything, and he thought Angus had been starting to feel the same.

Perhaps Angus only studied because it meant being close to him. While that was a pleasant thought, it was wrong. If he left, what would happen?

"If you wait, you will not see each other or work magic for even longer." Cadmael's words sounded friendly, but the threat was clear.

Angus glanced at the priest-in-training. "I'll spend the time getting to know him better. I think Saka should too. These are our lives."

"There's more than your lives at stake. The world is icing over, and there is war between magic users. Decide. Now."

"What will happen if we do nothing?" Saka stared at Cadmael. Magic shouldn't be rushed. And Angus was right. If they killed Angus and brought in another priest, the mage could be kept forever without ever being able to refuse.

The idea was horrifying.

Cadmael smiled in a cold and toothy way that Saka was starting to loathe. "We always need new pitz players to support the war effort."

Angus's eyes widened, and he glanced at Saka. "What happened to refuge?"

"You have been offered it. If you refuse to accept the terms, you can leave." Cadmael indicated the door suggesting they could simply walk out.

"And go where?" Angus said as though he were seriously considering it. "And what about my friends? Or have you already killed them with your game?"

"They are alive and well. Unlike you, they are not bound to a mage. They dabble in natural magic only. You are the danger."

Angus shook his head and glanced at the floor.

"The Mayan Empire will not allow unregistered demon magic users to run around. Bear in mind, Warlock Donohue, it is your country we are at war with. You are the enemy with your blatant disregard for the rebalancing of magic. We have tried to make up for the shortfall, but we can only do so much. Where once Vinland and the Empire were allies with much in common, we are now divided, which has left us vulnerable to those who want all magic banned." He took a few steps closer. "Let me say that again. All magic. The Sindu, who happily kill those who show or are even accused of having any magical ability, are gaining traction. What they don't realize is that magic users are needed to keep it from stagnating. Your college has created the greatest stagnant pond of magic the world has ever experienced. We are not fighting to turn back an ice age, we are fighting for our right to exist as magic users. Make your choice, *Warlock* Donahue." Cadmael spat *warlock* as an insult.

Saka was sure there would always be magic users. They would just get better at hiding it. But the human world was going to suffer before things got better, and he couldn't take Angus away from it. Angus had to stay in his world and take his place as a magic user. He had treated Angus too much like a demon instead of like a human.

Angus faced him. While he didn't say anything, he shook his head slightly.

What did that mean?

"You aren't a sportsman," Saka said. Angus would die if he were to play pitz.

"No, but I am a magic user. A little warlock, a little mage, now to be a little priest." He shrugged. "How does it work?"

"You send your demon back, then Kabil"—Cadmael pointed at the man who'd been told to leave and stay and had chosen to obey Saka instead of the priest—"will open the void for the first time, and because he's met Mage Saka, it will open for him. It's not that different from when you first made the link to Saka."

Saka had wanted a bond with a warlock that time. This time he'd have to accept it. Like all mages, Saka had been taught how to turn away. But too many had done that because they didn't want to be bound to a warlock. If they hadn't shirked their duty as teachers, perhaps the Warlock College wouldn't have gone down such a destructive path.

Angus smiled as though he knew what Saka was thinking. Maybe he'd already realized that things could be made to go wrong. "And if it fails?"

"It won't fail," Cadmael said with far too much surety. Maybe the mages here didn't know how to turn away the bond, or maybe they were happy to make it. Saka didn't know enough.

Saka held Angus's gaze. It was a risky move, but if it were Angus opening the void he'd respond in a heartbeat. For a moment he wanted to go and take Angus with him and try for a different ally. Another trek could kill Angus, but staying here would kill Angus if they didn't obey or at least appear to obey.

Angus put his hand on Saka's chest and then leaned in and kissed his cheek. "Do not open the void unless it's me or Terrance. Trust me."

Saka returned the kiss. "This isn't worth dying for."

If Saka turned away Kabil, then what retribution would there be? Would Angus be thrown onto the pitz court regardless? It would be safer to accept the bond with Kabil—or at least safer for the moment and safer for Angus.

"It's my turn to save you." Angus opened the void.

Saka hesitated, but Angus gave him a small nod, which Saka reluctantly returned before he stepped back.

The stones were cool in Demonside, but he didn't stand and wait by the pillars for Kabil's summoning. He walked away as though his job were done, but that wouldn't be enough. Cadmael would make Iktan search for him, so he needed to leave the village and find a place to hide. That thought almost stopped his steps. He was running and hiding when he should be fighting. Was it a mistake?

Did Angus actually know what he was doing? He was young and untrained… but he was living among the Mayans, so maybe he understood them better.

He forced himself to keep walking past the two guards. He had to trust Angus that turning away Kabil was the best thing to do. Letting someone else save him sat wrong in his gut. He was so used to being the one to help Angus that he didn't like leaving him alone and unprotected. When he glanced over his shoulder and was unable to see the guards, he ran toward the village. He wouldn't have long to get what he needed and leave.

In town he kept his pace brisk as though he were doing something very important. From his room he gathered only a waterskin and his knife. He could live without the rest. Then he walked into the jungle, although his heart still wanted to be at the doorway, to be there for Angus.

A ripple ran over his skin—the tug of the void, calling him back to the doorway. But it wasn't Angus summoning him. The touch was unfamiliar and tentative and too far away because it was bound to the doorway made of stones. But he knew where the doorway was, could feel the pull, even though he couldn't see it. How far did the doorway's power reach? He was used to the void opening only a body length from him. He wanted Angus to be able to summon him without needing the doorway. He might have to walk for days for that to be possible.

Saka brushed aside the contact, knowing it would fall on another. At least that was the way it worked at Lifeblood, but he wasn't sure how it worked here. For a moment, guilt tightened around him, but he drew in a breath and kept walking. He had to trust Angus.

It was only when he reached the underground lake with the caved-in roof and the large things swimming far below that he stopped. Then he climbed into the branches of a tree until he was hidden.

The urgency that had filled him fled and left him hollow. He'd abandoned Angus to face the consequences of their plan. Cadmael would be unimpressed and demanding answers. Saka should've ignored Angus and accepted Kabil. It would have been safer in the short term. And what of Terrance? Angus truly thought he could play pitz and win, but Saka held no such hope. Nor did he want his warlock to play their game. What would happen now that he'd turned Kabil away?

His chest wanted to cave in. He couldn't lose Angus.

Knowing Angus had made him more human and more selfish. Where once he would've sacrificed everything for magic and his tribe, now he weighed each cost. Angus had deemed it a worthy risk and he was willing to pay for their shared illusion of freedom. But now that they had committed to this course, going back would only make it worse.

He was a failed mage and a coward.

CHAPTER SIX

ANGUS'S PALM was still warm from the heat of Saka's skin. He'd wanted to speak with him longer—have longer to hold him and longer to plan what they should do next. He curled his fingers to hold on to the heat, knowing that even if he opened the void to summon Saka, he probably wouldn't come, not the first time anyway, and maybe not for several days.

Adrenaline made his heart quicken. This was as dangerous as standing up to the college. He was almost certain that when Kabil tried, Saka wouldn't respond. They had agreed, and though he knew Saka didn't like it, it was something Angus had to do. He wouldn't share Saka with someone he'd just met. That place was for Terrance. And he refused to think about the game and what could happen. He couldn't think that far ahead.

If Saka didn't respond to Kabil's summons, what would happen to Saka… and to him? His stomach knotted, but it had to be like this. He didn't want a stranger, a Mayan priest they didn't know and couldn't trust, to have any kind of power over Saka—but Terrance….

For a moment in the desert, they had briefly talked about more between the three of them, and he held on to that. When they were reunited, they would see what kind of magic they could draw up.

But he didn't give a damn about magic right then. It had never done anything but complicate his life. No matter how interesting or amazing it was, it always came at a cost, and he was running out of ways to pay.

All he had left was his life, and he was sure the Mayans would happily take it.

They didn't need him. He needed them. They could turn him over to the college, but he'd rather die here than in Vinland. He was a traitor to the core.

He turned to glance at Cadmael, hoping to stall the moment for as long as possible. "So what happens now? What's the point of all of this? Aside from making sure you can control me and supervise me?"

"It's not about control. Supervise?" Cadmael nodded. "You never finished your first year at the college. You've trained with demons. Your magical education is a patchwork of ideas. Like Vinland, we have training that is required for your safety as well as everyone else's. Vinland took the idea of formal training from us."

"Why didn't they take the shared-demon idea?"

Cadmael stared at him. "They did at first. They took the idea of payment and rebalancing as seriously as we do. But…." He shrugged. "Something went wrong, and they twisted the ideals to build power. Magic isn't about power."

"I know, and I'm happy to learn from you."

"I know you are. That doesn't mean we want to share knowledge with you. You think of magic as a small thing. Of individual acts. It's not." Cadmael touched his heart. "Everyone has magic, but not all can access it in life."

The cult of death and blood. He'd hoped that was Vinnish propaganda to stop people from fleeing south, but so far, it was looking like the truth.

"Kabil, focus on Saka and open the void," Cadmael commanded.

Kabil had the decency to look uncomfortable. Because he didn't want the stigma of having a Vinnish warlock and a red demon? Or because he knew he was unwelcome and taking another man's place?

It was too soon. Saka needed a chance to get away from Iktan.

Angus didn't know how well Saka was guarded or how closely he was watched. "So that's it? We don't get to know each other first and discover if it's truly a good fit?"

"Usually that would happen," Kabil said before Cadmael could get a word in. Kabil had said a few things that Cadmael didn't like, which only made Angus more certain he'd made the right choice. Since he had to make one, and Kabil could be someone interesting to get to know.

"This is different. Don't you want to be free to walk around and see your friends?"

He did, but not at the cost of Saka's freedom. If they were bound to a priest, neither of them would be free. Angus hadn't been free from the moment he started showing signs of being able to use magic, long before he was sent to college.

"I do. I want to see Terrance." Was it love or was it desperation that made him say that? It didn't matter if he died. Angus wasn't ready for Terrance to be gone. He'd never be ready. Maybe it was love? How did he love Terrance *and* Saka? Or could he love neither of them properly?

"You can see him before the game."

To say goodbye? No. Terrance would win. He had to. Angus hadn't said goodbye to Saka either. What if that was the last time he saw him? Would the mages across the void do something to him? He tried to think of other options, other plans they could've made in those few heartbeats, but he came up with nothing. They'd done the best they could, but would that ever be enough?

"Open the void, Kabil," Cadmael ordered. "What are you waiting for?"

"I didn't think we'd be doing this today. I thought—"

"It doesn't matter what you thought. This is what is happening."

Kabil moved his hand, palm down, like he was wiping away a circle. The void shimmered open. For a moment nothing happened. Kabil stepped back perplexed, but the void remained open, and no demon came through.

Angus had to concentrate on breathing. His chest was tight and his ribs were crushing him with expectation. When Angus had first opened the void, Saka had wanted a warlock because he wanted a connection with someone inside the college—a spy. If Angus hadn't been suitable, Miniti would've have ordered Angus's death.

Both sides treated life as though it were nothing but a coin to spend.

It didn't have to be that way, yet the alternative wasn't popular either. That was perplexing.

"Something isn't right." Kabil frowned. "Shouldn't he be here? Shouldn't a guard be leaning through and checking?"

Cadmael turned his head and fixed Angus with a glare. "Go through and get your demon."

Angus smiled. Saka was ignoring the summons. "So you can abandon me there?"

It would be a slow death. Weeks in the making unless they could find another tribe of demons to take them in. The horror of the first trek, the way the scarlips had stalked them, looking for an easy meal, the thirst and exhaustion and sunburn. It was all too fresh in his mind.

But if he stepped through, he could see Saka. Maybe. But Saka had turned away the connection… so which demon had it settled on?

A demon armed with a bow and arrows stepped through. His fur gleamed golden in the lights, and his antlers arched gracefully over his head. While clearly a soldier or hunter, he didn't look half as intimidating as Saka.

Angus bit his lip to keep from smiling. Something had gone wrong. This was now Kabil's demon, and the demon wasn't a mage. Priests were supposed to have mages.

"What is… why are you here?" Cadmael spoke in his native tongue, giving up his accented Vinnish as though what was said was none of Angus's business.

Angus's ear burned as the magic trapped in the jade let him hear and understand every word. If Cadmael knew he had it, it would no doubt be torn from his ear.

"The void opened, and I needed to cross. I couldn't resist any longer. It's never happened before." The demon glanced around the room, and his nose twitched as his confusion clearly became concern.

Cadmael rounded on Kabil. "Did you even try to summon Saka?"

"Yes." He sounded offended. "This is unacceptable."

Cadmael closed his eyes. "It's not unheard of, though it is less than ideal. Was the red horned demon, Saka, not at the doorway?"

What was the doorway? The void opened near a demon. It should've opened near Saka regardless of where he was.

"He came back through and left," the demon said.

Cadmael's gaze slid to Angus, and Angus fought the urge to step back from his cold glare. There was nowhere to run to, and he was tired of running. He crossed his arms as though bored because he couldn't understand what was going on or what was being said.

"Your demon was supposed to wait by the doorway to be summoned." Cadmael spoke in Vinnish.

"Doorway?"

There was a moment of silence as the Mayans realized that Angus didn't know what they were talking about and they clearly weren't sure if they wanted to share. It was Kabil who spoke first. "We made doorways in Demonside so the void can only be opened in those places."

"It is important that we work together. Since we can open the void, it was fair that the void only open in fixed places... for safety," Cadmael finished.

That made sense. So if Saka wasn't there, he knew that, and he'd fled.

"That's not what we're used to. A misunderstanding." Angus shrugged.

"Summon him so we can fix that," Cadmael said.

"He's not at the doorway." The hunter had just said that.

"He'll feel the call and return. That is how it works."

But Angus knew Saka wouldn't answer, and they had no way of communicating. While he'd never wanted a demon or to be a warlock, suddenly the idea of not having a demon was akin to cutting off his arm. He was quite attached to Saka and had become used to depending on him whenever he had a question about magic. They were more than mage and apprentice and more than lovers. Saka had become enmeshed in his life in such a way that trying to cut him out would kill him. Without Saka, death might be nice… peaceful.

He couldn't fight for magic and stop the ice on his own. He wasn't even sure he could do it with help. It wasn't even his responsibility. He was a no one, and there were institutes and warlocks and priests who knew far more than he did. They should be doing something, anything, to put things right. Instead they were putting sanctions in place and hurting ordinary people.

"I can try." That was all he could do, so he tried. The void opened, but without Saka at the doorway, it shut just as fast. In that moment he felt Saka before he was brushed aside. The rejection stung, even though he knew it was for the best.

More of that awful thick silence followed.

Cadmael looked at the soldier demon. "I will send you back. We will sort this out."

The demon nodded and didn't need to be asked twice to leave. He hastily stepped through the void and back to Demonside. Angus wished he could follow to avoid whatever was going to happen next.

"You will stay here until Saka attends."

Then he would be here when the world iced over and they all died.

"Kabil has a demon now. What does it matter?"

"His demon isn't a mage. We can sever that bond."

"I thought that could only be broken with death." That's what he'd been told by the college. Was there another way?

"That is correct," Cadmael said, his voice as smooth as the polished glass on the outside of the temple.

Angus's mouth dropped open before he could close it. "You're going to kill the demon?"

"I have no choice. You can blame Saka for not obeying."

No, he wouldn't blame Saka. "Why can't he train to become a mage instead?"

Kabil and Cadmael glanced at each other, but it was Cadmael who spoke. "Not all are suited to be a mage. Surely you know that. Not every life can be saved. Death has worth and meaning."

Not to the people who do the dying.

"I will show Angus some of the city so he may understand. The Vinnish treat death as something to be feared and avoided, not something to be embraced," Kabil said.

Angus couldn't imagine ever embracing death.

DUSK WAS SMOTHERING the city by the time he was allowed to leave the temple, and he was sure he was only allowed to leave because it was clear Saka wasn't coming. Cadmael had ignored Kabil's offer to show Angus more of the city—neither of them were in his favor—and Angus had been returned to his apartment and ignored for the last few days. Was Cadmael hoping the isolation would make him more compliant?

The air hummed with insect life as though nothing were wrong with the world, but the sky was an odd, sickly green. Angus had been watching from his balcony as the sun set. He had nothing more pressing to do with his time, and he'd yet to work out how to escape from his tower prison.

Not that anyone called it that.

The magic dampeners were featherlight on his skin, not like the ones in Vinland, and he was tempted to experiment to see what would happen if he did some magic. Would alarms go off? Would he get a visit from Cadmael?

He was in no rush to see the priest.

He ran his finger along the balcony railing. Terrance was out there somewhere, Saka was unreachable, and every breath hurt. He'd lost the people he cared most about. What was the point? What exactly was he fighting for?

He didn't give a shit about the correct use of magic, but he believed everything should be kept in balance. He didn't really care who was in power in Vinland as long as they weren't screwing it up for everyone else.

Maybe he was just fighting for himself and the right to live his life the way he wanted. In that case, he was doing a shit job of that too.

Suddenly the hairs on his arms drew tight and the temperature dropped.

He lifted his gaze to the green, boiling sky as a flash tore across. He shielded his eyes with his hand, and the familiar feel of magic tingled across his skin as though he were raising power. It had been so long that he gathered it to him just to feel the rush. The scar on his chest warmed and then burned.

Then the breath was taken from his lungs.

His back hit the glass door, and the building shook like the magic-laced air was trying to pulverize him.

Panic made him throw up a circle in defense, but it wasn't enough. Sirens and alarms were going off. Then as quickly as it had hit, the wave of magic started to recede and drag everything with it. The magic Angus had pulled to himself wanted to flow out of his body.

That was not a good thing.

Nails scratched the inside of his veins trying to tear all magic from him. It hurt worse than Demonside slowly draining him, but the result would be the same. He resisted and used everything he had to keep the magic within him. When his body wasn't strong enough anymore, he reached out to the building, to the magical dampeners and the wiring beyond. Light bulbs hissed and cracked, and the building shook like it was being ripped in two.

His teeth were going to be pulled from his head, and his nail beds ached, but if he let go, even for a breath, he was dead.

Whatever was happening was trying to kill him by taking the magic that was part of him. He hadn't survived for this long to be taken out by some kind of storm. He pressed his nails into his palm deeply enough to cut. Drawing blood didn't bother him anymore. His own had been spilled so often. He peeled himself off the door long enough to run his palm and his blood over the railing to create another line of defense.

The dragging sensation faded. The building still quaked, and other buildings did too. It was as though the ground were trembling.

Was there a spell in the storm to harvest magic?

His breath came in hard pants, and he was on his knees by the time everything went still and the sky brightened to pink. Alarms echoed across Uxmal, and his apartment was ringing as the dampener screeched its warning.

His head was ready to split open, and red stained the front of his shirt. He peeled it away from his skin to see that the mark Saka had carved into him had been torn open.

Around him, the metal and stone glowed. He should go inside, but it was too noisy in there. He'd be better off trying to heal himself outside. Something hot and sticky hit his lip. He wiped it away with the back of his hand, not surprised to see more blood staining his skin.

He lay down on the warm, glowing patio to rest.

That he was alive seemed amazing, but if that storm happened again tonight, he would be fucked.

<h1 style="text-align:center">CHAPTER SEVEN</h1>

Saka held the telestone in his palm. He wanted to speak to someone back at Lifeblood, to know how his tribe fared—not that they'd ever let him be their mage again. No tribe would have him. They'd never trust him.

They might be right.

Was he still putting Arlyxia first, or just one human?

Angus hadn't tried to summon him in two days. He should be glad, but he was concerned. He'd know if Angus were dead… wouldn't he?

Wek returned with two small, scaled animals with strangely naked tails. They were good eating even if they looked odd. "I didn't see anyone. Maybe they've stopped searching."

For the first few days, he'd worried that Iktan would find him and drag him back to the doorway so Kabil could make a bond. But that hadn't happened. Either they weren't looking for him or they didn't care, neither of which seemed right. There was something else going on.

"I have placed a few more stones." While she hunted, he'd walked all day to place another stone and then return.

They would need to make a decision soon—leave the place they'd come to for refuge or stay.

If he was far enough away from the doorway he could answer Angus's summons, but Angus wouldn't be able to come to him, or he'd be stuck in Demonside. The Mayan solution of having an anchor wasn't entirely without merit. He hadn't lied when he claimed they'd spoken of inviting Terrance into their bed—though neither of them had thought of what it might mean beyond that.

He didn't want to dwell on what might be happening with Terrance. Perhaps that was why Angus hadn't contacted him.

Wek started to skin the creatures. "Did you want to try and reach Tapo?"

Saka put down the stone. "I do not know anymore."

Wek put her hand over his, her fingers slippery from the animal's fat. She opened her mouth, but the words never came out.

They were swallowed in a sudden cloudless deluge of bitter-tasting rain.

CHAPTER EIGHT

IN THE MESS HALL, plates rattled off the counters as an alarm sounded. Water bounced in Terrance's glass. Panic blossomed and was fed by confusion. He felt the tremor in his chest as though someone or something were thumping him on the back. One of the other pitz players—a man who was sure to die in his first game—ran to the windows.

Terrance didn't get closer to the glass in case it blew in or out or otherwise shattered. Beyond the glass the sky was a bruise, green and sick with shadows of purple. Nothing good could come from something that looked like that. He'd never seen the sky such a peculiar shade. And the vibrations in his chest hadn't stopped.

"Do not go outside. It is not a quake," a female voice called over the speakers.

Terrance had no desire to go outside. The building was protected. He'd felt the magic as soon as he'd arrived. Out there was just the toxic sky and whatever it had brought.

"There's someone out there," the man at the window said.

The man outside staggered toward the building. Blood streamed from his nose and ears.

No one moved to help him. They'd been ordered to stay in. At the training school, it was best to obey orders. It was a sports camp taken to the extreme. Everything they ate and did was scheduled, every workout and training session logged. He'd expected a disorganized mess given that some of them would die—why waste time and money on the soon-to-be dead?

But that wasn't the way training was viewed at all.

The person outside fell to the ground, motionless. Then the tremors stopped, and the clouds rolled away and returned the sky to the pinkish spill of sunset.

The alarm shut off, but the ringing echoed in Terrance's ears, and the beat of his heart was still too quick. Something big had happened, but he didn't know what.

The mess was silent. No one moved, even after they'd been given the all clear.

"Can we go out now?" someone asked, but he didn't wait for an answer. The man walked toward the door and pushed it open when no one stopped him. Then he crossed the ground where they did their morning sprints to kneel by the man's side.

Terrance hoped the wounded man was alive. He didn't know why, when everyone at the school knew there was a good chance they'd die. Some volunteered themselves, and some were criminals who'd been given a choice. Terrance probably fell into the latter category.

The man who'd run outside picked up the body and brought him in. "He's alive."

Sighs of relief filled the air, and talk resumed.

Terrance sipped his water. His mouth was dry, like he'd been in Demonside too long. "What was it?"

All heads turned toward him. His fair skin marked him as an outsider, but for the most part, no one had held it against him. They were all there to play. But now there was a prickle of animosity.

"That was a Vinnish magical weapon." The speaker glared at him as though Terrance were responsible.

"Clean sweep they call it," someone else said.

"Knocks out anyone outside and kills those with magic in their blood. He was lucky he didn't have magic."

Terrance swallowed. If he'd been outside, he'd be dead. From the way they were looking at him, it was best they didn't know that. Next time they might shove him outside, regardless of orders. "I'm sorry."

There was nothing else he could say.

He couldn't leave the mess until he'd eaten his required nutrients, but no meal had ever tasted so awful. He was sure he would pay for the Vinnish clean sweep tomorrow during training.

CHAPTER NINE

THE HEAT from the stone balcony seeped into Angus's skin. He opened his eyes, and for a moment, he couldn't work out why he was lying down and why he couldn't breathe through his nose.

He pushed himself up, but his head felt like it was the size of the moon. The sky had darkened to inky black, but the building was glowing. He wiped at his nose, and dried blood came off on his hand. There was blood all around him and smeared on the railing and doors.

There was magic everywhere.

It pulsed in the building like a living thing. Magic should naturally gather in places, but it hadn't here. No magic had gathered in his apartment the whole time he'd been in Uxmal.

The scar on his chest burned as though it still held magic, and blood was seeping out of his skin. He placed his hand over the wound to heal it, but then he hesitated. The magic was all around him. He could use it, but he wasn't supposed to.

Screw that and Cadmael's rules.

His skin cells divided and knitted to heal the scar. It had been torn open by whatever had happened, and that wasn't a good thing. He healed the cuts on his palm and then made sure that the blood vessel in his nose wasn't going to spring another leak.

Insects buzzed around him, drawn by the blood and magic-created light, and he squashed them as they landed on his skin. He wasn't ready to get up, but he didn't want to be eaten alive either. With a grunt and far too much effort, he grabbed the bloodied railing and pulled himself up. It took a moment for him to feel steady.

The apartment door swung open. Cadmael was wild-eyed and looked ready to kill. He strode through the apartment toward the balcony. Angus curled his fingers and drew magic to himself. He really wasn't in the mood for the priest's shit, nor did he want to fight.

The two soldiers remained by the entrance as Cadmael opened the glass door and closed it behind him, giving the illusion of privacy, even though the guards were watching. "What did you do?"

"Me? What was that… that storm?" He didn't even know how to describe what had happened. "It was trying to drag the magic out of me."

"You were outside when the clean sweep hit?" Cadmael's face became a mask of horror.

"Yes." That seemed like the correct answer. It was also the truth.

"You should be dead."

Yet here he was only *feeling* like death. "I held on to the magic."

"How?"

When they had first entered the Mayan Empire, he'd had a medical exam. The doctors had seen the scar, but hadn't asked about it. "I used a focus, and when that wasn't enough, I used the building. What is the clean sweep?"

"That is the weapon your Warlock College has made." Cadmael paced closer. "Nonmagic users become incapacitated. Magic users get the magic and life sucked out of them."

"Where does the magic go?"

"Back to Vinland. With every strike they injure the population, kill those who would stand against them, and gather more magic."

The weapon his father had hinted at was real and terrifying. He shouldn't have survived, but he had, although he felt bruised inside and out. He really wanted to lie down, yet he also wanted to celebrate. *Later.* While Cadmael was talking, Angus wanted information. "You've been hit before."

"A different city, smaller and on the coast. The Nations have been hit too. That is what you're fighting against, what we are all fighting against." Cadmael put his hand on the wall, and Angus was sure he saw the wall pulse. "You resisted somehow."

"I wasn't going to get dragged out with the tide."

Cadmael nodded. "You do realize that you have fried the building's circuits? It was designed to prevent magical buildup, and you have... filled it."

"Would you rather I died?" His life was a terrible inconvenience to so many, though he was starting to enjoy being such a disappointment.

"Usually this magic is funneled through the temples. We have priests on duty all the time in case of an attack."

"But they can't get it all."

"We get what we can to stop Vinland from becoming stronger and to return magic to the demons. But it's not just one strike. We're getting reports that several countries have been hit tonight. They're already backing away from the sanctions and giving Vinland what they want—anything to stop Vinland from targeting them."

Vinland was bullying everyone. Without strength in numbers, no one would stand against them. "That won't stop the ice. The weapon has to be stopped."

"With every strike we're able to learn more about the weapon and where it originates." Cadmael glanced at him. "You healed yourself. You can help to heal others."

"I thought I wasn't allowed to do magic." He was still waiting for Cadmael to issue some kind of punishment to him for frying the building and surviving.

"I'm making an exemption. The hospitals will be overflowing with injuries. Clean yourself up."

Angus was tempted to refuse, but he wanted to get out and see how magic was actually used. More than that, he wanted to use magic.

He missed the feel of it flowing through him, so he nodded. "How many magic users are dead?"

"We don't know the official numbers, but you saved the ones living in your building."

Angus allowed himself a grim smile. He got no thanks or praise, but he hadn't expected any. He went into the bathroom and closed the door. The walls cast enough of a glow for him to see by, so he took a moment to examine the remains of the damage. He looked worse than he felt, considering how close to death he'd been.

Had Terrance been outside at the time of the strike? If he asked, would he be told? Or did Cadmael not even know? There would be more important people to worry about.

Terrance was either alive or dead.

Angus chose to believe that he was alive, because the other option would shatter the fragile calm he was holding on to.

Why weren't other countries doing something? Attacking back? Anything? From his little balcony, it seemed that the Mayan Empire was doing nothing but watching people die. He pulled off his shirt and dropped it on the shower floor so he could clean the blood off his chest. The scar was smooth beneath his fingers, and the skin glinted as though flecked with metal, the way it had since Saka made his mark.

He was sure that if he tried, he could erase Saka's claim on him, but he didn't want to. And the mark had been useful more than once when he needed to anchor magic. He scrubbed his skin and face and tried to be ready to face Cadmael again. That he was being asked to help was either a sign of trust or desperation, but he was hoping it was the former.

In his room he dragged on clean pants and shirt and put on shoes.

Cadmael was on the balcony, staring out over the city.

"I'm ready." He wasn't sure he was, but he never had the luxury of time.

"You will be moved tomorrow. Somewhere with better protections."

If he was moving, he wanted more than better protections. "I want to be able to watch the news and learn what's happening. I can't keep living in the dark."

"You'll be housed with the other priests undergoing training. Kabil will show you around. If you leave the city, there will be no second chance. Do you understand?"

Angus nodded.

"Say it and mean it." There was a resonance behind Cadmael's words, as if they were laced with magic.

The magic still clung to Angus, wrapping around him and making his skin tingle with power. The leftover residue from the clean sweep made Angus feel like he could raise an entire field of crops on his own.

In that moment he was glad he could help heal people, because being alone and wondering what was going on would be terrible. Maybe for a few minutes he'd stop thinking about Terrance.

"I understand." The words were simple, but he could taste the magic.

"Now I have your word. Words shouldn't be broken."

Angus's eyes widened. "What magic is that?"

"Magic you have yet to learn." Cadmael entered the apartment. "Come. They'll be expecting us. Someone will collect your things."

None of the things in the apartment were his anyway. The furniture had already been there, and the clothing had been given to him. He was quite happy to walk away and start over. Again.

One day he was going to have a home.

With a sigh he followed Cadmael out of the apartment and down the stairs. The elevators weren't working, because he'd ruined the building's circuits.

There was chaos on the street. Sirens sounded in the distance, and people were rushing around, looking for friends and family who'd been caught out. That was what *he* should be doing, but he didn't know where his friends were… were they alive.

"Where are Lizzie and the others?" Were they together? Cadmael had said they weren't a threat, but that didn't mean they were safe.

"Someone will check on them."

The temple was lit up, and that was where they headed, not the hospital.

"I thought I was going to help heal."

"When the hospital temple is full, the wounded come to any temple. All have priests, and even though we all have our specialties, we can all heal and help."

Angus bit his tongue for a little longer and then tossed caution aside. "And Terrance?"

"I don't know. The pitz school is protected. If he was indoors, he'll be fine."

That wasn't an answer. *Had* he been indoors?

"I want to see him." He needed to be sure Terrance was all right.

"You will, before the game."

He didn't want to ask, but the word fell off his tongue. "And when will that be?"

"After this?" Cadmael shook his head. "Sooner than it should've been."

Angus wished he hadn't asked. He didn't want the game to ever come, even if that meant he never got to see Terrance again. At least he'd be alive.

CHAPTER TEN

W ITH W EK'S help to make sure he didn't damage himself, Saka used the telestone to reach across the sands, although they weren't on the sand yet. They were still in the blue swath of jungle where the tribes connected to the Mayans lived.

He'd walked out into the sand yesterday to place another stone. What he found was chilling. Two pillars reached for the sky, much like the doorway Saka had seen outside the town. But there was no town and no magic around the pillars. They were all that remained of what had once been there. A few pieces of wood stretched out of the sand like fingers, but they had once been homes. Had the jungle once reached that far? He placed the stone at the base of one of the pillars and returned to their camp.

In his mind he felt all the stones of the web he'd made humming with energy. For a moment he was tempted to reach back to where Miniti and his tribe would be. But he didn't. Couldn't. He'd connected to Iktan with the assistance of several other mages, but now he only had Wek. Looking back wouldn't be of any use. There were no answers in the place he'd once called home. He needed to explore farther.

Someone brushed against his mind, and then Mage Iktan was there.

Saka almost dropped the connection. They'd avoided all mages and other demons for days, though only narrowly. This swath of jungle-coated hills was well habited. Saka didn't know how closely they worked with the Priest Cadmael, and he wasn't prepared to make himself known and ask.

Iktan lifted his hands. *I am not here to hunt you or hurt you.*

Then why are you here?

I could ask you the same.

Saka's body was aware of the breeze on his skin and the shifting of leaves that let the sun warm small patches of his body, but his mind was full of Iktan. He'd reached to talk to someone farther away who could add to their knowledge, not to talk to those who would drag them back.

I have been feeling your call for a few days, Iktan continued, *and this time I thought it best to respond. What are you trying to do?* .

There was no point in avoiding the question. *I want to deepen my understanding of what is happening. I was hoping to speak with some other, more distant, tribes.*

Iktan nodded. *In the same way you reached out to me. You didn't have to leave to do that. Your human has been given a place.*

I had to leave. And he wasn't entirely sure that Angus was safe.

You did not want to bond with the priest.

I have Angus. He didn't need another…. But Angus needed another.

We do not always agree with our human counterparts, as I'm sure you've experienced. Iktan bared his square teeth in something close to a smile. *Mages do not believe the bond should be forced, and we will not force you to accept it. No mage will turn you in.*

Some of the tension loosened. Iktan had told the truth about not wanting to drag him back.

Though soldiers, demon and human, acting under orders, will lack the level of comprehension required. So you would best be careful as they are looking for you, Iktan added.

Thank you for the warning.

We are all acting to save Arlyxia. If you go much farther away... say where the river sinks into the pool... you will be out of range of the remaining active doorways. So, should Angus open the void, it will open near you.

Saka nodded. They would pack up and relocate. He didn't want Angus entering the village to look for him. *I found a doorway in the desert. What happened to the tribe that lived there?*

Iktan was silent for a moment. *The desert expanding is just one symptom. The doorways are ceasing to work. There used to be many doorways and many mages. Now there isn't enough for the priests they are training.*

He didn't need to travel far to learn. All Saka needed to do was trust that all mages wanted what was best for Arlyxia. Even Usi was doing what she'd thought best by wanting to kill all humans to rebalance.

Can you stop humans from coming through the doorway?

Yes. The expression on Iktan's face became serious.

Saka exhaled. That could change everything for his tribe. *The warlocks are trying to kill the Lifeblood tribes, my tribe. A doorway could save them.*

The making of a doorway isn't easy.

What if it wasn't a doorway, but Lifeblood Mountain itself? No warlocks would be able to get demons. They wouldn't be able to open the void at all.

I don't know. Iktan flicked his ears. *There may not be enough magic left to even make one. The ones that remain are very old.*

There was more that Iktan wasn't saying. *Has the skill been lost?*

Iktan's silence was the only answer Saka needed. He wouldn't be able to tell his tribe how to block the warlocks.

Iktan glanced down. *The doorways do more than localize travel across the void. They control the flow of magic too. I do not know if they do harm or good.*

My people may not survive a second war with the warlocks.

Our people may not survive. You see this place and think we are untouched. I see tribes with no children all crowding into an ever-shrinking area. I know you do not trust me or my priest, but I think we need you.

I can do nothing while in hiding. He wasn't helping anyone by not accepting his fate, not even Angus. He was supposed to put his tribe first, not his desires. *Does the bond work? You do not feel trapped with two humans?*

I only work with Cadmael. The other is there just to open the void so he can go back. I understand your reluctance.

Saka doubted that. *I will consider the matter further. Cadmael will not be happy you are helping.*

He will not know. I hope you find the answers you need before it's too late. Then Iktan was gone.

Saka opened his eyes and rocked as though the ground were shifting beneath him. The wave of dizziness passed.

Wek put her hand on his shoulder and peered at him to see if he was all right. "Who did you speak to?"

"Iktan. We need to move farther out." Seeing the panic on her face, Saka put his hand over hers. "We're safe. But we need to get out of range of the doorway."

"And we still need to talk to someone else."

"Yes." They needed to do something. At the moment they were doing nothing, and despite the recent downpour, Demonside had dried a little more. He saw the signs every time he crossed from desert to jungle. The sand was creeping closer. Iktan had confirmed that even this part of Arlyxia was dying.

Without a human, he wasn't even rebalancing.

Saka frowned. "Have you seen any of the mages rebalance?"

She scowled for several heartbeats. "No. I didn't see any signs of it either."

The downpour had been a rebalancing from Humanside, but even that hadn't been enough. For the first time, he wondered if anything they did would be enough. Perhaps they had passed that point, and Arlyxia was too far gone.

CHAPTER ELEVEN

THE ROOM REMINDED Angus of his college room back in Vinland, except for the turquoise walls and wood floor. There were sheets on the bed, and there was nothing else in the room but his dirty clothes where he'd left them in a pile before his shower. At the moment he didn't care about the mess. He just wanted to sleep.

After not using magic in weeks, maybe months, he'd forgotten how exhausting it could be. He wasn't sure how long they spent crossing the desert, but he knew he'd been in the Mayan Empire for several weeks already. He was relieved the priests in charge hadn't let him heal anything complex, but he'd done his bit and hopefully proven that he wasn't a threat or a danger.

He dropped the towel he'd worn from the communal showers and got into bed. He didn't remember falling asleep, only that he woke sweaty and tangled in his sheets to someone knocking on the door. The blinds had been left open, allowing bright sunlight to stream in.

"Just a minute." He pulled on yesterday's pants, even though they weren't clean. He really needed more clothes. He'd been wearing three outfits in rotation, and now he didn't even have them because they were in the apartment. That would be the day's mission—get clothes.

Angus yanked open the door.

Kabil stood on the other side. He lifted his eyebrows. "I thought I'd better show you around and give you a timetable so you can attend classes."

Angus blinked. He wasn't ready to slot into college life. "Um… unless they're given in Vinnish, I'm not going to understand anything." That was a complete lie. Angus was still wearing the jade in his ear.

"You don't know how to translate?"

Angus stared at him. He wasn't awake enough for this, and he hadn't had coffee in weeks. He shook his head. "My things are at my old apartment. I need clothes. I need…." He needed a life instead of skulking around trying not to get killed.

Maybe going to college was what he needed. He could be a normal nineteen-year-old for a while.

"I'll lend you a set of clothes. Then I'll get you set up here then take you out." Kabil smiled, but it was small and secretive. "I think there are some things you'll be interested in."

"Like what?" Angus was instantly wary. "And why are you helping?"

"I was told to. I'm interested in working for the Intelligence Temple, and getting to know an actual college-trained warlock was an opportunity I couldn't pass up." Kabil gave him a quick once-over. "Cadmael said you're headed for the Hospital Temple?"

"Yeah." He'd wanted to be a doctor before he was forced to be a warlock, but this was feeling too easy, too neat. He should grab the chance with both hands, but he wanted to reach for Saka and Terrance instead. "What about the debacle with Saka?"

"It will be sorted."

"You aren't annoyed?"

Kabil twisted his lips. "Yes, but mostly no. Cadmael shouldn't have pushed."

"Yet he did."

"And I am still to watch you."

"I thought you were here to help me?" Was Kabil someone he could trust or not?

"Same thing, really."

No it wasn't. "So you learn Vinnish if you want to go to the Intelligence Temple?"

Kabil nodded. "But I speak five other languages too. Most Mayans speak at least three. I'll get the clothes and meet you back here shortly," he said and walked away.

Angus grabbed his towel off the floor. He'd shower and hopefully, by the time he was done, Kabil would have gotten him some clean clothes. Then he'd follow along with whatever Kabil had planned. Maybe he'd be able to find out where Terrance was and if he was alive.

KABIL WAS WAITING by the door with a small pile of clothes. While some people wore suits, many didn't. The most common clothing was loose drawstring pants—almost demon in style, or did the demons get them from the Mayans?—and a shirt that was more tunic and didn't unbutton all the way down. He'd seen a few people wearing dresses. All the clothing was bright. The more expensive-looking clothing was in finer fabric with colorful borders and patterns on the sleeves.

Angus slipped into his room to dress and turned the cuff of the pants up twice. Kabil was a little taller, and Angus was thinner, but otherwise it wasn't too bad. He slipped the sandals on and ran his fingers through his hair. Hopefully by the time they were done, his things would've been delivered and he'd be able to have a shave and brush his teeth. He picked up the card he'd been given. It was his identification and bank card all in one. He'd noticed that most people wore it around their neck, but he wasn't sure how to use it, nor did he understand what Cadmael had meant about *base wage*. Did everyone get a fixed amount of money even if they did nothing? Was he getting paid to go to college?

It didn't make sense, but he didn't want to ask too many idiotic questions.

Saka would shake his head and tell him it was better to ask, and he'd be right. What would he say to this? He'd probably see it as a great learning opportunity, which it was. But he'd only learn if he asked the right questions.

Kabil was still in the corridor, doing something with his phone. He traced over the screen in quick strokes. When he finished whatever he was doing, he glanced up. "Ready?"

"Sure."

"You've missed today's classes. They run six days a week from six to one."

"Six in the morning?"

"Yes. Leaving the afternoon free for self-study and relaxation."

He hated the place already. No one should have to go to class at six in the morning.

An hour later they'd gathered up everything he needed, including books. He'd gone to pay for them, only to be told they didn't pay for books. He was expected to take care of them and return them. Damage would be billed as would nonreturn. But he couldn't read the books anyway. They were filled with indecipherable glyphs—pretty to look at but not much use.

His timetable was also in glyphs.

He was so screwed. He was going to be that person who failed everything. They didn't use magic the same here. The rules were different, he didn't have a human to share Saka with, and there was most definitely no sleeping with his demon. The only place his kind of magic was acceptable was in Demonside, but he wasn't a demon or a mage.

Kabil showed him the doorway where demons could be summoned and where students could go to Demonside. "So I can't summon Saka from anywhere?"

"You can… but you aren't supposed to until you graduate. If you want to see him, you can go through here. They will log you out. The void is opened three times a day. There is only one doorway on the other side."

"Then it must get very busy." Or was the demon village they'd first arrived in the one that was linked to Uxmal? He wasn't sure how that all worked. If he got out a map, would Demonside neatly overlap with

Vinland and the Mayan Empire, or was it more to do with where magic was used? Were there demons who lived without ever knowing about humans?

Kabil shook his head. "Aside from here, there's only one other, and that's for public use. They open the void frequently so you're never going to get stuck there."

"Then why do I need an anchor if the doorways are so well regulated?"

"Because one day you may not be near a doorway or your demon may not be near a doorway. That and because magic is worked better with three. How do warlocks manage if they don't even have a mage?"

Angus glanced at his toes. "To draw up magic, they drain the demon." He didn't need to add that they often killed their demon. Vinnish warlocks had a reputation.

"Is that why you started…?" Kabil's dark cheeks took on a reddish tone.

"That was to rebalance. You only rebalance in blood and souls." But sex had become an easy way to draw up magic. He probably had started relying on it too much. Saka had said so, and Saka was usually right about magic. He'd rather be taking lessons with his demon than here.

"That isn't true. We focus much more on keeping magic circulating, which is why we've been a little more protected from the growing glaciers. We work with our mages to gather magic. I believe you call that wizarding?"

Not really. "Close enough."

"Let's go into town. I'll show you how to use the tram and where to buy clothes and food, and then I'll take you somewhere special."

He had to ask while there was a chance for Kabil to change his plans. "Do you know where Terrance is?"

Kabil paused and then sighed. "Yes. No, I can't take you. People in the pitz school don't get visitors until the day before they play."

"Did he survive the attack?"

"I've already asked Cadmael for you. He hasn't replied."

Angus closed his eyes. "I need to know."

"There are lots of people looking for loved ones. Hundreds died last night. Thousands were injured. Buildings were damaged in the shock wave. I don't think you understand how devastating the weapon is. The only reason our fatalities were so low is because we've been creating and installing wards in public buildings and as many private buildings as we can. But we're still rolling out the devices. We learned fast after nearly all the priests in Ekab were killed.

"The Nations have been hit hard, particularly those that use demonology. We've been looking at ways to neutralize the clean sweep with them, but… but they are fracturing. The people who don't use demon magic are trying to break away from those who do."

"I'm sorry." He should've taken his father seriously when he claimed they were weaponizing magic. Angus hadn't thought it possible. But the Mayans were doing plenty with magic that he hadn't thought possible.

Kabil shook his head. "Let's go out. You can tell me what Demonside is like."

"You've never been there?"

"Only for excursions at school or with the Training Temple."

"Why is everything a temple?"

"Any *official* organization that deals with demonology is a temple."

That implied there were unofficial places. "So where are we going?"

"The entertainment plaza," Kabil said with a smile.

ANGUS LEARNED how to swipe his card to buy a ticket for the tram, despite not being able to read a single thing. Instead he memorized the symbols. Kabil bought him a lanyard so he could wear the plastic card around his neck like everyone else.

The tram rolled down the street, and people got on and off. As they made their way through the city, Kabil pointed out the damage done by the shock wave.

"If you look to the left, the red building with the frieze of ball players is the pitz training school."

Angus's heart leaped into his throat. Terrance was so close and yet unreachable. Angus stared out the window until the red building was gone.

How did people go past it so casually? "Will they all eventually die?"

"We all eventually die. But no."

Angus frowned and looked at Kabil. "I thought the game was played to the death."

"Some are. Some are just played. Excitement is generated either way. The final match is always to the death. Did you expect an endless tide of blood?"

He wanted to nod, but he didn't. "So he may not play to the death?"

Kabil winced. "He has been put in that division. The crowd will want to see Vinnish blood."

People on the tram looked at them more than once. They would know they were speaking Vinnish even if they couldn't understand it, and their stares were as hard as knife blades. If Angus were to walk about on his own, some might let their anger and frustration out on him, even though he wasn't to blame.

Angus couldn't keep apologizing for his country. He needed to do something to stop them, but if the best priests and other magic users had failed, what could he do?

He stared out the window, barely listening to Kabil. He might no longer be locked up, but he wasn't exactly free to wander. Kabil touched him on the arm at their stop. Angus followed and stayed closer than he probably needed to, but he took note of landmarks so he'd know the stop for another time. They went into a few stores, and Angus bought some extra clothes. Kabil explained that everyone had a weekly allowance and that he'd need to buy any luxury food items. The food they were served in the mess hall would be very basic.

He let Kabil pick what he needed. That included something that wasn't coffee but would wake him up, although Angus wasn't convinced that anything made of cocoa and chili was going to be a good drink first thing in the morning. With the shopping done, they entered the plaza proper. Demons and humans walked through the plaza, shopping and talking as though it were perfectly normal. Angus wanted to stop and watch, but Kabil didn't pause at any of the stalls, nor did he take Angus inside any of the buildings that framed the outer area, even though he said there were movies and plays and bars there where people and demons could socialize.

Together? How could they exist so closely but not be intimate?

Demons were treated differently here, as if they weren't different at all. He wanted to linger, but Kabil led him on. They slipped through another archway and into a much smaller courtyard. This one had a more private feel. There were stalls, but they seemed to only sell alcohol.

"What is this place?" There were more demons there, and magic was thick in the air.

Kabil smiled. "This is where humans and demons mingle much more… *closely*."

The way he said *closely* implied something more than mingling. "Cadmael said that shouldn't happen."

"It shouldn't happen between a mage and priest… or warlock." Kabil glanced at Angus. "What title do you use?"

"I don't know." He hadn't thought about it. He didn't want to be a warlock, never had. But he wasn't a priest either. He wasn't Mayan, and one day he'd like to go home… to even have a home.

Kabil made a sound of disapproval, as though Angus's preferred title was a major concern. "There are no prohibitions on any other human getting close to a demon. We keep the magic moving in any way we can. In the same way that humans are curious about demons, they're curious about us, and people come here to find out. Some come here on a regular basis, especially those with magic in their blood but no formal training."

"So wizards can do whatever they want."

"No. Lay priests can't do anything but offer charms. We regulate magic for safety. But we also make training free. We want people to develop their skills. Most of the humans here have no magic but want to experience some. I thought you might like to come because you like demon sex."

Angus lowered his gaze as heat rushed to his cheeks. It had never been about liking demon sex. He wasn't sure he even liked it the first time, because it had been so wound up with rebalancing. It was unlike anything he'd done before—intense and heady. The memory was enough to make his blood heat.

"Go on. Find a demon. I'll wait."

"But I'm a… I have a demon."

"Yes, and you can't have sex with him, but there's nothing stopping you from being with a different one. There are male ones here. You do prefer men?"

He walked away and had his card scanned so he could buy a drink. The alcohol was dark and bitter and cut right through him. He wasn't sure he'd be able to stomach a second cup, but he'd need more than that to continue this conversation.

Kabil followed. "You don't want to be here."

That wasn't entirely true. Angus was intrigued. "Do the demons?"

Kabil stepped back, horrified. "We do not enslave demons. They come here to take back the magic they gather. Small-scale rebalancing has a place, and magic circulates as it is supposed to. You have enough money for a visit if that's what concerns you."

Angus finished his drink with a shudder that ran all the way down his spine. Whatever that was, he wouldn't drink it again. He should've gone with the red option, and he would soon if Kabil kept talking. "It's not the money."

"No one watches… unless you like that."

"You've been here?"

"Once, just to see what it was all about."

Angus shook his head. "I… umm… I couldn't. Not with anyone but Saka."

"But you have Terrance? You are intimate with him too?"

Did he still have Terrance and Saka? Or had he lost everyone he cared about? He hadn't seen Lizzie or the others since they arrived. Words formed, but they melted. He sighed and went with the simplest explanation he had. "I love them both. I'm not going to pay for random demon sex."

He knew he shouldn't love them, but he couldn't help it.

"Oh." Kabil glanced away. "Don't tell Cadmael that."

Angus hadn't wanted to tell anyone. He'd never even told Saka. It was a mistake he wouldn't make again.

"Let's soak up the magic, and then I'll teach you how to create a translate talisman." Kabil bought two more drinks—red ones—and they sat beneath a tree.

Sounds of sex and laughter drifted out on the night air. The hollowness inside Angus expanded. Kabil had brought him out to have fun, and all he wanted was to go back to a time when the people he loved were sleeping on either side of him. Sure they'd been slowly dying in the desert, their life and magic being leached out, and they'd been too exhausted to do more than sleep, but each night Saka had been on one side and Terrance the other. He should have said something then, made it clear how important they were to him.

"Saka gave me this." He lifted his hair to reveal the jade spike in his ear. He'd healed the ear, but the jade still got hot and made his ear throb.

Kabil smiled and nodded. "He shouldn't have, but I guess you'll have no problem understanding the lectures."

"No one will understand me. How much are you going to tell Cadmael?"

"About a third of the priests speak Vinnish. Though most will probably ignore you. As for Cadmael, I'll answer his questions, but I won't volunteer information."

"Why?"

"Because what we've been doing has only stalled the ice age, not stopped it. You don't do magic like the others. You survived the clean sweep. No magic user has ever done that. It scared Cadmael."

Angus bit back a laugh. He wasn't scary at all, unless his inability to use magic properly counted as terrifying. "I want to see Saka."

"Then you'll need to go through the doorway to him. You don't have approval for that."

"I'll summon him." Or at least he'd try. How long until Saka would respond, or would he think it all a trap? He needed to speak to Saka… or maybe he didn't. Maybe he could get a message through to him.

"He hasn't been responding when you try." Kabil sipped his drink. "Cadmael will reach a point where he sends you across to sort this out."

And Angus wouldn't be surprised if Cadmael left him there. At the moment that didn't seem like an all-bad idea. He sighed and slumped against the wall, still not sure what to do next. But he had to do something, and tonight seemed like his best chance. "How long until the next attack?"

"They won't attack Uxmal for a while. They've been moving from city to city. The Institute for Magical Studies and World Council of Demonology will probably make official statements over the next couple of days."

"But they won't do anything. No one is doing anything."

"Bombing another country and killing innocents isn't the first step."

"It's what Vinland is doing to everyone else."

"And we're not them." He turned the glass in his hand. "Military strikes are planned. This latest act of aggression might be enough to make it happen. My uncle belongs to the Military Temple. He said that, despite the magic, it would come to blood on the ground. He knew the Vinnish wouldn't stop."

"It's not the people. Just a few at the top."

Kabil lifted his gaze. "Your people could've stepped up fifty years ago or ten years ago. But they didn't. So few did so little, even as the noose tightened. Did you not realize something was wrong?"

Angus stared at his drink. It was sweet like berries with a burn that almost made him sweat… though that could be the humidity. "I thought it was normal. I didn't realize how broken my country was." He downed the rest of his drink. What was normal anyway?

He didn't feel like a freak for enjoying sex with Saka or Terrance. People came here to lie with demons and demons to lie with humans. Those demons went back to Demonside to take gathered magic with them. Angus stood. "I've changed my mind. I'm going in."

He didn't wait for Kabil to answer. The scent of heady perfumes and the sweet roil of sex magic washed over him. He drew a breath and couldn't help but be aroused. The magic in his blood crashed around his body seeking an escape. His dick hardened in anticipation.

A few of the humans eyed him warily. The demons were more intrigued. Angus checked out a couple and decided on a feathered male with teeth like little knives. He walked over and pretended he'd done that a million times, when he had no idea what he was supposed to do.

The demon stood and beckoned without a word, his erection pressing against his pants. Angus followed, his heart beating so fast he was sure it was going to explode in all the wrong ways. But he needed to get this done before he changed his mind.

CHAPTER TWELVE

THE NERVES WERE the same as before any game. Terrance couldn't sit still. Instead he paced and ran through the different plays he'd been taught. It was a relief that everyone had been trained the same, graded the same, and placed into their appropriate divisions. It seemed that the results weren't rigged. But then, the game was close to sacred, and cheating was probably not a good look.

He knew enough to understand the commands and to ask for simple things. Only a few spoke Vinnish, but for the most part, he kept to himself. After the attack few wanted to associate with him. While it stung, he understood.

There were to be three blood matches—one from each of the divisions. The losers would die at the end.

He didn't know when that happened or how, and he wasn't that keen to find out, especially since everyone expected him to do the right thing and give up his life as some kind of apology for the shitty behavior of the Vinnish warlocks.

Fuck that. He never went onto the field, or court, to lose.

For the first time, his life actually depended on winning. All those other games he'd played—the finals in grade school, the matches for the selectors from the colleges—they didn't mean shit.

If he hadn't been so wrapped up in what he wanted—to get out of Vinland—he might have seen the bigger picture. He ran his hand over his freshly shaved head. He didn't like that or the loincloth uniform. He was used to wearing a whole lot more.

Well, he had gotten out of Vinland. At least he could check that off his wish list.

The door opened in the hall where the players waited, and people walked in. His heart got stuck on one of his ribs and quivered there like a dying bug. Not long to go now. This was the last visit from a family member—only one per player. Everyone was entitled to one, but not everyone would get a visitor.

Some of the men were sitting down on the sides of the room as though they didn't care that no one was coming for them, and a couple he knew to be criminals had offered themselves to the game for a chance at a reduced sentence.

Terrance couldn't stop himself from scanning the steady stream of brown-haired visitors as they entered. He couldn't raise his hopes. That would be stupid. He had to focus on the game and keep calm, yet tension jangled his nerves. It was no different from any other game. He couldn't think about the consequences, only of what he needed to do. But he didn't believe the lies. It wasn't just any game.

It could be his last.

He shook out his hands, trying to shed the nervous energy, and he was about to turn away from the door and the desperation that made him want Angus to be there when he saw familiar red hair.

He couldn't have stopped the smile if he tried. He only just kept himself from walking over. Then he gave up. He met Angus halfway and wrapped his arms around him. Maybe if he didn't let go, it would all stop. He'd wake up and they'd be back at college, wrapped around each other in bed after spending too much of the night talking about magic and demons.

"I almost didn't recognize you." Angus brushed his palm over Terrance's head. "It's rather dramatic."

"It's regulation."

"I like the uniform." He smoothed his hand down Terrance's bare back.

"Thought you would." For a moment his world was normal. He was going to play a game, and his boyfriend was there to watch. That was a good thing. *Think of the good things, the ones worth living for.* "There's protective gear for the actual game."

Angus blinked, and his eyes were too shiny.

"Don't," Terrance muttered. If Angus broke, then he might also.

No one else was shedding tears about what was about to happen. Around them, everyone was happy and talking as though there were no room for sadness. For everyone else this was their thing. It happened frequently and was considered an honor to play—only model prisoners could even apply—and not everyone who volunteered was accepted. He didn't want to cheapen that. If he did die, it would mean something. He wasn't sure what, but something.

But it would hurt Angus. Terrance swallowed the swelling in his throat.

"I was worried after the attack. That was all," Angus said.

"That was…." Close. It had been far too close. He'd been outside only half an hour before. They all had. "I thought it was an earthquake at first."

Angus still hadn't let him go. His arms were looped around Terrance's waist. "What happens after the game?"

"I don't know. Maybe I have to keep playing." He hadn't asked, and he didn't need to know until after the game. He had to focus on today. "What about you? Are you still locked in your tower?"

"No, I'm back at college… Training Temple." He shrugged. "I've been trying to piece things together and get in touch with Saka. He won't answer my summons, but I've sent him a message."

"So you don't have an anchor?" Was there still room for him? He wanted to know more about what was going on, but he didn't want those thoughts tumbling in his head when he needed to concentrate on the game. He just needed to know he was wanted.

"You will always be my anchor." Angus kissed him softly on the lips and didn't pull back. They stayed like that for a moment, sealed together from hip to lip.

Screw it. If he was going to die, he wanted more than that as his last kiss. He cupped Angus's head and kissed him hard. Angus's mouth opened to him, and Terrance took everything that was offered.

There would be a feast later, after the games. He'd get a chance to celebrate.

His lungs burned, but he didn't care. Angus moved against him and pressed close. The loincloth would hide nothing, but the need in his blood was a magic all its own. It wrapped around him—around them—but it wouldn't keep them safe.

A bell sounded. The visit was over.

He drew back a little, not ready to let go. "I'll see you after this." *Hold on to that thought.* If his teammate fucked up and let the ball touch the ground, Terrance would kill him before the ritual sacrifice.

Angus didn't look convinced. His mouth was set in a thin line.

"Playing ball is what I'm good at." Was he good enough? He'd won games during training. That had to count for something.

"I know." Angus nodded and forced a smile that was more grimace.

People were leaving. Angus held his hand, and Terrance squeezed it hard. "I'm glad we made it here. I love you."

"I love you too."

The bell sounded again. Terrance released Angus's hand and stepped back.

This death had honor. Being shot like a dog in Vinland would have had none.

TERRANCE COULDN'T SEE the game being played, but the charge in the air was something close to a thunderstorm. The magic rippled over his skin. There were no dampeners to stop the magic from gathering. Instead it roiled over the ground in a mist he could feel but not see.

There were cheers and gasps. The blood matches were spread out during the event, but it didn't seem to matter. Even if the stakes were low, the anticipation of the crowd still fed the magic.

Terrance fiddled with his helmet and checked his forearm and knee guards and the protective girdle around his waist. The damage one of those heavy balls could do to an unprotected belly had been explained in graphic detail. He hadn't understood many of the words, but the pictures had been more than enough—that and feeling the weight of the ball every time he trained.

They had all worn bruises from training until yesterday when they were healed and shaved in preparation for today. His muscles didn't ache, and his skin wasn't split… for the moment.

He flexed his fingers. *No grabbing the ball and running to the end for a try.*

The game ran for a set length of time. Points were deducted for too many bounces. It was over if the ball became dead on the ground, but it could be won if the ball was put through the hoop that was set six meters above the ground… and immediately lost if the attempt was unsuccessful.

While he'd taken a few stabs at getting the ball through the hoop during training, that was not the strategy for today. He glanced at his partner, a man who had been doing time for fraudulently claiming the base wage of his dead brother. Both of them were expected to die.

Clearly the Mayans didn't think highly of thieves or traitors. How many people had bet against them?

It didn't matter.

He breathed in and exhaled. His nerves were giving way to pregame focus.

The crowd outside went quiet. What had happened?

An eruption of cheers rippled through the air.

"Hoop!"

It was the only word Terrance understood among the shouting, and it was all he needed. The elite team before him had put it through the hoop. There was no way he could live up to that. The man he was partnered with stared at the floor already defeated.

"Live," Terrance said. That was all they had to do. They didn't need to be marvelous or awe-inspiring. Just live. He ignored the worm of reason that reminded him that if they lived, the other team must die.

He didn't know them. He couldn't care. If he did, he'd have told them their rules were cruel and that no one should die.

With the other game over early, the thief and he were ushered out onto the court.

If the air had been charged in the waiting area, out here it was thick. Magic beaded like dew on his skin. He wanted to lift his gaze to look for Angus, but he didn't. They had to bow before the priests and the mayor of Uxmal. He didn't understand what was said. It was just part of the ritual, and he didn't care. He was trying to settle himself.

When he'd planned to use international rugby as a way to defect from Vinland, he'd known he'd be playing for his life. But he never thought it would be so literal.

The priest stopped talking, and the crowd cheered as the players went to their sides of the court. The stone walls around the edge were high and smooth and the hoop as distant as the sun.

They had gone through plays and drills and learned to keep it simple and clean and as bounce free as possible. The strategy was for survival, not glory. But he hadn't realized how much magic would be here. If he used it, he could ruin Cadmael's plans for him in under a minute. But he'd never used magic while playing. It was forbidden during rugby, and players wore dampeners to prevent it, though there were ways to cheat.

Magic hadn't been mentioned during pitz training, but he didn't have time to think about it as the ball was thrown down and the game was on. Beyond keeping the ball moving, all thoughts fled.

He used his forearm to push the ball high to his partner and his hip as it came back to him. They were trying to move into the territory of the other team to score points, and the other team was trying to get the ball. Sweat rolled down the sides of his face, and the air was sticky and loaded with magic. The other team got the ball and looked like they were going for the hoop. Terrance used his body to block them and hoped his partner would be there when he sent the ball his way. It bounced once… but the man got under it and used his knee to send it up. Terrance ran to get in place. They were still near the hoop. Should he?

If he failed....

No, keep playing. He started to use the magic that clung to him to direct each strike. He hadn't used magic in a while, but it was like breathing, and magic made his every strike more accurate and more powerful. Then he used it to be that little bit faster. When the other team went for the hoop again, his partner was there first.

The other man was desperate not to lose. If the other team got it through the hoop, it would be over. If Terrance failed, it would also be over. But he had magic, something his teammate lacked. Their deaths would be on his shoulders if he didn't try.

His teammate nodded.

Their opponents were better than they were or more desperate.

Terrance had put the ball through the hoop in practice. This should be no different... but it was completely different. The hoop seemed higher. People were watching and expecting his blood to be spilled. For once, he wanted to disappoint the crowd.

He couldn't breathe as they passed it between them and tried to get into position. He ran at the wall and then relied on his partner to get it to him at just the right moment. It only counted as a failed shot if the ball arched up to the hoop and missed. Any player could run at the wall and gain height. So Terrance moved toward the wall and increased in speed with every step. He had to trust a thief.

The other team realized what they were planning and tried to check Terrance so he couldn't reach the wall.

He grinned at the man and barreled through him shoulder first. He'd been tackling for over a decade. The man went down, and Terrance picked up speed, launched himself at the wall, and moved his feet up the almost-vertical surface. Magic boosted his height. His teammate sent the ball toward him and Terrance pushed off the wall, gathered every drop of magic he dared, and used it to send the ball off his forearm and toward the hoop. He dropped to the ground like a stone, hands to the dirt for stability, barely able to breathe.

He didn't want to see if the ball went through or missed.

CHAPTER THIRTEEN

THE BALL BOUNCED between players while the air thickened and crackled. Magic was all about emotion. Capturing the excitement and anticipation of the crowd and being able to use that would be a massive piece of rebalancing. Angus breathed it in. His skin tingled, his own tension fed the magic, and the magic amped his anxiety.

It seemed like a lifetime ago that he'd been part of an orgy at Lifeblood Mountain, and the magic gathered had been tremendous. He'd never thought he'd feel anything grander, but this was far bigger. The magic was sharp on his tongue.

If this happened in Demonside, he'd be able to see it, thick and roiling. On the human side of the void, it was only a feeling, like electricity over his skin. In all the times he'd watched rugby on TV, he'd never stopped to think about the emotional buildup.

Terrance must have. That was why all players wore dampeners to prevent cheating.

None of the four pitz players were wearing anything to stop them using magic. Did that mean they could if they were wizards? There was no way that ball was going through the hoop without magic, and the other team was trying hard. Their desperation was a living thing that chased them around the court. While he could barely follow the game or its rules, he knew it was all over if the other team put the ball through.

The jade in his ear was hot and burned his earlobe as it tried to translate all the words around him. He wanted to yank it out, but he needed to hear every word. He didn't want to watch, but he couldn't look away either. His gaze tracked every step Terrance took, and he winced every time the ball connected with Terrance's body and he passed it to his teammate.

He bit his lip. He wasn't going to make a scene, no matter what happened.

Terrance wanted to be afforded the same respect as the other players. Before they entered the I-shaped court, a priest had spoken about the honor of sacrifice.

It was easy to keep track of Terrance because his skin was paler than the others. Too many spectators had shouted "Death to the Vinnish" when he stepped onto the court. Angus hadn't turned to see where the words had come from. He kept his gaze fixed on the court. The crowd urged the other team on. They wanted Terrance's blood—his life—all because of where he'd been born.

They weren't the ones responsible for the ice age or the clean sweep. They had tried to fight it, but they hadn't done enough.

He shouldn't have spent so much time in Demonside. He should've realized the underground didn't want to stop the college. The underground was infected with college warlocks who wanted to seize power for themselves. All of it had been brewing since the first demon war, long before he was born. Everyone else was collateral as the powerful tried to take more than they ever needed.

Terrance took control of the ball. Something was different this time, though Angus couldn't say what. He watched sports for the aesthetics of the players, not for the rules, and the rules here were vastly more deadly than he was used to. He didn't doubt Terrance's fitness or skill as a sportsman. Terrance knew how to get in the right place as the ball was passed between him and his partner.

But then he ran at the wall, and Angus stopped breathing. What was he doing? Was he going for the hoop? If he failed....

People were cheering—for failure or success, Angus didn't know. The words became lost in a roar of rising emotion, a tide of magic that needed direction. And Terrance was a warlock who'd had wizard parents.

The ball spun off his partner's arm toward Terrance, who met it midair in a move that should've been impossible, that *was* impossible without magic. The ball hit his forearm and was redirected toward the hoop, still high above.

The crowd took a collective gasp. It would be counted as an attempt, and failure would end the match. While the other team had made some effort to get close, they hadn't taken a shot at the hoop. Had they pretended the hoop was their plan to force Terrance's team to act rashly?

Angus's heart stopped beating as the ball flew through the air and silence filled the court.

It was going to hit the edge and bounce away. Terrance would be killed. Angus closed his eyes. He couldn't watch. He couldn't breathe. His pulse was loud in his ears.

He'd led Terrance there and promised him safety. Instead he'd brought death.

The sharp, hungry magic in the air choked him. It pressed against his skin like needles seeking blood.

"It's through," someone near him said as though they couldn't quite believe it.

Angus didn't. It had to be a cruel joke. He opened his eyes and looked up as the ball bounced on the ground and rolled away, untouched by any player. The siren sounded, and Terrance stood and hugged the man he'd been playing with.

Around Angus people were yelling about how the ball had gone through. He let himself breathe again. The game was over, and Terrance got to live.

Angus's face split with a smile. He wanted to whoop and shout and celebrate. People were cheering, but it was different from what he knew. They weren't joyful because their team won. They were more admiring of the shot, for the game. Everyone there understood the stakes and that death wasn't something to celebrate.

Life was worth celebrating, and Angus wanted to climb down and hug Terrance.

The other team stood proud, but grim, their fate sealed. All four players gave a small bow to the audience, to the watching priests and mayor.

Angus was sure Terrance glanced at him as he left the court. He went to rise so he could find Terrance, but Kabil placed a hand on his shoulder.

"Stay to the end. Understand the importance," Kabil said.

Angus twisted around to look at the man in charge of watching over him. He'd thought he'd lost Kabil, but clearly he hadn't.

"I don't want to."

"Do not disrespect their sacrifice. There are only three more matches, though after that shot, it may be hard to gather that level of attention."

The hard bench bit into the back of Angus's legs as he watched without seeing. He didn't care about the game. He'd been there for Terrance. But one didn't leave a ritual halfway through, and while it might be ordinary citizens watching and playing, it *was* a ritual.

Would Cadmael find a way to make Terrance pay for surviving?

Angus swallowed, his mouth dry. He was contributing to the magical buildup. But where once he would've become lost in it, his feet were firmly grounded.

The final siren sounded, and the three losing teams that had played for their lives walked back out, stripped of their protective gear and helmets. Terrance wasn't among them.

His chest eased a little. He shouldn't have doubted the sanctity of the game. Even Cadmael wouldn't stoop into forcing Terrance's death.

No fear washed off the losing teams. The crowd treated the players like heroes as they followed the priest.

"Now we can go. There's a small temple out the back where the rest of the ceremony is conducted," Kabil said in his ear.

"I'd rather see Terrance."

"He'll be back at the school."

No. He played and won. That should be it. Angus's stomach turned. He was wrung out, as though he'd given too much. Maybe in his fear for Terrance he had. He should eat, or at the very least, drink something.

He followed Kabil and the small crowd to the base of the temple. It was small, little more than a raised platform, but built the same as the much bigger ones. On top stood two priests, and magic shimmered around them. That was where much of the energy had been channeled. The void was already open. It was a black tear at the top, and one by one the players were led up.

And beheaded.

Angus looked away. He'd seen death too often. He knew the worlds needed rebalancing, but this….

With every death, he felt the surge. This wasn't one death. This was like the death of hundreds. The games had gathered the magic more effectively that anything Angus had ever experienced. A little from many, with only a few vessels to contain it until it could be released.

No drop of blood was spilled on the stones. It all went across the void. With the last death, the void was closed and the pressure of the magic was gone.

He should be glad that the Warlock College had never thought to use the rugby games to gather magic. But that was wizard magic, and they wouldn't touch it. Priests used both.

Even if they held games once a week or every day, it wouldn't be enough to rebalance what Vinland had taken. What would happen if Vinland timed a clean sweep during a match?

"Death matters," Kabil said. "We all die, but we don't all make it count."

All Angus could do was nod. He was living, but he wasn't making it count. If he died, all he'd be was the defector who'd hidden in the Mayan Empire and hoped someone else would find a solution.

He wasn't even brave enough to step onto the court and put his life on the line for a cause he'd once believed in. He needed his demon. Had Saka received his message? The demon in the entertainment zone had been perplexed that Angus didn't want to have sex, and the language barrier had made things harder. All he could do was wait for Saka to respond. While he waited, he'd find the others, even though Cadmael didn't want them to talk.

First, though, he had to get Terrance out of the pitz school.

CHAPTER FOURTEEN

THE RAIN FELL HARD. It was sticky as it hit Saka's skin—blood magic, more than he'd ever felt in his life. The effect was instantaneous. Plants grew as he watched. The scale of the magic returning to Arlyxia thrilled and terrified him. How many humans had died to feed this rebalancing? Had the warlocks attacked? He used the magic flowing freely to push his mind through the telestones.

He didn't reach wide as he had the very first time he tried, when he injured himself in the process. With each attempt he went in a set direction, only spreading wide when he'd almost reached the end of his ability.

Most of his attempts returned nothing.

The one tribe he had reached had told him they wanted nothing to do with humans. If demons had never worked with humans, perhaps none of this would've happened. But magic would've still moved between worlds, and humans would've still dabbled, and an unskilled user could have done much damage.

Today there was someone with him, but not making contact. It didn't feel like Iktan, though Saka occasionally felt him there, silently giving strength to Saka's attempt. If he pushed a little further, maybe the other mage he could feel would be able to make contact.

Wek made a sound of disapproval that he ignored. He knew when to stop, and he was almost at that limit.

The mage made the connection just before Saka was about to give up, but it was a fragile thing. *I have felt you over several days.*

I am seeking wisdom from other tribes about Arlyxia and what is to be done.

Nothing for us. The mage opened her mind, and Saka saw the bodies of the tribe. Demons with metallic gold skin, orange scales, and wings so delicate they were almost transparent… lay in the sand for the scavengers. *Not enough magic for us to draw up water. No help to come. The people of the grasses are gone.* She smiled hollowly, her hunger making her eyes too big in her face. *Though there have been no grasses for my lifetime.*

Panic gripped him, and he almost lost the connection. *I will send help.*

It will be too late. I have waited for you to get close, so someone would know what became of us.

Where are you?

She moved and her attention wavered. Then he saw what she was seeing—a map of Demonside like Miniti had. It showed water and meeting points, but it seemed to cover a bigger area. *This was made by our travelers. Humans we once worked with before they stopped coming. We had a network of stones too before we folded in on ourselves and stopped speaking to other tribes. We shouldn't have stopped. That was our mistake, and it has cost us dearly.*

Saka stared at the map and tried to commit it to memory. He would piece together a map that covered all of Arlyxia and note the tribes and who their humans were. *Which country of humans did you work with?*

I fear they no longer exist. Their own people didn't trust magic users. Some lived here until they died. She shook her head. *Some mages once said humans cannot be trusted with magic. They get a taste for it and then cannot live without it.*

For all that he didn't trust the Mayans, their way was at least more respectful. *Where on the map am I?*

She pointed to the edge. *This way.*

Have you heard of Lifeblood Mountain?

We were trying to reach there. She pointed to a triangular mark on the map. *I am so close... but I will not make it.*

You are alone.

I am. I have been drinking the blood of those that have died, but the scar-lips are getting braver.

Will no one from Lifeblood come for you? When had his tribe become so untrusting?

They will not answer. Perhaps they are also dead.

No! He wouldn't believe that. He took a moment to compose himself. *That is where I am from.* In his heart he wanted to return one day, but only when Vinland was safe for Angus and only if the Lifeblood mages stopped demanding the death of all warlocks.

I am sorry. Her sadness echoed in Saka's mind.

So am I. I would come to you if I could.

You have. She bowed her head. *Thank you. I have not died alone.*

He didn't see the blade, but he felt it as though it were in his own skin and the heat of his blood was spilling out onto the sand. He gasped, but the connection weakened as her life ended.

He reeled back until he was aware of the ground beneath him and the tree root that bit into the back of his thigh. Wek steadied him, but he wasn't ready to talk.

"Are you all right? Did you push too far?" She lifted his chin to search his eyes. "What did you see?"

"Death."

CHAPTER FIFTEEN

The last time Terrance had been in this room, his life had hung in the balance. He wasn't sure it was different today. Cadmael was in another of his bright pinstriped suits—they seemed to be popular with the men and women who favored more formal attire.

It was the first time Terrance had bothered to dress properly in weeks—training was always done in a loincloth—though a summons to the Intelligence Temple wasn't the occasion he wanted to dress for. He was sure he wasn't going to be rewarded for his outstanding performance on the court.

Everyone at the school was stunned at his win, including his trainers. He'd since learned that magic was the only way to get the ball through the hoop, though it was something they never trained for nor did they select players who were magically trained. If it happened, it happened. Had Cadmael thought him too stupid to use magic to save his life, or had it been another test?

He'd been using magic since he first sensed it, much to his grandparents' horror. It happened only six months after his wizard parents disappeared, and he had no doubt that the college had killed them. Even as a child, he'd understood the danger of what he could do and what would happen if people found out. His grandparents encouraged him to concentrate on sports instead of magic.

For that he would be ever grateful.

Hopefully they were still alive. These days he didn't put any faith in hope, only in things he could touch. He'd like to touch Cadmael's throat and squeeze until his face matched the purple of his shirt. Terrance curled his fingers but otherwise didn't move. He was tired of games. They should concentrate on more important things.

Cadmael had watched Terrance silently from the moment he walked through the door. Perhaps Cadmael was about to toss him through the void. There were worse places, and he was sure Angus would get him back from Demonside.

He didn't know what they'd do after that. They needed a plan.

Their first plan had been to flee Vinland, then to make it to the Mayan Empire. But all they'd done since was try to find their feet and live. This wasn't home or even a safe place, and nowhere would be safe until the Warlock College was a footnote in history and a warning to magic users that nothing was free.

If the silence was meant to intimidate him or make him want to talk, it was failing. Terrance had played with wizards and warlocks and pitted both sides against each other for too long to fall for that game. He could wait. He had nothing more pressing to do.

He'd been used before to keep Angus in line. Even the threat of death was nothing new. Cadmeal would have to try harder.

Cadmael took a few paces forward but didn't get too close. Had he watched the game? Weeks of training had rebuilt the muscles Terrance lost on the trek across Demonside. The drills had made him faster, and he could ignore pain—he'd learned to do that years before.

There was nothing Cadmael could do to him that would hurt, except put Angus in danger. If he put Angus on the court, Cadmael would see exactly what a third-rate wizard with a talent for ball sports could do with a Mayan head. It would bounce quite nicely off his elbow. Terrance bit back a smile.

"Congratulations on your win." The words were almost said

sincerely, but the tightness around Cadmael's lips and eyes gave away how he truly felt.

"Playing with balls and saving my ass is what I'm good at." He'd saved his partner's life too—this time. But his win had condemned two others to death, which had stolen the glory and left him feeling sick. For all that he'd tried to adapt to their mindset around pitz and death, he couldn't quite get there.

Cadmael nodded. "You made a good team, a team people would like to see play again. Although, given that you have put the ball through the hoop once, I'm guessing that doing it every time will no longer be a challenge."

"I play to win. If that's the best way to win, then that's what I'll do."

"I thought warlocks didn't use magic like that."

Terrance smiled. "I only became a warlock because they offered me a scholarship. College isn't free in Vinland. My grandparents couldn't afford it, so I decided that getting a demon was a price I would pay for getting to play rugby." He didn't add *and eventually getting out of Vinland.*

"But you don't have a demon."

Aqua, the scarlips that he'd tamed with his blood, had been killed by the college, and Cadmael knew that. It had come out when he was first questioned. "Not currently."

"You will not be able to play pitz again. Once someone has revealed their talent for magic, it is forbidden. They are supposed to train to become a priest."

Terrance allowed his grin to form. "I would be happy to get a demon. I believe we've had a conversation very similar to this."

Cadmael shot him a glare. "I do not believe that bonding with Saka will be possible. He has vanished."

Angus had said something about getting word to Saka, but he hadn't wanted to hear it because he'd been getting ready to play. Wherever Saka was, it couldn't be that far. Saka wouldn't leave Angus.

Terrance shrugged. "I'm sure he'll turn up. He's probably doing magey-type stuff. He was always very magey. Magic and tribe first and all that." Terrance had heard Angus's frustration more than once, but it was always tinged with admiration and a little jealousy. Saka had a place, something they'd never have in the Mayan Empire. But the trek had revealed that Saka did have a heart beneath that tough metallic hide. Terrance had seen the love he had for Angus, and for a brief moment, he had been allowed to step inside that warm bubble.

He wanted that again.

He was never going to get all of Angus, and that was fine. He wanted to be his anchor in the human world, the one who made sure Angus could always get back and the reason he wanted to come back.

Terrance wanted to stand with Angus, bring down the Vinnish warlocks, and grind every last one of them into dust.

"Maybe," Cadmael said. "But he refused the bond with the chosen priest."

Saka not blindly obeying? Terrance wasn't even surprised. "He clearly doesn't want a priest." Terrance didn't blame him.

"You will become the anchor for another priest, not Angus."

"And if I refuse?"

"You may not be allowed to play pitz anymore, but there are other ways for you to die. Criminals are often sentenced to death, and with the world in such disarray, the death penalty has become more necessary."

"Do as I'm told or die."

"Yes. I knew you'd see reason."

Fuck that. He'd seen it all before. "I want to be able to see Angus."

"I'm not unreasonable."

"We came to help, if possible, not to be treated as criminals."

"You defected, and your loyalty has always been to the highest bidder. You, out of everyone, are the one I will watch. One stumble—"

"Yeah, I'm dead." Terrance crossed his arms. Some things never changed. "You aren't the first and probably won't be the last to make that threat."

"Then why?" Cadmael frowned.

"Why what?"

"Why not change—swear loyalty and mean it?"

"Why should I give my loyalty to people who are not loyal to me?

Who will throw me over for the slightest reason?" No one had ever kept their word. His parents had promised to return, but they never did. His grandparents, who promised to love him no matter what, were terrified of what trouble he'd bring to their door. The underground had promised to keep him safe, but they had their own agenda. And the college had vowed to overlook his parents' sins if he just did a few things for them.

Angus had cared enough to fight for him, and Saka had helped him in the desert.

"Perhaps you need to show it to get it in return."

Maybe, or perhaps most people thought he wasn't worth it. He certainly wasn't going to vow undying loyalty to a man who tried to end his life. If Terrance were a cat, he'd be burning through his nine lives, and as a human, he was just bloody lucky. Luck and timing and a little magic could go a long way. "If that's all, I'd like to get my things. I'm guessing there's a room for me at the priest college near Angus?"

"We'll talk again soon."

"I'm sure we will." Like everyone else, Cadmael wanted something from him. Like everyone else, he was going to be disappointed.

The Training Temple didn't bring the relief it should have. There was another set of rules, and he hadn't learned enough of the language to get by. He didn't even want to be there, but it was the only way he was going to be able to see Angus.

Terrance dumped his limited possessions on the bed and walked straight out of his room. There were no locks on the doors, and while he didn't have anything worth taking, he didn't like it. But if he asked for privacy, Cadmael would just assume he had something to hide.

As he walked down the corridor, he had no idea how he was going to find Angus. There seemed to be an endless number of doors, and he couldn't knock on each one. Well, he could, but it wouldn't be smiled upon.

The priest he would eventually anchor for—which would never

happen—was supposed to be acting as his guide and supervisor, but the priest hadn't shown up, and Terrance wasn't going to wait around.

When he turned a corner, he came face-to-face with a young woman. She saw him and stopped in her tracks. Then she widened her eyes in terror and stepped back.

Terrance forced a smile. His head was shaved, but he didn't think he looked that bad. "Have you seen Angus?"

A rapid stream of Mayan flowed from her lips. Clearly she didn't speak a word of Vinnish. Doors opened.

It was his turn to step back, but even if he ran for his room, there was no lock and he wouldn't be safe from a mob.

But the mob didn't attack. Some grinned. He could understand the word pitz and very little else. Maybe they were impressed with his win? But they weren't smiling. Maybe they were *un*impressed because he was Vinnish? That was probably closer to the truth.

The group gradually parted and Angus stepped through. The tension thickened, and for a moment, Terrance was sure the mood was going to turn from suspicion to violence. But Angus smiled and said a few words in Mayan and the onlookers drifted off and returned to whatever they had been doing.

Angus walked over and took his hand. His fingers were cold. "No one expected you to win. They're impressed, but it's rather a bad omen, given that you're Vinnish."

Terrance frowned. "I don't see how a game has anything to do with the war."

"They're wondering if all of Vinland is filled with magic users."

"Cadmael knew I was trained. He should never have put me there." But Cadmael hadn't realized that Terrance could use the magic around him the way a wizard could. While the priests knew about warlocks, they didn't seem to know a lot about wizards.

Angus nodded. "But they don't know that."

"True." Everywhere he went, people didn't trust him. He glanced at Angus, and his doubts resurfaced. Terrance wasn't loyal or good at anything except saving his own ass. He didn't deserve a man like

Angus, but he couldn't walk away. He loved Angus, and he needed to believe that Angus loved him.

So he stepped closer, not sure if Angus would accept his embrace, but when Angus did, Terrance let himself relax. "I've missed you."

Angus was silent for several heartbeats. "I thought you were going to die."

Terrance swallowed hard. There was still a good chance that they would all die. They didn't fit in here, and no one really wanted them. As glad as he was to be out of Vinland, the Mayan Empire would never be home. "Yeah. I'm hard to kill."

His grandmother had called him stubborn and often warned him that it would get him into trouble. But he couldn't keep his head down and pretend obedience.

"I'll show you around. Did they assign you someone to help you settle in?"

"Yes, but they haven't turned up yet. I don't really want the grand tour." He held Angus's hand. "I found you, and that's enough."

Angus smiled. "How about I show you where my room is. That's pretty important."

Terrance grinned. "That's the only room I care about finding."

Hand in hand they walked around the corner and down another corridor that looked just the same. It was like one of those nightmares where there was no way out. He was never going to be able to find his room again, but he'd worry about that later.

Angus opened a door. The room was exactly like Terrance's, but there were books on the desk and clothes on the bed.

"You're already studying." Terrance flipped open a book. The page was a mess of glyphs. He stared at it and willed it to make sense. "You can read this, already?"

"No, but I've learned what the glyphs mean. They're sounds, not letters. But because I don't speak Mayan, what I read makes no sense." He picked up what looked like a piece of glass the size of his palm and placed it over the text. The glass went dark, as though filled with blood-colored ink, before words appeared in Vinnish.

Terrance had seen plenty of magic and used it himself, he'd never seen anything like that. It was so ordinary and yet so powerful.

"What is that?"

"It was developed to break codes during the first demon war. The Mayans were spying on us. This one has been keyed to translate to Vinnish. It wasn't easy, and that's my blood doing the translating. Kabil showed me how to do it."

Terrance glanced at Angus. "Kabil?"

"The priest Cadmael wanted Saka and me to bond with. He tried to force it while you were training, but Saka and I refused. Now I can't get hold of Saka, and he won't answer my summons. Maybe he's not safe. I hate not knowing what's going on in Demonside. I don't know if he's alive, but I think I'd know if he were dead."

"What of the message you sent?"

"I have to go back tomorrow and see if there's a reply… or if it even got delivered. Hopefully there'll be some news. You should come. It's an odd place."

"What do you mean?" Everything in the Empire was odd.

"There seems to be quite a trade in sex between humans and demons, to keep the magic flowing, apparently."

Terrance frowned. "But you got in trouble for that."

"Because there's a rule that priests shouldn't have sex with their demons."

"Why?" If the magic should be kept flowing, wouldn't it be better if it were allowed? Some of the rules around magic seemed arbitrary.

"Because it can ruin a working relationship." Angus leaned on the desk, his feet apart. He gripped the edge until his knuckles whitened, and kept his gaze on the floor. "I want you to be our anchor, but what if it all goes bad? I've broken so many rules already. My knowledge of magic is a mash-up of bits and pieces. I'm not anything, and yet people want to know what I am."

Terrance stepped between his legs and cupped his face. "You're you. Your relationship with Saka is something to be envied."

"Even other mages thought it was too much."

"He loves you."

Angus grimaced. "If he does, he shouldn't. He told me that early on. A mage always has to put his people first."

"Which is why he left his tribe to take us across the desert. I think the time for discussing relationships has passed. We're in this together, no matter what." Somehow they had to put everything right. He didn't trust the Mayans any more than he trusted the Vinnish warlocks.

Angus looked up and gave him a weak smile. "I thought we'd be safe here. I'm sorry."

Terrance kissed him. "Nothing to be sorry for… unless you're quitting and wanting to make a home here." Angus loved learning about magic. It was the kind of place he could be happy. "Are you enjoying this?"

Angus nodded. "It's more what I thought magic should be like. I want to go to the World Council of Demonology and learn what other countries do. There's so much more. Mages should be at the council. And if they had been, then maybe we wouldn't be in this mess." Angus's eyes were bright, the way they always got when he talked magic. He thought it was something good.

Terrance wished he could agree, but magic had never brought him anything but pain. "People will always abuse power."

"I've been watching the news. Countries without magic abuse power too. They kill those they suspect of using magic. With the way things are now, there have been more killings—anyone who looks different or acts different. New Holland is under attack from the north because the nonmagic-using alliance wants to take over and destroy them. With so much magic tied up by Vinland, there's a fear they will crumble. The world is a mess."

"It's not your job to fix it." They just needed to survive and stop the college—and even that would be better left up to people who knew what they were doing.

"I know. I can't sit back and do nothing, but I don't know what to do. We can't run again."

"This will never be home." They would always be outsiders. If the whole world turned on magic-using countries, they'd be caught up in that net.

"You want to go home, back to Vinland?"

Did he? All he ever wanted to do was leave, and now that he'd left, the rest of the world didn't want him either. "Not as it is at the moment. The magic they've taken needs to be released."

"They set off another clean sweep yesterday."

"I didn't feel it."

"Farther north, at the border. The Mayans returned fire—not with magic but with ordinary bombs. Thousands are dying."

"The whole world is at war." He leaned closer to Angus, and Angus slipped his arms around him. If the magic users didn't fix the mess, they'd be wiped out by those who didn't understand and didn't want to understand.

CHAPTER SIXTEEN

THE LUSH JUNGLE after the rain was a lie. It gave the demons false hope. The death of the golden mage reverberated through Saka's body as though it were his own. If the demons did nothing, it would be. He painted Lifeblood Mountain on the map on the wall of the tent. The distances weren't correct. He was only guessing. He knew how hard it had been to reach Iktan via telestones from Lifeblood and how long it had taken him to walk, but he was stronger now and able to reach farther with the stones, even though he had only Wek to help. Perhaps the golden mage had been closer than Lifeblood, but she was still too far away to reach them.

He painted the symbol for Lifeblood and then added another for the Vinnish warlocks. He did the same for the jungle-clad hills they were living on now and made a symbol for the Mayan priests.

Saka closed his eyes and tried to recall the map the golden mage had shown him. He needed to capture as much detail as possible. If only he'd had longer to talk to her. She'd said her people had once used telestone webs, that what he was doing wasn't a new idea.

He added a little more to the map. It was imperfect, but it was better than what he'd had before. He couldn't sit and wait for the desert to claim him the way it had the mage with the golden skin. He would respond to Angus's next summons, and he would accept the bond with the priest. It was all he could do, though it filled him with no joy.

"Iktan might have a map." Wek dropped a fresh kill nearby. It would be their dinner.

Saka stared at the tent and the map of Demonside. He nodded. Iktan might be able to expand Saka's knowledge. "I think it is time to go back."

Wek didn't look convinced, but she skinned the animal and got it cooking while Saka finished working on his map. When the fire was crackling and the meat was cooking, Wek finally spoke. "Do you still believe Vinland can be stopped?"

He wanted to say yes, but he didn't know anymore. "Perhaps it's too late." Did he want to spend his last heartbeats fighting the inevitable? "If Vinland can't be stopped, what do we do? Surrender?"

He'd spend what was left with Angus. Perhaps it would be better to live for a time on Humanside. Let the magic pour out of him instead of wilting slowly like the golden mage. He hadn't thought about how he wanted to die, but no option appealed.

"We kill as many warlocks as we can and die in battle."

Saka smiled at her. There was a certain appeal to that. "I will contact Iktan and see if we can go back. There's nothing more to learn out here." And he didn't want to spend more time away from Angus. His life might be too short to waste even another day.

Iktan didn't respond immediately. When night embraced the jungle with the darkest of purple, Saka tried to will sleep to come. The night was too still and humid to sleep in the tent so, as he had so many times before, he made his bed on the ground and watched the stars appear in the darkness. He was resolved to start the walk back to Iktan's tribe in the morning, no matter what. But he was unwilling to accept that getting a priest as an anchor was the only way forward.

What had happened to Terrance?

By not responding to Angus and by cutting himself off from the tribe, he was blind in one eye. The lack of knowledge worried at him.

As sleep started to creep closer, his telestone called to him. He felt a hum in his bones and a physical craving to touch it, but he didn't answer immediately. It felt like defeat to go back and accept what Cadmael had planned for him. He was a mage, not an apprentice. But he had nowhere else to go, and he didn't want to die alone, swallowed by the sand. He wanted to be able to talk to Angus, to hold him. He missed him.

Saka reached out and placed a hand over the stone. He wished he could talk to Angus as easily. He'd never spent so long without him, even though he'd probably spent too much time *with* him, treated him too much like a demon… like a lover.

Mage Iktan. Saka went with the formal option, since he was going to have to beg for a place.

Mage Saka. Iktan inclined his head. *I have good news. Angus has sent word.*

Saka ignored the hiccup of his heart. How had he sent word? *What did he say?*

He wants to see you. You are far enough away that he will come to you, not to the doorway.

How will he get back? He didn't want Angus to be stuck here again.

You can return to the village with him.

And once I return? Why was it this easy to come back? He'd expected that Iktan would no longer want him around.

We can talk about it when you are here. Iktan hesitated. *When you return I will not be able to stop Cadmael from forcing the bond with an anchor.*

I know, and I accept that. That was the price he'd have to pay to have Angus. *I have learned nothing good.*

But you have still learned, and others will want to know what you have discovered in your time away.

So that was the mistruth that had been told—that he had been learning, not running away. Lying was dishonorable among mages, and yet it seemed to be coming more easily. *I hope my absence did not cause you trouble.*

Cadmael was not happy, but I stressed that mages have work to do here.

We do not exist for a priest's pleasure. Do you wish to send a message to Angus?

There were so many things he wanted to say, but he wanted to say most of it in person. *I await your arrival.*

That was the bone-deep truth. He craved Angus in a way he'd never wanted anything before. He didn't want to hold tightly to the hope that Angus would be with him soon, but he couldn't stop the flutter of need that followed.

And I await yours, Iktan said.

The connection broke, and Saka was alone with his thoughts. He folded his hands on his belly and stared at the stars. The stars would still be there, even if Demonside died. Perhaps there were other demons on other worlds. Perhaps something would survive.

Where once he'd believed that everything had a time and place and that he'd happily give his life for his people, Saka knew he wouldn't be able to die with the dignity of the golden mage. All he had left was his life, and he would fight until the last breath was torn from him and his heart ceased to beat.

CHAPTER SEVENTEEN

TERRANCE'S WIN had two immediate effects, aside from getting him within touching distance of Angus. The first change was that people on the street recognized Terrance and either smiled and nodded at him or called him something that sounded like *Vinnish pig*. Angus wasn't sure the jade earring translated that properly.

The second effect was that Lizzie worked out where to find them. Any player who got the ball through the hoop was moved to the Training Temple. She approached Terrance and Angus on their way to the entertainment quarter to meet up with the demon who'd taken the message to Saka.

Angus hugged her hard and didn't want to let her go. "You survived the clean sweep."

"Of course I did. I knew something wasn't right and took shelter." She grinned.

Angus hadn't. He'd watched the roiling sky like an idiot and had barely survived.

"You have been a hard man to find," she said to Angus. Then she nodded at Terrance. "Fortunately he can't stay away from fame and glory."

"That's why I'm here—to make a name for myself as I save the world." Terrance spoke with a smile, but there was a bite to his words. "Have you seen the others?"

"Where have you been staying?" Angus wanted to be able to find her again.

"I was told my magic was insignificant, and then I was placed in a boarding house until I could decide what to do with my life." She shrugged. "I have no idea where Reece and Emma are."

"Shit. I was hoping you'd all be together." Once they were reunited, Angus still didn't know what they were going to do.

"That would be too easy. I'd been hoping they were with you." Her smile fell away. "Maybe they didn't survive."

That killed the mood. He should be used to being disappointed and to having things snatched away, but he wasn't ready to believe that Reece and Emma were dead. "We need to find them. It can't be that hard."

"Trust me, it is." She crossed her arms. "So where are you going?"

"The entertainment quarter. Hopefully to get a response from Saka."

Lizzie frowned, and as they made their way to the entertainment quarter on the tram, Angus told her what had happened with the clean sweep and about the anchor requirement.

It was still light when they got off the tram, but the air had cooled and the insects were attempting to bite exposed skin. The bells around his ankle chimed as he walked. Their familiar sound was a comfort.

People glanced at the three of them. Their fair skin made them stand out, even though Terrance and Lizzie both had dark hair—or Terrance would have when it grew back—right then it was little more than stubble. Distrust was evident on the Mayans' faces. They were the enemy.

Angus wanted to tell them that it wasn't his fault and that he was trying to fix it… but he wasn't.

They slipped through the market, and Lizzie marveled at the demons strolling around. "Can you imagine what they'd say about this at home?"

"Nothing good." Many people were brought up believing demons were killers, only after human blood… which they were now, because they were trying to save their world. "Did you want to come in?"

Lizzie and Terrance both said yes. Angus didn't warn them about what was inside, but Terrance blushed, and Lizzie's eyes went wide.

"I should be shocked that you'd find a place like this, but I'm not," Terrance said.

"I didn't find it. My helpful *guide* brought me here because he thought any demon would do." He half expected to see Kabil following them at a discreet distance.

Lizzie smirked.

The furred demon that Angus had seen last time walked over. "I'm glad you came back."

Angus nodded, and Lizzie bit her lip trying not to laugh. Angus knew what it looked like, but it was better if it looked like he was following his skitun tendencies than passing secret messages. Besides, no one here was skitun. The Mayans didn't have a slur for people who fucked demons. It was allowed and people enjoyed it.

Angus followed the demon into the small room. "You got a response from Saka?"

"I gave the message to my head Mage, Iktan."

Angus groaned. That meant Cadmael knew.

"He passed it to Saka. Iktan said to let you know Saka awaits your arrival." The demon lowered his voice. "He isn't near a doorway."

Angus bit his lip and frowned. Away from the doorway. He knew that the doorway limited travel to protect the demons from humans arriving everywhere. But if Saka was away from the doorway would Angus arrive where Saka was?

"Thank you. I hope you won't get into trouble."

The demon looked at him. "Why does Saka not come here if he wants to see you and you want to see him? Not using a doorway is dangerous."

"It's… it's not that easy." Though he wished it were. Saka would stand out too much among the furred and feathered demons.

"Best of luck." The demon walked out of the room, leaving Angus to follow.

Lizzie and Terrance were waiting outside the building.

"That was quick." Terrance grinned.

"Got what I needed."

Lizzie gave a strangled laugh.

"You two are terrible. I'm trying to do something useful, and you're carrying on." He stalked off, but they caught up.

"We're having fun. It's in short supply," Lizzie said. "I didn't think I'd ever get to see you again."

Angus stopped and turned. "You wanted to?" After everything that had happened?

"Yes. They want to keep us separate, but I want to make sure we don't get lost. Mostly because I know you'll come up with some stupid idea that will stop the warlocks."

Angus stared at the ground.

"You are thinking of something?" The worry in Lizzie's voice was clear.

"Like what? Bombs are being dropped on Vinland. The warlocks are using a weapon that sucks magic back to them and kills those with magic. What can I do?"

Terrance put his hand on Angus's back. "You were outside and survived. That's something."

It wasn't enough. He wasn't even sure how he'd done it, and no one else thought it was worth talking about. "Luck."

"Then you must be the luckiest man alive." Terrance kissed his cheek.

"I'm sure others have survived." They must have.

Lizzie stared at him. "I'm not sure they have."

Maybe no one else had survived a clean sweep, but he couldn't worry about that. He had to get to Saka. "Saka wants to see me, so I need to find somewhere to get across." He needed time to open the void without being detected.

"Just go through at the temple," Terrance said.

Angus shook his head. "That's fixed to the doorway in Demonside, and Saka isn't there."

"Will you get in trouble if you just go?" Lizzie's eyebrows drew together.

Angus didn't answer. He didn't need to. They all knew the answer.

"What if you get stuck there?" Terrance held him a little closer.

"I won't, because you will open the void to summon Saka. You will be the anchor."

Cadmael was never going to allow it, so they had to act before the priest made it impossible.

The pitz court in the park was empty. It seemed like as good a place as any. There was a residue of excitement and angst there—not enough, but better than nothing. There was no point in waiting another day or thinking through details that would only give way to worry.

Angus hugged Lizzie. "Find the others."

She nodded. "Cadmael will have your blood."

Angus forced a smile. "Probably." He faced Terrance. "I'm leaving you too soon."

He was always leaving Terrance. For a moment he considered not going. But that would mean admitting the Empire could be home and that he was willing to share Saka with just anyone. But he didn't want to do that. He wanted to stop the warlocks and go home to Vinland— with Terrance. Saka, could then go back to Lifeblood, and everything would be right. Angus held Terrance tightly and kissed him hard.

"This time I know how to get you back. I'll give you one day or until Cadmael starts breaking my fingers or whatever they like to do here."

He was putting Terrance in danger again, but as usual, Terrance wouldn't step aside. Angus didn't deserve such loyalty or love from anyone. "You're really all right with this?"

"I don't have another plan. Lizzie?"

"I've got nothing. I think I need to get a demon. Then at least I'll be moved to the Temple with you two. Ask Wek if she'll have me? I know I'm not Norah, but maybe she wouldn't mind."

Lizzie, who never wanted to be a warlock, was now ready to cross that line. Wek had been devastated after losing Norah, her trainee. Was she ready for another human?

"I will." Angus drew in a breath. "Let's break some rules. Unless you'd rather start walking away and pretending not to know me?"

Terrance kissed him. His lips felt warm and desperate. "While safer, that would be infinitely less exciting." With a last taste, Terrance pulled away. "Go."

Terrance and Lizzie took several steps back, and Angus closed his eyes. The last time he opened the void, he almost died in the desert. His skin prickled with anticipation, and his stomach knotted. This wasn't even close to his previous dumb ideas. This was dangerous, banned, and possibly deadly. Cadmael could arrest Terrance and Lizzie and leave him in Demonside to die.

Angus glanced over his shoulder. His friends were leaving him, and Saka was waiting. Without his demon, Angus was nothing but a wannabe warlock/mage/priest without enough skills to do much more than save his own skin.

With barely a blink, he tore open the void, but no sirens sounded to announce the breach. Cool air rushed toward him, and the darkness beckoned. The familiar scents of Demonside mixed with the unfamiliar notes of the different vegetation of the jungle tribes.

He swallowed hard and stepped through, not sure where Saka would be. He had to trust Terrance would get him within a day. Angus blinked and tried to work out where he was. The jungle was bathed in starlight and shadows. A tent covered in markings was pitched near what could only be described as a hole in the ground that looked like it had no bottom. A few paces to his left, and he'd have been over the hole. He shivered.

The void closed, and he was once again in Demonside. For a moment he breathed easily. It was like coming home.

Saka stepped around the tent, his horns gleaming in the starlight and his metallic skin shimmering. He was very much alive. The tension that had knotted Angus's stomach eased so he could breathe again, but in that same heartbeat, he had to wall himself up so Demonside didn't suck the magic from his body and leave him nothing but a broken husk.

The time when he had enjoyed letting go and being part of something bigger had slid through his fingers. He missed rebalancing the way it had been in Saka's bed.

"I wasn't sure it was actually you who sent the message," Saka said.

"But you replied anyway." He never doubted that the message had come from Saka.

Saka gave a single nod. "And you came."

Angus took a couple of paces toward his demon. "Where are we this time?" He recognized the jungle, but he didn't know how far it spread or how close they were to the demon village that was connected to Uxmal.

"Several days walk from the village and the doorway that you would know. There is a smaller settlement two days away."

"Not that far, yet Iktan hasn't dragged you back."

"We have an agreement. I will be returning, so you can return through the doorway." Saka moved closer.

"Terrance plans to open the void tomorrow, if you respond to him." Or if Saka didn't want to, he'd walk back to the town with him. Cadmael would force a bond with a priest, and it wouldn't be Kabil. There would be no more stalling or wriggling out of it, and Angus was sure Cadmael would find some way of forcing Saka to accept the bond instead of turning it away.

"He is alive? He played?"

"Yes and yes." Angus wanted to tell Saka about the game and the ritual and the emotions the blood had soaked up.

But Saka's face became serious. "Terrance being the anchor is not approved."

"No. I'm not very good at following rules."

"I've noticed." Saka took his hands. His skin was warm and rough, and a shiver traced over Angus's skin even though the night was warm.

Magic and lust coiled through him. He wanted nothing more than to rebalance and enjoy the time he had with Saka without thinking about the death of Demonside. But that was impossible. All magic was tied to Demonside, and its use had to be paid for. He enjoyed the paying far too much and didn't understand Cadmael's warning not to get entangled with Saka when it was clear there was no ban on human-demon relations.

But he'd also seen that there was much more to rebalancing. They needed to think bigger.

"So we have a day before Terrance wants you back."

"Not just me." Had Saka not been serious in the desert? "Didn't you want to see what you could do if you had two humans to rebalance with?" He hadn't forgotten. And he'd thought too much about it while he was alone and missing his lovers. Magic pushed against his skin, following Saka's thumb as he rubbed in small circles.

The corner of Saka's lips turned up. "It is a curiosity that I would like to sate."

What would it be like to watch Saka and Terrance? Would it kill him? He was able to taste what it must be like for both of them, to know what was happening but not be part of it.

He was the worst boyfriend… and he wasn't much of an apprentice either.

Everyone else managed to follow the rules of magic—expect for the college warlocks. Maybe *he* was a warlock.

Saka closed the distance between them. His chest almost touched Angus's. "Tonight I have you to myself."

"Yes." For weeks he'd been looking forward to being alone with Saka. "Tomorrow I'll tell you about the game."

"And I'll tell you what I have learned and maybe we'll have enough to make a plan."

"Maybe." In the soft starlight of Demonside, plans and danger seemed far away, and he didn't want to let anything intrude on their time. He brushed his lips over Saka's, and the demon returned the kiss. With every touch and taste, the kiss became more demanding.

Saka put his hand on Angus's hip and drew him closer. The pressure of his fingertips betrayed his need. Angus put his arm around Saka's neck, glad that Saka still wanted him, despite all the time and distance that had been between them.

Where once it had been about need—the need to rebalance and the need to teach Angus about magic—now it was so much more. He rocked his hips so he could feel the hard length of Saka pressing against his hip, and a shiver of longing raced through him. It had been too long since he'd been in Saka's bed.

The magic he'd brought from the human side of the void was trapped in Angus's body. It bubbled, seeking a way out. While memories of the trek still played out in his dreams, he didn't need to hold it all in. It was only a day….

Unless something went horribly wrong.

Saka traced Angus's cheek with his finger. "You don't need to rebalance."

Angus rested his forehead on Saka's. "I want to, and I should. I've been using magic as I study." He was hard and ready and wanted more than a quick fuck. He missed the times when Saka could keep him on edge for hours until he begged to come.

"I can feel your worry."

Angus gave a small nod. "What if no one opens the void for me?"

"The doorway opens regularly."

"Unless Uxmal gets attacked again, and all magic users get killed." But if everyone he knew were killed, what would be the point in returning? No, he'd go back to Vinland and take down every last warlock responsible, even if it took him the rest of his life.

"There are other doorways." Saka cupped his face. "Do you fear Demonside now?"

The awe that he'd felt the first time—the heat and the visible magic, all the different demons, learning the truth—was still there but tempered with the knowledge that this place would kill him. It wasn't home and never could be, nor was it a safe refuge. "I respect it and the people who live here."

"You share that with the Mayans. Their way of using magic is more similar to mine than I'd thought."

Angus covered Saka's hands. "I can't stay here. I want to be able to go home. Don't you?"

Saka was silent for several heartbeats. "Yes. But I can't go back until the balance is reset."

"I know." Angus kissed him hard. "Let me give a little to rebalance."

He didn't want to say out loud how much he liked to feel the magic trickling from his body as he came, or describe how it made the release more intense.

Saka slid his hand down Angus's neck, leaving a trail of heat, and then down his arm. Their fingers touched briefly, and then he traced the length of Angus's dick through his pants. "Just a little. Arlyxia is so hungry for magic that it may take too much. Stay in control."

Angus bit back a groan. He was sick of being in control and sick of the expectations people had of him. He had no idea what he was doing.

Saka's lips were whisper-soft against his cheek. "I mean it. You should be able to feel the draw on your magic. The need is stronger than usual."

Maybe it wasn't all pent-up desire. He let himself sink into Demonside so he could feel the magic. It was there but barely moving. The rest was all heat and dryness. To him it was thirst, not hunger, and he couldn't sate it. He wasn't sure that anything could. He pulled back. He couldn't let go, no matter how much he craved it. "I'll be careful."

One day it would be nice to come here and to let go completely and know that it wouldn't kill him. If the magic were rebalanced properly, humans would be able to spend longer in Demonside. The longer they spent, the more they would keep the magic in balance.

Saka undid Angus's pants and eased his hand inside. His skin was rough on Angus's hard, heated flesh.

Angus smothered a groan. "Should we go into the tent?"

"Wek is sleeping."

"No one stands guard? What about the riverwyrms?"

"They're different here. They stay in the river. Don't swim in the water holes. That's where humans get sacrificed, and the wyrms expect the food." Saka kissed Angus's neck and then between his collarbones. "Let's move away so we don't wake her."

Most likely she was already awake. Angus didn't want a silent audience, so he let Saka lead him away from the tent and toward some broken pillars. Vines wrapped around them with a resonance of old magic. Saka pulled off Angus's shirt and dropped it on the broken stones and then drew Angus down.

A sigh slid from his lips as Saka's mouth closed around his dick. He swept his tongue over the slit and around the crown and then took him deeper. Angus closed his eyes and stopped trying to hold back the magic that wanted to bubble out of him, but he remained in control enough that it was only a trickle and not a rush.

When Saka slid his tail up Angus's inner thigh and brushed against his balls, lust tightened low in Angus's belly. Heat and need surged and made it harder to hold on to the magic. It was so tempting to let go and not worry, but if he did, Demonside would swallow him whole. Angus ran his fingers over Saka's horns to the cool, sharp tip. He hadn't spilled blood for Demonside in a long time, but tonight wasn't the night for that kind of magic. He moved his fingers away, and Saka released his cock.

Saka moved over him, pressed his hips closer, and rocked against Angus. Angus tugged at Saka's pants, but Saka drew back, out of reach, and he stroked and teased with his tail.

It was hard not to writhe and want more. Angus's breath was already coming in short pants. "I thought you wanted me to be careful?"

It was hard to concentrate on keeping the magic in and not get swept up, and Saka wasn't making it any easier.

"I do. You are out of practice."

He was, and he smiled. "I'm sure there's a way for me to practice more."

But he didn't want it to be about magic all the time. Angus pulled Saka closer and kissed him. He needed to taste him, and this time he managed to get his demon's pants undone and free his cock. He wrapped his fingers around the rough shaft and stroked, knowing what Saka liked, even though he could hold out forever or something close to it. It was a control Angus didn't think he'd ever be capable of —he always ended up enjoying himself too much.

He pushed Saka over so the demon was on his back. Then Angus kicked his pants off so he could straddle him, and he leaned over and pressed Saka's hands to the ground with his own. Saka could shove him away at any time. He was far stronger. And while Saka would never beg for release—they had tried that once, and it remained the only time Angus had ever been the one doing the fucking—the idea that one day maybe Angus would be able to bring Saka to that point was intriguing. It was also a much-needed distraction from how desperately he really wanted to let go.

Saka watched him, and the stars reflected in his black eyes.

Angus rolled his hips, relishing Saka's rough skin against his. Saka traced along Angus's asscrack with his damn sneaky tail. Angus shuddered, and precome slicked his dick.

Saka grinned. "Perhaps what you need is a tail to help you."

"You could stop using yours." But he didn't want that. He liked the tease of the tail circling like a finger, ready to press deeper.

Saka didn't stop.

Neither did he. Angus would slide past the point of stopping unless Saka forced him to. Angus half expected that. Saka liked to torture Angus that way, and it was always good when he did. The release was that much better, and that much more magic was rebalanced… which was exactly what they wanted to avoid.

He tried to keep a firm hand on the magic as he ground against Saka, but as the climax tore through him, so did the magic. He came hard—his back arched and his chest was as tight as though it had been years and not weeks.

Saka freed his hand, dragged him close, and kissed him hard. He thrust his tongue deeply into Angus's mouth as his hips bucked, and hot come pooled between them as Saka gave in.

Angus groaned and battled to rein in the flow of magic. He grounded himself in Saka's kiss and the feel of his skin to close himself off from magic and Demonside bit by bit until it was barely a trickle. But he wasn't ready to lose the lingering ripples of pleasure just yet.

He rested on Saka, and Saka looped his arm over him.

The humming of insects filled the night air. Angus's skin was sticky with sweat, but he didn't want to move. As soon as he did, the moment would be over and they would start talking about how to stop Vinland.

Angus just wanted to live and breathe in peace for a few more moments and listen to the rapid beat of Saka's heart before it slowed to something more respectable.

Magic leached out of him, and he didn't stop it. Instead he held on to the pleasure for one more heartbeat. Then he put up the wall and protected himself from the thirst of Demonside.

Saka lifted his head and looked at him with a faint smile on his lips. "I should start teaching you again."

"You don't need to find an excuse for me to be here. I like being here." He wanted to say more, but he swallowed it down.

Saka placed a soft kiss on his lips. "I know."

CHAPTER EIGHTEEN

WHEN IT REACHED noon and no one had asked where Angus was, Terrance was convinced they'd gotten away with it. He'd go to the park that night and open the void to Saka, and it would all be fine. But he'd have a demon again, making him a warlock or something, and Saka would kill him if he ever hurt Angus.

Of course he didn't plan on hurting Angus, but people he loved got hurt. It terrified him that Angus was quite capable of putting himself in harm's way without a second thought. He'd much rather be protecting Angus than wishing him good luck.

At least if they shared a demon, he might have a better chance of preventing Angus from destroying himself to save the world. That wasn't their job. Smarter, more-qualified people were trying to save the world—not that bombing other countries was the smart thing. The whole world was fighting and finger-pointing, and no one seemed to have a plan for how to get the magic back to Demonside.

Leveling Vinland wouldn't work. The magic would still be tied up. But Vinland was deploying a clean sweep every other day, it seemed, causing death and injury and stealing even more magic. Mayans were trying to find a way to stop the clean sweep, but it wasn't working.

What if nothing worked?

The world was reaching the point where the ice age wouldn't be stopped even if the magic were rebalanced. Thousands more would die of starvation if the cold remained in place. And people in Vinland were dying too—the sanctions had hit them hard.

He found it too hard to watch some of the stories from around the world. There were worse places to be than the Empire, so while the Mayans didn't trust him, he tried to feel grateful to be alive… tried.

At dusk he made his way to the pitz court. People were playing, and they invited him to join, but he didn't want to. At least their words were making more sense. He was getting used to the rhythm and flow of the language. When he caught himself understanding, the shock made him lose track of what was being said and he had to fight for every word again.

Eventually the park emptied as people went home. He noticed they checked the sky like they were waiting for it to turn the sick green color that indicated an attack.

Terrance walked onto the court and stood in the center. What if he fucked up?

Sweat blistered on his back, despite the chill in the air that he hadn't felt before. The glaciers were creeping closer, villages were being abandoned, crops hadn't ripened, and in some places, they couldn't be planted because the soil was too hard, too frozen.

He had to get Angus back. They had to do something, even if they didn't want to. There had to be a way to end this.

Terrance hadn't opened the void in months. He needed a circle on the ground as a focus, but he didn't need to walk it. He pulled the pencil out of his pocket and drew a large circle on the ground. It was more of an egg—art had never been one of his strengths—but it would do. Then he drew in a breath and centered himself.

"Summoning someone?" Cadmael's voice came out of the gloom.

Terrance's calm shattered. He fisted the pencil as though it were a weapon. He doubted he'd even get the chance to make one hole in Cadmael if it came to a fight.

Cadmael stepped onto the court, and for a moment, his face took on a look of reverence. Pitz was more than a game, and even before the imbalance, it served a very important function. "I did wonder how long you'd leave him there."

"We agreed a day."

Cadmael nodded. "A sensible amount of time, given the situation. We don't recommend staying overnight to tourists. I'm sure Angus knows what to expect and how to deal with it better than most."

Terrance nodded. He hoped Angus did. "Are you here to stop me?"

"No. We have people watching all of you. You aren't the only defectors, but you don't seem to be liars. You aren't passing information back. Or if you are, you're doing it in a very clever way that we haven't been able to determine."

It took a moment for Terrance to realize what he was being accused of. "You thought I was helping the college? They killed my parents."

"You have helped them before." Cadmael paced a little closer.

"I did as they asked, nothing more, because I like living."

"There are some who'd like all defectors locked up until after the war. Most of us don't feel that way. You know your country better than anyone. You should be helping to fight."

"But you won't let us."

"You're a danger to yourselves. You know just enough magic to do a few minor things, but not enough to understand."

"Me? Yeah. I never wanted a demon."

"The best magic users don't. They understand innately what it means. Angus never wanted one either, yet he risks everything for Saka."

"He knows he has to do something."

"What?"

"I don't know."

Cadmael put his hands behind his back and took a couple of steps forward, careful not to disturb Terrance's egg circle. "Find out."

"Spy on him."

"Help him… allow me to help him." Cadmael's smile was too bright, too hungry.

"Why would you help him?" While Cadmael and his friends in the Intelligence Temple could've left them for dead in Demonside, Terrance doubted they'd been rescued because the Mayans were super friendly. Military and magic ruled the Empire. Everyone had to do two years' service. He'd learned more about their culture in pitz school than he had anywhere else.

"Why do the Vinnish want him back?"

"What?" Terrance's knuckles were starting to hurt, but he kept his grip on the pencil.

"The Vinnish have offered ransom for him. He killed his father, a high-ranking warlock, and he helped liberate demons that were to be sacrificed. The warlocks don't retrieve many of those who are taken to Arlyxia, but they retrieved Angus only to have him betray them."

"They retrieved him because of his father." Not because of anything Angus had done.

Terrance was half tempted to ask how much the ransom was. "Why are they offering a ransom?"

"So they can get him back and punish the traitor would be my guess." Cadmael didn't seem like the kind of man who guessed.

"You won't hand him over?"

"I haven't yet. Besides, if the Vinnish want him, he's more valuable to us."

"What do you want him for?" If Terrance brought Angus back, there was no telling what Cadmael would make him do. But if he didn't bring Angus back, Demonside would be a death sentence.

"I don't know yet. You tell me." That smile again.

"And if I refuse?"

"I'll have someone else open the void and bond with Saka." Cadmael indicated the shadows behind him. He wasn't alone. "I know Angus doesn't want that. Nor does Saka. I don't think you do either. You love Angus. What I don't understand is why he loves you."

That made two of them. Terrance shrugged. "I thought you didn't want me involved."

"I expected you to die. I underestimated you. I won't make that mistake again." The knife edge of the words was sharp and hard. "I suggest you get on with it. I don't have all night." Cadmael pointed at the egg circle.

Terrance sighed. While he hadn't been looking forward to it, at least by being the anchor he could protect Angus from priests like Cadmael.

"You've open the void before, had a demon before. What is the problem?"

He might fuck it up and end up with a random demon. "I've never done it with intent to get a specific demon."

"You have, every time you opened the void for your demon. You just didn't realize. You know Saka. Bringing him to mind should be easy. He is the only demon of his kind in the area."

That was true. Terrance gave Cadmael a nod and focused on gathering up what magic was whispering through the trees around him. There was more in the air here, more than in Vinland, but the Mayans made a point of keeping it moving.

He'd never wanted to be involved with demon magic again, but now he wasn't sure he wanted to play sports again either. Although the energy of the crowd… maybe it didn't need to end in death.

The hairs along his arms prickled and pulled tight as the magic gathered. The tension in his gut swelled. He couldn't screw up. If he did, Cadmael would get someone else to be the anchor, and that would be a disaster.

Terrance thought of Saka and tried to bring up every detail he could, from the way he looked at Angus when he thought no one was paying attention to the way his hand had felt in Terrance's and the promise that there could be more between the three of them. He bit his cheek to keep from smiling.

Then he reached for the void with his mind, to a place where the magic could punch through the gap between worlds. The void tore open with a rush of cold air and shimmered darkly within his egg circle. He couldn't step across—not unless he wanted to be over there with Saka and Angus. Although, at the moment, that didn't seem like an entirely bad thing.

But where had he opened the void to?

Each breath made his ribs ache. Who or what would come through?

CHAPTER NINETEEN

Saka felt the pull as the void opened, but it wasn't Angus opening the void because Angus was walking next to him. They were on their way back to Iktan's village, as Saka had promised.

Saka was sure it was Terrance summoning him, but he took a couple of breaths to get the feel of the summons before he allowed the connection instead of turning it away.

Angus glanced up as the void opened before them.

Wek stopped too. "So we don't need to make the trek at all."

"That opened for me," Saka said. He sighed. Now he had two human warlocks. Twice the teaching. Safer for the humans. Was it safer for him? Unlikely. "I had best go through. I will not be long." He glanced at Wek.

It was dangerous with just the two of them, but a demon on their own was an easy target for predators. While Wek was a good hunter, other things were also good at hunting and tracking. There might not be packs of scarlips here, but there were other things with long naked tails and bristly fur and things that flew and had talons like knives and hungry beaks.

"I'll stay." Angus bit his lip. "Terrance is your… your human now too."

Yes he was. What had been discussed was now reality, though even Angus seemed unsure.

"I won't be long." Saka kissed him with a quick brush of lips and then stepped through the tear in the void.

Despite knowing who was summoning him, he was still careful. His hand was on his machete, and he was ready for trouble. There was every chance that Angus's absence had been noticed, so he expected to arrive in a room with several unhappy priests. Instead he was outside, in a circle so weak it wouldn't have stopped a plant from growing out of it. Terrance stood in front of him, but someone was behind him. Saka didn't need to turn to know who. "Priest Cadmael."

"Mage Saka. So glad you could finally find the time to respond."

"I have been busy." He kept his gaze on Terrance, even though he wanted to have an eye on Cadmael too. Why was the priest here?

"I heard." Footsteps, and then Cadmael came into view. "A risky strategy."

"You are not supposed to force a bond. What you did was wrong." Any magic user who broke their own rules, that they claimed were for the protection of their people, should feel a modicum of shame.

Cadmael glanced at Terrance. "My intent was correct. It is dangerous not to have an anchor. You wouldn't want Angus getting stuck across the void."

"Nor would I want him having to work with someone not of his, or our, choosing."

"And you choose *this* man?"

Terrance's face hardened, and he shot a glare at Cadmael.

"Yes." Saka knew enough about Terrance—the good and the bad— to accept him as his human. "He will learn." He gave Terrance a smile. Magic wasn't all naked rebalancing, although Saka wasn't sure how much Angus had told Terrance.

"Some people shouldn't learn."

Saka's gaze slid to Cadmael. "I was working with a college warlock before you were born. I have been involved in the fight against them. I know that the kind of people who shouldn't learn magic are the ones most hungry for a taste. Terrance is not one of them."

How the Mayan weeded them out, he didn't want to know, though he could guess. The college had cultivated a need for power, corrupting them young and ensuring they'd never speak out.

"Agreed. But there are other things to be wary of," Cadmael said carefully.

"Like the way you asked me to report on Angus?" Terrance finally spoke. He looked like he was going to crumble, but it took strength to reveal what he'd been asked to do instead of hiding it and obeying.

"Yes. That." Cadmael's expression soured.

"My judgment is sound," Saka said with a smile. "We are not the enemy, Priest. We all want the magic rebalanced and our worlds healed. It doesn't matter if our way of using magic is different from yours."

"Their way is what has caused the damage."

Terrance shook his head. "I have always paid for the magic I used. Angus has rebalanced more than his share too. We understand."

"You aren't properly trained," Cadmael snapped.

"And we never claimed to be." Terrance fisted something in his hand, but otherwise didn't move. "All we wanted was refuge so the warlocks wouldn't kill us."

"They will be trained, but you have made that harder, cut them off from their friends and tried to stop what was happening naturally." Saka didn't remember any mages at Lifeblood ever talking about anchors, but it made sense. He also liked the doorways and wanted to learn how to make one to protect his people… if his people were still there.

Cadmael's lips twisted. "Cement the bond and be done so Angus may return."

There was nothing to do to cement the bond. Vinnish warlocks spoke a few words that held no magical sway, but he didn't feel like reciting them.

"Thanks for responding." Terrance offered his hand.

Saka clasped it. "It will be a pleasure."

Cadmael looked at them. "No blood offering?"

Saka held Terrance's gaze. "Another time."

He stepped back into the void before Cadmael could demand more, but his hand shook until he fisted it and regained control. He felt as though he were swimming in riverwyrm-infested waters and couldn't reach the shore. It was only a matter of time until he was eaten. The void closed behind him, and the heat of Arlyxia wrapped around him.

Angus and Wek had waited for him.

"It's done?" Angus studied him.

"It is. He will open the void for you in a moment. Cadmael has asked him to watch you."

"Of course he did, and Terrance would've agreed because there would've been an accompanying threat."

"These people are not our friends," Saka said.

"They're not our enemies either." Angus shivered, and then the void opened in front of him.

Saka stepped closer. "Did you feel the tear?"

"Yes." Angus rubbed his arms as if he were cold.

"Now you need to learn how to turn it away so it doesn't open near you. It might save your life."

"My next lesson?"

"There will be several. I need to think about what will be most useful."

Angus frowned. "I don't know what I need." He gave Saka a bitter grin. "A way to take back all of the magic Vinland has been stealing?"

"If it were simple, it would've been done already. Go before Terrance thinks you're never coming back."

They shared a final embrace, and then Angus stepped through. Saka watched and waited for the void to close. It took several heartbeats. Terrance needed to learn how to close it after himself, which wasn't easy when traveling to Humanside. It was much easier to close it in Demonside. He stared at the place where Angus had been standing, and he sighed.

Cadmael would want blood. It was just a matter of when.

CHAPTER TWENTY

"This man is a Vinnish spy." Cadmael forced the kneeling man to look up by grabbing a handful of his hair.

The man didn't look that Vinnish. While Terrance's coloring was darker than Angus's, he still had that square-jawed look and fair skin. This man had a narrow face and dark eyes. Angus glanced from the man to Terrance and then back to Cadmael. "How do I know you're telling the truth?"

"He's not. I'm a refugee, like you." The man stared up at Angus, pleading.

"You can look for yourself." Cadmael released the man's hair.

Over the last week they had been learning about mind reading. It could be done gently—a sort of sifting through the top layer as they had done in class. He'd tried with a few different people, and they tried on him. But Saka had taught him how to conceal. He knew thoughts could be hidden or faked—at least they could be during a cursory examination.

He'd experienced something much more painful and in depth at the hands of the college. Angus stepped forward. He still needed to touch the person to look into their thoughts.

"You could've planted fake thoughts," Terrance said. He trusted Cadmael as much as Angus did, which wasn't a whole lot.

Angus knew Terrance had told Cadmael some of what they discussed. For the most part, he didn't care what Cadmael knew. He wasn't doing anything wrong.

He'd started to study the videos of the clean sweep and its after-effects.

A few priests in Merida had tried to harness the magic like he'd done. They'd been cooked from the inside out. It was rather more gruesome than he'd thought—Cadmael had helpfully supplied the details. Angus couldn't explain how he survived, despite writing down exactly what he'd done and how it had felt so Cadmael and others could learn from it. It was an experiment he wasn't keen to repeat, but if he didn't, he wouldn't know what worked.

"Sorry," Angus murmured as he pressed his consciousness into the subject's.

The top layer was fear and imprisonment. The man had been caught a week ago, just before Angus went to Demonside to see Saka. His earlier memories were jumbled, possibly hidden. The man remembered Vinland, but not a part Angus was familiar with. He had a memory of arriving in the Mayan Empire, but none of fleeing from Vinland.

There were other people in his thoughts, but Angus couldn't see their faces. Then one image bloomed sharp and clear.

Wanted alive. Angus Donohue.

Angus jerked his hand back.

The man grinned. "If not me, then someone else. Traitor."

"World destroyer," Angus replied. How could people live with themselves when they saw the hunger and hurt on the human side? And the damage done on the other side of the void compounded the devastation.

"Humans will survive. Not all, but some. We will be better—stronger—without depending on demons."

"You aren't even a warlock. Do you really think they care about you? You're fodder, a pawn in a game for control." How could the man be so blind?

Terrance put a hand on Angus's arm. "You can't save everyone."

Angus blinked and looked at Cadmael.

Cadmael was thin-lipped. "Take the prisoner to Demonside. Finalize the bond."

"Finalize?" The bond was made. And while Angus was itching to get back to Demonside, he didn't want to keep leaving Terrance behind. Terrance should come too… he needed to do stuff with Saka. Angus really wasn't sure what, only that he didn't like the idea of being left out, the way Terrance had so often been left out. He bit the inside of his lip to keep the grimace off his face.

"Kill me." The man nodded at Cadmael. "He wants you to kill me to keep the blood off his hands." The man didn't seem too concerned about his death. Maybe he didn't think it would happen.

"Why do I need to kill?" Angus didn't want to kill anyone.

"A sacrifice is always made to the demon who is giving up his freedom to work with us. Even your warlocks once made sacrifices," Cadmael said as though they were discussing the possibility of rain.

Vinnish warlocks had made sacrifices, but they were animals, not people. He'd read about them in the books in the library. More recently, criminals had been sent to die in Demonside. Traitors like this man.

"Would Saka want this, in his name?" Terrance didn't sound convinced this was a good idea either.

Angus wanted to say no. Maybe Saka would want a sacrifice now that he was a mage to two warlocks, if only to rebalance a little of what had been taken while they trained. They would never refill the bucket one drop at a time, not when the hole at the bottom couldn't be plugged, but Angus nodded. "He would. For Demonside."

"Saka is back in the village. Go through the official doorway, so your leaving and return can be checked off. Try to avoid accidentally slipping away." Cadmael looked at Angus like he had a bad habit of taking off to Demonside, although he had only gone the once. "Guards will take this man through for your ritual."

"He won't do it. Traitors are weak," the man sneered.

"He will if he wants to earn his place." Cadmael fixed him with a glare and then turned to Terrance. "Or he will."

Terrance shook his head. "I'm only the anchor."

Cadmael shrugged. "We will see who becomes the anchor. You have an hour to prepare."

An hour wasn't long enough. Angus put the bells around his ankle. There'd been a time when he'd never taken them off, and now it didn't seem right to wear them unless he were leaving the Training Temple or going to Demonside, even though no one else did. But they'd been a gift, and they had become a good luck charm as well as a riverwyrm deterrent.

He picked up the bone-handled knives that had been given to him when he fought for his life after his father had stabbed him. While the scar on his stomach was gone, the memory hadn't faded at all. His father had tried to kill him, and while Angus hadn't held the blade that killed his father, he had delivered him to the demons.

"Are you actually going to do it?" Terrance sat on the chair and watched Angus get ready.

Angus shrugged. "Do I have a choice? If I don't, I fail Cadmael's test and disrespect their way of paying for and using magic. If I do, then… then…."

"Then you kill a man."

He nodded. It wouldn't be his first kill, but it would be the first by his own hand. Was there really a difference? Saka always talked with reverence about those who volunteered to die. Death was respected and necessary. The Mayans knew that too. He'd been raised to believe that living was more valuable and that a warlock's life was worth ten times that of a wizard. "What would you do?"

"You know the answer." Terrance pressed his lips into a thin line.

Angus nodded. Terrance would act to keep himself safe and do as he was asked to live and have the chance to fight. Angus was tired of fighting. He just wanted to live. "Do you trust Cadmael?"

"No, and he doesn't trust anyone either. I never realized until now how much Vinland is feared and hated."

The Vinnish were the reason that other countries hated magic users, but it hadn't always been that way. Angus had been able to learn more than he ever had at home, where knowledge was controlled. But the Mayan had watched it unfold and documented the college takeover. It was a chilling read.

When his father was his age, the college was just a place for teaching, not the power behind the government. But the World Council of Demonology had done nothing, or at least nothing effective, and by the time the Institute for Magical Studies stepped in, it was too late. The ice was creeping, spreading.

He didn't want to be another person who watched and waited and hoped something changed, so he strapped the knives in their red sleeve onto his forearm. They were demon in make and style. He hadn't seen any Mayan priests wearing knives, though he knew they must own some, since shedding blood and souls was their preferred method for rebalancing. The bone handles were cool as he brushed his fingers over them, but the blades were clean and sharp. He made sure to keep them that way.

Angus lifted his gaze. There was only one way he would get his life back. "Tell Cadmael I will do what he wants. I'll do whatever it takes to stop Vinland. But then it's over, and we owe him nothing."

"That's what he wants to hear."

"Then let him hear it." The sooner he did it, the sooner it would be over. The ice would retreat, the Warlock College would be out of business, and Vinland could pull itself together. He could use what he'd learned to help instead of kill.

"Do you mean it?"

"Yes." Angus forced a breath out between his teeth. "Let's not be late to the execution."

Terrance grabbed his arm as they reached the door. "Let Saka do it."

Angus knew Terrance meant well. There was worry in his brown eyes and tension at the corners. There would be no coming back from this. It was a line drawn in the red sand of Demonside that couldn't be uncrossed. It was also usually the line that made an apprentice into a mage.

"Saka trained me for this. It's an offering to him. Either I do it or you do it." He held Terrance's gaze. The anchor didn't make the kill. He wasn't sure Terrance could hold the knife and draw blood from another, despite having done it to himself.

Terrance didn't say anything.

Angus nodded. "I'll do it. I'll do what needs to be done." He opened the door and started toward the doorway in the Training Temple. He trusted that Terrance would follow, though he wanted to be anywhere else. But there was nowhere else he could go.

The air in Demonside was dry in his throat. Angus's tongue stuck to the roof of his mouth, and his palm sweated around the bone handle of the knife.

He expected there to be a ritual place—like Lifeblood Mountain—but this wasn't up a hill. It was a shaded valley. The sun was overhead but barely sliding past the tree leaves. Somewhere nearby was a nest of blue-and-yellow insects that reminded him of bees, although they were about three times bigger.

Iktan and Saka stood on opposite sides of the stone platform. Like the one on Lifeblood, it looked like a single piece of rock, but there was no hole in the middle to feed the mountain. This rock drained off toward a massive hole in the ground. There was a name for underground lakes, and ones where the roof had caved in and left a dangerous opening to a watery death, but he couldn't remember it or what they called the creatures swimming in them.

Iktan had pulled him aside and told him what he needed to do, and Saka had reminded him of what it meant to him and his tribe.

Angus fucking knew. He got it, but it would be easier if he didn't.

Terrance stood opposite him, but he wasn't looking at Angus or the man who was to die. Instead he stared at some vague point to

Angus's left that made Angus want to turn and see who was behind him.

They were waiting for him.

The man had lost his careless attitude when he was brought across. He'd begged, but the soldiers brought him here and tied him to the rock. There was even a little spot where metal flowed out of one corner to create a loop. The man was calm now, but Angus had done that. He used magic to make him quiet.

He thought he'd need the quiet to concentrate, but it was too quiet. The insects hummed and filled the air with the beating of their wings. The leaves whispered their tales, and water lapped at the rock walls of the deep lake. Something in there was moving, waiting, and Angus was sure he could hear the man's rapid heartbeat echoing off the rock. His fear was still there—his body knew what was coming, even if his mind had been sent elsewhere.

Get it done, Donohue.

Angus glanced at Saka and gave a small nod. Terrance wouldn't look at him. *Fine.* He'd deal with that later. Did Terrance really think he couldn't do this or that it would break him? Angus wasn't weak, and he'd spent months training as a mage. Saka had been his first victim when it came to cutting and pain.

He drew up a circle around them, and it snapped into place with a familiar crack of blue light. Visible magic… he'd missed it.

He took half a step forward and flicked the knife over his bare wrist. The blade caught the sun as a couple of drops of his blood fell. He should say something, but words were pretty much useless. Magic was about intent, not pretty speeches and fancy arm waving—though the warlocks liked the spectacle of both. The blood hit the stone in a flash of ruby light, and the scent of metal was on the air.

Terrance lifted his arm as though he were a wooden toy. His expression was blank and his focus internal. It was a look Angus had seen before—one that he'd probably worn many times in Demonside. Terrance wasn't used to the way demons did magic. He'd never seen the rituals or been part of it, and while he believed in paying for magic and keeping the balance, this was something else.

Angus ran his thumb over Terrance's skin, and golden magic followed, dulling the nerves so there'd be no pain. A fingerbreadth to the side there was a pressure point that he could use to make someone scream. He made a small cut, and a few drops of Terrance's blood fell toward the stone. Before they'd even hit, Terrance had pulled his arm away from Angus's touch.

Saka held his arm out, but Angus didn't use magic to take away the pain of the nick.

That was the easy part—the part where they were all equal, bound in blood.

Now for the offering—a deposit in the magical bank they'd be drawing from, a sign of good faith, just like the rabbits warlocks had once given their demons. But this time the sacrifice was human... and Angus wasn't a demon.

How could the knife be so cold? He wanted to wipe his slippery palm, but he didn't want to show that weakness, not while Iktan was watching. As head mage he had to be there. That Cadmael did not was a relief, though Angus had no doubt Iktan would report back. The giant bee things were quiet, or maybe his heartbeat was too loud. He put a hand under the man's chin and tilted his head, and the man whimpered, but held still.

Just like a rabbit.

He stared at the skin until he was able to see the bright nerves beneath and the pulsing blood. It had taken him a while to learn how to see. Usi had made him practice again and again on Saka. They were lessons he'd never forget, but the magic illuminated where he needed to cut. *One cut.*

The knife was so slick with sweat that he was probably going to screw this up. Better to wipe his hand than make a mess. He switched the knife into his other hand and rubbed his palm on his pants. Ready to make the sacrifice, he didn't wait for his palm to become sweaty again. He grasped the knife.

The slice was deep and sure, and magic poured out of the man in a thick, glinting ribbon of red.

Angus had to speak. "An offering for your service, Mage."

"It is accepted," Saka replied as formally as if they were on Lifeblood. "You have been my apprentice. Now you are a mage by the tradition of my people."

His apprenticeship hadn't been long enough. He knew less than half the magic that he needed to know.

Iktan's attention snapped to Saka. Making Angus a mage hadn't been part of the plan, but it had been Saka's. When Angus arrived and told him what was going to happen, Saka had reminded Angus of what it would mean.

But Iktan didn't say anything, and the blood stopped flowing. The man was dead.

Angus really should've asked him why he believed in the warlocks' cause before he cut his throat. Why would anyone want the world to be wrapped in ice and Demonside to be dry and dead?

He dropped the circle, and the gathered magic rolled out like fog and trickled away until it was so well dispersed it seemed to vanish.

Iktan and Saka picked up the body and took it to the hole that was easily half the size of a pitz court. It was several seconds before there was a splash.

What followed shattered all silence and calm—the splashing and deep reverberation as the creatures fed. The knife almost slid from his hand to land in the puddle of blood that was still draining.

Terrance turned away, even though they couldn't see the creatures devouring the corpse. That was a small mercy. As fast as it had started, it was over, and the animals returned to whatever they did between meals.

Angus swallowed.

A feast had been prepared in town, but he wasn't sure he was hungry.

CHAPTER TWENTY-ONE

THE ROOM in Saka's house wasn't well lit, but Terrance didn't mind. He didn't want to look at Angus anyway, and he wasn't sure he could without something close to disgust or horror showing on his face. He thought he knew Angus, but the man who'd held the knife and killed was a stranger—a mage.

But Terrance was human… and Angus was still human. Yet in that killing moment, he'd been as cold as any warlock who decided who should live and who should die.

Angus dried his face and hands without looking at Terrance. He'd scrubbed his hands hard, like they were covered in blood, even though they weren't. "You're very quiet."

They'd barely spoken. Saka and Iktan had talked on the way back to the village. Their conversation about maps and telestones hadn't held his attention enough to stop him from reliving the instant the blade had cut deeply. He rubbed his thumb over the small cut Angus had made. It would heal on its own and wasn't worth the cost of magic, but he wouldn't let a scab form. The more he rubbed, the redder it became and the more blood oozed out. He needed to leave it alone and stop picking. "Thinking."

"Don't."

"Is that what you did? You stopped thinking and just did as you were told like a good little warlock?"

Angus crossed the floor in three steps. His voice was low and edged in razors. "What would you have had me do? Let him go? This was for the demons, not the priests. It's their ritual for giving up their freedom to work with us."

"Saka wouldn't have wanted death." He kept his voice equally low, not knowing who was on the other side of the thin wall.

Angus shook his head. "Don't talk to me about what Saka would want. I've seen him kill humans on Lifeblood. I know how to use the knife for pleasure and pain because he taught me."

Who was this man? "I thought you were learning how to heal."

"I have been. But that's just one part of the same magic."

"You don't even care. You've justified it in your head. Now you're a *mage*."

"Is that what you're pissy about? Do you think I wanted that? I'd like to have skipped the whole thing. I don't like death or magic drawn from fear and pain, but sometimes it has to be done."

"I've heard warlocks say much the same." Terrance stood. He needed to get out. Celebrating was the last thing he wanted to do.

Angus grabbed his arm. "There's a difference between justifying and making peace with what has to be done. That man was a spy, and he was looking for me. There's a price for my return to Vinland. What do you think will happen to me when I'm there? Will they give me some wine and have a little chat or will they peel the skin from my body and return me piece by piece to Demonside?" Angus released him. "Maybe you'd like to collect that reward."

"Don't be stupid."

"What should I be? Cold like a warlock, or stupid like some kid who never even wanted magic in the first place? I'm not that person anymore."

"I can see that. But have you stopped to think about who you're becoming?"

"I told you I'd do what it took to return the balance, and I meant it. I never meant to drag you into it."

"What do you want from me?" Was he an afterthought? A convenience? Angus had never made him feel like that, but how well did he really know him. How could he love someone who killed so easily?

"A friend. A lover. Someone who wasn't part of this. I want more than this." Angus flung his hand out and then let it fall to his side.

"What more is there?"

Angus had everything—power and status—and he could use magic far better than many of the third-year warlocks Terrance had known. The college had wanted him watched even before he was taken by Saka on the day of the demon summoning. That's why Angus had gotten a fucking mage as his demon. No one got a mage as their demon… except maybe the Mayans. No warlock.

Maybe Angus wasn't a warlock after all.

Terrance didn't know what he was.

"What did you want from life? To play rugby and to defect. You've done that. Now what?"

"I don't know." Terrance had no other plans because he couldn't make any while they were perching on the whim of the Mayans. They could be knocked off at any time, and they'd land in the hungry mouths of whatever waited below. The moans of the things in the hole still echoed in his bones. He had no doubt they'd haunt his sleep too. "I was only ever a rugby player trying to find a way out."

Angus should never have looked twice at him, but they were stuck together. He wanted that, and he still loved Angus. He just didn't know how to love him right now. He couldn't brush the murder aside as being for ritual or magic or the greater good. Maybe he'd never believed in any of that. There was no greater good. There was only one life, and it was for the individual to make it good.

"I don't believe that. You have magic and a good heart. You could do anything."

Terrance shook his head. "I can't be like you."

Angus looked at the ground. "I wouldn't wish that on anyone."

CHAPTER TWENTY-TWO

ANGUS STRAIGHTENED the suit he'd been given. He tugged at the cuffs and tried to feel comfortable. But it was constricting. He'd only ever owned one suit, and that was for his grandmother's funeral when he was sixteen. It wouldn't have fit him now even if he had it. This suit was Mayan style—blue with fine purple stripes. It was nice enough, if one liked bright suits. But he was getting used to seeing them, and they were prettier than the gray or black clothes his father had worn —no Vinnish man would wear anything so bright and bold.

He combed his hair and did his best to make it look something close to civilized. It was full of blond streaks from the desert and well past time for a haircut. He should've done that yesterday, but he liked the way Saka ran his fingers through it and pulled him close for a kiss.

That was all that had happened after the feast.

With his blood full of the demon-brewed alcohol, he'd wanted more and so had Saka. They stole a few kisses but couldn't do more because it would be wrong to exclude Terrance, especially with him there drinking silently and waiting to go back to Humanside. He'd barely made eye contact with him or Saka. Angus pressed his lips together.

He'd wanted to stay the night. He'd thought that, with the three of them finally together and not fighting for survival….

But no. Terrance was still doing his best to avoid him.

There was nothing he could do about his hair or Terrance at the moment.

He had no idea what he was going to say to the World Council of Demonology either, but Cadmael had asked him to speak. They were holding a meeting in Uxmal, though only a few knew about it because of security concerns.

There was a knock on his door. He turned, but the door opened before he could say anything. His back stiffened at the intrusion, but then he smiled as Terrance stood in the doorway. "Come in."

Terrance hesitated and then stepped into Angus's room. "You look good."

"I look like I'm playing dress-up." Though his father would never have let him dress up in his suits.

The corners of Terrance's lips curved up. "But you look good doing it."

Angus had become far too used to loose-fitting demon-style clothing. He felt trapped in the fabric and buttons. "Thank you."

Such a formal thing to say when usually there'd have been kisses instead of words. He fiddled with the buttons on the jacket. Things had never been this awkward between them, and he wasn't sure what to do.

He had to believe he'd done the right thing. The alternative was too awful. But he wasn't a murderer. He was a mage. Was he going to have to talk about that with the WCD?

Saka had warned him that there were things mages couldn't discuss with nonmages. Where was that line and would someone explain it to him at some point?

Terrance leaned against the wall. "Do you think they'll cave to the demands of the Institute for Magical Studies?"

"I don't know." As the most powerful demonologists, the Mayan Empire and its affiliated nations had a strong voice, but if the whole world turned against them, would they stand alone?

The knowledge of demon magic would be lost if no one used it, and that would only strengthen Vinland. That was what he needed to say. While they couldn't fight magic with magic, they needed the knowledge and the ability to rebalance. Eventually someone would have to return the magic to Demonside.

"You know Lizzie is here now?"

Angus nodded. He didn't want to know what Terrance had told Cadmael to get that boon.

"Well… I just came to wish you luck, not that I think you'll need it."

"I do, and I appreciate it." Had Terrance forgiven him? Or at least reconciled what had happened? He wasn't sure if he should ask or wait.

Terrance scuffed the side of his sandal on the wood floor. "I shouldn't have called you a warlock."

"But I am."

Terrance shook his head. His hair was growing back. The dark fuzz that covered his head was long enough to tickle his palm but not long enough to wind his fingers through. Would he get that chance again or would there always be distance? "They act for personal power. You don't." He lifted his gaze. "The college didn't lie about what demons do, but they didn't tell the whole truth either. The sacrifices are needed. I guess I wasn't ready to see the reality."

"If the worlds are in balance, then there would be fewer and death wouldn't be necessary. Blood would suffice. There's going to be another pitz game." The priests were calling for volunteers, and they weren't hiding how dire the situation was.

"I heard. More death matches. Too many people are dying to rebalance."

"People are dying from the *im*balance and from the cold and the lack of food. Without rain we'll soon be out of water. Then it will be only days until the cities are filled with corpses. The warlocks are killing more in their quest to control all magic than the demons or the Mayans ever could."

"You have no doubts?"

Angus drew in a breath, but there was no anger or shock left in

Terrance. "I do, about everything. I don't know if I'm doing the right thing. What is that anyway?"

"I meant about the cost to you. You *are* doing the right thing, but I see the changes. You aren't who you were when I first met you."

"No one had tried to kill me back then. I didn't know what the rest of the world was like." How ignorant he'd been, how trusting in his country and his father and even the college and the underground. Now he trusted so few. "You don't like who I've become."

Angus couldn't go back. He wouldn't.

"I'm getting used to it. Though I think I'll be happy to leave you and Saka to do the magic."

"All of it?" Angus lifted one eyebrow. "Magic can be fun. Rebalancing more so." Or was he only remembering the release and not the agony of all-consuming lust? Pleasure had burned away any feelings of pain.

"For the moment." Terrance held out his hand.

Angus closed his fingers around the offering. "I know you never wanted another demon. Thank you for being my anchor."

"I couldn't let anyone else do it. Saka would've killed me." His eyes widened as he realized what he said.

Angus tightened his grip. Was Terrance afraid of what would happen in Demonside? "He only takes willing offerings. You have nothing to fear from him." Angus stepped in closer. He wouldn't let anything happen to Terrance. "I'll see you when I get back?"

They hadn't spent a night together since their trip to Demonside to cement the bond.

"I'd like that." He kissed Angus's cheek. His lips were warm, and for a moment, Angus could believe that everything was all right between them. It was a kiss to the cheek, as though Terrance weren't ready for more, but Angus wouldn't push. Perhaps they could talk about something other than magic, and slowly things would go back to the easy way they had been. That thin thread of hope was all he had to hold on to as he headed to the meeting with the people who could decide the fate of all demonology users.

· · ·

THERE WERE five people in the room. A tall woman who represented the African Union of Demonology, a fair-haired man from New Holland, a woman in a bright pink-and-yellow striped suit from the Mayan Empire, and two men from places Angus wasn't familiar with. From what had been already said, it seemed that their homes were surrounded by countries that had either banned or persecuted magic users, and they were being pressured to halt their use or face sanctions or war.

"We have to be seen to be taking positive steps, even if there is nothing we can do to stop Vinland."

"No matter how careful we are to rebalance, any demon-driven workings are being viewed as problematic. The Union is in danger of disintegrating, and one member country's recent election has swung toward those who want demonology banned," the African woman said.

"As we've seen before, that leads to all magic being banned and the users persecuted."

"Knowledge then goes underground or is suppressed, neither of which is beneficial."

Angus tried to follow the conversation between the five. There were a few priests and government observers. Every so often someone would be invited to sit before the table, where they'd be questioned about politics and the use of magic and asked to offer a solution.

"Perhaps we should put a halt on demonology until Vinland is stabilized," the man from New Holland said. "Not that I think that would stop the threat on our northern borders. The nonmagic users are being opportunistic, since we can't effectively defend ourselves with magic." His mouth turned down. The lines around his eyes made him look old, yet his hair wasn't gray.

"Could Ma—" The African woman glanced at the paper in front of her again and frowned. "Mage Angus Donohue come forward."

A few people glanced around to see who would get up. When Angus heard *mage*, he also wondered where the demon was. Then he realized they were calling on him. Cadmael must have listed that as his title, which meant Iktan must have told his priest. That conversation must have been interesting. The title didn't sit well. It was too big for him, but what else could he be called? He wasn't a warlock or a priest, but he didn't feel like a mage either. He didn't know enough.

With his heart beating hard, he stood and made his way to the chair, glad he couldn't see the people behind him or hear them over the pounding of his pulse.

Breathe.

It was no worse than facing the college, and these people weren't going to dig around in his head. He'd faced Miniti and lived, and he'd faced the council of mages. He would be fine. But they were all highly skilled magic users with years of experience who understood the way the world worked.

"A human mage," the woman said as she studied him.

Angus nodded. He kept his fingers laced together in his lap to keep his hands still and tucked his legs under the chair so he wouldn't fidget. He'd been called to the principal's office once at school when he got a little payback on the school bully. The other boy never received a day of suspension, because his father was a well-connected warlock. But Angus had spent the last two weeks of the term with detention every afternoon. His father, despite also being a well-connected warlock, had thought Angus deserved the punishment. They hadn't been speaking at the time, and detention hadn't improved their relationship. Angus should've known then that nothing he did would make his father happy. Would it be any different at this meeting? Would they judge him and find him unworthy?

A bead of sweat rolled down his spine, and his stomach tied itself into ever-more-intricate knots.

"Tell us how you came to be a mage when you should've ended up a Vinnish warlock."

He couldn't explain that it was an accident, although that was the truth.

But mages should always tell the truth. If he was going to be called a mage, he needed to act like one. While it was never his plan, he couldn't walk away now. If his story helped at all, it would be worthwhile.

Angus drew in a breath. "It was sort of an accident...."

CHAPTER TWENTY-THREE

TERRANCE WENT with Lizzie to a café that had become their place to get away from the Training Temple. She stirred her hot chocolate without much enthusiasm, and he couldn't even be bothered to stir it or to drink it. He hadn't gotten used to the heat from the chilis. He really wanted tea, but that was hard to find. Chocolate supplies were dwindling despite the priests' efforts to protect the crops.

"What if this is it?" she asked as she stared at her spoon.

"What do you mean?"

"This is the end. There's less than a month's worth of drinking water. If the priests don't magic some up, we'll all be dead a few days after it runs out. Some people are saying we've already reached a tipping point with the ice and it's too late. This meeting with the WCD isn't about solutions, but about curtailing demon magic." She looked up. "People are worried. Even here they're starting to suggest that maybe it's time to let magic go."

"Magic is a part of the world. There will always be people—wizards—who can use it."

"And maybe that's fine." She shrugged. "And we shouldn't be tying ourselves to Demonside."

"You worked with the mages and you still think we should walk away?" He might have done the wrong thing in taking the bond with Saka, but it had been for Angus, not the demon. Terrance wouldn't be able to live with himself if Angus got stuck in Demonside. This way he could summon him back.

"I don't know. I thought that maybe I should get a demon. Wek is supposed to get a priest even though she doesn't want to. I understand her reluctance. I'm not ready for a demon." She cupped her hands around her mug. "We're ruining their world."

"And ours." He took a sip, but the chili and chocolate didn't excite his taste buds. It was like mud, thick and cloying. "When Vinland has all the magic, I don't think they'll use it wisely."

Lizzie lifted an eyebrow. "Really? What gives you that impression?" She rolled her eyes. "If you were in charge, what would you do with all that magic?"

The right answer was "return it to Demonside," but the college warlocks wouldn't do that. "I would make sure that there were no wizards left."

"While no one knows for sure, I think we can assume those rumors are true."

There had been reports that wizards were being rounded up and killed. He'd come to the conclusion years ago that his parents were dead. If he'd stayed in Vinland, he'd be dead too, as would all of the other trainees.

Terrance nodded. "Well, I'd want to make sure that other magic-using countries would either join me or be flattened. I'd want to be the single magic-using power."

"So treaties?"

He shrugged. "Or threats. I mean some countries are already tearing down their magic users or passing laws or voting in antimagic governments. A world without magic."

People like Lizzie and him would have nowhere to go. The Mayan Empire was strong, but could it fight a war against Vinland or would it fold? Without its temples it would be vulnerable, because much of its society revolved around the use of magic.

Without magic there would be no Empire. It would crumble, and

Vinland would take over. Angus had already realized that. He'd saved them by taking them to Demonside, and he was speaking to the WCD to argue that they needed demon magic.

"I don't want a world without magic." *Or Angus.* Something inside of him squirmed and made his stomach roil as though the hot chocolate were poison. Angus would keep pushing until he died trying. Terrance had watched him learn new skills and had heard the stories from Saka. The more Angus learned, the harder he pushed.

It was his job to make sure Angus didn't go too far. He wasn't just Angus's anchor to this world. He had to make sure Angus wasn't consumed by magic.

Lizzie frowned. "What's wrong? Would it really be that bad? Magic belongs in Demonside, not here."

"And not in the hands of warlocks. It needs to be returned."

"How?"

He had nothing. Not a clue. "We kill the warlocks?"

"The last Mayan strike team was tortured and killed by warlocks."

The media had recounted the story with horror, but no one knew what to do.

A man walked toward their table, his blond hair bright in the sunlight. It took a moment for Terrance to recognize Reece, and he smiled. Lizzie and he had been asking around, searching for Emma and Reece. Word must have reached him.

Reece sat, his lips stretched into a painful smile. "Just act like we are having a nice chat."

"What?" Terrance's smile broke, and Lizzie closed her hand around her spoon like she planned to use it as a weapon.

"You have been asking about me, and word reached some other people—people who are interested in talking to Angus."

"He's rather busy today. I'll let him know." Terrance's gaze flicked over the occupants of the café, but they all looked ordinary. "Which people?"

"People who will kill me tonight if Angus doesn't come to the entertainment quarter." Reece didn't turn his head, but his eyes darted to his left.

Terrance didn't look over until he lifted his cup. Then he risked a glance. The hot chocolate was cold and slithered down his throat. He saw man and a woman chatting as though they were eager to get to know each other better. They didn't look Vinnish.

"I may not be able to drag him out."

Reece's forehead crumpled. "First me, then one of you will be next. They *will* get to him. Don't fight it."

Lizzie leaned forward. "Where's Emma?"

"Demonside. She figured she was safer there." He glanced down. "If you hadn't looked for us, they might not have found us."

"Angus was worried about you," Terrance said.

"We didn't want anything more to do with magic or Demonside. We nearly died out there. We were trying to be normal." Reece's voice broke. "We'd taken jobs at a farm and were making a new life. These people won't stop. Angus has pissed off too many warlocks."

That must mean he was doing something right. Terrance went to speak, but Reece shook his head.

Reece stood. "Bring him. If you tell anyone, they'll make sure you don't get to speak again." He leaned closer. "Traitors get their tongues cut out." He stepped back. "Bring him or there will be blood on your hands. I did tell them you'd be better bait."

"How am I supposed to get him there?"

"Tell him I have news. I'm sorry." Reece walked out of the café. He'd barely reached the door before the couple got up and followed.

If he did nothing, Reece was dead. And he'd be used as bait next. If he delivered Angus, then Angus would be dead.

Urgency prickled over his skin. He should do as they asked.

"We have to tell someone," Lizzie said.

"I like having a tongue." He wouldn't be able to kiss without it, but he wouldn't have anyone to kiss if he turned Angus over. "Maybe we shouldn't have looked for them."

"Too late now. If you take Angus out tonight, I will kill you." She pointed the spoon at him. "I know enough blood magic to empty you out slowly."

"So many offers of death today." He finished his cold drink and finally enjoyed the afterburn of the chilis on his tongue. He couldn't go to the Intelligence Temple. No doubt people would be watching. "I think we should get back to the Training Temple. I need to talk to Kabil about that telestone homework."

"You still can't use one?"

"No." But that wasn't why he wanted to talk to Kabil. Kabil could get word to Cadmael, and Cadmael wouldn't want Angus snatched. "But Kabil is a very good tutor."

He was sure doing the right thing wouldn't go unpunished. But the punishment would be better than living with the knowledge that he'd destroyed the one chance they had of stopping Vinland.

"For the record, this is a bad idea." Terrance didn't like Cadmael's plan. Too much could go wrong. Cadmael had come to the Training Temple, ostensibly to talk to a class of students who wanted to join. But that was for show.

Terrance pressed his tongue against the roof of his mouth. He was going to miss it.

Angus was still at the meeting with the WCD. "Angus should know what's going on."

Cadmael shook his head. "No, because then he will act differently or want to do something reckless, like save Reece."

Terrance winced. Cadmael was sure that Reece was dead no matter what. If he lived, it would be purely by chance. "And Lizzie?"

"The fewer who know the truth the better. We don't know who the spies are. How well do you know her?"

Terrance opened his mouth to argue, but Cadmael had a point. "You thought I was the risk."

"If you hadn't come to me, I would've been proven right. I'm still surprised." Cadmael scowled as though it weren't a pleasant surprise.

Terrance still wasn't sure it was the right thing to do. "You'd better protect him."

"I will."

"Why? Why do you care?" He needed a reason to trust Cadmael.

"Because he's done things that no one else has managed. There hasn't been a human mage in centuries. He survived a trek through Arlyxia and a clean sweep."

"You want to know how."

"I think it's important to investigate." Cadmael looked out the window. "Go and meet him. Tell him Reece contacted you and wants to meet up."

CHAPTER TWENTY-FOUR

THE SLANTING EVENING sunlight was too bright for Angus after being shut in all day. Too much talking had made his throat rough, and too much listening and struggling to grasp the enormity of what was happening around the world had blossomed into a headache that made Angus long for silence.

He'd be quite happy to lie down and see no one for the rest of the day.

As he walked toward the tram, he unbuttoned his suit jacket and slung it over his arm. Terrance was waiting by the stop, and Angus's steps faltered. How had he known where to come?

"I didn't expect to see you here." He leaned in and gave Terrance a quick kiss, well aware that there were plenty of people watching the two Vinnish oddities. He had no idea what the five people from the WCD thought of him. While he'd left out some of the more personal details, he hadn't been able to hide the nature of his relationship with Saka. Now everyone knew he was a demon fucker. He'd heard those words muttered over lunch. Even though people could dally with demons, not everyone approved of it, and some thought the practice disgusting. That was fine. No one was forcing them to get close to a demon.

"Cadmael told me." Terrance took his hand and gave it a squeeze.

The hairs on the back of Angus's neck lifted. "Really?"

"Yeah. He was at the temple and said you might like company on the way back. I know we planned to meet up this evening anyway. Did you want to get dinner? A drink?"

That didn't sound entirely like Cadmael, and Terrance was being a little too friendly given their recent distance, but maybe he was trying to make it up to him. "As glad as I am to see you, I don't think I'm up for going out."

The headache that had been a dull throb had exploded, and all he really wanted to do was get back to his room and lie down. He couldn't even face using magic to get rid of it.

Something flickered across Terrance's face. "Was it that bad in there?"

"It wasn't good. Interesting... in a terrifying 'I never knew the world was so screwed, and I don't know if magic will ever be viewed the same' kind of way."

"Demonology."

"All magic." Every magic-using country was being scrutinized. "But they're condemning the killing of magic users."

"I'm sure those being beheaded or hanged are glad about that. Maybe they should actually do something."

"What? Squabbles are escalating to battles everywhere." Angus raked his fingers through his hair. "I'm tired. Let's grab something to eat on the way back." He smiled at Terrance. "Maybe I'll feel better after some food and we can keep our original plans."

The tram slid to a stop, and they got on. Angus slumped into an available seat while Terrance stood. There was a pinch between his eyebrows as he glared out the window. Angus was pretty sure Terrance wasn't seeing anything that was whizzing past.

"I've arranged for us to meet up with Reece tonight," he said without looking at Angus.

Angus grinned as the tension left him. "Why didn't you say?"

"It was supposed to be a surprise."

"When did you hear from him?" Reece had survived the clean

sweep, but Cadmael would be annoyed that they were reconnecting with their friends.

"Today."

"And Emma?"

"Is in Demonside, apparently." Terrance didn't look at him.

"Oh… why?"

Terrance shrugged, his gaze once more on the window.

The prickly feeling that something wasn't right resurfaced. It needled Angus's skin and pressed into his heart. He reached up a hand to capture Terrance's fingers. "There's something else."

"No."

That was a lie. He let his hand fall away and leaned back in the seat to study the man who'd watched him for the college and the underground before he became his lover. Maybe he was a fool for sliding into bed with Terrance, and letting him share Saka. Cadmael had been worried. Had he been right?

He didn't want those thoughts. He wanted to believe that everything was all right, but ever since the sacrifice, everything had felt wrong. Everything had been off-kilter in ways he couldn't quite explain, and he had no idea how to fix it. This morning he'd thought the gap was being bridged, but it was as wide as ever.

"Do you not trust me?" Was it him? Was he so obsessed with magic that everything else ceased to matter? He was always taking off to Demonside. "I know I'm not always around—"

"It's me."

So it was him. Whenever anyone said "it's me," they meant "it's you" but were trying to be kind. "Do you regret joining Saka and me?"

Terrance sighed and shook his head. "It's me you can't trust."

The tram lurched and stopped. People got off, and others got on. Angus stared up at Terrance.

"What do you mean?" he managed to murmur when the tram moved again.

"I can't say."

"Then I won't go." What was going on? "What is Reece up to? What have you done?" He needed to be able to trust the man who held his life in his hands when he went to Demonside. He should be able to trust the man he loved. Did Terrance not love him? The fragile world he'd built around himself was starting to crumble. This time he'd be left holding nothing, and he refused to let go that easily. He needed more than magic and stopping Vinland in his life.

Maybe there was nothing more or couldn't be anything more until Vinland was stopped. Even if he did find happiness, it could all be snatched away. One clean sweep and it would all be gone.

Terrance closed his eyes. "What I had to." He pressed his lips together. "Cadmael swore me to secrecy. I shouldn't have even said that."

Angus's stomach contracted like he'd been hit, and nausea spread through him.

Of course Cadmael was involved. He should've realized by the way Terrance had been sent to collect him. That Cadmael and Terrance had teamed up was a little more concerning. Angus scowled and concentrated on his sandals. He curled his toes against the leather. He had two choices—defy Cadmael and have a much-needed rest, or go out and see what happened.

It would be safer and smarter to return to the Training Temple.

But he wasn't known for doing the safe or smart thing, and he was curious to know why Terrance and Cadmael had reached some kind of truce. Cadmael didn't trust Terrance. Where Angus saw a man who'd survived the only way he could in a country that wanted to imprison wizards and corrupt warlocks, Cadmael, saw him as a man without morals or spine. And now?

If survival had always been Terrance's skill, what game was he playing? What threat had been made?

He was the anchor. He was essential.

"Are you using me?" What was Terrance trying to get out their relationship… if they even had one?

"No… I love you. Not everything you do, but if it needs to be done, you do it." Terrance's fingers ruffled Angus's hair. "I'll make it up to you, I swear."

Angus would go out because that was what he did. He knew a

storm was coming, and instead of going into shelter, he'd meet it head-on. He lifted his gaze with anger simmering in his veins because Terrance wanted to share secrets with Cadmael and not him. Terrance should trust Angus enough to confide in him. He pressed his lips together. If magic had taught him anything, it was that nothing came for free.

Angus wasn't paying this time. He nodded, and his voice was glacier cold when he spoke. "You will."

THE ENTERTAINMENT QUARTER was already busy. While Angus wasn't the only man in a suit, he still felt overdressed. When they'd first arrived in Uxmal, the air had been sticky and ripe. Now it was dry and cool, and leaves were dropping from the trees. The sweepers tried to keep on top of the litter, but they were failing. The sky was visible through the branches where once there'd only been canopy.

The jungle was drying, and they were running out of water. The impact of the spreading ice was discussed at length. Everyone was suffering, but instead of everyone fighting Vinland, they fought each other. Some were embracing Vinland and hoping not to get a knife in the back.

Angus glanced over his shoulder. He was on guard, even though he should be relaxed.

Terrance gripped his hand tightly. "Please try not to look so spooked."

"Right. Wouldn't want to mess up your plan." He forced a smile, as though they were heading for a fun night out, but his temples throbbed with every beat of his heart. The scar on his chest burned from the magic he'd gathered to him as they sat in silence on the tram. He was ready for whatever happened, or at least he hoped he was.

While Reece might be there, Angus was sure it wouldn't be for a chat. Terrance hadn't gotten lucky and found Reece—someone wanted them to meet. They stopped at an outdoor bar with bright orange lanterns strung from the trees. Terrance sat at a table and flicked through the menu. "What do you want?"

Angus eased onto a stool, rested his elbows on the table, and massaged his temples. He let a little magic slide from his fingertips. Treating the headache, or at least masking it for the moment, would help him in the long run. "Whatever."

"You really didn't want to come out tonight."

Angus lifted an eyebrow. "My brain is trying to pry open my skull, and now I'm kind of freaking out about what's going on."

Terrance's grin was tight, but his voice was soft and sad. "I'm sorry."

Angus jerked his head in a harsh nod, and his head protested. He wasn't ready to forgive.

"I'll go and order." Terrance stood.

Angus took the menu out of his hands. "No. I will. I'm not sitting out here on my own. What do you want?"

"The chicken tortilla."

"I'll get two of them and the usual beer." He didn't wait for a response.

As he waited to order at the bar, he watched as Terrance scanned the crowd as though he were looking for someone. Reece? Would he arrive soon? Or later, after they'd had something to eat? Behind the bar, the kitchen was bright and the staff were chatting and laughing. Someone's kid had taken their first steps. Someone else was trying to pick an auspicious day to get married. Despite the way the world was teetering, people still had lives and were intent on living them. What else could they do?

He really needed to live a little, but there was no time. Every day was spent cramming in as much magical training as he could. He wasn't sure what he needed to be ready for, but the need to know everything had never been so strong.

He ordered and paid using the card around his neck. It hadn't taken long to stop reaching for his wallet. He didn't need it in Demonside, so not having one here was no different. As he made his way to the table he saw Reece walking over.

His face was fixed in a smile. And while Angus hadn't had a lot to do with Reece except on missions for the underground, he knew enough about him to know that Reece rarely smiled. He was one of those guys who always looked grumpy. Something was up, and it wasn't good. Reece's smile widened when he saw Angus, and Angus drew a little more magic to him. The heat from the scar was almost unbearable, but his headache had receded. He'd get through whatever came.

He reclaimed his stool and waited for Reece to sit.

"Good to see you." Angus meant that. He didn't wish Reece ill.

"Yeah… this isn't how I planned on seeing you." Reece's smile remained fixed.

"What *did* you plan?"

"Well, I was thinking of never seeing you. Maybe sending you a thank-you note for getting us out."

"Now you can thank me in person." Angus stretched his lips into a wide smile, knowing he was failing at making it natural. The area around the bar was getting busy, but they'd been to the area enough to know that this was one of the quieter bars in the middle of the week. "We ordered. Did you want to get something?"

"In a minute." Reece glanced at Terrance.

Terrance picked at a hangnail and dragged the strip of skin back.

Angus flinched and looked away. His gaze caught that of another man, and he could tell the man had been watching them. The man's eyes widened.

Shit. He really wanted his dinner before whatever Reece had planned. His stomach grumbled.

Terrance ripped the skin off with a wince, and blood welled. "I told you I owed you."

Angus grasped Terrance's hand. The magic in the blood was like nothing he'd ever felt. It wasn't fear or lust or even the excitement from a whipped-up crowd, but it didn't matter. He could use it. Something whistled through the air, and Angus threw a magical shield over his back. Something glanced off it and hit the floor—a dart tipped with green feathers.

Reece took off.

Terrance dragged Angus off the stool to the floor. The stones bit into his knees. He didn't drop the shield, but he needed to see what was going on. There were people running everywhere, and he lost track of Reece.

Reece had set them up. Angus swore.

A man lifted the dart gun to his lips, and Angus lashed out with streak of magic that knocked him off his feet. Someone barreled into the table and knocked him and Terrance over. His shoulder crunched on the ground, and metal flashed. Angus raised his hand, but it was too late. The blade was pressed to his skin.

"Come quietly, warlock, or die here."

"The reward is for me alive." He had wrestled for control with Saka too many times to just lie there. With a squirm and a hip flick, the man was off him. Terrance scrabbled for the knife and got there first.

Angus got to one knee, his pulse a hammer in his head and the magic leaving him too quickly. He needed more. Terrance pressed a blood-slicked hand to his.

He didn't know whose blood it was, and he didn't care. Magic shimmered in it.

He brought up the shield, trusting it without being able to see it. He stood up and made himself a target. Terrance stayed at his back with the knife.

"You want to take me alive? Come on. I don't have all night. I have other plans." Magic crackled across his fingertips. He didn't expect anyone to take him literally, but desperation made people do things they wouldn't usually do. He wouldn't have chosen to trek across Demonside, but it had been the only way. He was not being dragged back to Vinland where death would be slow and painful.

Where was Cadmael?

He wasn't there, but his people were. The fight was between three men—one now on the floor and several others who weren't wearing the green uniform of the military but looked like they knew what they were doing in a fight.

No one ran at him.

"Come on!"

The scuffles died down. Cadmael's men had two of the attackers on the ground. The man who'd held the knife to Angus remained on the ground until someone hauled him up to take him away.

Adrenaline made his hands shake. The blood was drying and tacky on his skin.

A man walked over.

Angus kept the shield up. People were staring, curious about this piece of impromptu entertainment.

"I thought you'd go to Demonside," Terrance muttered, "not fight."

"Fleeing didn't cross my mind." He was done with running, and Demonside only offered the illusion of safety. Besides, he wanted to know what had pushed Reece to this and why Terrance had insisted he come out, knowing that people wanted to kidnap him. "You owe me an explanation."

"You'll get it."

He would or he'd send Terrance to Demonside so Saka could get the truth out of him on the end of a blade.

The man stopped a few steps away. "You can drop the magic."

"Can I?"

The man pulled out his ID card. He was a priest. "I work for the Intelligence Temple. Mr. Erikson informed us there would be an attempt to take you."

Angus swallowed. Terrance had gone to Cadmael. For a moment he couldn't believe it. "Is that true?"

"Yes. I couldn't solve it on my own, and I didn't want Reece to be killed by them."

Angus dropped the shield. "Where's Reece?"

"We'll look for him," the priest said. "We'd like to escort you both to the Intelligence Temple."

There went the plans for the dinner he hadn't wanted.

"Can someone heal my hand before we go?" Terrance held up his palm. Blood flowed from the wound—he'd cut his hand to give Angus more magic.

Angus grasped his hand and used the rest of the magic he'd gathered, along with Terrance's own worry and sorrow—that was the odd taste of the magic—to do the rest. He'd truly been afraid that Angus would hate him or at the least want nothing more to do with him.

"There. Good as new." Except for the scar. Terrance would have to get rid of that when he was ready to move on.

Terrance ran his thumb over the scar and then glanced at Angus and nodded. He made no effort to erase the reminder.

The men who'd attacked them were being taken away as the people around them, who had been enjoying their dinners, milled around, unsure if they should leave or stay.

The priest held up his ID card. "It's safe to sit down. Danger's over."

Everyone was staring at Angus. He could feel their distrust like a wave wanting to drag him under. He hadn't caused the fight, but he'd been at the center.

A waitress walked up to them, her hands full. She glanced at the man from the Intelligence Temple and then at Angus and put the tortillas and beers on the table.

The tortillas smelled spicy, and his mouth watered. He needed to eat, but not there in the open.

"Can we get them to go?" Angus asked. He didn't want to eat with everyone watching from the corner of their eyes and whispering about the Vinnish warlocks.

The woman looked at him as though he were stupid. "We don't do that."

"The sooner we're gone, the sooner you can get back to business," the priest said. "Please make an exception."

Angus picked up the beer and downed half of it in a few swallows. It was exactly what he needed, possibly followed by several more while lying on his bed and letting Terrance make up for this disaster in as many ways as he could think of. His gaze slid to Terrance, but he was scanning the surroundings as though there were still a threat. They were safe. A man from the temple was with them. Without magic to prop it up, the masking of his headache slipped and his skull ached again.

The waitress picked up their order, and gossip wrapped around them until she returned. They followed the priest toward the street and out of the entertainment quarter. Suddenly warning rippled over his skin and then quick footsteps made him turn to see someone running toward them. Panic grabbed his throat, and he reached for magic too slowly. He regretted that beer.

The priest who accompanied them from the bar suddenly pressed a knife to Angus's back. "Not so smart, warlock."

Without magic, all he had was the hot food and leftover beer, so he lurched forward and swung the bottle. It connected with the knife and shattered, sending glass and beer everywhere. His breathing came in pants. The broken glass didn't stop the priest—if he was even a priest. He pressed forward with the knife, and Angus stumbled back, still grasping the broken neck of the bottle. He threw that, and the man sidestepped out of the way. But then he went oddly still as an arrow appeared in his neck.

A green-clad soldier climbed out of a tree, arrow nocked and ready to fire. The priest fell to the ground, his expression stunned as he lay twitching and struggling for breath.

Angus felt much the same way. He put his hands on his knees and tried to slow his pulse and dull the headache so he could think and focus without wanting to fall over. Terrance was several steps away with the man who'd been running toward him, the man Angus had been ready to lash out at. Was this one to be trusted or were they all Vinnish spies and Mayan traitors? He'd heard rumors of priests who envied the power of warlocks.

"Thank you," Angus said to the soldier. So far he was looking like the most trustworthy person there. He was also the one with the best weapon.

The people who planned the meeting with Reece had expected it to go wrong and had brought in either a fake Intelligence Temple priest or one they had in their pocket. Either way, without some immediate help, the priest was dead. He should be questioned.

The soldier checked the wound, and there was too much blood. "I don't want him dead. Can you stem the bleeding until help arrives?"

Sirens were drawing closer, and Angus wanted to leave the man to bleed out slowly, but the soldier was right. "Terrance, want some practice?"

Healing wasn't Terrance's strength, and healing was painful even with a skilled practitioner, but if someone couldn't soothe the pain as they worked, it was twice as bad. In an emergency, a healer would skip the soothing for survival, but this man didn't deserve any comfort.

Terrance gave a single nod. "Yeah."

The other man, the one who'd run toward them—to warn them?—approached slowly as if expecting Angus to lash out with magic. "I was hoping the traitor in our ranks would be revealed. Lozim has shamed us all."

"You'll excuse me if I don't trust you right away." Angus really wanted the rest of that beer, but magic and alcohol didn't mix at the best of times, and this was nowhere close to a good time. He shouldn't have drunk anything until he was safe in his room.

Lozim lay on the ground and gargled in agony as Terrance attempted to heal him just enough so he'd survive questioning by the Intelligence Temple. Angus had no sympathy to spare. His fate would've been worse if he'd been taken to Vinland, and Lozim wouldn't have lost any sleep.

CHAPTER TWENTY-FIVE

THE MAP now covered most of Saka's tent. With the help of Iktan and the other mages, he'd been able to reach farther across the sand. But the news wasn't any better. Many tribes were struggling to survive. Those without human contact seemed to be doing a little better than others, but they were all in dire need of rebalancing.

He had symbols for the human countries, and he was sure that Angus would know them and they'd be able to match them up. He could've asked Iktan to get a map from Cadmael, but Saka wasn't sure Cadmael would supply a map, and Iktan didn't offer.

While Iktan worked with his human, he still had autonomy and saw to his responsibilities as a mage. Most of what the mages did now was make sure there was water and food, both of which were becoming harder to source. And predators were stalking closer to the village as they grew desperate.

Demons from smaller villages were flooding in. Doorways that had stood for longer than anyone knew were no longer working, which horrified many demons because the priests would randomly appear. Although Saka was used to that, the priests were equally horrified by the change. With no doorway they were dependent on their anchors to return them to their side of the void.

The Mayans were so used to coming and going freely that the idea of waiting in Demonside was abhorrent.

There was no longer a steady trickle of humans seeking healing or simply visiting. The only people who crossed the void now were priests, and they were just as desperate for answers as everyone else.

Iktan and five other mages—the most senior in the area—paced around the painted tent. They had nothing more to add, and they all agreed that pushing further would risk damage to the brain. They were concerned when Saka explained what had happened the first time he stretched himself over the sand via the telestones. Words had been hard to find and form, and he'd needed to heal himself before he tried again. He didn't tell them that he would've died if not for Wek.

"We need to make copies of the map," Saka said. "We cannot lose this information again."

The golden mage still whispered in his dreams. She showed him the map and talked about lost things.

Iktan nodded. "It needs to be made in stone."

"It needs to be on cloth and carried far," said another.

While it was important to know where all the tribes were and who they worked with, that alone wouldn't save them. It would be useful only when they were safe.

"If the doorways are failing because there isn't enough magic to sustain them, perhaps we should take the magic from the many and devote it just to one." Saka drew in a breath because his idea wasn't complete and he didn't fully understand the magic that operated the doorways. He should be learning about them, not speaking about them. "If there were just one, could we shut it and stop the flow of magic to Humanside?"

All the mages stared at him.

They were like him, but all different. Their feathers and scales and fur were the obvious differences, but it went much deeper. Their magical workings with their humans were unlike what he'd grown up with.

But to close Demonside and halt the flow of magic would go against everything they believed and the Mayans believed in.

"The flow of magic is needed," the woman with the crest of red feathers said. Niri had explained to Saka that the doorways operated because of the flow of magic but that setting them up took great skill and not all locations were suitable.

"The flow of magic to Humanside is killing us. The closure of the doorways need only be temporary and only one way. Magic must be able to flow back to Demonside." It was the only solution that Saka had been able to come up with. It wasn't so much a solution as sticking a finger in the hole of a leaky jug while water still poured from the spout.

Iktan shook his head. "Every tribe would need to act, and most do not have doorways."

"We have a network of telestones. They can direct thought and more." He'd tried a few things, like growing ynns—the staple food for many tribes—from a distance, feeding them magic through the telestones.

Niri tilted her head. "We bind all tribes to our doorway."

"Yes." It was as awful as it sounded. Saka held his hands palm up. "I do not see any other solution. If we wait much longer, there will be no tribes left to contact. There will be no demons."

"Can it even be done?" a brown-and-red scaled mage asked.

"I don't know. But I cannot sit around and wait for the humans to do something," Saka said.

"There will be games tomorrow and a new tide of magic. As long as pitz is played, we will survive," the scaled demon said.

Iktan scowled, and his ears flattened. "Then perhaps with the tide we should make an attempt with the local villages and see if we can link their doorways to ours."

"If their doorways are closed, their priests and humans would be stuck here."

"We can't close the doorway without discussing it with them."

"It is our world, not theirs. Our magic bleeds through, and they have failed to return it." Saka fisted his hand. "While some do the right thing, many do not. We must protect ourselves."

"And what would your human—your mage—say?" Niri crossed her

arms and glared at him. She didn't like the idea of a human mage, even though Saka had explained that Angus had done what was required to become one, according to the customs of Lifeblood.

"He would agree."

"I believe Cadmael would too, though he would want to make sure that any humans who are here could get back."

"If we control the doorway, then we can let them return." How hard would it be to open the door so the humans could go home?

"I hope so. To trap them here would not behoove us."

"The priests will have limited power without us."

Saka smiled. "They will have to resort to using what is already there, like the wizards of Vinland and the many magic users around the human world who shun demon magic."

Iktan glanced at the demons gathered around the tent. "So we will shut down and link all local doorways to ours tomorrow?"

One by one the mages nodded.

"I will spread the word that we are attempting to slow the flow of magic." Iktan held Saka's gaze. "I do not know if I want it to work."

"If it fails, we have at least tried something, learned something."

Perhaps that was all they could hope for.

CHAPTER TWENTY-SIX

ANGUS DIDN'T WANT to go to the pitz game. He still wasn't comfortable with death and sacrifice being treated as entertainment. But Terrance insisted they go as a mark of respect for the players and their sacrifice. Because he had played, he understood what it meant on a much more personal level, and Angus hadn't been able to come up with any argument that didn't make him sound heartless.

While Terrance's life wasn't up for grabs this time, Angus was no less tense. Maybe it was the atmosphere around the court. On the roads leading up to it, vendors were selling food and drink. Others were taking bets on the matches and players. It was business as much as magic. In that regard it was no different from the rugby matches he was used to watching. In the stands the excitement and tension were thick. He could grab the energy and use it if he wanted to.

Everyone knew the reason the matches were held and understood that they would run out of water soon without them. This match would be used to bring rain and rebalance. And there were more blood matches than last time—more deaths.

When they arrived, the first few games had already been played.

Because they were considered priests, or would become priests, they sat in the reserved area. The distinction between magic users and others was clear. And while there were those Angus would've called wizards, they used their magic in defined ways that never crossed into the territory of priests. They were the ones who sought out demons in the entertainment quarter to gather magic for their charms and simple spells. His life would've been better if he'd been a wizard. But the college would eventually have found him and killed him. He'd have been caught up in the purges that were happening in Vinland, and worldwide, as fear got the better of people.

Angus raked his fingers through his hair, forced a smile, and tried to enjoy the game for what it was and not think about the fate of some of the players. The atmosphere thickened with each match, whether it were fatal or just for show. Although he didn't want to become caught up in it, the magic prickled along his arms and made his heart beat faster with excitement.

Toward the end of one of the fatal matches, he stopped watching the game. He heard the cheers and groans and knew it was still being played, but something else had caught his attention.

A small patch of blue sky had become bruised. There was a gray green smudge in the cloudless blue. At first he thought it was nothing —perhaps a cloud for the promised rain. But as he watched, it swelled. Then clouds bled through the blue sky and spread the green sickness. He elbowed Terrance hard in the ribs. "I think a clean sweep is building."

"What?" He cheered as the ball went to the other team. Not even dragging his attention from the court for a second.

Angus didn't want to start a panic if he was wrong, but if he was right…. Terrance wasn't going to be able to do anything. "I'll be back." He gave Terrance a quick kiss on the cheek so as not to distract him.

"All right." Terrance glanced at him. His eyes lit with fervor from the magic and brewing excitement.

Angus stood and made his way up the stairs. He'd only gotten halfway before someone in the crowd started yelling "clean sweep." Everyone looked up at the green clouds, and the ball hit the ground— usually the end of the game. No one cared who won. No judge called out the result. People started to flee to find shelter. Priests fled to the small temple in the sacrificial area.

He should go with them and be safe. But the magic was still around the court. It had been carefully gathered, ready to be used. When the clean sweep unleashed, there'd be even more available. He watched the sky as an idea formed. He could return it *all* to Demonside, not just the magic gathered during the games. Open the void and then shut it before the clean sweep could suck everything back to it. If the void was open when that happened, the clean sweep might suck out what magic was left in Demonside, which would be disastrous.

That the clean sweep was launched during the game meant someone had told Vinland. He hoped that Lozim, the traitor priest, was paying for his crimes and his pain wasn't going to waste.

Terrance raced toward him. "We need to get inside."

"You go." Angus used Terrance's shirt to pull him close and kiss him hard. "I'll be fine."

"No. You aren't going to stand out here and take it on." Terrance tugged his hand.

Angus stood his ground. "I'm not fighting it. I'm going to send the magic to Demonside."

"If it were that easy, then why has no one else done it? Come on." Terrance tugged him again, and the crowd jostled Angus closer.

He put a hand on Terrance's chest. "Because I'm the only one who's survived. I only survived because of this." He pulled aside the shirt to show the mark Saka had made. The scar glinted as though metal were in his skin. "Be safe."

"I'm not leaving you." He gripped Angus's hand and squeezed tight.

"You have to." Priests were calling to them. They'd close the doors soon. "I can do this. Tell them what I'm going to do."

"What if you don't survive?" Panic widened Terrance's eyes, and for a moment, Angus hesitated. He could hide with the others and wait until they knew more, but every day they waited was a day wasted.

There were many times when he'd thought he wouldn't survive.

He had to do something with all of his good luck, and this would just about use the rest of it up. "I guess I'll die doing something good?"

Terrance shook his head. "Don't be so careless with your life. Please."

Maybe he was a mage and ready to use his life for Demonside. "I think you are the only one who'll miss me." He gripped Terrance's hand hard and didn't want to let go, but he had to. If Terrance stayed outside, he'd die.

"That's not true. The college really wants you."

Angus managed a small laugh. "I'd hate to disappoint them."

"Please. Come with me. Let the priests do this."

But the priests weren't doing it. "I can't. I don't know why the mark works, but it does."

"Maybe we should all get one tomorrow."

"You can ask Saka to carve his name into you next time you see him." He released Terrance's hand and gave him a shove. "Go."

Angus turned to watch the sky. He couldn't watch Terrance leave, so he tuned into the magic. He felt Terrance hesitate and then run. Would he get other priests to come and drag Angus in?

As the sky thickened and roiled, the air became sharp enough to cut his tongue, and the court emptied, he wondered if he was doing the right thing or the stupid thing. Just because he'd gotten lucky once didn't mean he'd be able to repeat it.

Sirens went off around the city, warning people that they were about to be hit.

Angus walked down the steps to stand at the edge of the court and stare down at the bare sand and the rubber ball the size of a human head.

He drew in a breath and tried to settle his heartbeat. There was no way to warn the demons that there'd be a huge influx of magic rushing through their doorway, and he hoped no one would get hurt.

Carefully he gathered the magic in the court to himself. The ball rolled toward him and the clouds did too, searching for where the magic was. How much control did the warlocks have once the clean sweep was unleashed? The clouds sank lower.

For a moment he did nothing but stand at the railing by the edge of the court, staring down at the sheer drop to the sand below, and draw everything he could to him. The scar on his chest burned through his ribs and branded his heart with the heat. While the pain made it hard to breathe, he didn't stop. He had to be ready to open the void when the storm unleashed—too early and it might halt, too late and it would suck the magic from Demonside. The storm could kill Saka and everyone there.

He took a step back, knowing it was too late to seek shelter, but that he could still survive even if he did nothing. Terrance would be telling the priests about his plan. But at least Angus was trying. While they generated emotion and death and helped to rebalance, the games weren't enough.

Even if he succeeded, it wouldn't be enough. But it would be something.

He grinned up at the clouds and lifted his hands. Magic sparked across his fingertips and made them tingle. If he were in Demonside, the magic would be bright around him.

"Well what are you waiting for?"

The clean sweep hit him hard, and he fell back onto the stairs, his breathing tight. Something was broken. A rib? He fought his way upright as the tide of magic swept over him, drowning him, smothering him.

One breath.

Two.

He opened the void, and the ground went from under his feet as the tide swept him up like he was seaweed. He clawed at the chairs, but he wasn't strong enough, and his back burned with every breath. His fingers slipped as the storm pummeled him, and the magic rushed to Demonside where it belonged.

The void beckoned.

He couldn't close it from this side. All he could do was close his eyes and let go.

CHAPTER TWENTY-SEVEN

THE CLEAN SWEEP was unleashed but never reached the building. Terrance glanced at some of the others. The storm was raging, and the small temple shook with the force of the magic, but the weapon didn't unfurl the way it had before.

What was Angus doing?

He shouldn't have left him out there alone, but there was nothing he could do to help. His unwillingness to dig deeper into magic meant Angus was facing the clean sweep by himself.

"We should do something to help." He didn't expect anyone to reply. When he'd told the other priests that Angus intended to stay and return the magic to Demonside, they had been horrified or assumed Angus had a death wish. They didn't want to do anything that might risk their own lives.

"What? If we go out, the magic will be sucked out of us and we'll be killed."

But the storm wasn't at that stage… not yet. How long until it turned? He was fast, but probably not fast enough to run to the stands and grab Angus and haul him to safety. Angus would resist and make it harder. He didn't want to be saved. He wanted to act. The longer

Terrance stood there doing nothing, the more he needed to do something until finally the itch to act became all-consuming.

"I'm going out." He stepped toward the door.

Two priests blocked it. "No. This door isn't getting opened until it's over."

"He's out there alone." Panic pitched his words higher than usual. He didn't like that fear was twisting him up inside. It was fine when *he* was facing death, but not when the man he loved risked his life. He couldn't deal with that and didn't want to.

"His choice."

It would take only seconds to attack and defeat the men physically, but they were already gathering magic to them. It whispered over his skin, waiting to be used. Terrance didn't need to see it to be able to feel it, and he'd never be able to take them on magically.

He lifted his hands as though giving up and then sprinted toward them, intending to barrel his way through.

A magical charge ran through him and took his legs out from under him. His cheek hit the floor, his muscles twitched, and a groan formed.

One of the priests leaned close. "Next time it will be fatal."

"Vinnish warlock probably wanted to kill us," another muttered.

He tried to console himself that Angus had survived the first time, and he would survive this. But something wasn't right. He lifted his head and tried to get his arms under him, but they were jelly, and his breathing was still erratic.

"The clouds are breaking up," a woman said.

"But it never hit us?"

"That's not right." Chatter erupted around the room.

Terrance forced himself to sit. His thigh muscles were still a little twitchy. The clean sweep had been neutralized. "Angus stopped it."

No one moved to open the door, so Terrance got to his knees and paused a moment to steady himself. The sky was clearing, returning to the bright, painful blue that promised no rain.

It was only when every cloud had melted away that Terrance

stood. He walked to the door and glared at the two priests who'd stopped him before. Neither moved. "I'm going out."

This time no one challenged him.

The door squeaked as he shoved it open. He swallowed and checked the sky again, but it was clear. Nothing was going to happen to him, so he let the door swing closed behind him and made his way to the stands around the court, expecting to see Angus sitting there exhausted and triumphant.

There was no one there at all.

"Angus?" He jogged down the stairs and peered down. The rubber ball was against the wall, but there was no Angus.

"Angus!" He had to be here somewhere. Where else could he be? "Angus!"

His voice echoed off the stone walls and came back at him. He was too late. If the clean sweep had destroyed Angus, surely there'd be bits… evidence. But there was nothing. Had it somehow swept him up and taken him away to Vinland? That seemed unlikely because the storm had never turned.

Where had all the magic gone?

His stomach hollowed out as the answer hit him—Demonside. Angus had let it all go, so he must be there. Terrance needed to get to a doorway.

Screw that. He'd open the void right here.

He had nothing in his pocket to make a circle, so he would have to rely on will alone—something he'd never been very good at. Angus was probably fine. He'd be walking through the doorway at the Training Temple while Terrance fretted. He worried at his lower lip and flexed his fingers. What if he wasn't walking through the doorway? What if he wasn't walking at all?

It was his job as anchor to open the void for Angus. Even if he did open the void, it would go straight to the doorway, not to Angus, but Angus should've opened the void to the doorway too. Angus should've been here, not in Demonside.

Had something gone wrong?

He closed his eyes for a moment and weighed up his options, but everything led back to the same place—the doorway. There was no point in breaking a rule when everything would be fine and he was freaking out for no reason. Angus knew what he was doing.

Terrance uncurled his fingers and sighed as he tried to let go of the knots of worry that had drawn tightly around his gut. He'd go to the Training Temple and wait.

Angus was probably already there, wondering what was taking him so long. Cadmael would want to know what had happened. He smiled. Angus's idea had worked.

Sirens trilled through the city as he got on a tram and hurried back to the Training Temple. He checked Angus's room and then his own, but they were both empty. The knots tightened. Maybe he hadn't come through yet, or maybe he'd gone straight to see Cadmael. There was an easy way to check.

He ran to the doorway, which was guarded by two soldiers, as usual. Then he scanned the log, but Angus hadn't signed in. Maybe he'd been in a rush.

"Did Angus come through?" he said in Mayan. "Red hair and spots?" He didn't know the word for freckles. How could he not have learned that?

"No one has come through," one of the guards said.

"Are you sure?" That wasn't possible.

The soldier scowled at him. "Of course I am."

"But…." Maybe he was hurt… or spending time with Saka… or…. There had to be a reason, but every reason he thought of ended with blood and death.

Saka would look after Angus on that side. So why were his insides knotting with the kind of fear he usually reserved for when he was tied up and in serious strife?

He stepped away from the soldiers and their knives and bows. Sweat trickled down his back, and his heart beat fast from the run and the panic that wouldn't let him go. Something wasn't right, but who would believe him? His mind churned over names until he settled on Kabil.

He turned and sprinted to Kabil's room, but he didn't respond when Terrance knocked. Was he at the Intelligence Temple? Cadmael would be there. Terrance needed to tell someone or go through the doorway himself.

He opened Kabil's door and peeked inside. The room was empty of life. Books were piled on the desk and a notebook lay open, but he couldn't read Mayan, and he didn't care what it said. He picked up a pencil and wrote a note that would hopefully be found soon.

Angus was outside during the clean sweep. He wanted to try something, send the magic to Demonside, I think. I've gone through the doorway to find him. He might be there.

Terrance.

It was a shit note that explained very little, but he didn't have time to write an essay. He left the door open, so Kabil would know someone had been there, and he raced back to the doorway. He was a sweaty, panicky mess when he got there. The soldiers scowled as he put his name in the logbook so there would be a record of him leaving. He shouldn't be going. He was the anchor.

The cold of the void was what he needed to cool his blood, but it was gone too fast. Instead the heat and sweet air of Demonside enveloped him as soon as he was through.

Six mages stood around the stone platform. On either side of Terrance were stone pillars that he remembered from their rescue. Back then he hadn't known it was a doorway that limited comings and goings.

The mages looked at him, and he stared back. It seemed that he had interrupted something. He was relieved to see Saka, but there was no sign of Angus. His heart edged higher in his throat.

"Why are you here?" Iktan asked.

Terrance turned to him. "Angus… he should be here."

"Why would he be here?" Saka's voice was level, but his words were cautious.

"There was a clean sweep during the pitz game." That was when he realized the ground was wet and the stones slick. The air was more humid than he'd ever felt it, like moisture would bead on his skin at any moment. Fuck, he was thirsty. He swallowed, but his throat was dry. "Angus stayed out to try and send the magic here. It rained? It worked?"

"It was more than usually comes through from a pitz game." Iktan's ears flattened as he spoke.

"Where's Angus?" Why was no one freaking out? "Why are you all here?"

"He opened the void to send the clean sweep through?" Saka stepped forward and took Terrance's hand to stop him from waving it around.

"Yes. Well, that's what he said he was going to do." Terrance licked his lips. His breath was still coming in short pants. He should have known better than to come to Demonside without water, sunscreen, or hat. He wasn't prepared for a search and rescue. Or was he over-reacting?

"The magic didn't come through this doorway," Saka said looking to Iktan.

"That was odd," Iktan concurred. "By rights it should've."

"So he came through a different doorway?" Still no one was doing anything. The mages were all standing, still waiting for him to leave. "He was in Uxmal. It should've been this doorway. Why isn't he here?"

Saka closed his eyes. His chest lifted as he took a deep breath and then spoke. "He is here, and he isn't dead."

"How do you know?" Though if anyone would know, it would be Saka. He wanted to shake the answers out of the demon. How could he be so calm?

Saka opened his eyes and stared at him. It was too easy to fall into the bottomless black and get lost in them.

Saka tightened his grip on Terrance's hand. "Because I can feel the connection, and if you tried, you'd be able to too."

Terrance lowered his gaze to his sandaled feet. He probably should've tried that. "I knew something was wrong during the clean sweep, but I didn't go out and help him." But if he had, he'd be dead. He couldn't do what Angus did.

"That he is alive after facing a clean sweep is no small achievement," Iktan said.

Terrance lifted his gaze. "But if he isn't in Uxmal and he isn't in town… where is he?"

CHAPTER TWENTY-EIGHT

Every breath hurt like someone was driving a knife into his back. There was a lump on the back of his head that felt like half a rotten orange, and he was saturated. Water dripped off his hair, landed on his nose, and rolled down until it fell off the end. He lay on the stones, staring up at the sky, and let the rain pummel him, only forcing himself upright when it stopped.

He'd come through *a* doorway, but not the one he should've come through at the village. The stones on the ground were broken, and one of the pillars was half crumbled. But he recognized the view because he'd been on his back when he was here with Saka.

That time had been infinitely more pleasurable.

He touched the lump on his head again. It had stopped bleeding, but he was more concerned about his ribs. Breathing hurt... and he was alone.

Wek wouldn't be nearby in a tent half hidden by the trees, and Saka wasn't going to suddenly appear.

This old, supposedly broken, doorway was several days from the nearest village. He took a careful breath and tried not to let panic take hold. He might as well have been on the other side of Demonside. No help was coming.

He reined in his thoughts. That wasn't true. Terrance should be able to open the void for him. He must have realized he was missing, but no one had come for him. What was the point of having an anchor if it didn't work when it needed to?

"Come on, Terrance," he muttered. But with every heartbeat his hope sank. Terrance would be expecting him to come through a doorway. Would he have realized something was wrong?

If he had… why was he not being the anchor?

Angus sat and waited for the void to open, but it didn't. He couldn't sit and wait, and he didn't even know how long he'd been there, exhausted and unable to move as the rain fell and flattened him to the stones. He'd brought the rain and he'd bathed in that satisfaction but despite the heat in the air and the steam rising from the ground, he was cold to the core. He'd always been told not to wander alone in Demonside. Aside from what he was wearing he had nothing with him—his ankle was naked of bells and he had no knives. If he stayed put, predators would see him as a wounded, easy target, which he was.

He needed to do something, get himself to a doorway—one that was open to Humanside. This one was supposed to be dead, but it had worked well enough for him. He pressed lips together in a grim smile. Maybe he'd *made* a doorway with that rush of magic.

He knew what he didn't have. What he did have were clothes that covered him fairly well, so at least he wouldn't burn too fast and sandals, also useful.

He checked his pockets but found nothing.

His ID card was still around his neck, but he couldn't buy his way out of this trouble.

He forced slow, shallow breaths while his heart beat hard, driven by fear. Terrance would've already noticed he was missing. It wouldn't matter where he was, he was far enough away from the working doorway that the void would open near him, just like it had when he came through to Saka. All he had to do was survive for a little while.

But he had a limited amount of time before Demonside sucked the magic and marrow out of his bones and left him a husk in the…

jungle. At least there were trees, and he kind of knew the path Saka had taken to get to the village. He could make his way there, and he had to believe that Terrance would open the void soon.

He used the pillar to stand, but each breath was a fresh pain. He wasn't going to get far with broken ribs or be able to fight off predators, and any magic he used would hasten his death.

Angus leaned against the pillar and reached for any magic he could. Then he brought up a circle around the doorway. It crackled as blue and bright as always and felt familiar and safe. He gritted his teeth to ready himself for the pain of healing. He wanted to spill blood to help, but he knew he had to work with magic drawn from around him, not from within him. It was much harder to wield, but even a half-healed bone was better than one that was totally broken. Heat laced through his back, spread along his ribs, and constricted his breathing until stars bloomed in his already-tender head. Tension locked his jaw, but he pushed on until he felt the bones start to knit.

He held out for another two heartbeats and then quit and leaned on the pillar for support so he didn't crumple to the ground again. A sob escaped, but his breathing was easier.

The circle fell, and he was slightly less wounded but still alone in Demonside. His stomach rumbled, but he had no food, and it had stopped raining, so he had no water. Even with all the magic in the world, without water he'd be dead by tomorrow.

CHAPTER TWENTY-NINE

Kabil had been waiting for Terrance at the doorway when he came back from Demonside. He was annoyed that Terrance had been in his room and horrified by the note. They went to the Intelligence Temple straight after but were forced to wait for Cadmael because there was some other crisis happening. The doorways in other cities weren't working, but if they weren't working, why couldn't he get to Angus?

Terrance ran his hand over the fuzz on his head. What was going on?

The round mat on the floor was his focus for the circle, and the void shimmered open. Once again a guard stuck his head through and rolled his eyes, unimpressed that Terrance was trying a fourth void opening in minutes.

"Are you thinking of Angus?" Cadmael asked again.

"Yes," Terrance snapped.

"Then he must be within the area serviced by the doorway." Cadmael glanced at the jade skull on his desk. "I need to respond to this." He placed his hand on the skull and closed his eyes.

Terrance glanced at Kabil. "What do we do now?" The area serviced by the doorway couldn't be that big.

Kabil put his finger to his lips.

If it weren't for the stupid doorways, he'd have been able to open the void next to Angus and they'd be having dinner and laughing about how Terrance had freaked out.

Cadmael's features twisted, but not in anger. He was supposed to know everything, and Terrance didn't like to see his confusion.

Cadmael jerked his hand away, and his scowl deepened. "More cities are reporting that their doorways no longer work."

"What do you mean? Our doorway works," Kabil said, his concern echoing Cadmael's.

"People can go through, but they end up at our doorway in Arlyxia instead of their own. What exactly did Mage Angus do?" Cadmael stared at Terrance.

"I wasn't with him." If he had been, maybe Angus wouldn't be lost in Demonside. "He said he was going to send all the pitz magic and the clean sweep to Demonside. He didn't want the Vinnish to take that magic." It was a hasty but good theory. And Saka was sure Angus was alive and had vowed to get him back. If it had been any other demon, Terrance wouldn't have trusted their word, but Saka loved Angus enough to leave his tribe. If that didn't count for something, then nothing mattered.

"Maybe the pathways were overloaded," Kabil suggested.

Maybe, but Terrance didn't think so. "There were six mages gathered at the doorway when I went through." Not one of them had answered his question about why they were there. Had they been about to bind the doorways?

If all doorways went to the same one, how big was that area? They'd never find Angus before Demonside drained him of magic or something ate him. He had to think. Before his thoughts could get too wild, he drew in a breath. "Unbind them or something. There has to be a way for me to reach Angus, otherwise what's the point of being an anchor?"

"If the mages bound them, we can't unbind them. Doorways are set up by priests and their demons. To create one takes a huge amount of magic," Cadmael said as though speaking to a child.

"I don't care about the doorways. How do we get Angus back?"

Both priests were silent for too long. Finally Kabil spoke. "If the mages have limited void opening to one doorway, they must be trying to limit the flow of magic."

"In theory, they can then close the one doorway," Cadmael said.

Terrance didn't need that explained. Demonside would be shut with Angus on the wrong side.

CHAPTER THIRTY

"IF WE CLOSE THIS DOORWAY, we will not be able to open it." Saka stood almost toe to toe with Iktan. It would never end in a fight, but it was coming close.

"You are only worried because your human is out there."

"Would you also not be worried if your human were out there?"

Iktan shrugged. "Cadmael knows the risks."

"Angus did this to help us. To trap him here is a death sentence. It would also be foolish when he is the only one who can redirect a clean sweep to us." It was a small strike at Vinland, and it had only returned a fraction of the stolen magic.

Iktan's ears twitched in annoyance. Saka had wrapped the tip of his tail into the leg of his pants to prevent such an obvious sign of irritation. "If we leave it open, Cadmael may come through and demand answers."

Saka crossed his arms. "Let him. And tell him the truth. We must protect what we have left. They can still rebalance, but they cannot come and go as they please anymore."

"Except that is what you want for Angus," Iktan muttered.

Saka inclined his head, admitting that was a flaw in his argument. He wanted to protect Demonside, but he also wanted to save Angus.

"On the third evening we will shut it. He will be dead by then if he has not been found." Iktan sighed. "If we spread the word, the humans still on this side will have a chance to get home. We will do what is right."

"Send a message with them. Tell Cadmael what we intend." It was important that the priests understood.

Iktan's ears twitched again. "Not everyone is as close to their priest as you are to yours. While we work with them, we would not risk our lives to save them."

If Iktan wouldn't send a message, Saka would. The priests needed to know the truth if they were to continue working together. Angus would need human allies.

But first he had to find Angus. He had a direction, a pulling in his heart when he reached out. "You will allow demons to help with the search?"

"I will. Winged hunters can fly out in the direction you indicated to see if he is out there." Iktan touched Saka's arm. "We may already be too late."

Saka wouldn't believe that. "Angus has been trained in how to survive. He is alive."

The lessons had been a great cause of frustration and grief between them, but Saka had refused to let his heart get in the way. This time his heart was far too vulnerable.

CHAPTER THIRTY-ONE

ANGUS PICKED up a piece of rough stone that had fallen from the broken pillar. It was dull and gray, nothing like the stones he'd once chosen, which had been smooth and colorful. But he didn't care what it looked like, only that he already had a connection to this place and these stones, and he intended to exploit it so he didn't have to use as much energy to create a telestone.

He put the stone in his pocket. Every movement made his skull thump, though the head injury was just a bump and not worth healing. He'd have been worried if there were no lump and just the pain. Terrance had once told him that indicated internal swelling, which was most definitely not good.

Terrance hadn't opened up the void for him to return, which was the whole point of having an anchor—someone on the other side to open the void for him. It worked when they did it at the pitz court in the park, and it should be working now... unless something had happened to Terrance.

He couldn't worry about that until he got to the village, and he had to survive to get there.

When Saka sent demons out to look for him, they'd need to know where he'd been and which way he'd gone. He glanced at the fallen rocks and then the trees. It would be easier to move the rocks off the doorway site and then make an arrow out of them on the dirt. He made sure to put it in the clearing so winged demons could see it— not that he'd seen any signs of a search party yet.

They will come.

That kept him going when he squeezed his shirt for any lingering moisture from the rain. His head pounded from the injury and the thirst, and it was only going to get worse, but he couldn't even attempt to draw water up until he'd walked away from here and was ready to rest for the night.

Shit. He was going to have to walk at night and rest through the day as he had before to avoid the heat and sun.

For a moment he considered staying where he was, but he quickly decided against it. If there was no search party because they thought he was dead, he needed to get himself to any village.

He glanced at his arrow and made sure it pointed toward the village. Then he set off.

There were rivers. Maybe he'd be lucky enough to find one. Yeah, and maybe he'd stumble across a three course dinner laid out just for him.

When the sun set, the insects came out. They filled his ears with their humming and nipped at his skin. He shuddered and hoped that he wouldn't have to pick larvae out of his flesh... again. His mouth was dry, like he'd been eating sand, and the headache was blinding. Every heartbeat hurt. He'd given up singing as he used to do when walking in Demonside. There were no riverwyrms, so what did it matter?

He needed water and a rest before he could continue. The trail was still a narrow thing, and the canopy blocked the stars and cast everything in deep, velvety shadows. He hadn't even made it to the next clearing, and there was no chance he would make it to the village anytime soon. It would take too many days. That thought alone made him want to sit and rest, but Saka had warned him about that urge. It was better to keep moving and keep to a routine.

A drop of water fell on his head, and something scuttled above him in the branches. Water was caught in the leaves. He'd feel better after a drink, and if there was water up there, it would be easier than drawing it out of the ground. He reached up and then bit back on his gasp of pain as he pulled himself up onto the branch. Starlight made the leaves gleam like emeralds, and rain had been captured in the cups formed by the leaves. Swarms of insects hovered around the tiny ponds, and other scaly things were catching them with long tongues.

Angus stayed still and watched. If he drank the water, it was going to be full of things—eggs and larvae and the bodies of adult insects that had fallen in. He peered into the pond closest to him. It was going to be crunchy water—more of a meal.

He needed to eat. His stomach was a hard knot of hunger, but even his stomach wasn't sure about the wriggling life that was forming in the pond. When it rained in Demonside, life happened fast. Things woke and bred and laid eggs and died or hibernated to wait for the next rain.

The water would be undrinkable soon, putrid or dried up. He should make the most of it. *Easy dinner.*

He repeated the mantra, lowered his face into the cup, and drank. The insects got stuck in his teeth, and he had to chew or swallow the lumps. He gagged but kept going. He needed the water. When that cup was empty, he moved to another one and another until his thirst was quenched and his stomach full of wriggly squirmy things that tasted sour when he bit them.

It was only as he sat and watched the tongued things eat that he wondered if the insects were toxic. Too late now, and at least he wouldn't die of thirst. Reluctantly he slithered out of the tree.

Knowing there was water above him that he could get anytime he was thirsty, he walked faster. He had to cover as much ground as he could before daylight brought the heat and sun.

. . .

HE DRANK several more cups of water during the night and ate the contents, convincing himself that food was food and hunting would be impossible without the magic that he didn't want to use. He gagged each time but kept it down. When the sun finally arced higher, he was exhausted.

Whenever he stopped to drink, he used the stone in his pocket to carve an arrow and Saka's mark into a tree. He'd handled the stone all night, ready to throw it if he needed to. A number of things had stalked him, nothing had come close. His singing voice wasn't that appealing.

Or he was still too alive for them to risk attacking, which was a pleasant thought.

He stopped at a rocky outcropping that looked like it once would've held a stream. It was as good a place as any to rest—he was in the open where he could be seen, and if he curled up near the rock, he'd have a sliver of much-needed shade. It was that or get back under the canopy where he wouldn't be seen if a winged demon flew overhead.

He lay down with the rock, his stomach gnawing at his insides. He hadn't eaten enough. By nightfall the water in the leaves would be undrinkable. Another night alone. He squeezed his eyes shut as they burned. Tears would be a waste of water.

Pull it together, Donohue.

He sniffed a few times. He was a mage. He'd studied magic, but it wasn't enough to save his ass out here. Where was everyone? Had he killed all the demons when the magic rushed through? Was Terrance in trouble for letting him remain? Why hadn't he opened the void?

He swiped away a tear and forced his attention to the stone he'd been carrying. It knew him now, and he knew it. He'd committed every bump and sharp edge to memory so he could hold it in his mind perfectly, down to the fine crack. It wasn't a perfect rock, but it was much like him—it hadn't broken and it had once been part of something bigger.

He was part of Demonside while he was here, and magic was part of him. He was a mage, a warlock, a wizard, and a priest—a human in a place that craved his blood. He used the rock to make a tiny cut on his hand and fisted it as the blood smeared the surface, careful to only let the smallest trickle of magic out and then drew what was around him close. There wasn't much to be grabbed, and he hoped it would be enough.

He poured all of his focus into the stone, determined to make it work, and pain exploded in the back of his skull.

It was dark when he woke, and a blanket of insects lifted off him when he moved. His skin itched, and his eyes were almost swollen shut. The stone was warm in his palm and something nagged at the edges of his mind.

Saka.

His lower lip split as he murmured the word. While his body clamored for water, he ignored the physical and instead reached for his demon with a desperation that surged from deep within him. He let the magic flow until he felt Saka there, until Saka was as clear as if he were standing near him.

Saka smiled. *I knew you could survive. Where are you?*

Angus tried to call up a picture of the clearing and the dried-up spring. *Not close enough to the village.*

You are well?

Mostly. He'd been worse, though he wasn't brave enough to look at the color of his eyes. *I need to draw up water.*

I'll keep in contact. I'll send people your way.

You know where I am?

Yes. Stay where you are. Saka broke the connection.

As relieved as Angus was, he was still alone and no closer to getting across the void.

The moon was high when he gave in to the thirst. He cut his hand again with the stone and placed his bloody palm on the spring. The water was there, not too deep. He could reach it with a little more magic, so he drew from all around him, including the trees. A whispered apology would never make up for what he was doing.

A few drops of water fell from the edge, and he licked them up and used his enjoyment to feed the magic. Any strong emotion could draw up magic, but desperation was not the best. Pleasure had always been the one he could work with, and this was no different. The drops became a trickle that cooled his skin as it splashed over his face. He laughed and wet his shirt and hair.

Not long now until he was found.

A snuffling sound made him turn hopefully, but it wasn't a village demon.

On the edge of the clearing was something the size of a dog with a long ratlike tail. Its face was short and mostly mouth. It padded closer, following the path he'd taken into the clearing that morning. Angus moved up onto the rocks as quietly as he could. The creature swung its head in his direction and snuffled closer on its long spindly legs.

All he had was the rock and magic… and hope.

That was more than he'd had the day before.

The creature came closer and drank at the new stream.

I gave you that. You shouldn't be hunting me.

It lifted its head to stare up at him.

"Shoo!"

It didn't shoo.

He was not going to be eaten by a thing when help was on the way and he was sure he could hear voices and the beating of wings in the jungle—that or he was delirious from lack of food. Maybe he hadn't spoken to Saka, and it was all in his mind. He could call him to be sure but that wouldn't prove anything because he could be making it all up.

Shit.

The creature moved around the side and lurched up at him, a double row of teeth visible in its open mouth. Angus inched back, but there was nowhere for him to go. If the creature kept making that squealing noise, others would come. Maybe it was calling all its buddies to come—to the feast.

"Go away." He kicked out as it lunged again. It was quicker than he was and grabbed his ankle.

Something went crunch, and Angus screamed.

The creature tore his sandal off and came back for more. Angus threw his only weapon—the telestone—and put magic behind the strike. He didn't care if his eyes lost their color. If he was going to die, he'd rather do it on his terms and not as living dinner.

The telestone hit the creature between the eyes, and it stopped and crumpled.

Angus didn't move. He wasn't even sure that he'd be able to stand. His foot wasn't in its usual position.

No sandal, no telestone—if help didn't arrive soon, he would open a vein and be done with it.

CHAPTER THIRTY-TWO

"He's resting." Saka's lips were drawn down.

How hurt was Angus? Terrance needed to know. As soon as word arrived, he came through the doorway. "He's all right, though?"

Saka was silent for a moment. "A dhur bit his ankle. There is damage we can fix… but it will never be the same. He would be better having your doctors cut it open and mend it."

"There's no magic for healing now. No magic at all." The WCD had given their verdict, and it had rocked every demonology user. "The use of demon magic is forbidden except for rebalancing."

Many feared it would never be allowed again.

Vinland had ruined demonology, and possibly magic, for everyone, yet the warlocks were still having a tantrum. While they hadn't used another clean sweep on the Mayans, they had bombed a city close to the border in retaliation.

Cadmael was furious about the verdict and the realignment of the doorways. The feeling of helplessness was growing. It was a thing that prowled the streets and kept people up late. Terrance was starting to worry that it would never be all right and that Angus was going to kill himself trying. Maybe it was time to give up, but he could never say that to Saka.

"Your doctors can still operate to fix it," Saka said. "Your doctors need to do something. It's complicated. No demon can fix the injury. I asked."

"Why not? You healed him when he was stabbed. You can fix everything."

"I can't. Magic can't heal what isn't there." He paused. "Healing only helps speed up what the body is doing—stemming blood flow, knitting skin and bone and muscle, fighting tumors."

"But you do surgery."

Saka nodded. "We do. We cut out things that have gone septic or remove limbs too damaged to save. We then heal what is left. I can heal what is left, but I cannot recreate tendons and muscle that have been ripped away."

"Oh." It was bad beneath the bandages.

"If I could, I would. You know that."

Terrance closed his eyes as he tried to think up a solution. He was much better at following orders and game plays. He shook his head and opened his eyes. "If we were somewhere else, the doctors would do something, but the Mayan medical system runs on magic."

Some would say they were too dependent on it, but their society had been built on trading with demons and allowing the flow through. It was what magic probably should be, certainly better than the Vinnish method.

Saka snapped his teeth together and looked away.

Terrance narrowed his eyes. "You haven't told him."

"He's been resting."

"Fine. I'll tell him, but I know what he's going to say." He'd want the injury fixed before he threw himself through the void and risked death again. He wouldn't rest and recover even if they tried to force him. Angus was too tangled up in the struggle.

While he'd once dreamed of getting revenge on the college for the disappearance and murder of his parents, it had been just that—a dream.

Saka nodded. "That does not mean he shouldn't have the choice."

He led Terrance to where Angus was lying. The room wasn't big, but it was airy, and there were gaps in the slats to allow a breeze. A stone glowed in the corner and cast the room in soft light. It was Saka's room, Terrance realized. His things were on the table—knives, glass orbs, and the machete he sometimes carried. He forced his gaze to Angus so he could study how badly he was hurt.

His heart became lodged in his throat. At first he thought something was seriously wrong as Angus's skin looked bark-like, but it was some kind of paste that had been smeared everywhere.

"Is it that bad?" Angus's voice was soft.

"You look a little grubby."

Angus laughed. "To soothe the insect bites. It works."

"You're not in pain?"

"No, but only because they did something. I know my ankle got chewed up. I do still have a foot?"

"Yes." Terrance touched the toes on the clearly damaged foot. A bandage had been wrapped around the wound, and a dark stain had spread in several places. Terrance couldn't help. He wasn't a doctor, and he didn't know what was wrong. He sat on the edge of the bed and brushed his fingers over Angus's hand. "I tried to reach you. To be your anchor."

"I know."

"I tried, but the void kept opening in the village. I should've been able to get to you before this."

"The mages have brought all the doorways here. I went through an old one, that should've been broken but had somehow become part of the linkup."

"Why didn't you come through it?"

"Because it wasn't open in both directions. No one can open the void from this side." He squeezed Terrance's fingers. "Don't feel bad."

But he did. He couldn't get to Angus when he was injured. "I should've been able to open the doorway you went through."

"I'm not a demon, and you don't know that magic. There was nothing you could do... but you can tell me what's wrong with my foot. I know it's bad."

"They can fix it," Terrance said too fast when it wasn't even the truth.

"I know they can't or they would've already done it. What did Saka say?"

"How do you know he said anything to me?"

"Because he wouldn't speak to me," Angus said softly.

Terrance looked away. It wasn't like Angus would notice. His eyes were closed and his entire face covered in the paste. "If they magic it better, it won't be right, and Saka says you'd be better getting a surgeon to operate." He paused. "But the WCD has banned demon magic. You'd have to rest and heal in the hospital after."

"There's still natural magic that doesn't draw on demons."

"Yeah. But the Mayan hospitals are in a bad way because of the ban. If we were in Vinland—"

"We'd be dead."

"True." Terrance's lips pulled into a grim smile.

"I'd rather get it fixed now. Getting treated at a Mayan hospital isn't an option. I'd be low priority because it's not life-threatening. Even if I did get seen quickly, I'd still need to come back here to heal, and that won't be possible. The doorways are being jammed. We don't have the days to wait, Terrance."

Terrance nodded. He expected Angus to go for the quick fix, but he wanted him to stop and be safe. If he was in the hospital, he wouldn't be running around, trying to get himself killed.

"Please don't tackle a clean sweep again." He blinked hard, his eyes burning. "When I couldn't open the void to you, I thought I'd lost you forever." He leaned over and hugged Angus, sticky paste and all. He could live without magic but he couldn't live without Angus.

"I won't." Angus lifted an arm and returned the embrace. His fingers brushed the back of Terrance's neck. "I don't need to."

"Why?" Terrance glanced up, but Angus's eyes were still closed, sealed shut with the paste. He didn't believe for a moment that Angus was quitting.

A smile formed on Angus's lips. "Because I know how the clean sweep works, and I'm going to make one to deploy."

Terrance blinked, not sure he'd heard right. The words rolled around his head as he tried to make sense of what Angus had said. He was aware of the rise and fall of Angus's chest, the beat of his heart and the way his own had almost stopped. Angus wanted to make a clean sweep—wouldn't that be even more dangerous?

"We can take back the magic the Vinnish have stolen," Angus continued.

"That doesn't sound particularly safe."

"Magic isn't safe. That's why there are rules." Angus leaned up and kissed the top of Terrance's head. "Your hair is getting longer."

Who cared about his hair? "Does Saka know this?"

"Not yet. While I'm resting I'm working out what I need to do, creating the right kind of spell."

A spell. "You're relying on words?" Words were nothing, a simple focus for wizards who couldn't handle the small amount of magic they could grab.

"Not words, but a way of unleashing and pulling back. I need to control the tides."

How could one man control the tides? Was it all a fever dream? But Angus didn't feel overly warm, and he seemed lucid. "Surely you need more than one person?" The college had many warlocks at their disposal. If a few died in the process, they probably didn't worry.

"I do. I felt the warlocks controlling the spell, their anger as it hit me. They knew it was me. They didn't expect the void to open and take what they were using." He smiled again as though it had all been worth it.

The warlocks had recognized Angus. That knowledge chilled and terrified Terrance. The warlocks had already sent people to capture Angus, and after this they would be furious. "This isn't your war to fight."

"It's everyone's, but I know how to do it."

Terrance shook his head. "Even if you take the magic back, what's to stop them from taking it again?"

Angus was silent for a moment. "The clean sweep kills people who have magic. There would be no warlocks left."

Terrance's heart stopped. "And where will you be? How will I be able to get you if you're stuck here?"

Angus was silent for several heartbeats. He couldn't tell Terrance where he'd be. He would worry, and rightly so. "You'll be here too."

"How will we get back if the demons have closed the doorways?" He wasn't liking Angus's plan at all. Cadmael was furious that the demons were locking up the doorways so they all opened in one village.

"The doorway will probably collapse with the tide of magic."

"This isn't a plan." It was suicide.

Angus smiled. "But it will only take one wizard who wants a demon to open the void and reestablish a doorway."

CHAPTER THIRTY-THREE

ANGUS'S BONES ached from the healing of his ankle and foot. He wiped away the worst of the paste that had coated him and inspected the damage now that the skin wasn't hanging off it like so many white-and-scarlet ribbons.

The scars were red and angry, thick around the back of his leg, and his foot was kind of stuck. He couldn't flex it. The tendons had been ripped out by the creature's many teeth, and magic couldn't create new ones. He wasn't sure human doctors could either. Bitterness bubbled up, but he pressed it down. He was lucky to be alive… to have a foot at all. While he could no longer run, at least he could walk. That would have to be enough.

The paste and the night of rest had given the insect bites time to fade, and they were no longer itchy, swollen lumps. He needed to scrub the rest of the paste off and wash his hair—look presentable when he talked to the mages. Wandering outside in only his underwear and the residue of the paste wouldn't do him any favors, and he needed their support. He examined the remains of the suit, but it was a ruined mess, and he wasn't entirely sad about it. There were clean clothes in another pile—demon-style pants and a shirt.

Wearing just his underwear, he held the clean clothes in front of him and made his way to the bathing house. His steps were awkward as he tried to get used to the lack of movement in his foot. He didn't want to drag his leg, and his step was heavy and rolling, but it was better than lying in a hospital and spending weeks recovering the nonmagical way while the world froze. He didn't have weeks, and neither did the world.

They probably didn't have days.

He took as long as he could in the shower, which wasn't nearly long enough. When he was clean, his skin was unblemished by bites and his head no longer hurt. He searched for the lump, but he couldn't find even a tender spot. How much magic had been used to heal him? More than he could repay today.

But if his idea worked, he would return everything. If.

He needed to share his idea with the mages to see if it would hold up to scrutiny. Did he know enough, and was he strong enough? Doubts nibbled at his thoughts. The confidence he felt when he talked to Terrance had faded in daylight. There were so many ways it could go wrong… assuming he even got the backing of the mages and the priests.

And if he didn't?

The water shut off and he stood dripping for several breaths.

If he didn't, there was nothing more to do but watch the world go to war and magic users get slaughtered. He sighed, flexed his fingers, and watched as bright, golden magic sparked across the tips. He stepped out of the cubicle and found Saka waiting next to his clothes and holding a long wooden staff.

He held it out to Angus. "You might need it."

He might. It would make his steps easier. But at the same time, he didn't want to be dependent on something when he knew the warlocks would strip him of everything.

"Thank you." The staff was smooth and made of the bloodred wood that was so common in Demonside. He felt the weight of it as he held it, but he couldn't imagine walking around using it. If he'd had it sooner, he could have used it to fend off the creature that bit him. His knives and bells would've been a good idea too. It might be a good idea for him to always dress as though he were about to go to Demonside, as he had when he worked with the underground.

"What are you planning?" Saka leaned against the wall. He appeared calm, but his tail twitched.

"Planning?"

"You were talking in your sleep. Asking for the mages to listen to you. I am listening."

Angus hadn't decided if he was going to tell Saka first or ask to speak to all the mages at once. He picked up his pants and pulled them on, but his foot made it awkward. He'd never thought much about his feet before, but now they were everything. He sat on the bench with his clothes and held the staff in front of him. He'd been wondering how best to bridge the void. Maybe a simple stick would be enough.

He looked up, knowing Saka would wait for him to speak until the worlds died.

"I know how the clean sweep works. I want to use one against Vinland and return the magic to here." He rubbed his palms over the smooth red wood. Who had made this for him?

"How would it work?"

"I'd need to be in Vinland and open the void."

Saka sucked in a breath and looked away. "You can't go to Vinland. They'll kill you on sight."

"No they won't. They'll make an example of me. It will give me the time I need."

"And if it doesn't, you're dead."

"We're already dead if we do nothing."

Saka knelt before him and put his hands over Angus's. "You are a mage, but you do not have to give your life for Arlyxia or even for your world."

"I don't plan on dying."

"But you might." Worry filled Saka's black eyes. Angus had never seen him look so desolate.

"I might've died in the desert or when my father stabbed me or when the riverwyrm attacked or if the underground had turned me over to the college." He cupped Saka's cheek. "Someone needs to do this."

"Get the priests to. It is too much for you." Saka bowed his head. "My heart is cut in two—for you and for my people. I do not want you to do this, but no one else can go to Vinland in your place."

"Mages shouldn't have families, I know. But here we are. I need to talk with the mages. This isn't something I can do alone. I need you." If they all turned away, then he would fail.

Saka nodded. "I will gather them. I could not have had a better apprentice or a lover with a braver heart."

Angus kissed him, and Saka pulled him close. The staff pressed against Angus's chest. "You made me see magic as it should be. I should be thanking you." He sniffed as his eyes burned. It wasn't goodbye yet.

SAKA, IKTAN, and four other mages, including one that looked like a snake with a feathered crest, sat in a circle. Angus formed part of the circle, but while they had been studying for years, he was a nothing who'd had a bit of good luck… or bad luck, depending on how he viewed the last year of his life. He tried to move his foot. While there was no pain, it still didn't move. He needed to stop testing it and move on.

For the first time in his life, he wouldn't be able to run away.

Worse, he was running—hobbling—toward danger.

He explained how the clean sweep worked and how he'd create one to deploy on Vinland.

The mages were thinking. At least they hadn't said no or gotten up and walked away. If they agreed, he'd have to actually do it. Cold rushed through him and stole all the courage he'd gathered to simply take a place in the circle.

"You are sure you can create a clean sweep?" Niri, the snake mage asked.

"Yes." And if he couldn't, then it would be too late anyway.

"You should do a practice first," Saka said.

"The spy would learn, and the warlocks need to think I've been defeated." That was the worst part of this plan. At some point he was going to have to tell Terrance what part he would play. Angus didn't look forward to that. He wasn't looking forward to any of it, but who else had been inside a clean sweep and survived?

"If you fail, all the magic will be dragged out of Arlyxia and given to the warlocks. You were a warlock."

"And if we do nothing, all the magic is bleeding across anyway."

Mages offered their comments and doubts but none were helpful.

"No one has offered an alternative idea," Saka said. "All we can do is shut the doorways and hope the humans deal with Vinland. That is less of a plan and more of a refusal to help."

Iktan's ears flicked. "I do not like it, but I do not have another idea."

"I don't like it either." Saka held Angus's gaze. There was more in his words than anyone else would hear. "But I will do what needs to be done. I will do what you ask."

Slowly the other head mages agreed to the plan, but only if they hammered out the details before Angus left Demonside. He bowed his head, grateful that they would share their knowledge and add to his plan instead of leaving him to flounder alone.

It was late by the time Angus was done talking with the mages. He was surprised to see Terrance still in Demonside and even more surprised to see Emma with him.

"I'd heard you were here. I'm so glad the Vinnish didn't get you." Emma hugged him.

"They almost did… you knew?" And he'd be walking into their waiting arms too soon.

"I fled, but I had to open the void to get away. I've been making my way here with some of the other humans who are stuck now that this is the only doorway."

"If you opened the void…." A frown formed. "Then you must have a demon."

"Yes." She looked away. "Not a mage, just an animal. So I guess it's like not having one at all." She didn't appear thrilled with having a demon. "I won't be using it for magic. That wouldn't be fair."

Her eyes were dark, although she'd been in Demonside for several days. The skills she'd learned on the trek were saving her life again. If she went back across now, the priests would push her into doing magic or she'd be killed when his clean sweep sucked the magic from her.

"Don't cross the void yet. Stay here."

"Terrance said you were planning something." She stared at him for a few seconds. "Try not to die."

He smiled. "I'll do my best." But it wasn't a promise he could make, because he didn't know what would happen. It was all very well to think about it and discuss it, but a weapon like the clean sweep would've been tested on a small scale before becoming a city destroyer. He wasn't going to get that chance.

"Did you want to eat?" Terrance took his hand and led him away. His fingers were warm, but his smile was tight.

"You waited for me."

"Of course I did. I want to know what stupid thing you're going to do next so I have a chance to prepare. I know I won't be able to stop you."

Angus wasn't ready to talk about the plan yet. The mages needed to do some more work on the doorway situation. They needed to be able to shut down Demonside, and he needed to get to Vinland to deploy the weapon. Terrance was not going to like what Angus needed from him. "Let's not worry about that tonight."

He gave Terrance's hand a squeeze.

They were in Demonside, they were alive, and he wanted to make the most of that while he could.

"What did you have in mind?" Terrance watched him with a tilt to his lips that suggested he knew.

"I have to pay for the magic that was used to heal me."

"That was a lot of magic. Are you sure you're all right?"

"Fine, but you could help." Angus grinned. "It can feel pretty good."

There was a flicker of hesitation, but then Terrance shrugged. "Fuck it… we might be dead in a few days."

Angus shook his head. "No. Don't do it because of that reason. Do it because you want to."

Terrance stood in front of him. "I don't know…."

"Just me. Saka can watch… unless you don't want him there."

"He should be there."

Terrance's nerves washed over Angus. The first time he'd ever rebalanced with Saka had been part anxiety and part pleasure. "But he doesn't need to be. I want to show you that magic doesn't have to hurt or be about blood and pain." While he still had that chance. They wouldn't all be dead in a few days, but *he* might be. He put his palm on Terrance's cheek. "Magic can be good."

But Terrance had been pulling away from him since the last time they were both in Demonside. The sacrifice had been too much for Terrance to witness.

"You say, after nearly dying. I see magic hurting you."

"Magic didn't hurt me. That was an animal." Angus stepped closer. "I miss you." They should be closer than ever, but the gap between them had widened. And if what he was planning did kill him, he wanted Terrance to remember something good about him and have a nonmagical connection to Saka. They'd both need someone to lean on.

And he needed both of them.

Angus dropped his hand. He didn't want to waste his last night in Demonside. Tomorrow they'd go home and make plans, and the mages would work to close up Demonside, tribe by tribe.

"I miss you too, but I'm not cut out for this. I can't help you the way you need. I can't be a mage or a priest." Terrance glanced down. "You should've accepted Kabil as your anchor."

"No. You're what I need. You don't need to be or do anything special. I've never wanted anything else. You've always been there when I came home—the anchor who keeps me from getting swept away." While Saka was the lure of magic and Demonside.

A sad smile formed on Terrance's lips. "This is it, isn't it? You're going to do this thing as soon as we get back."

Angus nodded, and his eyes were hot. "Tonight is ours. They were going to kick us across the void after dinner, but there are some parts to finalize in the morning. So what's the point in going and then coming back?"

"Plus you said you told them you'd rebalance."

The mages knew exactly what kind of rebalancing that would be. But, unlike the priests, they didn't care.

Terrance frowned. "Can two humans rebalance without a demon?"

"Yes." Angus didn't know what he'd do if Terrance made him choose. He didn't think he could. Maybe it would've been better to go home for the night and finish preparing. Terrance was the distraction Saka always talked about. Mages didn't have family. They weren't supposed to fall in love, because love messed up your priorities and the tribe had to come first.

Saka had held their hands in the desert and said that he'd like to rebalance with both of them. That day seemed so long ago—a faded memory—when they were running from warlocks and toward possible death. This time Angus would be running toward the warlocks and certain death.

At the time, Terrance had seemed interested. Angus had thought about it many times while he was alone and safe in bed, but it wasn't Terrance who'd changed. It was him. He wasn't the first-year warlock-in-training he'd been when they met. Maybe he was pushing Terrance too far.

He opened his mouth to speak, but Terrance kissed him—not with the light brush of lips that was appropriate in the middle of the demon village—deeply and hard. Their teeth clinked together as their tongues met. Was that a yes?

"I don't want you to die," Terrance said against his lips. "I want you, and I love you… but you scare me."

Angus closed his eyes. "I'm scared too."

Part of him was paralyzed with fear, and every so often, one of its tentacles would wrap around him and squeeze until it was hard for him to breathe. He had to fight to keep moving forward and think only of the next step—much like crossing the desert.

If he did nothing, the world would freeze and Demonside would die. They were out of time and options. Tomorrow would come soon enough. There was no point in worrying about it.

"I think everyone is scared. Some are just better at hiding it." He brushed Angus's hair aside and kissed him again. "The world needs you. I know that, but I wish it didn't." He rested his forehead on Angus's. "I don't want to lose you. I'm not afraid of the world dying, I'm afraid of *you* never coming back."

Angus closed his eyes but didn't speak. He bit his lip, not sure what to say that wouldn't make it worse. Terrance's parents left him because of magic, and now he was doing the same. But there was nowhere safe to hide, and he didn't want to sit back when he could help.

Terrance drew in a shaky breath. "I agreed to be the anchor because I wanted to taste what it was that you and Saka have. I want to be part of it." Terrance laced his fingers with Angus's. "That hasn't changed. Everything else has."

CHAPTER THIRTY-FOUR

Saka's room and his bed had been cleaned since Terrance saw Angus the night before, wounded and covered in gunk. Holding tight to Angus's hand, Terrance stepped inside. He didn't want to keep pushing Angus away but drawing him close was just as hard. There was power around Angus, as there was around the priests and mages and warlocks, and it made a part of Terrance squirm uncomfortably. He'd never been that good at magic and had never wanted to be good at it. Angus loved him, but he didn't know why.

He was never going to be a magic user like Saka.

He had no idea what he was going to do for the rest of his life when the fear of destruction was over. He was terrified that he'd be left holding memories and nothing more.

He wanted to pin Angus to the bed and keep him there so he didn't go and do the dumb thing he'd planned. A selfish part of him didn't want to lose him, even if it meant destroying two worlds. But he didn't want to stop Angus from doing what he needed to. He didn't want to be that person—the one who stood in the way because they were too selfish and too mean to think about what their lover wanted. And Angus wanted to do this. He *needed* to. The uncertain warlock-in-training he'd been was long gone.

"You're thinking about it too much," Angus said with a smile.

Terrance wasn't thinking about it at all—that was the problem. He was worried about what was coming instead of taking full advantage of what he had. He forced out a breath. "I've never done sex magic before."

"It's not that different from blood magic. It's about emotion." Angus trailed a hand up his forearm, and Terrance's skin tingled from the light touch. "It's slower... more controlled." Angus smiled. "Well, someone needs to be in control."

"Have you ever been in control before?" It was hard to imagine Saka letting Angus take over. Terrance couldn't imagine ever being in that position.

"Yes." Angus stepped in close so his lips brushed Terrance's ear when he spoke. "Even Saka can be made to quiver with need."

"Where is he?"

"I told him to give us a little time alone." Angus kissed Terrance's neck.

"And then?" Terrance snuck his hand under Angus's shirt and pulled him firmly against him. How much longer did they have? His mind wouldn't settle. He had Angus now, and that had to be enough. He was so tired of making do with scraps. He wanted a life, a family, and everything else he'd been denied.

If Angus succeeded, *they* could have all of that.

And Angus needed him. Angus needed him so he could walk out and be what he needed to be and then return. *Get your head in the game, Erikson, or kiss it all goodbye.*

In that heartbeat Terrance knew they were saying goodbye in case Angus didn't make it back. He closed his eyes.

"It doesn't matter what happens later." Angus looped his arm around Terrance's neck and pressed his lips pressed against Terrance's.

Terrance responded—not because he should, but because he wanted to. He was the anchor, and that meant reminding Angus why he needed to live and come home. "Will he watch or join in?"

"If you want."

He didn't know what he wanted. He'd never had anyone watch him in bed and he'd never had more than one partner—not that he hadn't thought about it. And he'd definitely wondered what it would be like with a demon. In the entertainment quarter it had been tempting, but it wasn't just any demon or any human that he wanted. He'd stopped being with other people when he'd started sleeping with Angus. He didn't actually remember making that decision. It just happened.

He shouldn't have wasted all that time being horrified at the sacrifice. He should've accepted it the way Angus had—he'd done what needed to be done. Terrance should be good at that, but it had always been about what he needed for himself. Angus cared about everyone else.

"Did you really want to rebalance, or do you want me?" He toyed with the tie on Angus's pants. Was it just magic tonight or something more? He felt needy, and he hated it, but he couldn't hide it, not when everything was about to fall apart. He also didn't want to make things harder for Angus.

"Both. It's the same thing here." He moved against Terrance, and the building heat spread through his blood. "But here you can see what's happening. The orbs will fill with raised magic and make it easier to control."

Terrance glanced up to see the glass balls hanging from the ceiling. He'd seen them on the trek and wondered why Saka would bring something so unnecessary, but they weren't decoration. Sex magic already sounded complicated.

"You don't have to worry about the magic. You just need to enjoy." Angus brushed his lips in a hint of a kiss that left him wanting more. "And try not to come."

Terrance threaded his fingers through Angus's hair and took the kiss. "That doesn't sound like fun."

"It's better if you wait. It's… it's like falling apart completely for a moment."

"Are you saying Saka is better in bed?" Had he been failing all this time?

Angus laughed. "No. Ritual is different. There's intent. When we're together it's because we want to be. I used to think it was a good idea to keep it all separate, but I don't think it is. You and he are entwined through my life, equal but different. I'll stop if you don't like it."

"I'll probably like it because you're doing it." He knew Angus had been part of a demon orgy—that he'd done it once and decided it was too much for him—but that seemed like a lifetime ago. Terrance hoped the two of them, maybe the three of them, wouldn't be too much for him.

"I haven't done anything yet." A smile danced over Angus's lips as he brushed Terrance's thigh with his hand but didn't go any farther.

That wasn't true. The nerves had settled, and lust was sliding through his blood. His skin sparked where they touched, and his dick was already thinking about what was to come. How much better could sex get? "You're teasing."

"We could strip and get to it, but holding out is that much harder."

"You can't make someone wait."

Angus's eyebrow quirked up. "I begged the first time."

Terrance swallowed. He didn't beg. Saka wouldn't beg. "Why? What did he do?"

Angus considered him for a moment. "Nothing really. I'll show you, if you want. Get on your knees."

His heartbeat quickened as he knelt, still fully clothed, on the hard-packed dirt floor.

Angus swept his fingers over Terrance's hair and then down his neck. "Can I take your shirt off, so I can feel your skin?"

"Yes." Why even ask? They had undressed each other many times without a word being spoken.

But Angus didn't take it off right away. He traced the edge of the fabric and down Terrance's back as he knelt behind him. Terrance's breath hitched as Angus lifted the hem and skimmed his ribs with his knuckles.

He'd barely been touched and he was hard. He glanced up, but the orbs were merely reflecting the light, not capturing any magic.

"I haven't put a circle around us yet." Angus kissed the back of Terrance's neck. "Shall I?"

Once the circle was up, it would become ritual. It was already feeling different, and not just because Terrance was having sex in Demonside for the first time. "Yes."

He wanted to see the orbs light up. He wanted to see the magic Angus loved more than life. He wanted to understand.

The circle shimmered blue around them and crackled with a life of its own. It was only then that Angus drew Terrance's shirt off. The scrape of the fabric over his skin drew a shiver. He shouldn't be feeling so aroused, but it was the anticipation of not knowing what came next. He was tempted to ask, but he didn't want to break the spell that held them.

He'd missed this connection with Angus. The distance between them had been painful, but he hadn't known how to bridge it. He'd never been this serious with anyone before… never trusted anyone.

Angus smoothed his hand over Terrance's stomach and swept across the front of his pants without pausing to touch where Terrance wanted to feel Angus's hand. So he grabbed one and pressed it against his dick.

Angus gave a small laugh. "If I had a tail, I'd grab your hand and stop you from doing that. You're supposed to relax and enjoy." But Angus didn't take his hand away. He rubbed the head of Terrance's cock through his pants. The fabric was coarse against his skin.

There was no part of him that was relaxed, but he tipped his head back to rest against Angus's shoulder. A little part of him screamed that everything was going to hurt after this. It was a mistake. His heart would be broken when Angus left—diced up like steak and scattered for scavengers.

He didn't want to leave this room. While they were here, they couldn't be torn apart.

His breathing quickened, and need spiraled low in his belly, and Angus slid his hand away. Terrance was about to grab it, but Angus nipped at his neck and then soothed the bite with a kiss. This was a very different side of Angus.

It wasn't boyfriend Angus. It was Mage Angus. This was how Saka had introduced Angus to sex magic. Terrance glanced up at the orbs. There was a faint glow to them. Something was happening because of what they were doing, or more correctly, because of what Angus was doing.

Terrance closed his eyes and sank into the sensation. His skin prickled with the anticipation of each touch, and when Angus dipped his finger beneath the waistband of his pants, his breathing hitched. Fingertips barely grazed his hard flesh, but his hips jerked.

Angus moved closer, so there was no gap between them. The hard length of Angus's dick rested along the crease of Terrance's ass, and he pressed against it, hoping to tease Angus into action.

Angus released a shuddering breath that swept over the back of Terrance's neck. Angus wanted, but not as much as Terrance needed. He could feel each bead of precome as it slid down his shaft. All he wanted was Angus's hand around his dick, and even then it would only take a few strokes.

Terrance licked his lips. He wanted to say something, but Angus shoved both his hands down the front of Terrance's pants, and the relief was instant. He thrust into Angus' fingers, and then Angus pressed his fingertip against him. The edge receded and left him hanging there. He could barely breathe, and he needed more, so he tugged his pants down and freed his cock.

The orbs were glowing now, lit by the magic of his desperation. Was he enjoying it? It wasn't what he'd thought sex magic was—he expected more sex.

Angus kissed the back of his neck and then the side. His lips hovered over Terrance's pulse, and he placed one hand over Terrance's heart and the other on his stomach. Terrance rolled his hips and made a low noise of need.

He wanted Angus's mouth or his hands or anything… even his own hand. But that would be cheating somehow, so he had to wait. But he couldn't. He kept silent for a couple more breaths and then gave in.

"I can't do this. I want you." He turned and faced Angus. Beyond

Angus and past the crystal blue of the circle, Saka was leaning in the doorway, watching. Terrance hadn't heard the door open.

Angus cupped his chin and turned his head away from Saka. "Lie down, and I'll give you what you want."

For a heartbeat he was torn, and his gaze darted to Saka and back to Angus.

"He's been there since you pulled your pants down."

Oh.

Angus moved to kiss him, but their lips didn't touch. "Someone has to make sure I don't screw up."

"I don't think you *could* screw this up." He lay down. The floor was hard and warm against his back, and his pants were tangled around his knees.

"It is possible to release too much magic. I need to know when to stop. You need to remember to shut it off." Angus drew the offending pants off the rest of the way and straddled Terrance, still fully clothed.

From that position Terrance couldn't see Saka, but he knew he was there watching. Was Saka jealous? Terrance had been jealous for a time, but now he wondered what it would be like to see Angus with Saka. The idea was as exhilarating as it was terrifying, and it was completely different from knowing that Angus had a lover on both sides of the void. Those worlds had well and truly collided and could never be separated.

Angus smoothed his hands down Terrance's stomach. The scars on his ribs from when he used to pay for the magic and feed his demon were healed, but he didn't know enough to remove them. He could ask Saka how. He could become better at magic… but he wasn't sure that was what Angus needed, and it wasn't really what *he* wanted. All he wanted was Angus, even if it was part-time.

But he needed him now.

Angus came so close to touching his dick that it jumped every time.

"Please," Terrance murmured.

Angus smiled, and his blue eyes were bright. He wasn't afraid or unsure. Angus was in control and enjoying it. He'd always been pretty, but now he was luminous. There was an aura around him, as though he could do anything. He leaned a little closer. "I think you just begged?"

Terrance drew in a breath to argue, but if it got him what he wanted, he'd keep his mouth shut.

Angus lifted his eyebrows and caressed Terrance's tight balls and then slowly traced along his dick to the tip. He swiped a little of the fluid there, brought it to his lips, and licked his finger clean.

He was dead. He pulled Angus close and kissed him hard, tasting himself on Angus's tongue. "You're killing me."

"Mmm. Ask nicely." Angus wrapped his fingers around Terrance's cock and gave the smallest stroke.

Terrance shuddered, and Angus pressed that spot again. Terrance bit back a curse. The room was lit like daylight. All that magic rebalanced. How much was it? Enough to pay for Angus's healing?

"Say it," Angus said against Terrance's lips.

Terrance threw back his head and arched his back, desperate for relief from the torture. Angus kissed his collarbones, licked the dip between them, and then moved lower and followed the line that carved between his stomach muscles until his lips were almost where Terrance wanted them. Terrance watched, unable to look away as Angus stuck out his tongue and licked, not at the head of his dick, as he hoped, but at the small puddle of precome on his belly.

Terrance fisted his hands. *Just say it. It's not that hard.*

The words wouldn't form. Angus grinned, moved a little lower, and flicked his tongue over the crown. Terrance lifted his hips, needing to feel the heat of Angus's mouth, but Angus drew back.

Terrance groaned.

Angus glanced up, his head tilted a little to the side as though he were listening or checking something. For an awful moment, Terrance thought Angus was going to get up and leave him like that. Instead, Angus moved over him to lie against him. He kissed him deeply, his body almost vibrating with need.

Terrance drew in a breath as the need to come rippled through him and Angus drew back and straddled Terrance's hips.

Fucking asshole.

Angus ran his palms up Terrance's chest. "It's going to feel so good when you do come."

It was going to feel good to get Angus on his stomach and drive into him. He covered Angus's hand with his.

"Just say it."

"Or what?"

Angus pulled his hands away. "I'll watch you."

Either way he won—he got to come. The need twisted inside him like a creature trying to get out. Either way he lost. He wanted Angus's touch, but he'd be handing over a tiny piece of control. He'd put himself entirely in Angus's hands. He'd have to trust Angus completely.

Terrance closed his eyes. He already trusted Angus, didn't he? It shouldn't be this difficult. When he opened his eyes, Angus hadn't moved. His pants were jutting forward, damp where the tip pressed against the fabric. Yet he was in control. Terrance glanced at Saka, still in the doorway, and their eyes met for a moment.

Saka would take over as soon as Terrance was done, and then it would be Angus writhing with need. Terrance swallowed and smiled. "Please... with your mouth?"

Angus shifted back and grasped Terrance's cock. He licked the slick slit and then swallowed him. Terrance couldn't help himself—his hips lifted off the ground, and he thrust up a couple of times and then gave in.

His climax tore through his body as his stomach muscles contracted and he groaned as if he were dying.

Then he realized he was. It wasn't just come, it was magic flowing through him and out of him. It took him several breaths to clamp down on it as Angus released his dick.

His skin was still too tight, and every touch was too much. He closed his eyes, sure his heart was about to explode. That was what being boneless and spent meant. He shivered as a ripple of pleasure traced through him again. Then the room went dark, and he cracked open his eyelids.

The magic had left the orbs, and the circle was down. It was over. Disappointment swept through him. If it was over, Angus would leave him.

Angus leaned over. "You all right?"

"Yeah." That was the best head job of his life. Nothing was ever going to come close. Ever.

Angus had ruined him for the rest of his life. And he was never going to be able to forget it, which was exactly what Angus wanted. Terrance's heart stopped as pain lanced through him at the idea of losing Angus. He pulled him close and hugged him hard. "That was amazing."

"It wasn't."

"It was to me." He should have held out for longer, but that would've meant more magic gathered and more released from him, which probably wasn't safe. But that was definitely a better way to rebalance than blood and souls.

He cupped Angus's face. "You're amazing." Terrance kissed him and hoped Angus knew how much he meant to him. "And you're still hard. We should take care of that."

Terrance glanced at Saka and nodded.

The demon entered the room, and a new circle crackled to life.

CHAPTER THIRTY-FIVE

ANGUS GLANCED over his shoulder as the room shimmered blue. He hadn't made the circle, nor had Terrance. Saka had stepped into the room while he was making sure that Terrance was all right. Angus drew in a breath. He was still astride Terrance, the taste of him still on his tongue, his skin tight, and his blood hot. As much fun as it was showing Terrance how it was done, he'd known how it would end.

There were things that weren't being said between them. His possible death was a topic they were avoiding tonight. Even at the meeting of mages, no one had said it might kill him, but Angus knew that was a risk. It would be more magic than he'd ever controlled or channeled.

He wasn't ready for it.

He wanted time with Saka and Terrance, to enjoy what they had and what they could have if he lived. A lump formed in Angus's throat. He couldn't think about that now. They had tonight, and he was going to make the most of it.

Terrance ran his hands along Angus's thighs. He didn't stop short and deny Angus the touch he needed. Would Terrance join in or just watch?

Saka cupped the back of his head and tilted it so Angus was forced to look at him. Saka's eyes were black, and the blue of the circle flickered within them. A part of him wanted Saka to say no, to say it was an awful idea, to stop him from going to Vinland.

But there was no other plan.

Terrance cupped his balls and then traced his length, but Angus didn't need any teasing. It had been hard to stay in control and he wanted to let go and enjoy.

Saka pressed his lips to Angus's. They were warm and rough—familiar. He closed his eyes. If he never had to leave this moment, that would be fine. He'd be like a bug trapped in amber—happy forever. Saka probed his mouth with his tongue, and Angus parted his lips.

He gasped as Terrance pulled down his pants and wrapped his hand around Angus's shaft. His touch was cooler than Saka's, his skin smooth. It was too easy to roll his hips and thrust into the eager fingers. A little more was all it would take. His balls tightened, and his heart beat faster, eager for release.

Saka dragged him to his feet, and a groan slipped from his lips, but he didn't resist. He was sure no one would've said a word if he didn't rebalance for the magic used to heal him, but it didn't feel right not to, and he'd wanted an excuse to get Saka and Terrance in the same bed with him. It had been just an idea for too long, and he wanted to make sure he didn't have stupid regrets. So he found his balance, and Terrance pulled down his pants while Saka removed his shirt. Then he was naked between his lovers.

He suppressed a shiver of pure anticipation as he flipped through every possibility that he'd already put too much detail into. Saka slid his hand over Angus's belly but didn't dip low. He pressed against Angus, and Angus leaned back into the embrace. Then Terrance kissed him softly, as though he weren't sure he should he doing anything.

But Angus knew Saka wouldn't send him away or make him watch. His two lives and loves had imploded, and it was only with both of them that he could do what needed to be done.

He turned to face Saka to kiss him and then wondered if Terrance felt left out. Saka kept him from glancing back, but a smooth hand caressed the curve of his ass and then traced the crease, barely pausing over the tight ring of muscle. His breath caught as he waited for more.

It didn't come.

Saka drew back from the kiss, leaving Angus breathless and hungry for more. Then he put a hand on his shoulder, and Angus obeyed the silent command and dropped to his knees. He watched as Saka slowly undid his pants, let them fall, and then stepped out of them. His cock was hard and thick, streamlined from root to tip. There was no crown to tease.

Angus glanced up at Saka, but Saka wasn't looking at him. He nodded and his tail pointed at the shelves. Angus glanced over as Terrance stepped toward a familiar little pot, and then Saka cupped his jaw and brought his attention to the waiting dick in front of his face. Saka brushed his thumb across his cheek in a soft caress. This time his gaze didn't waver even as Angus took him in his mouth. Saka's skin was hot and rough against his tongue.

Soft footsteps grew closer. It was Terrance with the oil.

He took Saka a little deeper and released him slowly, working over his length and tracing over the tight skin of his balls with his fingertips. Saka didn't make any effort to stop him or change what he was doing, and Angus was sure Saka was doing it for his pleasure and not for ritual.

Angus didn't mind either way.

His damaged foot ached, unable to lie flat on the floor. Too much kneeling was taking its toll. He fidgeted to be more comfortable without stopping until a smooth hand ran down the back of his thigh and lifted that leg so he could place his foot flat. The change in position also gave Terrance greater access, yet Angus still flinched when Terrance touched his hole with slick fingers. For a moment it was too much, but he took a breath and sank into the feeling. Lips brushed between his shoulder blades, and much like he'd teased Terrance earlier, Terrance now teased him—one hand across his belly and the other circling and pressing deeper.

Saka ruffled his hair and then smiled and pulled away.

Angus gasped. His lips tingled from Saka's rough skin. He'd

expected more than such a quick taste. Then the one slick finger within him was joined by another, and he bit his lip as a wave of pleasure raced through him. His dick twitched, and for a moment, he hoped Terrance would stroke him or Saka would suck him… anything.

He forced a breath out between his teeth as Terrance withdrew his fingers. Then he took a chance. He stood and moved toward the bed, and when no one stopped him, he lay down. Saka joined him. He moved between his legs, took a hard kiss, and ground his hips against Angus's, but Angus needed more. He bent his knees and lifted his hips.

Saka didn't ignore the hint the way he did so often when drawing it out for ritual. Had they moved into something more personal? If they had, he didn't care. His demon pressed into him, and the stretch and friction of the rough skin drew a shudder that was part pleasure and part pain. He lifted his legs, and Saka thrust deeper. His tail curled and beckoned, and Terrance approached the bed.

Angus looked at him but didn't know what to do.

But Terrance did. He lay down and kissed him, explored slowly with his tongue as he reached for Angus's dick and stroked and rubbed his thumb over the slit. Precome leaked out and made each stroke slick. He should be trying to hold back, but Saka wasn't slowing, and he wasn't telling Terrance to stop.

Terrance shifted and tracked down Angus's body with his mouth until his lips were teasing the head of Angus's cock. Angus could barely breathe, but he held back because he didn't want it to end. When Terrance sucked him, it was almost too much. Terrance released him and stretched out as Saka slid his tail over Terrance's hip. Terrance didn't pull away from the demon's touch.

Each of Saka's thrusts was measured and deep. The room had brightened again as the orbs gathered the lust they created. Angus ran his fingers over Terrance's too-short hair, wanting to feel his lips on his dick again, and Terrance obliged. He sucked and teased him as though he were hungry for a taste.

So he didn't hold back.

He let the hot, fast release tear through him and unleashed the magic held in his body. Terrance swallowed and moaned. Before Demonside could suck him dry, Angus clamped down on the magic, but his body still trembled.

Saka gripped his legs, gave another few hard thrusts, and then gave in. His cock thickened and twitched inside him and then flooded his channel with come.

His heartbeat was erratic, and he was happy to revel in the shadow of his release. Terrance leaned over and kissed him. His mouth was salty and his skin warm.

Saka pulled out and lay on the other side of him, and Terrance leaned over and kissed him too. Then he flopped on the other side. They lay in silence, the way they had on the trek across the desert. But Angus had never felt that good on the trek. He wanted to hold on to it, so he reached out and grasped both their hands. There was barely room on the bed for the three of them, but they fit.

The orbs were lit, and the circle was still up, as though even Saka wasn't ready to let go. Angus closed his eyes. His body was heavy, and sleep was waiting for him. Then Saka kissed his cheek and released the magic. The air tasted like rain, and the room became almost black, lit only by the moonlight that slid through the slats in the walls. Saka got off the bed. Angus cracked open an eye to see Saka with a washcloth, and his lips curved. He should've known Saka would get up. Angus felt the cloth move up his inner thigh, bringing the lightest touch of magic with it.

Angus clamped his hand over Saka's wrist. "No magic."

He didn't want the tenderness erased. He wanted to hold on to everything. Then the magic dissipated, and all that was left was the cool touch of the cloth. He was aware of Terrance wiping himself, and then Saka eventually coming back to bed and curling against him.

Terrance kissed the knuckles of their joined hands. "You were right. Magic can be beautiful."

Angus smiled. He'd done something right.

"I am glad you're a mage. No matter what, you'll always have part of Arlyxia with you." Saka traced the mark he'd carved into Angus's chest.

The scar always glinted red, like it held some of Saka's skin. At the time, Angus thought it was made to prove that Angus was his. But it was because of the scar he'd been able to hold magic within him and reach into the clean sweep to feel how the magic worked and to direct it.

Saka covered the mark over his heart with his hand, and Angus placed his hand over Saka's. He didn't need the mark for there to be a bond.

Terrance's breathing deepened as sleep claimed him, and Saka soon followed. Angus lay awake and traced Saka's mark. It had saved his life so many times.

Then he ran through the plan again and again.

Terrance lay next to him, his face relaxed. Angus should be asleep too. He wanted to enjoy lying there, but all he could think about was the plan and the magic. He tried to sweep all that aside for tomorrow, because the sun would rise regardless of how much sleep he'd had.

Crossing the void would mean he'd have to tell Terrance what his part was, and there were never going to be the right words for that, and no magic could ever make it right.

CHAPTER THIRTY-SIX

Saka laid out the final stone representing each mage and where they'd need to be when the doorway was opened from Vinland. They were sharing the plan beyond the head mages—with all mages in the village. Fifteen had assembled, and hopefully more would arrive as word spread.

"Angus?" Was he paying attention? It was his plan they were working on, but Angus wasn't ready. It was dangerous magic, and he couldn't entirely hide his pride. Angus was his human. He was doing this for everyone, and his name would be remembered for generations.

Saka wasn't ready to let him go and face it on his own, yet he had to. While he'd made Angus a mage, their plan would be a test more grueling than any apprentice ever had to face on Lifeblood Mountain.

Angus looked at him. "This mark." He pulled his shirt aside. "It's a connection to here?"

Angus had fidgeted all night until Saka ignored the protest about no magic and sent him to sleep. If Angus remembered, he hadn't said anything. Was this what he'd been thinking about?

Saka nodded. At the start it had been about making sure Angus knew that he owed his life to him, but that was before Saka started caring too much. But it had also been about forging a bond faster and giving Angus a better way to control magic. "It is a way of binding a part of you to here."

"It's why I survived the clean sweep the first time. I can store magic here… like a focus. It allows the magic to flow through me."

It also tore open the scar when too much magic burned through.

"You can't hold all you need with one mark," Saka said. That was never the intention of the mark.

"What if I had more?" Angus glanced around the circle of mages.

"Still not enough to hold the magic required," Iktan said carefully, his ears flicked forward as though he were interested. Saka could feel the ground start to crumble beneath his feet, and he hoped he was wrong.

"But I'd have better control as I channeled it? I would be able to store more?"

Silence from everyone. Saka didn't know what to say, so he said nothing.

"I will have no weapons. They will put me in magic-dampening cuffs."

"And you will be relying on Terrance," Saka finished. That was the flaw in the plan, but there was no other way.

"I trust him," Angus said as he held Saka's gaze daring him to argue. Saka would've once, but he knew Terrance wouldn't do anything to hurt Angus, which made his job the hardest.

"So do I," Saka said. He'd watched them work together and had decided that Terrance could be left in charge of Angus's life. But there were so many ways it could unravel. He didn't trust the warlocks, and if they killed Terrance, it would all come undone. "What you are asking is to be bound more tightly to Arlyxia. For every mage here to mark you, to have a connection to you." He spread his hands and glanced at Iktan. "I don't know what that will do to a human."

Iktan's ears flattened. "Nor do I."

"I'll deal with that if I survive. I want to survive. I think that's the only way."

Angus had tried to explain the clean sweep to them, but

weaponized magic was something they didn't use, and it was hard to create new magic when none of them knew what it was supposed to feel like. There would be no trial of it either. It worked or it failed. They were saved or they were dead.

Given that they were dying slowly and there were no other options, the vote was unanimous. But horror gripped Saka and refused to be shaken off.

No one had said a word about it as they shared a bed, but they had all known it might never happen again. Losing Angus would be like carving out his heart. Even the thought wounded Saka in a way that was unbecoming to a mage.

The other mages were looking at him like he knew what to do. As Angus's mentor he needed to say something. He couldn't deny the request, not if it meant Angus lived. But lived how? How could a human be tightly bound to Arlyxia and still be human? If Angus channeled all this magic, what would be left of him? Saka nodded. "As you said, anything that helps. Do you remember the pain?"

Angus blinked slowly. "Something like that is hard to forget."

"You want to do that, for every mage?" He didn't want to see Angus go through that.

He held Saka's stare. "It will be worth it to live."

A part of him didn't want Angus marked by others. Angus was his. Saka looked away. All scars could be erased when the wearer was ready to move on, but Angus had chosen not to remove Saka's mark despite having the skill. "You will wear many scars."

"I know," Angus said softly. He brushed Saka's fingers with his own. "But only yours is on my heart."

"I will give you my mark," Iktan said carefully.

The other mages murmured their agreement and left to get their knives.

They would also need food and water for after. Saka waited until they were alone and Angus was sitting, staring at the stones that represented each mage. He ran his fingers through Angus's hair. It was so much longer than it had been at first.

Angus glanced up, looking grim. "Thank you for letting me sleep."

Saka smiled. It was the least he could've done. He'd take Angus's place if he could—go to Vinland and deploy a clean sweep, but he wasn't sure that even a mage with decades of experience could do what needed to be done. His eyes were hot and gritty as he walked away to get what he needed.

Terrance was still in bed. He watched as Saka collected his knives and a cloth. "What are you doing?"

"Finishing preparations. You will be leaving soon with Angus." He wanted to shake Terrance and tell him how important his role was, but he respected Angus's wishes not to say anything yet. "Keep him alive."

"I will. I swear."

Saka pulled out a blade. "With blood."

Terrance took the knife and cut his forearm with a calmness and skill that he'd learned when feeding his first demon, a scarlips, his own blood. "Whatever it takes."

"Whatever he asks," Saka said, knowing that Terrance would want to refuse.

"Anything." Magic shimmered in the blood.

Saka put his hand over it and healed it, leaving a scar. "So you don't forget."

Terrance gripped his hand. "I won't. I love him."

"As do I." He pulled away and strapped on his knives.

When he returned to the meeting place, Angus hadn't moved. It was as though he were going through the magic in his mind, repeating it until he no longer even had to think about what he was doing. If he were attacked he wouldn't be able to think about the magic. He'd just have to do it.

Saka offered Angus a hand, and he reached out without looking and let himself be hauled to his feet. "I should have said something to you first."

"You're a mage. You don't need to ask my permission. I don't know what the effects will be." He looked at the stones. "None of us know."

"I should've pressed my father for more details about the weapon, but I didn't think it was possible."

"He was asked, Angus. He was asked many things before he surrendered his blood and soul to Lifeblood." The man had tried to kill his son, so he deserved no compassion and had received none. The mages had shown no care for his suffering. Pain and fear were just as effective in rebalancing as lust and desire.

"I hope he died in pain."

Saka put a hand on Angus's shoulder. "That is not a good thought to carry."

"It's the truth. He and his kind have caused the deaths of many. I've watched friends die. I've suffered. Why should I wish him, or any of the warlocks responsible, a pleasant death?"

"Do not do this for revenge."

Angus nodded. "I do it because it's the right thing to do. Everything I love will die if I do nothing." He drew in a breath. "So I do it for love."

"Make sure Terrance understands that. Make sure he knows that you love him."

"I will. I do." Angus forced a smile.

"They are all returning. Are you certain you want this?"

"No. But when has that ever stopped me?"

Saka wished Angus would stop and wait until he was sure. If they survived, there would be time to remind him that a mage was meant to consider all the options. But there was no time, and no one had any other options.

While Iktan was the head mage, Saka was Angus's mentor, so he created the circle. It shimmered purple to stop any sound from carrying, and Angus closed his eyes and took some deep breaths. Then he pulled off his shirt. Except for Saka's sigil over his heart, his pale skin was unmarked and smooth, with a dusting of freckles across his shoulders. How many times had Saka kissed them? Run his hand down Angus's spine?

He stood in front of Angus and took his hands. He would take some of the pain—all of it if he could. He'd step through the void and unleash the clean sweep if he could. Saka didn't want Angus to do this but couldn't stop him either. Angus wasn't his apprentice anymore, and no training that Saka could offer would help.

Iktan stepped up, blade drawn. He placed a hand on Angus's upper arm to heat the flesh and start the magic. Then he carved his sigil into the skin. Angus hissed, and the sting flowed from him to Saka. While he couldn't ease the pain the way he'd have liked to, Saka could share it and lessen it that way.

Iktan healed the wound and left a dun-colored scar.

One by one, each mage stepped up to repeat the process down his arms and over his back. With each one, Angus's grip on the pain and his ability not to cry out lessened. He bit his lip until that bled too, and soon he was streaked in blood as though he'd already been in battle. When they were done, Saka used magic to dull the burn of all the cuts.

Angus's chest lifted with each shaky breath, and Saka gave him a little time to regather himself. There was one more thing to do.

He released Angus's hands and passed him a knife. "Make your mark."

Angus blinked struggling to focus. "I don't have one."

"You are a mage. You should have one."

Angus gripped the knife more tightly. His knuckles whitened, and he nodded and placed his hand over Saka's heart. Trails of blood were drying on his arms, but some still dripped into the dirt. Saka's skin warmed and became hot. Angus removed his hand and placed the tip of the blade against Saka's skin. He hesitated for a heartbeat and then scored the sigil that would be his—two open arrowheads that overlapped and pointed in opposite directions.

It was perfect for Angus.

Blood welled and traced down Saka's chest, but he was used to the sharp pain of the cuts and could absorb them. Angus placed his hand over the wound and healed it. The skin remained pale, almost white.

CHAPTER THIRTY-SEVEN

Angus's skin was tight and new, and his stomach was too choppy, like an ocean that shouldn't be crossed. He regretted eating both breakfast and the flatbread he'd eaten after the cutting to ground himself.

He ran his finger over his sleeve and felt the ridges of scar tissue. Each mark was a different color—some green, some brown, some orange, and Wek's bright blue. The patterns were bold on his skin.

"Are you sure you feel all right?" Saka brushed his fingers but didn't grab hold.

"Yes." Mostly. He glanced at Saka. The pale mark on his chest was clearly visible.

Angus had wiped most of the blood away, and his shirt was unstained. Yet as they approached the house Saka was living in, Terrance stood. His gaze flicked between them and locked onto Angus's sigil on Saka. Then his gaze shifted to Angus. His shirt hid them all, But Terrance knew. Angus was sure of it. Terrance nodded, his face grim. It would only get grimmer when they went back across.

"That's it? We're going?" Terrance asked.

Angus tried to smile, but he failed. He didn't want to go. Once he stepped through the doorway, he'd be handing his life over to chance.

Saka grasped his hand. "You could stay another night."

Angus shook his head. He could, but then he'd never leave. "You told me in the desert that it was best to keep moving in case one day of rest becomes two and two becomes giving up and death."

"That is true." But Saka didn't let go, and Angus didn't release him either.

"The last time I was here, all I wanted to do is leave. Now I want to stay and pretend the other side doesn't exist." Terrance put a hand on Saka's shoulder. "I'll bring him back. I swear."

"I hope that is a promise you can keep." Saka released Angus's hand. "You had best go. The mages and I will continue to close up all doorways in preparation."

If they weren't successful, then when Terrance opened the void, they would end up in the wrong place and he'd have no help when he needed it most. Could he do it without the mages? Maybe, but he didn't want to try. Nerves fluttered in his belly like winged hunters after prey. "You'll be ready?"

"Five days." They had agreed that should be long enough. If it stretched to ten, the mages were to assume Angus was dead. Much longer than that and the ice would be set, and no amount of rebalancing would fix it. The humans would have to wait for nature to take its course. Demonside would be nothing but a barren desert.

The leaves were falling in the jungle, and the trees were withering. Death was on the air.

Together they walked to the doorway, and Angus walked around it and committed as much detail as possible to memory. He made Terrance walk with him. "You need to be able to visualize this place. You might need to direct the void opening. Note the cracks and chips, the discoloration of the stones, everything that makes this place unique."

"Me? Why won't you be able to do it?"

"Hopefully I will be able to, but if I can't and you need to flee, you should come here." That made Terrance pay greater attention. He scuffed a toe over a crack, ran his hand over the pillar to feel the bumps and grooves.

"I think I have enough detail to find it in a jumble of pillars and doorways." He looked less certain than he had before, and worry pinched his eyebrows together.

Angus's throat closed. He was coming back. He had to believe that. This would not be the last time he was in Demonside. He hugged Saka. "Thank you."

He would not say goodbye.

Saka squeezed him hard and let him go. Angus took two steps toward the open void, but Saka grabbed his hand and pulled him close again.

Angus knew the words forming on the demon's lips. He didn't need to hear them. "Don't—"

"I love you."

The words struck deep in Angus's heart. He'd wanted to hear them for so long, but not like that. "You didn't need to say it."

"You have been wanting to hear it. I owe you that much." Saka rested his forehead against Angus's. "I have known for a long time."

"I know. I knew." He sucked in a breath that cracked his ribs. "I love you."

Saka stepped back. He looked like someone had thrust the machete through his stomach and were casually twisting the blade. "Go. Before I change my mind and keep you here forever."

"That has never been a threat." He handed Saka the staff he'd been using. He'd have to get used to not having one. "Keep it safe until I need it."

Saka smiled, but it didn't reach his eyes.

Terrance took Angus's hand. "Come."

Angus didn't fight. He let himself be led away. Just before they stepped through, Terrance spoke. "If you two had crumbled, we'd all be doomed. I don't want to see you hurting."

Angus bit his lip, which was still tender from the morning's cutting. Biting it had only added to the pain, but it was something he could control. He'd have to let go of that too. In Vinland he'd have no control.

The nervousness he'd been able to keep locked down bubbled closer to the surface. He glanced back just before he stepped through.

Saka was holding the staff, his gaze on the ground, his shoulders slumped.

He wasn't a mage in that moment, and he didn't know the answers.

It was only Terrance's grip on his hand that kept him moving. He was wounding the two people he loved more than anything.

The air in Uxmal was sharp and cold. It tugged at his thin shirt, and he shivered. The changes were happening much faster now. Had Vinland deployed more clean sweeps elsewhere in the world?

Terrance signed himself in at the doorway, and Angus did the same. The guards watched as though it were any other day. No one could know the truth or the plan would be undone.

Did Cadmael know everything or had Iktan kept his silence on mage business?

Terrance grasped Angus's hand, and Angus held on. They didn't have much time.

"We should see Cadmael. He won't agree to this," Terrance said as though Cadmael's disagreement was enough to stop Angus.

He would agree. Everyone was desperate. "No, I'll go later. I want to speak to you alone first."

Terrance's eyes widened. "I do not accept you breaking up with me before you do this."

Angus shook his head, a faint smile on his lips. If only that were all it was…. "I didn't break up with Saka, and I'm not breaking up with you either."

"Then what?"

"In private."

"Then it's nothing good." Terrance pressed his lips together.

"Don't be jealous… please." They walked toward Angus's room, hand in hand.

"I'm not."

"Don't lie either." They didn't have time to unravel the truth.

"Just a little. You marked him."

"He asked." And Angus hadn't been able to refuse. Maybe the extra connection would be a good thing.

"And if I asked?"

"I would." They went in, and Angus shut the door. He should've managed to come up with the right words, yet there were none. He could think about it until the world froze over, but the thoughts would never be complete. He shivered.

Terrance rubbed his hands up Angus's arms. "You should...." A frown formed, and his touch went from warming to curious. He pushed back the cuff of the shirt, and Angus didn't stop him. The scars would've been revealed at some point anyway.

"What is...?" Terrance pushed the sleeve up to Angus's elbows on both sides. His eyes widened. "Did they carve their marks on you?"

Angus nodded.

"All of them?"

"Yes."

The lines on Terrance's forehead deepened as he traced one of the raised scars that adorned Angus's forearm. "Did you sleep with them all?"

"No!" He pulled down his sleeves, though he would have if he thought it would help. How would Terrance judge him then? He let go of the annoyance in the next breath. Terrance didn't know the plan and wasn't a mage. He'd been waiting to learn what was going on, and he was afraid. "The marks help me hold magic and direct it."

"Saka didn't mark me... do you even want to?" Terrance didn't look at him.

Angus had thought about it. He'd expected Saka to, but understood why he hadn't. "I do, but after this." He put his arms around Terrance. "You don't mean less to me just because I haven't made you bleed."

Terrance hugged him hard. "I know... but why not before? What if there is no after, and I have nothing." Terrance pressed his face to Angus's neck.

Angus's resolve started to melt. He'd been keeping it together, but he was starting to break. He swallowed hard, but his voice still shook. "Your skin needs to be clear or the warlocks might not believe you."

Terrance looked at Angus, and a frown formed. "What warlocks?"

Angus held his gaze. "You're going to betray me to the Vinnish spies."

CHAPTER THIRTY-EIGHT

"No." Terrance stepped back as though he'd been tackled by an elephant. He'd never betray Angus. Was he joking? But Angus wasn't smiling. He seemed to be in pain, his mouth pressed into a line and his eyes haunted.

"You have to."

"No." Terrance shook his head. He wouldn't hand Angus over to the Vinnish. "They'll kill you."

"Hopefully not before I've completed our clean sweep, but to do that, I need to be in Vinland."

Terrance slumped onto the bed and raked his fingers through his hair. Had that been part of the plan all along? He should've been in those meetings Angus had with the mages. He would've said no. Had Saka agreed to this madness or had Angus not told him either? "Why can't you do it from here?"

Angus knelt before him on one knee because of his injured leg. He put his hands on Terrance's thighs. "Because I'm not going to be able to direct the magic from here to there."

"They can." They sent the magic rolling from Vinland to every country around the world. Nowhere was safe.

"And they've had time to perfect the magic. I get one chance to take back what they've stolen. I need to be in Vinland, and the only way for me to get there is for you to turn me over. I can't sneak in. We can't cross the desert, and there is no doorway."

Angus was making sense. He knew that. But he couldn't. "No. I love you. They...." His voice broke. They wouldn't treat Angus kindly, even if they didn't kill him.

Angus bowed his head and pressed his fingers into Terrance's thigh. "I know they'll put me in magic-dampening cuffs, that I'll be sentenced to a traitor's death." He lifted his gaze. "They won't get a chance to kill me, though. You'll open the void, and it will go to the waiting mages. They will overload the cuffs."

"You're assuming they don't kill me on sight. I left with you. I'm just as much of a traitor." The plan would never work. They were all doomed. They'd be better off making the most of what time they had left before ice covered the world and Demonside died. They should drink and eat and fuck until death consumed them. He'd rather die doing that than sending Angus to his death. But he couldn't say that, not when all the demon mages had agreed to this, and everyone still had hope for a miracle. He'd seen Angus survive when he should've died. He swallowed hard. It felt like a pitz ball was stuck in his throat. "This won't work."

"You can convince them. You've witnessed my many crimes and debauchery with demons. You have to."

"I like your crimes and debauchery." He liked participating in the debauchery part quite a bit. Terrance pulled Angus onto his lap and hugged him close. He never wanted to let go, and he certainly didn't want to hand him over to the very people they'd run from. "I don't want to be the kind of person who betrays their lover."

Angus stroked his cheek, and his words were soft. "*They* believe you're that person. I don't. I'm trusting you with my life, with the world. No one else can open the void for me."

Angus had known he'd never be able to open the void in cuffs. That's why he made Terrance memorize the stones and pillars. Angus might be wielding the magic, but Terrance had to be there to open the void or it was all for nothing. Angus's whole plan hinged on the warlocks not killing him the moment they set foot in Vinland, but the void didn't open to the village from Vinland.

"What if I can't. What if it goes to the wrong place?"

"You have a connection to Saka, and you know the doorway."

"But it might. Then what?"

"Then I do my best without the help of the mages. You can send me magic from Demonside."

He wasn't a good enough warlock… or priest… to be able to get that right. He was shit at magic and shouldn't be such an important part of the plan. And the plan sucked. It was all kinds of awful. But if the mages and priests had come up with nothing better, what was left? It was the final play in a game of pitz where everyone died if they lost. They were going for the hoop, but it was sixty meters off the ground instead of six.

He needed to know the plan. "And once the void is open, then what?"

"Then I'll strike Vinland and destroy where they're keeping the magic."

"Where is that?"

"It won't matter. The clean sweep will find it."

"Wizards and warlocks caught in it will die." So many around the world had died already. If they did nothing, many more would die.

Angus closed his eyes. When he opened them, the blue of his irises was as hard as the stone he'd given Terrance when they were dabbling with telestones on the human side of the void. "That will be on my conscience."

"I open the void, and the warlocks will attack." They wouldn't hold back. They would know he double-crossed them.

"You'll go to Saka, so you won't die. Two pillars make the doorway. You and Saka are mine. You'll hold it open, and I'll come through when the wave rolls back."

"Alive." Terrance stared at Angus and willed him to agree.

Angus was silent for a moment. "I don't know."

He wanted to tell Angus not to do it, but it wouldn't matter what he said. The mages had agreed. Angus had agreed. He was prepared.

Terrance traced the ridges of scars on Angus's skin. They were on his back as well as his arms. Angus was changing every day. The first-year warlock he'd met no longer existed. "You truly are a mage, putting the world first."

Angus pressed his lips together, but no smile formed. There was nothing left to smile about. When this was over, he wanted to hear Angus laugh again, see him smile without the shadow of worry.

Terrance sighed. He wasn't good enough. "I'll never be a mage. I want to be boring. I want a house and a garden like my parents had, and the most magic I'll do is making sure the plants are growing all year round." He didn't care if he never played rugby again. After playing pitz, he wasn't sure he could pick up a ball without thinking of death.

Angus put his arms around Terrance's neck. "That sounds nice... unless I'm not invited."

"Of course you are... and Saka. So when you finish doing your mage stuff—and putting Vinland back together—you can sit down and have dinner. You need someone to remind you that you can be selfish." He'd always been good at that. Angus had taught him that there was so much more, and now he was supposed go back to being that person, the one who thought only of what he wanted and keeping his ass safe.

Safety had been an illusion. Even the idea that he was somehow in control of his life had been false. He could refuse to do this, but Angus would be alone, and the plan would fail. He had to help. Only then could he be safe and selfish. Then he could have a home like the one that had been stolen when his parents were arrested.

He hugged Angus tighter and skimmed his hands over more of the scars. "Promise me you won't hate me if I do this to you. They'll hurt you."

"I won't hate you. I swear."

Terrance closed his eyes and rested his cheek against Angus's. It was wet. Now he knew why Saka had made him swear to do whatever Angus asked. Saka had known. *Asshole.* When he saw him again, there would be words... or tears.

"You will?"

Terrance nodded. "Yes." There was nothing else he could do. To help Angus he had to betray him.

They stayed locked together, unwilling to let go, until someone knocked on the door.

Angus lifted his head from where it had rested on Terrance's shoulder. "A moment," he called out. Then he pressed a chaste kiss on Terrance's lips and got up.

That was it. In his heart he knew that to pull this off, he wouldn't be able to hold Angus again until it was over. He didn't want to be hugging a corpse and wishing everything were different. He clamped his teeth together and tried to find the person he'd once been—the man who'd tell anybody what they wanted to hear and had quite happily worked for the college and the underground as long as his own skin was safe.

Angus opened the door. The person there said something Terrance didn't catch.

"I'll be there shortly." Angus turned to Terrance. "I have to see Cadmael."

Terrance studied Angus and tried to memorize every freckle on his nose and the way he held the door—casually, but his knuckles were white. He was worried but burying it beneath what he needed to do. He wanted to wait and have one last night… but they had to act before the world froze over. And he had to start the play. "I'll be gone before you get back."

Angus nodded. "Wishing you luck would be wrong."

They needed more than luck. "You don't know what it's going to be like."

He glanced up at the ceiling. "I have a pretty good idea. It's why I thought trekking through the Demonside desert was a better option."

"I don't regret that… or sharing Saka with you… or you with Saka. I don't regret any of it." When the college first asked him to watch Angus, he accepted because he was curious about someone who'd been retrieved. He wanted to know why Angus didn't remember a thing about Demonside. Then the underground wanted Angus brought in slowly, and he'd been happy to do it because he'd seen through the college's lies. He could've said no, but the college would've cut off his scholarship and probably arrested him. The underground wouldn't have helped him if he refused to help them.

He never had a choice back then, but his choice now was between Angus and two worlds. He was going to have to tell some very good lies… or maybe the truth would be enough.

"I don't want to know before it happens. Don't warn me."

Terrance nodded. "What if I can't protect you?"

"Then we've tried and failed."

"I don't fail." Terrance always came out on top. "I need to see if that priest is able to talk."

He brushed his fingers against Angus's, but he didn't stop for a kiss goodbye.

Lozim lay on a narrow bunk in a cell that had no window. He was reading as though he had no troubles. Lozim's throat was a knotted mess. Healing wasn't Terrance's strength, and no one had bothered to take the time or magic to fix the traitor further. Terrance leaned against the bars. "Your carelessness nearly fucked up months of hard work."

The traitor priest looked up from his book. "You." His words were mangled, catching on the scars that Terrance couldn't see. "If not for you, we'd have him."

"No, he'd have flitted to Demonside. He's quick to run." He'd never seen anyone open the void so quickly. He'd shown Angus how to do it without walking, but Angus had quickly raced past him.

Lozim picked up his book. "You're a traitor like him."

"Like you? Why is a Mayan helping the Vinnish?"

"Why would I tell you that?"

"Why should I trust you with the information I have? I need to speak to the people in charge before the demons and their *pet* retaliate." Was that too much?

"Aren't you his boyfriend?"

Terrance pressed up against the bars. "I have spent months watching him, getting close to him, and gaining his trust. After your ill-judged stunt, I had to act against you because I knew something was being planned." He shook his head and steeled himself for his lie. "Angus only loves demons. He's a traitor, not just to Vinland, but to all humans."

"Ah, got sick of you did he?" Lozim didn't look up from his book.

"I'm tired of playing along. I've done as I was asked by the college, and yet the only contact I get is that you want to sweep in and grab him. You have no idea what's happening." That was the truth. He'd learned to always add truth when playing both sides. "He trusts me. I can bring him in."

"I almost had him."

"Keep telling yourself that." Terrance turned away. He couldn't seem too needy. "He knows how to stop your weapons, and he's teaching others. Vinland will be defenseless. It will become another state in the Mayan Empire. Human blood, not demon blood, will spill."

Lozim put his book down and walked over, his bare feet soft on the stones. Terrance didn't turn. He strode away as though the conversation were over.

"Wait."

Terrance smiled and then erased it before he turned. "What? I need to find someone who'll help me stop him and who can get all the details out of him before it's too late."

Lozim licked his lips. "There is someone you could try, though she might kill you before you speak."

Terrance snorted. "Someone in the college really needs to sort out their resources. I should be getting a medal for the work I've done."

"Bring Donohue in, and you'll get whatever you want. The bounty is large."

"I know." He smiled slyly. "But I also know that the demons' plans are even more valuable." The college would experience those plans firsthand if all went well. But there were so many steps where they could slip and fall. One step at a time. Like crossing the desert, it didn't pay to think how far away the end was, only that it was important to take the next step.

"There's a woman. She frequents a chocolate shop across town, has a lot of contacts. You'll know her by the gold pin in her hair."

"Lots of women wear gold pins in their hair."

"It's an oak leaf."

That would be uncommon here. Terrance nodded and started to walk away.

"Tell her where I am. They're going to execute me tomorrow."

CHAPTER THIRTY-NINE

Angus put the bells around his ankle and the knives on his forearm. They'd probably be taken from him as soon as he was grabbed, but he wanted them anyway. He tested his ankle again, but it had no more flex than it had yesterday, and it never would until it was cut open and rebuilt. There would be no running away.

Cadmael had offered his surgeons for after Angus executed his plan. Angus had just smiled and nodded. It wouldn't matter after. Angus could walk. It didn't hurt. In Vinland his foot was going to be the least of his problems.

There were reports that a clean sweep would be deployed at Kaan Pech on the coast. Officially Cadmael was sending him to stop it, but they both knew it was a lie. The Vinnish were preparing their trap. Angus hadn't even been back a day, and Terrance had made contacts and started spinning his lies. They'd travel overnight and be there by morning. He'd be arrested before lunch and in Vinland a day or two after… or dead. Though he doubted he'd be killed so quickly.

His heart wouldn't settle. It bounced and rattled as he packed up a few things. There was nothing he really needed or wanted, but he had to pack clothes to make it look like he was planning a short trip and not a one-way trip.

Terrance had done his part and done it well. Angus wanted to say something, but he didn't know what. Congratulations was wrong. It hurt that he'd been so convincing so fast, but at the same time, Angus was grateful that step had worked. It was the one he was most worried about. He had no other way to get to Vinland. Though Cadmael had a few military options, none of them would get him and Terrance deep into Vinland where they really needed to be.

With their bags in hand, Terrance and Angus made their way to the tram that would carry them through the jungle to the coast. Not many people were on it. Smart people were staying home and close to protection. Only idiots ran toward danger and a possible clean sweep.

If they were being watched, they needed to be the happy couple, so their smiles remained fixed as they took their seats. He should be excited about going to the coast and seeing some more of the Empire. It was what he'd wanted, but they wouldn't get to explore the seaside town.

"This is it?"

"You didn't want to know," Terrance said without looking at him.

No, he didn't. He couldn't be expecting it.

Terrance glanced at him and squeezed his hand. "It's not too late to run away, find a cabin somewhere in the jungle, and hide there until the world fixes itself."

"Didn't they say it would take two hundred years for the ice sheets to recede naturally?" They'd be long dead before spring came.

"That was the shortest estimate. There are whispers that they never will if the magic isn't rebalanced."

Angus nodded. He knew that. He was trying to make conversation because they couldn't talk about what they actually should be talking about. He stared out the window as the tram started to move slowly through the city and gradually picked up speed.

"You should get some sleep," Terrance said. He didn't need to say why.

It might be a while before he could rest peacefully again. He laid his head on Terrance's shoulder. He was as solid as ever, warm, and he smelled like soap and nervous sweat. The calm Terrance exuded was only skin-deep.

Angus's stomach knotted itself around his other organs. His thoughts were lodged firmly in tomorrow, and there was no way he could rest. But he closed his eyes and tried to find a little calm.

Saka would remind him that tomorrow would come regardless, but he couldn't rest. No matter how many times he closed his eyes, he'd snap fully alert at the slightest sound.

He'd fight. He'd have to resist, and he'd have to say horrible things to Terrance.

"It won't happen until daylight," Terrance murmured as though he'd been trying to sleep too.

"I'm sorry you had to."

"Let's not do that." He put his hand on Angus's thigh. The heat from his palm soaked through but didn't settle his heart or unravel the knots in his stomach. "Just remember, no matter what I say, you know the truth."

"Same. Whatever happens—"

Terrance kissed him. "Happens. We're stuck on the rails like a tram. We go to the end."

Sleep still managed to be elusive, so by the time the sun rose and the tram stopped, Angus's eyes were gritty and his neck ached from resting on Terrance's shoulder.

The tram stop was right on the coast, and the ocean was spread before them. The water was as blue as the sky, and a day at the beach was so tempting. He'd expected to be able to see Vinland from the beach, but he couldn't. It was too far away... yet far too close. Someone came up and asked Terrance for directions. Angus glanced over, wondering why anyone would ask two people who clearly weren't locals. Terrance turned his back to him to respond.

His heart lurched. This was it. He started to turn, ready to fight, and then everything went black.

CHAPTER FORTY

Via the telestones they were contacting any tribe they could and asking that they direct all magic their way in preparation. Not all agreed. Some needed time to prepare. Saka and Iktan took it in turns to reach out across the desert to make contact. Even with the other mages lending their strength, it was taxing. A headache had bloomed in Saka's temples, and the doorway hummed with power.

Angus had three days before the five-day deadline.

While Saka tried not to think about it, he knew Angus would've been captured by now. Cadmael had crossed the void to talk with Iktan, and Saka hoped he had news, even if it only confirmed his worst thoughts. Angus would be on his way to Vinland or already there. He kept waiting to be summoned, but it didn't happen. The warlocks would be careful not to let Angus slip away.

Cadmael finished talking with Iktan and walked over. "He was captured in Kaan Pech as expected. They put him on a boat that we believe is heading to Vinland. Without magic we are blind."

"And your allies who aren't so dependent on magic, what do they say?" Saka's words were sharp.

"That the boat looks like it is heading up the coast toward New London."

Saka drew in a breath. "That's where the college is based."

"That's where they've been hanging traitors," Cadmael said, his expression as grim as his tone.

"Terrance is with him?"

"He walked onto the boat. We don't know if he's still on the boat."

Irritation and worry crawled over his skin like so many beetles wanting to find a way in. There was nothing he could do but wait. At one time he'd been good at waiting, at telling everyone else to wait and give him time to work with the underground. What a fool he'd been.

"And Lizzie?"

"Is safe. I have other priests who will accept Wek as their mage—a mage who already knows how to make a doorway."

"They know in theory." No one had made a doorway in decades according to Iktan. "Train Lizzie and Wek. They know each other well. They'll be able to make a connection. It has to work." It had to be Wek and Lizzie. Emma was staying here for the moment and already had a demon animal, and no one knew where Reece was. Cadmael suspected the worst—that he had joined up with the Vinnish. Saka thought Reece had vanished, which was smart when the Vinnish wanted his blood and the Mayans were none too happy.

"Iktan says you're closing the doorway at dusk."

Saka nodded. Lozim's blood would help seal it. While they didn't have all of the tribes, they hopefully had enough—enough that there would be very little magic leaking out. But it was incredibly hard to do. Someone would have to be at the doorway at all times to keep it closed and stop the magic from leaving. They would work in shifts, none of them leaving the area and all of them ready to act when Terrance came through.

While mages had come from nearby towns associated with the Mayan Empire, Saka didn't know if it would be enough or how draining it would be. The whole plan was like running into the desert at night without bells or weapons and hoping to survive until dawn.

Sure it *could* happen, though it was unlikely. But he wouldn't dwell on failure, because he wasn't ready to think about a life without

Angus. Maybe if it reached day ten, he would walk into the desert alone and unarmed. It would be a better way to die than to wait for Arlyxia to finish drying. He drew in a breath. He could plan his death later. For the moment he would cling to hope the way he should've clung to Angus. He rubbed the pale scar on his chest—a scar he'd never heal. He should've said he loved Angus a long time ago instead of keeping it to himself as though it were something to be ashamed of. He wouldn't make that mistake again.

"Thank you for your help," Cadmael said, "for bringing Angus to us."

Saka considered the priest for a moment, and bitterness filled his mouth like poison. He hadn't brought Angus here for any other reason than to find refuge. If he'd known the cost, he'd have never risked all those human lives to get here. "Remember your gratitude when this is done."

CHAPTER FORTY-ONE

THE WORLD WAS ROCKING, the air was too warm, and his head thumped with every movement. Something was wrong with him, but every thought scattered before Angus could form them up into a line and make sense of them.

Angus sank back into the moving darkness.

The next time he surfaced, it was easier and accompanied by an unhealthy dose of panic. He couldn't move properly, and his skin itched. The back of his head throbbed and stung when he moved it. Whatever he was lying on was hard. He went to touch the wound, to see how bad it was, but his hands were cuffed together.

His heart beat faster as the panic learned how to fly.

This was the plan. It was fine. His breathing quickened. He was suffocating in the dark, so he forced slow breaths, each one laden with salt and sea. He was on a boat, and he felt weird because of the magic-dampening cuffs. The magic in him was trapped and coursing through him, unable to find a way out. His bells were missing from his ankle, replaced with cuffs, and he couldn't feel the leather of his knife sheath on his arm. They'd taken his sandals too. So far they were all things he'd expected.

The panic didn't recede, but it was contained for the moment.

He breathed slowly in the dark. They were still moving, and the rocking made his empty stomach rise and fall with the motion. How much longer would they be traveling?

He needed a drink… and to pee.

With no magic to see what he was doing, he groped around and hoped they'd left something. After several minutes of running his hands over wooden surfaces, he realized he was in a small room. The walls were lined with shelves—all of them unhelpfully empty. His steps were more of a shuffle because of the cuffs on his ankles. Metal and plastic and secured with magic—that he could feel—they were the kind of cuffs that were considered unbreakable. They weren't like the simple wristbands that sports players wore to prevent cheating and that Terrance had learned to bypass. These were cuffs for serious criminals.

He leaned against the shelves as nausea and hunger waged war in his stomach.

They wanted him weak on arrival. They wouldn't give him anything even if he asked.

The great traitor, in his soiled clothes, was unable to use magic. He hoped they wouldn't drag him through the streets.

The plan, which had never been great to begin with, was becoming more flimsy than wet paper. Where was Terrance? At least he wasn't locked in here. Did that mean they trusted him, or was he locked up somewhere else? He needed Terrance to open the void. If he didn't have Terrance, it was all over.

Everyone was expecting him to do this thing, and he wasn't sure he could. He'd never had the chance to even practice. He traced the scar he could reach on his forearm and then Saka's mark on his chest. The mages thought he could. He was a mage.

And he still had magic, even if he couldn't use it right now.

He still needed to pee, but he could solve that. While it was awkward with cuffed hands, he peed on the door. At least he knew where that was. Then he wedged himself back on the shelf he'd been sleeping on, and he waited.

. . .

LIGHT CREPT around the doorframe and caught in the dust hovering in the air. Angus stayed still and kept his breathing soft as he listened. He hadn't heard a single voice all day. He assumed it was daylight and not a light outside the storeroom. His back and head ached from lying on the shelf. It was barely wide enough, and when the boat rocked, he thought he was going to fall off and into the puddle of piss.

His tongue was glued to the roof of his mouth with thirst—not the Demonside kind of thirst as magic was sucked from his body, but regular thirst. That was just as bad. If he'd been caught in the morning and it was now dawn again, he hadn't had anything to eat or drink since dinner the night they traveled. He'd had some water on the tram, but that was too long ago. He needed to be in better shape to work magic.

He gritted his teeth. It would only get worse.

A thumping noise became footsteps and shouting. Something was going on.

He wiggled off the shelf to be upright when the door opened. He could run at the person and try to escape, but if they were in Vinland, there was nowhere to go.

The footsteps got closer. He fisted his hands for defense and waited. The lock clicked, and the door swung open. Angus blinked at the bright light.

"Welcome home, traitor." The man spat. Saliva hit Angus's shoulder.

While the man was wearing a winter coat and hat, Angus was still in his lightweight Mayan clothing. The air on his skin was already sharp.

"I was on vacation," he croaked.

The man didn't laugh. He grabbed the chain between the cuffs and dragged Angus out of the storeroom and toward the ladder. "Up you go."

Climbing the ladder up to the deck was awkward and slow, and the rungs bit into his bare foot.

"Hurry up." The man hit him across the back of the calves.

Angus slipped and *accidentally* kicked him in the face. A smile formed even though there would be retribution later.

He didn't want them to think he had planned to be there, so he had to put up some kind of fight. He reached the deck and scrambled up as best he could. The man who'd been behind him kicked him hard between the legs, and the pain, like a knife to the balls, made him curl up like a dying bug. A cry escaped.

"Not so powerful now, are you?" He stalked off.

Angus couldn't breathe to reply, only groan. He closed his eyes and tried to will the agony away. When the pain dulled to a throb, he opened his eyes. They were tying up the boat, and Terrance was helping them. He closed his eyes to avoid seeing the man he loved ignoring him so well.

No... he should ask. He should be confused and hurt.

"Terrance." His voice was dry and not nearly as loud as he thought it would be. It didn't need to be louder. Terrance turned. His gaze was colder than any glacier, and for a heartbeat, Angus wondered if that was the truth and what they had was the act. "What's going on?"

"You're home to face your crimes." Terrance turned away.

"What crimes? I thought...."

Terrance glared at him, and Angus saw just the smallest fracture in his mask of hate. "You thought wrong."

"No." He forced himself to sit up.

"Shut up." The man who'd kicked him shoved him to the deck. "No talking."

"Water?" he pleaded, hoping for at least that. He was pathetic.

One of the men sloshed a bucket of icy seawater on him. "Water."

Angus gasped and shivered, and a few of them laughed.

It was only then he realized the real bite in the wind. Saturated, he started to shake. If he asked to be warmed up, they'd probably set him on fire. He forced himself to move out of the puddle of spilled water and tried to tuck his hands into his armpits to keep his fingers warm. He was usually worried about sunburn and heatstroke. Now it was frostbite and hypothermia that were the real threat. His toes were blue-tinged already.

His teeth rattled, and he couldn't stop them.

When two of the men walked toward him, he braced for another strike or some other horrible thing, but they hauled him up and escorted him down the gangway to a waiting vehicle. He was shoved into the van before he could see where Terrance was going. Out of the breeze and out of sight, he wrapped his arms around his knees and shoved his hand in his mouth to silence the screams he wanted to make. His breaths came in hard painful pants as the panic raced through him unchecked. He couldn't stop it even if he tried. His toes gripped the floor as the van started moving.

Fuck, this was a bad plan. But it wasn't a plan. It was a string of hopeful things and best outcomes all put together because there was nothing else… no one else.

If he failed, everyone would die.

He thought he might be at the college—the changing rooms looked familiar—but he wasn't sure. They stripped him and made him shower and left him waiting. At least they had removed the ankle cuffs so it was easier for him to walk around.

If he was at the college, the bars on the windows were new.

He opened a few of the lockers hoping for a forgotten packet of junk food or an energy bar or even a pack of gum. Nothing. But at least he'd been able to drink and the water had been hot.

No towel, though. All the colored scars were bright against his pale skin. Every time he touched one, he felt a little braver for that moment. Then it faded just as fast.

When the door opened, he put his hands over his dick, not that his hands would do much if they kicked him again, and waited.

Three men entered, and two were well-armed.

The other was a warlock. He crackled with stolen magic, but he held a clipboard like he was an office worker. "Angus Donohue?"

"Yes." There was no point in lying about it. They knew who he was.

"You are charged with the murder of your father and consorting with demons." The man looked up. "Plural?"

Angus was going to deny it, but it was technically true. One demon orgy, and it would be held against him for life. "Yes."

The man made a note. "Aiding the underground, defecting to the Mayan Empire with the intention of bringing down Vinland—"

"No. I was fleeing. I just wanted to be safe." That was the truth. Bringing down Vinland had been a dream back then, not a possibility.

The warlock glanced at him again. "Did you or did you not interfere with our gathering of magic?"

So they knew about that too. "Yes."

"With the intention of bringing down Vinland. You are also charged with the kidnapping of Terrance Erikson and forcing him to participate in demon rituals across the void. How do you plead?"

His list of achievements was longer than he expected. He hadn't realized they'd use everything against him. "Do I get a lighter sentence if I plead guilty?"

The man closed the clipboard. "You will be hanged at dawn."

"What about a trial? Don't I get a lawyer and a chance to defend myself?"

"There will be a trial. You will be questioned, and there are witnesses who will testify to your actions. It will be broadcast so all can see your fate."

He was going to be hanged. His throat closed.

"Nothing to say for yourself?"

He had lots of things to say, not that the warlock really wanted to hear. "The magic belongs in Demonside, not here. You are ruining two worlds."

The warlock stepped closer. His gaze skimmed over Angus's body and left him in need of another shower. "Skitun. Covered in their marks. Did you get on your knees and beg for their magic, or was your mouth too full?"

Angus stepped back.

He couldn't hide the scars—they shimmered in the harsh light, marking him for all to see—nor did he want to hide.

"Your father would be disgusted at you."

"Good. That means I've done something right."

The warlock considered him for a moment. "Your death will squash anyone who thought they could be like you." Then he turned and walked away.

People knew who he was? Were trying to be like him?

"Get dressed." One of the guards threw a pile of yellow clothing—prison garb—at him.

He pulled on the pants but couldn't get the shirt over his head because of the cuffs. "Can you undo the center chain?"

They'd cut his old shirt off. Angus had fully expected the knife to slip, but they wanted him alive to demoralize anyone who was fighting back.

The one who'd thrown the clothes at him shrugged. "No hiding what you are." He snatched the shirt away. His hand slid to his weapon. He had a gun and a baton. "Behave yourself."

The other guard put the cuffs back on his legs. Angus didn't move. He didn't want a beating that left him more damaged and weak. He needed to be smart.

The man stood and prodded him forward. "Out."

Between the two guards, he was marched out of the changing room and onto a field. His steps faltered before he reached what had once been the grassed area of the college's rugby stadium. There were two inches of snow on the ground and yellow clumps of miserable people scattered around. With no shoes or socks and no protection against the cold, no one there would last long.

Soldiers marched along the walkways where fans had once gathered to watch their favorite players.

Horror gripped him. "What is this place?"

"Where traitors wait for sentencing. You got processed fast. You'll only spend one night here." The guard gave him a nudge, so he was forced to step off the concrete and into the snow. "Enjoy."

The cold bit into his feet and his back. The pants were too thin to do much more than offer privacy. He wasn't sure he'd survive one night.

He started to shiver, not sure what to do. Standing alone wouldn't help him stay warm, and he didn't have the energy to move around. He hadn't eaten in too long. That left joining a huddle.

He made his way over to the closest one, his steps more of a shuffle. A few people on the outside watched him with suspicion. Some of them had black toes and fingers. How long had they been here? How many people were there, all waiting to be hanged? Did they know their fate?

Who were they? Wizards or members of the underground or just anyone who spoke up?

He pressed his hands into his armpits, but there was nothing he could do for his toes. "Is there a fire or food in the middle?"

The woman next to him glanced at him with dead eyes. "No. We take it in turns to be on the outside. Like penguins. You sleep when you're in the middle."

"And food and water."

"You're standing on it," she said and turned away.

Grass and snow? Eating snow would only make them colder.

"They throw food in when they want to see us scramble," the man on his other side said. "Leif. I'd offer my hand but...."

It was missing, and the other one had blackened fingers.

"Angus."

"It's not a pleasure to meet you, I'm sure," Leif said.

The man stared at him a bit longer, his gaze focused on the cuffs. Angus wasn't the only person wearing dampeners, but he was the only one he could see with his hands and feet linked. In the huddle someone said his name, and a ripple went through the people.

"Angus? Angus Donohue? You escaped to Demonside?"

He didn't know if he was going to get a hug or a fist to the face, but he couldn't run from what was coming. All he had to do was survive until morning. "Yes."

"Let him through to the middle." Someone pulled at his hand and tried to drag him forward.

"It's fine. I'll take my turn at the edge." He didn't need more enemies, but he wanted so badly to be warm. People were already grumbling. "I'm being hanged tomorrow anyway." The words felt odd on his tongue. Should he be more worried about that? He glanced down. If he were really being hanged, would it be better to lie down and freeze and cheat the warlocks of his death?

"The guards won't let you lie down, if that's what you're thinking. They like you nice and alive," Leif said.

The huddle parted, and Leif nudged him forward. "Go on. Take it while you can."

Angus edged through to the middle, apologizing as he went.

"You're lucky, you know. We try to give those who know they're about to get the noose some middle time," a woman said.

People shushed her.

Those in the middle were lying down sleeping, but they looked dead. They were thin and pale and bony.

But it was warm in the center, and the breeze didn't chew at him. "Thank you."

He sat and rested his head on his knees.

He was woken later by the cold snap of wind on his face as the huddle fell apart. Food was being thrown onto what had once been the grassed oval. He knew he should get some, but he couldn't be bothered to fight for a share when there wasn't enough anyway. It had been so long since he'd eaten that his stomach had given up.

People ran back to their huddle, food cradled like babies—limp carrots, dark moldy bread, and raw meat. The guards were giving them shitty food just for fun. The magic churned within him, scouring his veins but unable to get out. His nails cut into his palms.

Leif put his hand on his forearm. "They're already watching you. Don't give them a reason to come down and give you something special."

Angus accepted the offered bread and half a carrot from another. They were sacrificing for him because they'd heard of him. He wanted to tell them that there was hope, but if he spoke, the desperate whispers would reach the guards. So he stayed silent, ate the rubbery carrot, and forced down the bread. He'd need the energy tomorrow.

After he'd eaten he After he'd eaten, he tried to bring feeling back to his feet by rubbing them. Some of the others had shoes, but no one had coats. "If they want us alive, then why not put us in a proper prison and feed us properly?"

Leif laughed. "You're funny. The prisons are full, and we're eating much the same as everyone else. Where the fuck have you been?"

"Mayan Empire and Demonside."

"Well you picked a shit of a time to come home, son."

Yeah. He should've done something months earlier. He was positively fat compared to some. While they'd been eating whatever they could, he'd gobbled down tortillas stuffed with meat and vegetable on both sides of the void. "What happens at night?"

"They turn on the lights, and we keep our huddle going."

"Why not one big huddle?"

"Too hard to rotate."

The huddle formed up after people had eaten and relieved themselves around the edges of the field without any words being spoken. Angus took a place somewhere in the middle, despite being offered a place in the center.

"Tell us about Demonside. The desert and the demons," someone said.

"Yes. We want to hear the story from you."

"Is it all true? Did you really live with demons?"

"Are you a demon?"

"Um…." Where did he even start? What had people been saying about him? He thought for a moment and then decided to tell them the truth—all of it—especially about the heat of the red desert and the scent of the marketplace when he first arrived. This time he'd add all the details, the parts he'd left out for the WCD. "Well, I was one of those people who got snatched and taken to Demonside the first time I summoned a demon. Saka is his name. He's a mage."

And he was waiting. The whole of Demonside was waiting.

CHAPTER FORTY-TWO

IT WAS BARELY dawn when Angus was summoned by the guards. The huddle had released him and said goodbye. People cried and hugged him as though he were a beloved family member, when all he'd done was tell them a story. He'd slept a little during the night, and eaten a handful of snow for breakfast. His feet, that had been kindly wrapped in rags, were icy and painful.

The guards made him walk through the campus on footpaths slick with ice. The cold chewed on his bones, and he missed the warmth of his fellow criminals. His skin was tight, and the scars ached. He wished for the heat of the demons' hands on his skin. He could almost imagine it. He shivered as he walked, and each breath cut his lungs.

When he hadn't been talking or sleeping, he'd been running through what he needed to do. If Terrance wasn't there, he was going to swing like any other traitor. They wouldn't uncuff him, of that he was sure. Fear made every step harder. He didn't want to do this.

Why had no one talked him out of it?

But if he didn't try, who would? All those people who were waiting in the cold would die. The friends he'd made in one night didn't deserve to be hanged for speaking the truth. How many more were in similar stadiums hoping to freeze to death instead of being hanged?

He tried to swallow, but it was like the stale bread had become caught in his throat.

He stumbled on numb feet and the guard let him fall. The concrete path bit into his hands and knees, and the toes on his lame foot were hot from stubbing. He sucked in a couple of shaky breaths as blood warmed his palms.

"Get up." The guard nudged him with his gun, and Angus scrambled up as best he could before the guard could kick or hit him with the stock.

They got moving again. His toes hurt, and he didn't want to hobble, but with the cuffs and his foot, it was easier and faster. Did he want to hurry up and get it done or slow down and enjoy what could be his last few moments?

The sky was bright blue, the air crisp and cold. There were crows in the trees talking harshly to each other. There was no other life that he could see. The trees were sticks waiting for spring, and the building and parks where students had gathered were empty and silent. The bushes that created little nooks had been removed. The place was a hollow shell of what it had been.

He sighed, and his breath clouded. Every minute he spent outside he was dying. His body was cooling. How long did he have before he got hypothermia? He'd never worried about it. He'd looked up heatstroke and desert survival, but surviving the cold had never really been an issue. He wished he'd asked more questions in the huddle. But they'd wanted to hear him talk… they wanted hope.

A frown formed as he realized where they were going, and he glanced around to be sure of his landmarks now that everything looked a little different. But he was certain. They were going toward the woods where the students practiced growing their trees and summoning demons.

A flock of large black birds—not crows, they were far bigger than that—lifted out of the trees as they got closer, and as they got nearer he smelled something. There was a sickly rotting on the air, and the trees were malformed. He squinted and stared, his brain not wanting to process the truth.

There was nothing wrong with the trees. It was what hung from them that changed their shape. Bodies dangled from the branches. Some were more complete, others were being pulled apart by vultures.

Hot bile rose in his throat. How many bodies were there? How many had fallen when their necks gave way and were now beneath the snow?

The guard gave him a nudge forward. "Traitors' forest. Reminds the students to behave."

Shit… they were still bringing kids to the woods and teaching them to be warlocks. He was still a first-year student. Or was it now summer break? Summer with snow.

It was all fucked-up.

His feet didn't want to move. The guard nudged him again, harder this time, and Angus stumbled forward and stubbed the toe of his good foot on the ground. Heat and pain flooded through the numbness, and he bit back the curses and huffed out several quick breaths. Each one clouded before him.

There were people waiting beneath a tree—for him, he realized. This was it. But he'd stopped shivering. And maybe he wasn't as cold. Was that because he was dying or because fear was warming him up? He couldn't worry about his body. He needed to think about the magic—magic that he couldn't do because he was still wearing the cuffs.

His breathing became quicker, and he couldn't slow it. He wanted to run… but he'd get a bullet in the back, and then his traitor's hanging.

The people waiting didn't even glance at the bodies in the trees, because they were the ones who'd put them there. How many people had been hanged?

While there wasn't a body in every tree, their yellow clothing made them stand out against the dark trunks, and the breeze gave them life and rocked them. Branches creaked, and bones whistled, and the whole place felt wrong.

Several warlocks were bundled up against the cold. There were half a dozen armed guards in case he tried to run, though he was still shackled and half dead from the cold. His stomach cramped. He wanted to hunch up, curl up, and hide.

He wanted to go back to those few days when he'd been safe and happy. There had been a few. Hadn't there? He gathered them close—the moments when he was studying magic and Terrance was in his bed, when Saka was teaching him and showing him how to raise magic, when he was walking with the tribe and healing their wounds, the night they grew crops.

Was Miniti's tribe still alive or had they succumbed to the desert?

The day he first summoned a demon and met Saka—that was a good day. He hadn't realized how Saka would turn his life around and how beautiful magic could be.

He closed his eyes and tried to imagine these woods as they had been that first day. For a moment he remembered his uncertainty and how he'd tried *not* to summon a demon. And then Saka took him across the void. At the time he wouldn't have said it was a good day, but it had been the best. It was the day he woke up.

He opened his eyes. He could do this. He had to.

The guard forced him forward, toward a cluster of people around a tree. A man threw a rope over a branch where a box was already set up underneath. Angus slowed. They were ready for him so soon?

The guards brought Angus closer, and the cluster of people stepped back. It wasn't for him. There was another man in yellow. He stepped up onto the box and faced Angus. It was Reece.

"No."

Reece couldn't speak because of the gag. The guard put the noose over his head. Angus lurched forward, and the guards let him hobble closer. There was nothing he could do, but he kept trying to run toward Reece. "No." But no one listened to him.

How had they gotten Reece? When? Had they been on the same boat? In the same stadium? Or had Reece been working with them all along and this was punishment for his failure?

The guard kicked the box away, and Reece flinched and jerked and struggled. With his cuffed hands, he scrabbled at the rope as his face darkened. Angus stopped and stood rooted to the spot like one of the trees.

It was forever and a heartbeat until Reece went still.

He'd be next. All thoughts of magic and stopping the warlocks scattered. It was all Angus could do to breathe and not collapse.

The guard hauled the body higher and tied off the rope—one more person denied their cremation and left for the vultures.

His heart was beating too fast, and his body was too numb. Angus didn't want to die like that. He had to stop these people or at least burn up trying. It was the warlocks who should be hanging in dishonorable death, not those who stood up to them.

Where was Terrance?

The guards grabbed Angus's arms and hauled him forward. The murder of warlocks looked like black-clad crows hiding among the corpses. They turned to face him, their eyes too bright, lit with zeal.

The hangman grinned and picked up another rope. Despite the cold, heat raced up Angus's spine. He shuddered and tried to step back, but the guards held him firmly in place.

The hangman walked to the tree next to the one Reece was in and threw the rope over the branch with a skill that revealed far too much practice. Angus didn't want to think about the number of people who'd died there.

Angus's heart fluttered like a dying butterfly trying one more time to get off the ground. He drew in a breath. "No. Not that tree. I want one I grew."

Angus turned away to look for one of the trees he made with Saka. He didn't want to die at all, but he wasn't going to die randomly.

"What does it matter what tree?" the warlock in charge asked.

"The magic has burned his brain," came a familiar voice.

Angus glanced over his shoulder. For the briefest moment, Terrance held his gaze. Then he looked away. He was nice and warm in his woolen cap, scarf, and coat. Angus narrowed his eyes.

In that moment he hated Terrance as much as he loved him. He wanted to run over and ask him how well he slept and what he'd eaten now that he was back in favor. He settled for glaring and muttering under his breath the few Mayan swear words he'd picked up.

"Find your tree," the female warlock said. "It will make it more fitting."

He didn't want to do anything that would make her happy. But he wasn't ready for it to happen. Was Saka ready? What if he weren't? Had it been five days? His mind raced and tripped over itself as it tried to find its way. He'd be celebrating back in Demonside soon. It was like his time in the desert—keep moving and eventually he'd be there. But so much could go wrong.

He wanted to talk to Terrance. Shouldn't he be asking why? If he were really being betrayed he'd want to know. Even this show for the warlocks hurt him.

Angus shuffled away to look for his tree, and the guards followed close by, as though they expected him to vanish. The snow and mud soaked through the thin wrappings on his feet. He couldn't feel them unless he stubbed them. Blood spotted the front of his pants from where he'd grazed his knees, and his palms were raw. None of it would matter soon either way.

He'd grown several trees here, and he didn't care which one he found, but it had to be one of his. He glanced around to get his bearings and saw the twisted one that someone else had grown in that first class. Its loop was distinctive, and his tree, tall and straight, was to his right. He put his palm on it, glad that no other body had defiled it.

The guards kept pace and encircled him. *Good. Let them make the circle.*

The hangman grumbled about giving prisoners extra rights and special treatment.

"Are we ready to broadcast?" asked the female warlock as others set up a camera and microphone.

His death was going to be live to the people of Vinland and anyone else watching. At least Cadmael would know what was going on. His stomach twisted as he watched the preparations.

The hangman gave the noose a tug. "All ready, *sir*. Let's hope it doesn't chafe your fine neck."

Angus pressed his lips together as the box was brought over. He was not climbing onto the box. If he got up there and had his head in the noose, it was too late.

The camera guy gave the warlocks a signal, and Terrance looked like he was going to throw up. If Angus had more food in his belly, he might actually have done that. Instead he stood shaking with cold and fear. His hands were blue and blotchy, so he made fists and released them repeatedly. He needed to move and wanted to act, but it was still too soon. He wished they'd hurry the fuck up, because he was tired of waiting and being hungry and cold.

Sometime in the next few minutes he'd either be alive and victorious or just another hanged traitor and a warning to others. But it would be over, and he could say he tried, which was more than others had done.

"Warlock Angus Donohue. You are charged with—"

"I'm not a warlock." They were being broadcast, and he wanted people to know the truth and to remember. "I'm a mage."

A guard stepped forward and hit him in the face with the muzzle of his gun. Angus staggered back as blood filled his mouth where his teeth had cut his tongue and cheek.

"Warlock Donohue."

"Mage Angus," he corrected. "I will never be a warlock. Let that title be reserved for those who misuse magic."

The guard raised his gun again.

"He needs to be able to talk. To confess," the woman said.

"You admit to consorting with demons?" The man who was asking the questions kept going.

"I'm a mage. Of course I consort with demons." Hot blood ran down his chin. The heat was almost worth the pain.

The warlock signaled, and a guard hit him again, this time on the back. Heat flared and spread through the split skin and cramped muscles, bringing them back to life. He had the first thing he needed in the battle—something no warlock would ever consider.

They never used their own blood.

CHAPTER FORTY-THREE

Terrance fisted his hands in his coat pockets and winced every time Angus was struck. Why didn't he shut the fuck up? He wanted to yell at Angus, but he bit his own tongue until he tasted blood.

He had to watch silently, like he didn't give a shit. The warlocks were waiting for him to break and do something. Now he understood why Angus had ripped the whip from the warlock's hand even though Terrance wanted him to be passive. Angus hadn't been able to watch. Terrance tried not to gasp or make a sound as metal hit flesh again. The gloves stopped his nails from cutting his palms. No one there truly trusted him, and he'd end up in a tree if things went badly. But for the moment, they wanted him there. He'd disabled the dampener they'd put on him. Now it was just a strip of plastic around his wrist.

Maybe the warlocks were desperate to believe that they still had people on their side. What Terrance had seen since he'd been back—which wasn't much—was that people obeyed out of fear. They didn't believe in the cause, and they probably never had. What was the point of becoming the most powerful magical country in the world when half the population hated you and the other half was dying of starvation?

The warlock in charge turned to Terrance. "You, give us the evidence."

Terrance licked his lips and stepped a couple of paces closer to Angus—not enough, but close enough for the moment. He was aware of the camera's focus on him. He'd need to be a little closer to Angus and a little farther from the warlocks when the time came.

Angus glared at him. "You come to say how much you loved sucking my dick?"

"You made me do things with demons that I'll never forget." The night with Saka would be forever in his mind. Why hadn't he grown some balls and acted sooner? They could've had more fun, and he could've learned something that he could have used to defeat the warlocks.

"You took me to Demonside and did rituals with demons. They marked you as their own." Those cuts must have hurt, but Angus had let them. Angus had shed so much blood for demons.

Terrance took another small step forward, and Angus was watching him, but his expression had changed.

Did he get it? Did he see how amazed Terrance was to even be included in this stupid, deadly, dangerous plan? Someone always wanted something from him, but Angus had only ever wanted to be held. Terrance couldn't even do that properly.

"You dragged me and others to Demonside, two of whom died on your march to the Mayan Empire." He'd do it again. He'd cross Demonside to get to Angus. He'd do it alone if he had to. He'd nearly lost Angus once. Another tiny step, and he was almost close enough.

Angus stared at him, his cheek marred by a purple bruise, the skin swollen and split like overripe fruit. He lifted his hands and wiped the blood from his lip. It was crimson on his blue hands, and his body shook with the cold. "Why did you betray me?"

Terrance stepped closer. He wanted to give Angus his clothing and hold him until he was warm. This was far worse than they thought it would be. The guards were watching him now, expecting trouble. Maybe he'd get a bullet before he could do anything.

"Me? You dragged me into this mess and showed me demons. A

world that I'd never heard about." He lowered his voice to a whisper. "I could never betray you."

He called up the image of the doorway with its chips and cracks and imperfections. He was trying to reach a doorway far beyond Vinland's reach in Demonside. He had to believe that all tears in the void now went there, even from here, even though he knew that wasn't possible. He ran his tongue over his teeth and tasted the metal of his blood, the fear, and the magic. Then he ripped open the void in the gap between him and Angus and dove through before the warlocks could lift their weapons and fire.

He slid through to Demonside on his belly and flipped onto his back in case someone had followed. Relief at the sight of the stones washed through him. Cadmael pulled him up and shoved him toward one of the pillars.

Saka stood by the other one, ready to act. "He's alive?"

"Not for much longer. They're about to hang him." Terrance glanced at Cadmael and the demons as they got up from where they'd been resting and formed up into an arrow that spread beyond the stones. Cadmael sliced his palm open and picked up the staff Angus had temporarily used. He offered his other hand to Iktan, who cut both his palms and Cadmael's and then linked hands. The other mages did the same, linking up hand to hand and blood to blood.

Terrance drew a breath, tore off the gloves and hat, and gouged his palm with his nails deeply enough that blood speckled through. Then he placed his hand on the pillar. He and Saka needed to keep the doorway open for the duration of the spell.

Cadmael stepped up to the edge of the void and stuck the staff through. Although it was made of wood, it began to glow. The magic was flowing, but if they failed, there'd be nothing left of Demonside.

If Angus didn't survive, Terrance didn't really care if both worlds died.

CHAPTER FORTY-FOUR

ANGUS IS ALIVE.

The worlds tumbled through Saka and made his heart beat fast. He wanted to run through the void and help, but he was where he needed to be. If the doorway shut too soon, the magic would remain in Vinland, and that would be a disaster. His palm was sticky with blood as he placed it on the pillar and locked gazes with Terrance. He hoped that he had the strength to hold his side.

The magic flowed out and tore at the edges of the doorway so it wanted to shrink and close. Saka had to hold it so Angus could finish and get through. The magic rumbled beneath his feet as it was torn out of the ground and directed through the staff.

It had to work or they were all dead.

Bullets came through the void, and several struck Cadmael. He gasped and staggered but kept the staff steady as blood splashed onto the stones and fed the doorway.

They waited. If the magic didn't come back... if Angus didn't came back....

Saka rested his forehead on the pillar. Holding the doorway open was like trying to hold back a river with his bare hands.

CHAPTER FORTY-FIVE

Angus grasped the staff when it poked through the void. The wood burned his bloodied palm and linked him directly to Demonside. As the magic burned through him, the pain seared every nerve until it no longer hurt and magic tumbled from his other hand.

The cuffs heated and overloaded, unable to contain the flow that was forced into him. The scars the mages had made along his arms tore open, and the magic in his blood flowed from them. Silvery magic leaped between his fingers.

The guards started to shoot. Angus grunted as something hit him. Then he put up a shield that shimmered blue. He'd been hit but didn't feel the sting of the bullet. He was no longer cold or in pain, but that probably wasn't good news. He was probably dying, and only the magic was keeping him alive.

His fingers crackled, and he flicked the magic across all the humans alive in the woods, taking the magic from them, along with their lives. Their little circles offered no protection from what he controlled. They fell and lay still. Every tree with a body in it burst into red flames as Angus gave those who'd been hanged a proper funeral, the kind they deserved. Let carrion feeders feast on the bodies of the warlocks.

With the magic tearing through, fueling him, Angus knew what the warlocks wanted. There was nothing but magic, and nothing else mattered. But the longer he held it, the more damage it did. It would scour him on the inside until only useless skin would be left. He needed to find the rest of the stolen magic.

The metal between his wrists snapped as he flung out his hand and sent the silvery whip searching for the magic the warlocks had locked up. He doubled over and gasped as the magic left him and its tail disappeared into the distance. He drew in several breaths of the cold air that cut his lungs, and his shoulder burned from the bullet wound. He wished he couldn't feel the cold that needled his feet or the way his skin burned and bled, torn open by the magic.

If he hadn't had the mages' marks, Saka's mark would have ripped open through his chest to his heart and killed him. But he wasn't done yet. That was the easy part.

He yanked on the staff, and Cadmael released it. He couldn't see the priest, but he could feel him. Angus drew the staff through. That was the signal the mages needed to get clear of the doorway. He slammed the wooden staff down on the chain between his ankles and shattered it. Green magic spilled out and leached into the ground. He shouldn't be able to see it, but he couldn't deal with that now.

He was breathing and hurting, so he was alive enough to finish. Hot blood poured over his chest from the bullet wound in his shoulder. He should fix that before he lost too much blood, but the ground rumbled and shook as though there were an earthquake. Burning trees fell and sent golden sparks high into the air along with black cinders. The destruction was beautiful. Angus stumbled as the shaking intensified and grew closer, but he kept his balance because of the staff.

It wasn't an earthquake racing toward him. The magic had been released.

He turned to watch, but the magic wasn't a silvery ribbon. It was a monstrous creature that glittered and shimmered as it raced toward the void, determined to get home.

There was no way he could channel that and make it safe the way he'd planned. Nor could he outrun it. He hoped the mages were clear of the doorway.

The ground rippled like a bedsheet, and he stepped across the void, refusing to die in Vinland. The magic hit him in the back and carried him the rest of the way through.

CHAPTER FORTY-SIX

MAGIC RUSHED through the doorway and tore up the stones and ground where the mages had been standing only moments before. The doorway snapped closed with a bang that reverberated through the ground as the flood of magic broke the link between the worlds. Saka drew away from the pillar, and weakness dropped him to his knees. Terrance had slid to sitting long before, his hand still on the pillar.

Terrance lifted his head and dropped his hand. "Where is he?" His voice was rough.

Saka shook his head. He hadn't seen anyone come through, but that didn't mean no one had been caught in the body of magic. "I don't know."

Mages were already tending the injured, and Saka forced himself up to help. Maybe Angus was there, but what would he do if he wasn't? He needed a plan. No one could leave until the doorway was reset and the void reopened by Lizzie and Wek, neither of which had ever wanted a demon or a human.

He walked over and hauled Terrance up, and Terrance put his arms around him. "He has to be here."

If not, Angus was alone in Vinland. There was no way to get to him, not quickly or easily. By the time Saka did, it might be too late. Angus would have to open the void and summon him. Saka's stomach twisted itself into knots.

"He might be here." But Saka had seen the amount of magic that returned. If Angus had channeled that, there'd be nothing left of him. Clouds gathered in the sky, roiling overhead and promising rain. He kissed Terrance's cheek. He wanted to say it would be all right, but he couldn't tell that lie, even to himself.

A shout went up as the first drops of rain fell. But the demons weren't shouting about the rain, which rapidly became heavier and soaked through his shirt to his skin. They were carrying something— someone—toward the mages.

Still holding Terrance's hand, Saka went to meet them.

"It's Angus. His yellow pants," Terrance said.

As they got closer, Saka saw metal around his ankles and the blood on his skin, more red than white. Saka gasped, and his heart collapsed. Was he dead? He wasn't moving.

"He's alive," the feathered demon holding him said.

The rain became a downpour that drenched them all and washed Angus's blood off his skin to reveal the open wounds.

Saka pulled Angus close and took him from the demon. He didn't wake, and his body was cold and limp. "Where was he?"

"In the town, by your door," she said.

The magic had brought him home.

Terrance lifted one of Angus's blue hands. "He's cold. He was outside with no coat. They wouldn't let him. He needs warmth."

Saka carried Angus to one of the nearby shelters. They'd been rapidly built so mages could live close to the doorway to keep it sealed until Terrance opened it. The shelter had walls on three sides and two beds that were barely off the ground and barely beds. Water streamed along the floor. As soon as the doorway was remade, Angus would have to go back to heal. Saka wouldn't keep him here, no matter how much he wanted to.

He lit a fire while Terrance stripped off the wet clothes and bundled Angus up in sheets to dry and warm him. Terrance added the winter coat he'd been wearing. "I can't heal him."

"I will," Saka said. Terrance could close the wounds, but he didn't know what damage the magic had done to Angus. The cuffs had burned the skin around his wrists and ankles and left it blistered.

But Angus was alive. Someone brought the staff and propped it against the frame. It *had* been made of wood, but now it gleamed black.

What had Angus become?

CHAPTER FORTY-SEVEN

THE WALLS WERE PINK, and a beeping that wouldn't stop had woken Angus. Carefully he sat up, and his muscles protested like he hadn't moved and stretched in too long.

He needed to shut the beeping up, so he reached out a hand. Red magic lanced through the machine, and it went quiet. Angus closed his eyes so he could think. He must be in Demonside, since he could see magic… but where? And why was there a machine?

He cracked his eyes open again. He wasn't cuffed to the bed, so maybe he wasn't a prisoner. Then he sat up and swung his legs over the edge of the mattress. It was a human bed, and he was tethered to a very human-style drip.

Where the fuck was he?

His heart gave a panicked dance at the idea of being captured by the Vinnish again, but their hospitals weren't pink, or they hadn't been last time he'd been in one, which was over ten years earlier.

There were scars around his ankles and wrists that he'd never seen before, but his hands looked the same. He turned them over. One palm was marred by a wide flat scar. He fisted his hand expecting resistance, but it was fine, just marked. He flexed his feet and then stood up. One worked fine and the other… well, it was no worse than it had been, so he stood.

He was naked. Wherever he was, he couldn't run around without clothes. There were none in the room, so the sheet would have to do. He wrapped it around himself and then realized he needed to get the drip out of his arm before he went anywhere.

Somewhere nearby another alarm was going off, and footsteps pounded outside his door, drawing closer. The door to the room burst open, and people in an array of colors flooded in and then stopped and stared.

The machine sizzled in the corner and gave a pop. Angus glanced at it and then at the people. Oh. He was the reason for the alarm. "It woke me up."

No one moved.

"Can you unhook me?"

"I think you should lie down so we can check you over." A woman he assumed was the doctor walked slowly over, as though she expected him to do something awful.

"I feel fine." Did he not look fine? He had new scars, and the mages' marks were still etched on his skin. He probably looked a little worse for wear. He glanced at the hospital staff, at their bronze skin and dark hair. "I'm in Uxmal?"

"Yes," the doctor said. "What else do you remember? Your name? Age?"

"Angus Donohue." She shone a light into his eyes, and he pulled away. "Nineteen… maybe twenty. It depends on the date."

"You can see the light?"

"Of course I can. I can see you." He could still see magic. That wasn't right, but he didn't want to tell her that.

The doctor didn't look convinced. "What's the last thing you remember?"

"Stepping through the void." He hadn't expected to wake up. He clearly wasn't dead, and nothing really hurt. How long had he been there?

"Lie down, and I'll arrange some tests."

"I'm fine." He picked at the bandage that covered where the drip pierced his skin. If she wouldn't take it out, he would.

The door opened again.

"You're awake! I left to get lunch, and then the alarm sounded." Terrance pushed through the cluster of doctors and squeezed him so hard his ribs almost popped, but he didn't want him to stop.

"I was a little tired... needed a nap." He leaned into Terrance. If he was there, it couldn't be all bad. He allowed his heart to settle, and he relaxed into Terrance's crushing embrace.

"You've been here for two days and another in Demonside before the doorway opened. You were so cold I didn't think you'd ever wake." Terrance held him close, as though he were never going to let go again.

"Hypothermia. It was the blood loss that we were worried about," the doctor said.

It was only when Terrance drew back that the delight on his face flickered to something else for just a moment.

It was starting to worry him now. They were all treating him like there was something wrong. "Have I grown horns like Saka or something?"

He ran his fingers over his hair and then his face, but it all felt like his. His cheek was tender, and the inside of his mouth sore. There was a pucker on his shoulder from the bullet and the marks from the cuffs. He catalogued the new scars but couldn't find anything that should make them all so cautious. He had all his limbs, even all his toes.

Terrance grabbed his free hand—the other was still holding up the sheet. "No, it's your eyes," Terrance said. "They aren't blue anymore."

"Oh...." He shrugged. The blue would return now that he was on Humanside.

The doctor was still watching him. "I really think you should rest. You lost a lot of blood, and we couldn't give you any."

"Why?" The room was starting to feel a little warm and his head a little weightless. He probably should sit, but he didn't want to prove her right.

"Because we don't have that type. It doesn't exist on this side of the void."

Terrance squeezed Angus's fingers. "It's a demon blood type."

"What does that mean?" Was he going to die? Was he part demon? Was he going to be fine and his eyes would recover in the future? Even as his mind filled with questions he should care about, he actually couldn't find the energy to care. He was alive.

"We don't know," the doctor said. "No human that we know of has ever had demon blood."

Angus nodded, and the room bounced. "Well, I feel fine, so I'm going to find some clothes and…." He glanced at Terrance, hoping that there were some clothes and that he could get out of there, but maybe he should lie down. Terrance tightened his hold as though he realized that standing was more taxing for him than it should be.

"You need to see Saka. I don't think he's slept," Terrance finished for him but looked at the doctor.

She pressed her lips together and didn't look thrilled by the idea, but finally she nodded. "You need to be careful. Don't push yourself."

Angus lifted an eyebrow. He had no plans to unleash another clean sweep. It had worked, hadn't it? No one had said anything. Had it been for nothing? He pulled off the bandage, but the doctor removed the drip before he could pull it out. She shooed everyone out of the room and closed the door.

Then it was just Terrance and him, and he sat heavily, unable to resist gravity any longer. He stayed upright but grabbed Terrance's hand for security. "It worked? Is everything fixed? Tell me it wasn't all for nothing."

Terrance stood between Angus's knees. "The magic is returned. Already the ice caps are retreating. It might take a couple of years for them to fully regress." He glanced down. "The World Council of Demonology wants to speak to you. Vinland is under martial law until elections can be held."

"What happened to the president?"

"He's been imprisoned. There's not much news coming out. Peace-keeping forces have moved in. It could take years for us to have a home again."

But it was home. "And the college? The warlocks?"

"Those that were close by were killed. They're searching for the other head warlocks to arrest. You're a hero and a villain. All magic users in New London died." Terrance struggled to meet his gaze. "And in a few other cities too. There have been guards at the door, demon and human, in case someone wants to retaliate."

Angus sighed. He'd known there would be deaths, but he wasn't sure he wanted to know the numbers. He should find out, but he wasn't ready. Would they ban him from using magic? Had he been worse than the warlocks he'd been fighting?

He cupped Terrance's chin so Terrance was forced to look at him. "Why won't you look me in the eye? Am I that awful?"

Terrance helped him off the bed and to the window. The bed sheet fell away, and Angus didn't bother to pick it up. At first glance his reflection in the glass looked much the same as he remembered. It was only when he looked closer and put his nose almost on the glass that he saw what it was that was freaking people out. It wasn't that his eyes weren't blue; it was that they were entirely black, like a demon's.

Terrance put his arms around Angus's waist. "I'll get used to it." He kissed the back of Angus's neck. "I guess when you told those assholes you were a mage, you meant it."

Angus smiled.

"That was broadcast by the way. It all was."

"Even the fire?"

"Yeah. And if I'd watched the footage before seeing you, I would never have expected to see you again."

"Did you see the magic?" Maybe it wasn't just him.

"No. But I saw your skin tear open." He touched the ridges of the scars. "I saw the trees burst into flames and the ground shake. You didn't step through the void so much as get swept into it. You were thrown all the way into the village. When they carried you to the doorway, to the mages, we thought that was it. You looked dead. You were cold to touch, and your pulse was barely there."

Angus leaned his head against Terrance. "Do you think they'll let me walk out of here?"

If they wouldn't, he'd open the void and leave, despite knowing he was supposed to use a doorway. He had demon blood. Perhaps he needed to be in Arlyxia to finish healing.

"Not a chance." Terrance turned Angus to face him. "I'll meet you at the Training Temple after?"

"You won't come with me?"

Terrance shook his head. "No. I belong firmly on this side. I know that for sure now. But Saka is welcome to visit."

Angus kissed him. "I won't be long." He didn't want to leave Terrance again, but he couldn't force him to come.

Terrance held him tight for a little longer, and Angus didn't rush to pull away. He breathed deeply, knowing he was safe. Terrance's arms were strong, and he'd always be there to save him.

"The sooner you go, the sooner you come back." Terrance pulled away.

"You don't mind?"

"No." He kissed Angus. "Though you might want to put something on before you leave."

Terrance opened up the drawer beneath the bedside table. A pair of bright blue pants and a cream shirt were neatly folded there for him. "Here."

"Thank you." He should've known Terrance would make sure he had what he needed. The bells he wore around his ankle fell out of the pile of folded clothes.

Terrance smiled. "Someone left them lying around. Your knives are in your room at the Training Temple."

Angus didn't know what to say, so he hugged Terrance again.

"Get some clothes on before I'm tempted to break the doctor's orders and get you too excited." But Terrance was smiling as he spoke.

"I'm fine." He wasn't fine, but he didn't want to worry Terrance or prompt the doctor to come back and tether him to the bed again.

Terrance held him at arm's length. "You wouldn't say that if you'd seen yourself. Go for a visit but come back and rest. I'll see you this evening?"

Angus nodded. "I won't do any magic."

"I'm not going to ask you to promise that. Magic is part of you... more than I ever realized."

"More than I ever wanted." Angus pulled on the pants and shirt.

"Do you regret it?"

Angus closed his eyes. He didn't want to think about the cold and fury of the magic within him. "I have to believe it was worth it. The worlds are in balance."

He would reckon with the rest later. Today he'd appreciate being alive. He put the bells around his ankle. "You sure you don't mind me going?"

"Saka will be anxious to see you. He couldn't be here the whole time, but one of us was always here."

Saka would've had mage things to do. Angus gave Terrance another kiss and then opened the void and stepped through.

The doorway was as it had been... almost. The stones were more uneven and slick with rain, and the pillars were a little crooked. He tipped his face to the sky. The rain was sweet and warm, the way he remembered, and his clothes were glued to him in moments.

The soldiers at the doorway looked at him curiously at first. Then one of them took off running to the village, and Angus followed. If he walked carefully, the unevenness of his steps was almost unnoticeable, but running was out of the question, at least for the moment.

Saka met him halfway, rain beading on his skin like crystals. He stopped and stared, and Angus closed the gap and hugged him tightly.

It was a couple of heartbeats before Saka put his arms around him, but when he did, nothing else mattered. "Welcome back, Mage Angus."

EPILOGUE

WHERE THE FOREST full of corpses had been were only charred stumps. Angus walked through the grass and tapped his staff on the ground as he went, looking for the remains of his tree. In his pocket were two seeds.

He stopped and turned, and Terrance and Saka looked back at him. They were all wearing coats and hats. Saka's hat had horn holes. While the weather was warming, it was still cold.

"It doesn't have to be the exact spot," Terrance said, his breath huffing out in a cloud.

"No, but it should be." His eyes hadn't returned to blue, his blood type was still demon, and he still saw magic on this side of the void.

It had taken nearly eight months to get a formal thank-you and pardon from the WCD—for using magic during the ban—and to be invited home to help put it back together. Saka had finally made contact with the Lifeblood tribes, or what remained of them. He was desperate to get home, and this would be the shortest route. This doorway would be the first in Vinland.

Magic would be taught demon-style, where magic must flow and be rebalanced, and not like the Mayans' blood magic. Somehow he had ended up in charge of that. For the last four months he'd been working with others to put Vinland back together.

"I think this is it." It was where he'd stood cuffed and cold and waited to be hanged. He pulled out the seeds and handed one to Terrance. "You remember how to do this?"

"Easy." He leaned in for a kiss. "Gather a little magic."

Angus smiled. The three of them had done that before they came out. The scars hummed with trapped magic as he pressed the seed into the ground and reached for Saka's hand. Saka held Terrance's free hand, and the other hovered over the seed. Together they grew the trees that would form the doorway between Lifeblood and New London. It wouldn't be open like the Mayan ones. Instead it would have a simple lock to prevent people from taking what they wanted from Demonside.

Saka had been working with Iktan and Cadmael on different types of doorways.

The trees grew and arched together, branches twining. Satisfied, Angus drew back and embraced Saka. "I'll be back tomorrow to summon you and finish this."

"I look forward to it. Perhaps you could escape for a day afterward? The mages at Lifeblood would like to see you."

Angus glanced at Terrance, who nodded. "I'll try."

Saka tore open the void, and the sweet, spicy air of Demonside wafted through. It was tempting to go through and feel the heat. He hadn't crossed the void in weeks. Saying goodbye to Iktan and the demons in the village had been hard, but he'd needed to come back. Now that he was here, he wanted to see Lifeblood surrounded by forest the way it had once had been. But he didn't take that step. They had to do it right and follow the new rules.

The void closed, and Angus stared a little longer at the place where Saka had been standing. The grass didn't remain flattened for long.

Terrance took his hand. "Are you in meetings today?"

Angus nodded. "We're still settling some rules."

The countries that had turned against their magic users, killing or jailing them, were in trouble for violating the rights of magic users.

Magic users were entitled to use magic, demon or natural, but only if they followed the rules set out by the Institute for Magical Studies. The college had never mentioned those rules, but that wouldn't happen again. And people could no longer be forced into using demon magic.

All magic had a cost. All magic left scars.

"What are you doing today?" Angus asked.

"Trying to get your mother's chicken pie recipe for your birthday dinner."

"Good luck with that. Just let her make it." She'd been trying to make up for what had happened, even though Angus would rather move on. He'd healed the cuff burns on his wrists and ankles when the pardon came through, but he still wore the mages' marks. He liked the way people flinched when they saw him. He wanted them to see the scars and remember.

Hand in hand they walked past the guards who protected the field. Around the edges people had left wreaths for those who'd been killed there. There had been memorials for those who'd died in Angus's clean sweep. He'd given a formal apology, but he had no idea how many from the rugby field had survived. Their deaths were a heavy burden that he couldn't forget. He still woke up some nights shivering as though cold and drawing magic to him. Terrance would hold him until the nightmare faded back to a memory.

Slowly Vinland was starting to heal, at least on the surface, but some scars would take a lifetime to fade. He glanced back at the two trees in the field surrounded by the stumps. Some scars would never fade.

Terrance tugged on his hand. "Come on. I'll walk you to your office, Dean of Sex Magic."

Angus hated that title so much, and Terrance knew it. He grinned.

"Stop it." Angus shouldered him.

"Nope."

"Next time Saka is here…." He leaned and whispered a few words in Terrance's ear so the guards at the gate couldn't hear.

Terrance's cheeks turned red. "That's not possible."

"I think you'll find it is. And you'll beg for it."

"I don't beg."

Angus lifted his eyebrows. "You keep telling yourself that."

"I ask. You on the other hand…."

Angus shrugged. "I know when to give in."

They stopped outside Angus's building. His office was on level three and had a view of the field.

Terrance gave his hand a squeeze. "I'll see you for lunch?"

"Yes. Of course." They always had lunch together.

It had been months, but Terrance still found it difficult to let go. Angus didn't push him away when Terrance held him a moment longer. With a final kiss, they pulled apart.

If he'd known what summoning a demon would mean that first day, he liked to think he'd have still done it, but no one was that brave. He looked up at the building. They needed to finalize the rules before mages and priests could start teaching. He never wanted to be a teacher, yet here he was—no longer a warlock in training or a dangerous rogue, but a mage, and he wasn't going to shirk that duty.

So he carefully climbed the steps, knowing that no matter what he did, he had a home on both sides of the void.

THE WITCH'S FAMILIAR

THIS TIME JUDE SULLIVAN had done nothing wrong. He'd know if he'd fried the circuits of a city or taken out a hospital's electricity by accident. He hadn't even been near a hospital in years. The worst thing he'd done all year was charge his car for free. Why pay for electricity when he could call it to his fingertips?

Surely not even the Coven would give him a warning for such a minor misuse of magic?

They couldn't know about his trip to Vegas. Even if they did, he'd done nothing wrong. Nothing that would put the paranormal community in danger of exposure and start another round of witch trials—or worse. He understood why the Coven freaked out so easily, but what did they want? Him to stop using magic? As much as he'd feared it when his talents had first surfaced, he'd started to find uses for it. And it was cool being one of the few people who could call down lightning.

He tapped his booted toes, unable to contain the nervous energy as he waited to be summoned into the Coven boardroom. These days, the Coven had the appearance of a well-run business. Their business being the management of the use of magic and the protection of all paranormals—and punishing those who didn't conform. He forced out a breath. As much as he hated being summoned to see the board, they had protected him when his power had first manifested and he had shorted out a hospital. They hadn't done it for him, though. They'd done it to protect every other witch. No one wanted to end up being dissected by overly curious scientists.

Jude glanced at the other man waiting. What had he done? Or was he here for better reasons than an assumed screwup? Some came to ask for help. Some had debts to pay. He may not even be a witch. Maybe he was a shifter. The man didn't look at him; he was staring at his phone, so Jude couldn't get a look at his eyes. It seemed kind of rude to see if he had an animal aura around him when they hadn't even spoken.

This was a lot like getting called to the principal's office, except there would be three witches on the other side of the table demanding an explanation instead of one cranky old principal who was tired of seeing Jude and telling him to keep his mouth closed so he wouldn't get into trouble.

This was his fourth visit to the Coven. He shouldn't want to throw up at the mere idea of stepping through those doors, and yet something about being here always tightened his stomach and prickled his throat with heat. He'd never hurled on their nice carpet, but there was a first time for everything. He didn't like not knowing why he'd been summoned.

The secretary glared at him over the rim of her glasses, and he forced his toes to still. It was a pity he couldn't calm his heart so simply or stop the sweat from forming and rolling slowly down his back.

It was worse this time because he knew he'd done nothing wrong. Nothing that would put anyone at risk.

This was far worse than the first time when he hadn't even known witches existed or that he was one. He'd thought the MRI machine had malfunctioned. But it was he who'd had the malfunction. His magic had burst to the surface and shorted the hospital. He'd been terrified.

The Coven had brought him in and had given him a tutor so he could get his magic under control. Now he could feel the hum of electrons as they danced through wires and he could taste electrical storms. He liked them, as it meant he could stand on the roof of his apartment block and join in without anyone being suspicious. Most of the time, the only magic he could freely do was charge his phone and his car. He'd destroyed three cell phones learning how to do that. He stared at his hands. Having magic wasn't as great as he'd thought it would be.

He could cast basic spells, but he didn't have useful skills. He couldn't move objects with his mind, read minds, or control animals. They were the talents of different witches. Where once he'd have been called a storm god, now he was just a troublemaker.

"Jude Sullivan." The secretary stood. "They'll see you now." She opened the door to the boardroom. No phone had rung to alert her. She'd just known. It was creepy no matter how many times he saw that trick.

Jude got up and wiped his hands on his suit pants even though he knew no one would shake his hand. He gave her a tight smile that she didn't return, then he walked through the large double doors.

Magic swept over his skin like a coarse brush. They were already examining him. He would be found wanting. He always was. Whatever they thought he'd done this time, though, he was innocent. He was *almost* sure of that.

If he could walk out of the Coven unscathed, in a few more weeks his passport would be here and he'd be out from under their scrutiny. And somewhere else. Anywhere would be better. The doors shut behind him with a soft click, trapping him in the boardroom.

The room was well lit, but there were no candles or incense or other witchy paraphernalia. The room could've belonged in any successful corporation. Jude sat in the only vacant chair. Across the large wood table sat three witches he was too familiar with.

The man in the middle was Landstrom. He hadn't like Jude from the first time they'd met. Jude had no idea what he'd done to offend the witch—probably breathed wrong.

Holling was the dark-haired woman. She like the rules followed.

The other woman was Tomlins. She didn't ask him much, but then she didn't need to as she could rummage through his thoughts like it was a discount clothing bin. He hoped he had a large sign that read 'Innocent' up today.

Jude pressed his lips together, not wanting to say anything that might be misconstrued. They could talk first, but he was itching to ask why he was here. Again. His toe almost tapped the floor as the silence stretched a little further. He was about to crack and speak, but Holling got in first.

"Thank you for coming." She smiled.

Attending wasn't optional; he'd learned that the second time he'd been summoned and a snake shifter had been sent to bring him in. That hadn't been fun. "I couldn't turn down the invitation."

"Skip the games, Sullivan. You know why you're here. You can't stay out of trouble." Landstrom rested his elbows on the table. There was a smirk on his lips as though he was far too pleased with himself.

Jude swallowed hard. Seeing Landstrom happy could only be bad. "Actually, I don't know why I'm here."

Tomlins leaned over and whispered something, hopefully that he was telling the truth, but he was starting to doubt that now he was here. He'd clearly screwed up, and Landstrom thought he had him.

"You went to Vegas two months ago?" Holling asked.

Jude's stomach twisted, and a rush of warmth spread over his skin. How did they know about that? "Yes. I thought it might be fun."

And it had been. It had also been quite profitable. After months of practicing at local casinos to get the slot machines to cough out small wins, he'd gone for a Vegas jackpot. And had gotten it. The memory didn't make him smile now.

"You got very lucky," Landstrom said with glee. Landstrom wasn't talking about the cocktail waiter who'd visited Jude's room with a bottle of tequila.

"Yeah, you know how it is. Put a hundred bucks in and something falls out." He had played carefully, spent four hours at the machine, putting coins in and getting small bits back. He'd had to learn the machine and the way its circuits flowed. He'd had to make it look real.

No miracle win on the first quarter that would draw the wrong attention.

Tomlins shook her head.

Damn it. She knew that he'd rigged the machine with magic. He had to stop thinking about it, but it was too late. There was no point in playing innocent. "No one got hurt."

"You used magic for self-gain. You risked exposing the paranormal community, again." Holling sounded disappointed more than anything, as though she couldn't understand why he kept screwing up. It wasn't like he did it deliberately…

Landstrom looked like he wanted to stand on the tallest building in Seattle and crow his delight. "You're a hazard, Sullivan. From the first time we met you, to now, nothing has changed."

"That's not true. I'm careful. I haven't had any accidents. I haven't revealed magic to anyone." But they had covered up his errors before. It was hard to explain why a whole town, really more of a small city, suddenly lost power. Aside from charging things, he generally avoided using magic unless he had to, so that he didn't accidentally break something. Playing with slot machines had been a way of letting the need to use magic trickle out, and even then the first time he'd tried it the machine had broken. He'd fried its insides. The casino had given him credit, but it had been two weeks before he'd been brave enough to go back and try again. That time he'd gone home one hundred dollars richer.

"You're lucky the casino didn't investigate why their jackpot suddenly went off," Landstrom said. "You put us all at risk."

"They're meant to go off." It was random, wasn't it?

From the expression on the witches' faces, he wasn't so sure. Were they going to make him hand back the money? He couldn't. He'd already invested it. If he was careful, he never needed to work again. He could do whatever he wanted. When he left the country, they couldn't follow him, could they?

"You don't seem to understand how precarious our status is. If we are rediscovered, there will be a fresh round of witch hunts. Or worse, the military will seek to exploit not just witches but every other paranormal being." Holling spoke calmly and carefully. "Taking a jackpot may mean nothing to you, but what if every witch did it? If we all used our magic to get what we wanted, society as we knew it would unravel. We have to live within human confines."

Jude frowned, not sure where this was going. He did try to live like a human. He considered himself human, a human with magic. "What do you mean?"

"What we mean, what the Coven has determined, is that you are to be given a final test that will determine your fate." Landstrom laced his fingers and grinned

"What kind of test?" He'd never been good at tests. He'd barely passed the test the Coven gave all new witches to make sure they were safe to go into the world. Maybe he was dangerous.

"The Coven wants to test your commitment to the paranormal community," Holling said.

That didn't sound too bad. He didn't want to hurt the paranormal community or humans. "I am committed to the Coven. I don't want to be exposed." Or burned at the stake.

"Good." Holling nodded. "But this test won't be easy."

"What is it?" Would it be today? Panic squeezed his heart hard. He wasn't ready.

"You're to go to Mercy South in Colorado to find and stop the creature that's mutilating cattle," she said.

"What? How do you know it isn't a wolf or a bear or something?" This wasn't the kind of test an electro-mage should be given. He didn't know anything about animals.

"It's not. It's a paranormal creature of some kind."

A paranormal creature. They were making him actually protect the paranormal community by policing it. "How do I stop it?"

"That depends on what it is."

"Don't you have investigators for this kind of thing?" He didn't even know where to start looking.

"Do you want to quit already?" Something about the way Landstrom spoke sent a warning shiver down Jude's spine.

Tomlins glared at Landstrom. "We do have investigators. We are giving you this chance. Perhaps you would like to become one and put your magic to use for us."

He wanted to laugh. His magic had no use. But they were offering him a place with the Coven as though he could be useful.

"I'm not quitting." But he didn't sound as sure as he wanted to, and he felt even less certain. This was some kind of trap if Landstrom was happy. "But what if I don't want to be an investigator?"

Tomlins tilted her head. "Electro-mages are rare. Your skills would be valued."

Landstrom looked like he'd swallowed a frog and it was stuck in his throat.

What could he do that other witches couldn't? He was rare...how rare? No, he was going to travel, not get into bed with the Coven.

"We will send an investigator in two weeks. That is all the time we can give you," Holling said.

Jude frowned. "If I pass, I get to be an investigator?"

He wasn't entirely sure if that was what he wanted. Part of him never wanted to have anything to do with the Coven after this. The rest of him wanted to believe that he was a good witch and did have a place in the paranormal community. He'd never belonged anywhere.

Holling nodded. Landstrom scowled.

"And what happens if I fail?" If this was a test, there had to be consequences. What if he wasn't any good and he couldn't solve problems?

Landstrom's smile returned. "You will be stripped of your magic."